MYSTICA

Yet beauty, though injurious, have strange power,
After offence returning, to regain
Love once possessed.

(Milton)

MYSTICA

JULIA
TAYLOR-STANLEY

Weidenfeld and Nicolson
London

This is for John, who opened the window and showed me a different landscape.

With thanks to Iain, Christopher, Alex, Lorna, Carolyn and Valerie for their belief and support. And Melissa for pie in the sky.

First published in Great Britain in 1991 by
George Weidenfeld & Nicolson Limited
91 Clapham High Street, London SW4 7TA

British Library Cataloguing in Publication Data

Taylor-Stanley, Julia
Mystica
I. Title
823.914[F]

ISBN 0 297 84050 9

Printed in Great Britain by The Bath Press, Avon

VENICE

Like an injured bird that senses its fate, he lay there, motionless, not daring to move. Grey and white clouds of cement dust wafted around him like an impenetrable fog. Dense, surreal. Lukewarm fingers of blood traced the outline of his bruised cheek; broken limbs, now numb, felt as though they no longer belonged to him.

A smothering blanket cloaked his consciousness. He tried to resist the warmth, but the arms of oblivion proved stronger than he and reached out from a familiar no-man's-land, pulling him ever closer.

Black shapes now whirled in a frenzied mass around the abomination's head as she leaned over the stone balustrade, surveying her conquest. A perverse Juliet calling to her dying Romeo. Dark tendrils of ebony hair framed translucent features with an undulating halo. A creation of the phantom breeze which knew no boundaries. She was transformed – a living Medusa.

With open arms she floated down from her murderous vantage point, moving in for the kill. Her heart-shaped face lingered a breath away from his helplessness. She smiled knowingly. He suddenly understood, opened his mouth to speak but could utter no sound. Fine white dust covered his face; the silent scream contorted his features into a grimacing mask. He was terrified, yet somehow appeared comical, like a redundant circus clown.

CHAPTER 1

Miles sat on the bed. He stared at the oversized suitcases and thought about the last time he'd run away from home. As a child of ten it had felt very different. Exciting, an adventure. But then when all of life stretched ahead like unchartered territory that was an understandable feeling.

Despite heartfelt pleas, his parents had been adamant about boarding school. (For a cosseted child used to the protective bosom of his family, the terrors of rigid schooling and probable bullying were unthinkable.)

So he'd run away. Well, not very far actually. Miles had camped out in the summerhouse with four packets of corn chips, two Cokes and a tub of mint-chocolate-chip ice-cream. Enough to last at least four days he'd thought. Of course when he got hungry that night, he'd given up. They'd packed him off the next day.

This childish urge to stay at home with his parents had been the strongest emotion he'd ever experienced. How time changes things. Now he couldn't wait to get away from them.

He moved to the open window and gazed beyond dappled foliage, through the enormous spreading branches of the plane trees, to the glittering promise of the lake beyond. Wisps of cloud passed before the sun as shadows drifted across a bright green sea of lawns like silent ships making headway. Was he making headway? He very much doubted it.

He sighed and crossed the room, determined not to be depressed about his prospects. A little brown terrier lifted her muzzle dejectedly for a moment. Suitcases had a tendency to depress her. Miles bent down to comfort her. She ignored him.

'You're going to miss that plane if you don't move your tush . . .' Celia Hanson's voice rang out along the vast panelled hallway. Miles picked up one of the suitcases and made his way to the head of the stairs. He paused for a moment to look down at the prone terrier.

'It won't be for long, I'll be back before you know it,' he

whispered unconvincingly. She raised her liquid eyes giving him a look that could melt most boyish hearts at a hundred paces.

His mother, an elegant brunette, rushed down the hall clutching an Etienne bag and a brightly-coloured silk scarf. She glanced absently at her son, took the stairs two at a time with the taut grace of a gazelle and shouted orders in Spanish to a maid who made faces behind her back. Miles sauntered down the stairs and ran his hand along the mahogany rail. He still liked to slide down when alone in the house.

Juanita ruffled his golden hair as she passed him on her way up. She picked up the heavy suitcases and hummed a few bars of 'O Sole Mio'. Miles watched her with mild affection. 'I should be doing that,' he said. She was so thin her arms were like sticks.

She put the suitcase down and pinched his cheek. 'Oh sure. You with your oh so beeg muscles.'

Mrs Hanson, who was casually repairing her make-up in the rococo mirror, shot the maid a withering glance that warned against familiarity. Juanita shrugged.

'You be sure you don't get yourself into trouble. Venice ees the city of romance . . . those Italian beauties they weel go for you. You'll see.'

Miles blushed and turned away. She laughed at his visible embarrassment.

The terrier heard the laughter and believed her luck had changed. She raced down the stairs barking excitedly.

His mother snapped her handbag shut. 'Time to leave Miles,' she said giving her perfect reflection a final appraisal. 'Juanita get the other case – quickly.'

She bounded upstairs. His mother shook her head. 'One of these days we'll get some reliable help,' she muttered.

Ignoring her disdain, Miles walked through the carved oak doorway into pastel evening light. Celia Hanson's recently polished Mercedes convertible gleamed in the evening glow. The chariot waiting to whisk him away from the gloom of his troubles.

He heard the crunch of gravel as he opened the boot. Heavy footsteps demanded attention. Miles didn't turn around.

'I hope you have a good trip.' His father cleared his throat nervously. 'After all that's happened I think you really deserve this break. Just don't do anything stupid, that's all I ask.'

'What, don't do anything stupid like you did, you mean,' Miles said through clenched teeth.

'All right that's enough.' His mother opened the car door and slid behind the wheel, displaying long black-stockinged legs. 'I'll be back around eleven, darling, I have to meet that bore Marcia at Greene Street for dinner.'

His father's body relaxed slightly as it often did in her company. He bent down to kiss the top of her auburn chignon. 'I gave you the lire and travellers' cheques for Miles, didn't I?' He looked anxious.

'Yes I've got it, everything's under control – now come on Miles, get in for God's sake – we're going to miss that damn plane.'

As she started the engine, Juanita appeared in the doorway struggling with the remaining suitcase. She refused Mr Hanson's offer of help and hauled the case onto the tiny back seat.

'You send a postcard, eh! If you know what's good for you. I weel be very angry if you don't let me know what a great time you are having.' She winked suggestively.

Miles curled the corners of his mouth slightly.

As soon as his father placed a well-meaning hand on his shoulder and muttered a series of tense warnings and vague reassurances, Miles turned away and stonily contemplated the long, sweeping drive.

There was obviously nothing more to be said. Celia Hanson waved a dismissive hand and put her foot down.

As the car accelerated away, a slight cloud of gravel dust wafted into the eyes of the assembled party. They rubbed their faces and looked as though they were crying. In his father's case nothing could be further from the truth.

Miles put down the sun visor and took a last look in the vanity mirror at the mock Tudor mansion. His little dog was sitting in the middle of the drive, determined to make him feel guilty to the last. It worked beautifully.

He reclined the chair slightly and felt suddenly optimistic. Perhaps this trip wasn't such a bad idea after all.

Though the shelter of privilege seemed to be a permanent fixture, he would soon learn what it feels like to be out in the rain. Acid rain.

'Take It To The Limit' by The Eagles blared from his mother's car stereo as they sped over the Triboro bridge. Miles watched the Hudson glistening in the rose-pink glow and pictured the Grand Canal in his mind's eye. Celia Hanson looked at her son and tried to read his features. She turned the music down. Miles turned it back up. She swore and turned it down again. 'Miles, I really don't think it's a good idea, you finding your own way round Venice. It's hell at this time of year you know. Why don't you let me call Mario at the Danieli? I'm sure I can get him to find you something nice.'

Miles turned away and watched the mountain of steel girders rise up for what seemed like an eternity above him. He gritted his teeth slightly. 'I've told you I want to see the real Venice. You've got to let me do things my way. I'm not a little boy any more. I'm a grown man. For Christ's sake, stop trying to wrap me in cotton wool.'

His mother tapped the wheel rhythmically, 'You're not quite over things yet, you know. Doctor Steinberg said you could suffer after-effects for anything up to three years. Do you really think you know better than a leading neuro-surgeon? God, you can be so like your father.'

Miles clenched his fist. 'Don't ever say I'm like that bastard,' he said angrily. 'I'll never be like him. I'd rather die.'

His mother sighed heavily. She knew the emotional divide between the two people she loved was as wide as the Grand Canyon. 'Okay subject closed. But promise me if you run into any money trouble you'll go straight to the Amex office and have them notify me so I can wire you some more.' She touched his hair without taking her eyes from the road. 'Promise me, Miles, please,' she said softly.

He bowed his head suddenly ashamed of the outburst. He could hardly blame her for all that had happened. She'd been a tower of strength through all the traumas. He touched her hand and promised solemnly. Then with The Eagles duly reinstated, she accelerated abruptly and they sped towards Kennedy airport determined to enjoy what was left of their journey.

Celia Hanson tried to shake off a series of intuitive feelings which disturbed her. How long would it be before she saw her beloved son again she wondered? Why was she so worried about this trip? As he had just pointed out, he could take care of himself now.

Four hours later Miles was on an TWA flight bound for Marco Polo airport. As the plane groaned skyward on its laboured ascent, Miles faced the window. Cloud formations had created a stunning landscape of white mountainous peaks and far-reaching plains. He gazed dreamily at nature's achievement and wished he could step outside, to walk upon the misty breath of the gods.

'Here we are, sir – enjoy.' The cheery stewardess delivered his meal. He gazed at it disparagingly and prodded glutinous contents with a plastic fork. He took a bite. Surprise, surprise, it tasted exactly like the tray it was served on. He closed the lid and buzzed for the airline's answer to Miss America. She flashed a row of perfect gleaming teeth at him – no request denied. He asked for a pillow and blanket, determined if he wasn't going to eat he was certainly going to get some sleep. He put on his headphones. Peter Gabriel sang 'Red Rain'.

> 'Red rain is pouring down, pouring down all over me.
> I come to you defences down. With the trust of a child –
> and I can't take any more . . .'

Miles burrowed into the discomfort of his seat and closed his eyes. Inevitable memories flooded in as Gabriel sang about vulnerability. Lisa stared at him from beneath a curtain of blonde hair. Her arms were outstretched, fragile beauty still intact. He remembered how she had come to him with her sense of self deeply buried beneath teenage preoccupations with fat legs, better essays on Emily Dickinson and didn't he think her nose was too big. When she stopped trying to be somebody else he fell in love with her. He loved her nose and her legs, her sense of fun, the green eyes that misted over when he made love to her. He clenched his fist and tried to replace her image with one of the Venice of his imagination. Like a small child dreaming of the magic of a Christmas soon to be experienced, he imagined wondrous architectural treasures which were greatly removed from the neglected reality he would soon encounter.

At the airport his first impression of Italy was one of complete and utter chaos. He was ill-prepared for the bedlam. The tranquillity of the house in Stamford, Connecticut and his subdued college surroundings were as far removed from the Italian sense of order and calm as Bali is from the South Bronx. Tourists rushed around like headless chickens in a farmyard, with about as much sense of direction. They complained about the heat, the baggage delay and the inefficiency of the Italians. The locals scampered about for an entirely different reason, desperate to collect their belongings and run from the airport to escape the unbearable heat which only they knew was imminent at noon. These sweaty natives scrambled into buses and ran for water taxis, shouting in unintelligible Italian at dirty porters who shouted back in loud angry voices.

After what seemed like a chaotic eternity, an English courier waiting for a plane load of delayed tourists noticed Miles squinting at a phrasebook. 'Chi . . . mi porta al albergo?' he was whispering like a nervous actor who sneaks a last look at his lines before going on stage. The courier sauntered over and asked if she could help.

'Thank God,' Miles said gratefully. Her obvious composure was a welcome contrast to the shrieking mass. 'Yes, could you give me some help? I need to find a cheap hotel – somewhere central. Could you recommend something and maybe tell me how to get there?'

The courier tossed her blonde hair and suppressed the urge to laugh aloud at his naïvety.

'A cheap hotel in Venice in high season, you've got to be kidding . . .' She said this softly to spare his blushes. 'And as for being central, I suggest you find one near the Rialto bridge so you can throw yourself off because it's going to be hotter than Hades.'

'Oh Christ, it looks like I screwed up . . . I thought it would be easy to find somewhere,' he said with a groan.

Miles suddenly looked tired and vulnerable and the courier felt bad about her discouraging attitude. 'Look, don't worry. I'm exaggerating. I know of a cheap pensione near the Accademia bridge – it's next to a pretty canal, you'll like it there – lots of students like you around.'

He wondered if it was that obvious he was a student. 'Thanks a lot, but how the hell am I going to find it? I don't even know if I can find my way out of the airport to the taxi rank,' he said.

The girl laughed lightly and looked him up and down, taking in the pale golden tan and reddish blonde hair falling over his blue eyes. He was definitely a lamb heading for the proverbial slaughter. She decided to take pity on him.

'Look I shouldn't really do this, but if you want to hang on until my punters get here I'll give you a ride in our water taxi.' She looked over at the arrivals board hopefully and sighed. Her flight number was still an absentee. 'You can keep me company anyway.'

Miles sat down on a red plastic chair and took a limp handkerchief from the pocket of his well-worn Levis.

'That's really good of you,' he said as he mopped his now glistening forehead. 'I see what you mean about the heat.'

In her crisp white shirt and navy pencil skirt, she seemed unruffled by the clammy air. She smiled and straightened the papers on her clipboard. 'I was new to Venice once myself. It's a bit daunting at first but you'll soon get used to it.'

He looked at her pretty face and wondered who had helped her when she first arrived; he imagined a gaggle of leering Italians all fighting over the opportunity.

Some time later, when it had been explained what punters were and where they were going, they had a cappuccino and waited for the delayed plane. Miles discovered that Carole had been in Venice for three years and was due to go home to London at the end of the season. She gave him some invaluable advice about the gondoliers and pickpockets and warned him against eating or drinking anything in St Mark's because the prices were inevitably tripled by the restaurateurs. She also told him that once they got into central Venice he mustn't mind the smell because he would soon get used to it. He explained that his mother had prepared him by suggesting he wait until the garbage was about four days old and then put his head in the pail. Carole laughed and said that was highly appropriate.

Speeding across the lagoon in a water taxi, Miles felt he could forgive the place anything. In the early morning light it glistened like an iridescent jewel, resplendent with historic glory. St Mark's Campanile rose proudly against the bright blue skyline. As they cruised past a seemingly infinite parade of some of the most breathtaking buildings he had ever seen, Miles was glad he had come.

They drew closer to the Grand Canal and Carole pointed out some of the endlessly photographed landmarks to them. The island of San Giorgio Maggiore looked worthy of investigation. An elegant white building gleamed with promise. The Danieli hotel with its rose-pink façade looked typical of the kind of opulence his father insisted on when abroad. He gazed in wonder at the grandeur of this architecture and wondered if he stood the faintest chance of emulating majesty such as this when he became a qualified architect.

He resisted the urge to join the other tourists in a photographic frenzy. He had plenty of time. He stood behind the driver with the wind freshening his skin and savoured the delights of the city. They turned from the Grand Canal into a smaller waterway and eventually arrived at a quaint hotel called the Splendide. Miles thought it sounded rather un-Venetian but Carole's punters seemed duly impressed. With the holiday-makers safely unloaded, the water taxi accelerated through a narrow maze of canals. He gazed up at the dilapidated buildings. Tubs of scarlet geraniums lined the brittle windowsills, providing colourful shelters from the heat for the cooing pigeons. The canal was so narrow he wondered how the driver would deal with a boat heading in the opposite direction. He asked the girl and she pointed to a blue traffic sign: 'senso unico'. No chance of collision then, it was a one-way street. On a minute balcony an artist sized up the perspective of an old woman on the opposite side of the canal. Miles breathed a deep sigh of appreciation. He was about to relay his enthusiasm for the ambience when a sudden current of air filled his nostrils with an unbelievable stench. Waves of nausea rose up from his churning stomach. He put a hand to his mouth and hoped he wouldn't embarrass himself by throwing up into the murky water.

Carole watched his face take on the colour of the canal. 'I told you, you'll get used to it, don't worry,' she laughed.

'I'm not so sure about that, it's a damn sight worse than the garbage pail.'

Their driver dextrously negotiated the foul-smelling waterways as Miles regained his composure. Colourful laundry fluttered above them, an occasional lichen-covered face gaped mournfully from above a half-submerged doorway, cooking smells wafted from kitchens beyond open windows. Miles stared at his reflection as the boat slowed almost to a stop. Venice had been born from water and now that water wanted to reclaim its creation.

They turned once more into the glittering Grand Canal. A large wooden bridge loomed towards them.

'The Accademia.' Carole gestured towards the advancing structure.

They passed beneath its looming shadows then turned into another smaller canal lined with pretty Renaissance houses which had been painted alternately pink and beige. He turned a blind eye to the rubbish piled high at the side of the canal; some of the debris was floating in this aqueous rubbish dump.

The taxi juddered noisily as it slowed. Their driver manoeuvred the boat towards the slimy green landing stage and called out to a fat man who was sitting on the low stone wall at the side of the water. He devoured the remains of his peach and grudgingly wiped his hands on his dirty vest, then reached out to catch the rope. A small terraced house displayed its name, Pensione Katerina, proudly in neon above the front door.

'Is this it?' Miles suppressed a yawn. He felt suddenly sleepy.

'Yep . . . Katerina will take good care of you. Just say I recommended you and she'll treat you like a prince,' Carole said with authority.

The rather sullen boat owner helped Miles with his things.

'Molto grazie.' Miles proudly displayed the only Italian he knew.

'Arrividerla . . .' The driver grunted this indifferent reply.

'That means good-bye,' Carole shouted as they moved away, leaving Miles on the worn cobblestones. 'I'm with Thomson at the Splendide every morning between eleven and twelve. If you run into any trouble call me . . . Bye.'

'Bye and thanks,' Miles called after them. Well, this was it. He was on his own now. He stood before the shabby pensione and squinted up at the bright pink façade. The dilapidated building was certainly a far cry from home. The windows were grimy, dirty worn net curtains hung haphazardly, blowing against the shutters in the all too light breeze. He was soon to discover that a breeze in Venice during July and August was a rare occurrence. Inside he found the reception hall was far cleaner and more tasteful than the rundown exterior suggested. White painted walls gave an impression of Mediterranean coolness, and a large mahogany desk took pride of place. Registration cards were neatly stacked by a visitors' book. A brass bell for service suggested a modicum of efficiency in the downtrodden little hotel.

He rang for attention and looked around him. A cat wailed somewhere in the distance – the heat was suddenly unbearably oppressive. He longed for bed and wiped his forehead with the back of his hand. Several Byzantine icons adorned the walls. A shaft of sunlight caught the mounts and cast a pale golden glow on to the rough white plaster which he noticed was flaking slightly in places. The stern-faced icons, mahogany furniture and white walls brought to mind a small chapel. He wondered if the religious ambience was intentional.

From a doorway behind the large desk, an even larger woman struggled to come out of the doorway backwards. She was dragging something that seemed very heavy and muttered distractedly in a language that, even with his limited knowledge, Miles knew wasn't Italian.

'Can I help you with that?' he asked.

The gargantuan woman jumped up and straightened painfully. She wiped her face on the hem of her floral print apron and panted her distress. 'Such a fright you are giving me.' She peered at him, 'Da, I think you can help – thank you.' Her East European accent was thick. Miles helped her drag the heavy trunk into the hall and said jokily, 'What have you got in here, your husband?'

The hotelier stretched her back again with a low groan. 'No no . . . it is clean linen for the beds.' She smiled, resting chubby hands on endless hips.

'Right, well, that's a relief,' he said. 'An English courier, Carole, recommended your hotel – you must be Katerina?'

'Katy, da,' she beamed pleased he considered her establishment to be a hotel and not a boarding house. 'And you skinny man – who are you?'

'Miles Hanson.' He thrust his slender hand towards her enthusiastically.

She shook it warmly in her own huge one. 'You are most welcome to be here Miles Hanson. We will have to put some meat on those bones if you stay, da?' She squeezed his upper arm.

'You have a room then?' he dared to ask, trying to put an image of the witch in Hansel and Gretel from his mind.

'How long you stay?' She screwed up her eyes and peered at him, adding to the unflattering illusion.

'About a month – if you can spare a room for that long.'

'I think that will be good.' She beamed, a glowing beacon in unfamiliar territory. 'Well then, for you the best room I 'ave. You will like – you see. Come with me.' Katerina dragged her huge frame breathlessly up the stairs with Miles following. They came to a long airy landing with eight or nine doors leading from it. Midway down the passage, Katerina extracted a bunch of keys from her apron and unlocked the bedroom door. She threw it open with a grand gesture. 'Here,' she announced boomingly, 'All this space for you.'

Miles looked beyond her bare, slightly mottled arm into a room about the size of his bathroom at home. It had two picture windows overlooking the narrow canal. A linoleum floor masqueraded as marble. There were two small rugs. The furniture looked simple, minimal. The double bed, made from a blackened cast iron, was remarkably high off the ground – the white lace coverlet which had been carelessly thrown over it left a gap of at least two feet to the floor. He had a sudden mental vision of himself comically attempting to heave this grossly overweight landlady onto the bed and bit his tongue with mute amusement. He took in more of the room; a rickety writing table and chair had been thoughtfully placed in one window. The only other furniture was a rather ecclesiastical, ornately carved mahogany tallboy which he felt would almost certainly have been more at home in a vestry.

Katy noticed his admiring glance. 'It belonged to my husband's uncle. He was priest you know.' There was an ambiguous Catholic pride in her tone. Miles felt sure the icons must have come from the same source.

'You like all this?' Katerina enquired, sweeping her arm round the room.

'Yeah, sure. It's great . . . how much is it?'

'To you skinny one, 400,000 lire.' She watched him struggling to convert the amount into American dollars.

'Four hundred a month?' he asked hopefully.

'No, no. You are indeed new to Venezia, skinny one. Four

hundred dollars a week.' He look exasperated, 'With breakfast and dinner of course.' Miles did a quick mental calculation and accepted gratefully. If he didn't have to eat out he could make his money last for the duration.

'Now you will have some lunch with me and then you sleep – it has been long journey for you, no?' She shuffled to the door.

'Yes, I feel like I could sleep for a week.'

They placed his luggage in the room and he christened the dreary bathroom down the hall. After a lunch of assorted meats, cheeses and some very good bread, he sat in her little salon and talked obligingly with her about the rigours of running a hotel single-handed. He learned that when her husband died, years ago, she had been forced to take in paying guests to support herself. From time to time she wiped her damp forehead on the hem of her dress and fought for breath. Miles had the distinct impression her grossly overweight condition was unsuited to the oppressive humidity outside. While she talked, he gazed with curiosity at her collection of faded photographs in silver frames on the dusty sideboard and longed to ask about her background. Her accent fascinated him and he felt sure she had a few tales to tell. Good manners and weariness, however, kept him from prying.

Later, he found his room darkened by closed shutters. The bed had been turned down and a bottle of acqua minerale had been left on his bedside table. He took off his jeans, socks, and trainers leaving his white T-shirt and underpants on. Climbing under the cool sheets, he fell asleep almost as soon as his head touched the pillow. He dreamed fitfully.

He found himself back in his old hospital room, only this time he was merely the voyeur. His mother bent over his lifeless body. Her shoulders heaved with soundless weeping. Miles stood behind her and tried to draw her attention from the shell that had once held his soul. The harder he tried the more grief-stricken she became.

Someone knocked at the door. He tried to open it – it was locked. The knocking grew louder. 'Dinner in fifteen minutes, skinny one.' His landlady's voice penetrated the dream. He drifted in and out of wakefulness.

'Skinny, are you awake now?' Katerina knocked again.

'Coming!' he called out softly. He lifted his hand to his forehead – it was drenched in cold sweat for the second time that week. Glancing at his watch, he was amazed to find it was seven o'clock. He'd slept for five hours. After a hurried shower he made for the dining room.

It was a pleasant room with French doors leading onto a tiny but well-kept garden with a disused fountain. An askance Cupid posed somewhat camply for his admirers with one hand on his hip and the other gesturing into the air. His dry mouth formed an O. He looked as though he had recently been surprised by something or someone. On one side of the terrace wire ropes held a wilting vine which looked badly in need of watering. Small as it was the garden was loved. Any greenery in this part of Venice was a valuable commodity.

Katy looked up from her conversation with the other guests and let Miles take in his new surroundings for a moment before declaring: 'Now everybody is here and we eat, yes?' Miles sat down and sized up his dinner companions. They were an older man and identical twin girls with shorn hair and horn-rimmed glasses. All three sat rigidly at the dark wooden dining table with its blackened patina. They eyed this cuckoo in their temporary nest with hardened, unfriendly expressions.

'Everybody, this is Miles,' Katy beamed. 'You will all become friends, I'm sure.'

Miles seriously doubted it.

After some brief introductions he discovered the twin girls were German students aged nineteen. The older gentleman, their father, was accompanying them because, as he explained to Miles in broken English, Italy was no place for unaccompanied girls.

The girls stared challengingly at him as he attempted stilted conversation with their father. He was running out of metaphors to bridge the language barrier when Katerina struggled through the swing door with an enormous soup tureen. They watched the swirling sea of liquid washing the sides of the bowls as she ladled the steaming soup with a singular lack of dexterity. She presented Miles with his first course. He eyed the bright purple liquid nervously and asked, 'Is it borscht?'

Katy filled her own bowl. 'Made with red cabbage, yes. But borscht – no, not really. It is my speciality. Eat please, you will like.'

Although he detested red cabbage he spooned the soup into his mouth. Fortunately it didn't taste of red cabbage at all. It was more like a dyed French onion. 'It's great,' he said. Katy looked satisfied and mercifully conversation came to an abrupt end as everyone ate. Miles looked at the ten empty seats at the table and wondered whether Katerina had some unspoken code for accepting guests into her home. He surmised that if his dinner companions were anything to go by, it was far more likely that business was slack.

She cleared away their empty plates and returned with a monumental serving plate of spaghetti. 'And now spaghetti alla carbonara. Her proclamation would have been more suited to the arrival of the King of Spain. Her lack of modesty, however, was justified by the taste. It was incredibly good and Miles said it was the best he'd ever had. 'Where did you learn to make pasta like this?'

'I learn from Giorgio in the next street,' Katerina said mischievously, 'He deliver it to me – Silly Skinny.'

CHAPTER 2

After dinner Miles couldn't wait to explore. Far from being tired, he was on East-coast time. For him it was only four o'clock in the afternoon, so he felt quite energetic. He made for the Accademia bridge. The canal smelt like a recently used toilet. Miles held a hand to his face to fend off the stench. He had been warned not to stray from the popular tourist routes. It was easy to get lost in the maze of alleyways. Armed with a street map, he was determined that his sense of direction would prove to be less plebeian.

His destination was the inevitable St Mark's square known as the place where 'lions fly and pigeons walk'. It was undoubtedly one of the most famous of all Venetian sights. He was pleased his mother had advised him to read about the city before he set foot on these sacrosanct cobbles; there was a wealth of culture and architecture to be explored, but he was determined to experience the lesser-known Venice. He felt the books had given him a distinct advantage.

The route was well signposted and he felt confident he would reach his destination without problems. As he strode across a tiny bridge, the wavering sound of an accordion drew closer. A gondolier proferred his rendition of 'Santa Lucia', perpetuating the cliché that was undeniably Venice. He stopped to listen for a moment and watched reclining lovers pass beneath him. He didn't envy their passion – it had its price.

He walked on, taking in the twilight atmosphere. A handful of Italian youths passed by wearing the arrogance of a nation on their lapels. They sauntered down a darkened alley, their supercilious laughter ringing in the dankness. For a moment Miles was tempted to follow them. Wisely he decided it was early days yet and kept on the tourist route, watching all the time for the bright yellow signs which directed him through the labyrinth of small streets and alleyways. Eventually he reached a vast cloistered expanse. St Mark's. He strode across the square to a colossal decorative building with five huge domes.

This, then, was the famous Basilica. He gazed up in wonder at its squat but commanding appearance; with its Byzantine overdressing, lavish encrustations on each façade, and golden onion domes, it dominated the buildings around it. Only the Campanile could match its majesty. Where the Basilica was intricate and overwhelming, the bell tower stood tall and elegant. Uncluttered, with its understated exterior, it looked down upon its lavishly overdressed neighbour with what Miles imagined to be lofty disdain. They were a perfect match for each other, architectural opposites, like a rotund but beautiful woman married to a tall immaculate man.

In the well-lit square painters had set up rickety easels displaying their talents. They sat patiently awaiting the tourists who would appraise their raw genius. If they got lucky someone might buy their rather tacky impressions of the city – if not, then perhaps lunch the next day would be a simple affair. Nearby there were several orchestras. Each one was perched on a dais decorated with plants and palm trees. Sheltered from the cloying heat beneath canvas awnings, they played Lloyd Webber and Vivaldi in turn. Miles thought it was a dreadful choice of repertoire. A couple, who obviously disagreed, smooched past him. The woman laughed as the man dipped her. Miles wondered if his parents had behaved like this on holiday. A comic display of this nature would have been unthinkable at home.

He needed a beer. Despite Carole's advice about high prices in St Mark's, Miles strode across the square to the Café Quadri confident that at least at the moment, he knew exactly where he was going. He sat down and spent five minutes trying to get served. When the beer finally arrived it was at least cold. He wiped the condensation from the rim of the glass and thanked the waiter in Italian. He nodded and resumed his animated conversation with a pretty waitress.

Miles drank his beer and took in the surroundings. He felt glad he'd come here first. It had been touch and go – whether to see Florence first and bask in the warm sunlight of the campagna of Tuscany – or sweat it out in Venice. He knew how beautiful Florence was from friends' descriptions. But it was the majesty and mystery of Venice which had won him over, seducing him from the pages of coffee-table books. To Miles, the mists and sunsets belonged to the likes of Byron, Browning and Canaletto, not to the uneducated tourists who raped the city of its faded dignity. To him it would always be the Venice of the eighteenth century; the masked balls, the regatta, the Carnevale, the music of Vivaldi and Scarlatti. He imagined men and women in period dress dancing with regal composure among the cloisters where the vulgar orchestras now played for equally vulgar tourism.

He finished his drink and motioned to the waiter that he wanted to pay. He was given a small slip of paper. He mentally converted the total – the beer had cost him seven dollars and fifty cents. Daylight robbery, he thought, using a term which must have once been shouted in anger after a pickpocket. The waiter had shifty eyes and a beaked nose – he would have made an excellent thief. He left a small tip and headed back to Katerina's, watching all the time for the yellow signs.

It was now close to midnight and he was unprepared for the rather eerie atmosphere which prevailed. The absence of life didn't unnerve him, but he walked a little faster. The streetlamps, which had seemed perfectly adequate in the twilight, were now hopelessly dim. It was harder to read the signs in the darkened campos and calles. Miles put on his tortoiseshell reading glasses and walked into the square. This was one of the campos he had walked through earlier on his way to St Mark's – he was on the right track.

Sure enough he found a yellow sign pointing towards the Accademia. He followed the arrow diligently and in no time at all found he was hopelessly lost. Like most tourists he had come full circle. He stared in disbelief at the tiny bridge he had crossed only minutes before. Groaning, he took out his map and tried to read it in the dull glow of a shop doorway. The minute typeface of the street names defied identification in the dying light. Muttering to himself, he was suddenly aware of someone watching him – he looked up and saw a menacing form slumped against the opposite doorway.

A tall youth, dressed in black leather with threatening steel chains adorning his chest and thighs, inhaled on the cigarette in his mouth and thoughtfully illuminated his plumage for Miles's benefit. He had a startling bright green mohican rising a full eight or nine inches from his skull. Miles quickly folded the map and set off down the wide but empty street. There was no one to help him out with directions. Sooner or later he had to come across another one of those damned yellow signs.

He strode down an alleyway, cursing his stupidity. Muttering vague profanities, he turned the corner. A torn poster advertised a Communist Party celebration – red and gold symbols of unity were emblazoned across the decaying wall. Miles heard footsteps behind him and felt a little panicky. He thought of the five hundred dollars in cash in his back pocket. Why hadn't he left it behind? He swore and walked faster – he didn't want to run in case it gave the youth the incentive to mug him. Miles knew he was strong despite his lack of meat, as Katerina had put it, but he figured the youth was probably far more accustomed to gratuitous violence than he was. He quickened his pace and turned down another alley. It was submerged in almost total darkness. He couldn't see a thing. He stumbled over a bundle on the pavement. The bundle cursed in Italian. Miles looked down. 'Are you all right?' he asked, concerned. A hand shot out from the heap of rags and forcefully grabbed his arm. Miles tried to pull away but the man was too strong for him. His dirty face leered at Miles from the gloom – he held a syringe to his captive's bare forearm.

'I don't want your drugs,' Miles struggled to break free.

'I am sure you don't, my friend.' The man's voice was guttural. 'I am the user – I got AIDS. You give me your money or you get this in your arm, I give it to you, eh? This is mine, you see, capisci?'

Miles tried to take in what the tramp was saying. The bastard was holding a long slow death against his arm. He heard distant echoing footsteps and called out for help. His cry resounded through the empty streets. The tall youth appeared at the mouth of the alley and broke into a run. Miles was suddenly terrified – were they in league with each other? As the youth approached he shouted at the tramp, 'Leave him alone, Luigi, or I'll break your fucking arm fer ya.' The tramp immediately removed the instrument of death from Miles's skin. Miles rubbed his forearm vigorously and jumped up.

The owner of the mohican looked down at the defeated tramp and angrily shook his fist in the man's face. He relieved him of the syringe. 'You were doing yer AIDS routine again, weren't ya?' The tramp shook his head. 'Stupido . . . what did I tell yer before. I'll set the fucking carabinieri on ya.'

Miles stared at the youth and wondered if he had a gentler kind of robbery in mind. He brushed the dirt from his clothes and thanked him anyway. 'I thought I was on my way to a living hell.'

'Naw yer all right. That fucking dago mental – he's no more got AIDS than I 'ave. Well I didn't 'ave it the last time I got tested.' He spat into the gutter.

Miles was comforted by his seemingly friendly tone.

'Well, thanks again, I . . .'

The youth interrupted Miles's gratitude. 'Yer was lost, wern't ya? I was watchin', see. I thought I'd better follow yer and keep yer awt of trouble – where you tryin' to get to, mate?' The punk peered at him in the dim light.

'I'm staying near the Accademia,' Miles said cautiously.

'Well, I'd better help yer get back. There's a fucking good pub near there. Me mates run it – dagos but they're all right, not fucking mental like 'im.' He gestured behind him to the tramp who, despite the youth's warning, had bundled himself up again in readiness for another ambush. 'Yer can buy us a drink if yer like.'

Miles said it was the least he could do and the two of them headed for safer territory. On the way to the bar, the punk told Miles his name was Charlie Rice. 'Terrible, innit,' he sniffed. 'Me mates call me Grapper. It's a sort of drink here so whenever someone calls awt me name in a bar the bloody waiter gives 'em a drink.'

Miles laughed. 'Well Grapper, is that what you'd like to drink?'

'Fuck me, no – I drink bloody Scotch, dun' I.' The youth stuck some well-chewed gum on the wall, leaving a territorial mark.

When they arrived at the pub Miles was surprised to find it was only two streets away from Katerina's. 'If yer get lost again ask a dago for El Souk; everyone knows where it is. It's the only decent place round here, it's wicked.'

'Wicked?' Miles stared at the bright green plumage and wondered what kind of place would let Grapper in, let alone welcome him.

'Yeah – crucial,' Grapper said with a West Indian accent,

pronouncing it 'crooshaal'. He went through the doorway, gyrating in a manner which Miles thought closely resembled a limbo dancer preparing for an act of contortion.

The interior of the bar wasn't quite what Miles expected. It looked sophisticated, upmarket. The walls were bright green, it had tall chrome seats, and smoky Art Deco-type mirrors were everywhere. Several young people were standing at the bar drinking – the music was almost deafening. Above the din, two barmaids chanted Grapper's name in unison and wiggled their hips at him. 'Bellissima, bellissima.' He kissed their waiting mouths over the bar counter. Miles noticed that the green in his mohican was almost identical to the colour of the bar stools. ''Ere girls, this is me new mate . . . he's a septic tank but don't let that put yer off – 'ere Miles, this is Bella and this 'ere's Anna and ain't they little darlin's?' He smirked and leaned over to Miles. 'Don't worry about the septic bit – they 'ardly speak a word of English.'

The girls smiled provocatively at Grapper who winked and said 'Later.' Miles asked for two large Scotches.

'Very grande if it's for Grapper, no?' one of the barmaids said knowingly. The way she tossed her flaming red curls suggested she was intimate enough with him to know what he liked.

Grapper led Miles to a table to await delivery of the drinks. He told him that most places closed at eleven – this was one of the few places that stayed open late. Miles said it was no wonder the city had looked so dead. Grapper explained that most riotous activity took place privately. While he talked about the seedier Venice, Miles studied his companion. Beneath the menacing exterior he was actually quite good-looking. He was also much older than Miles had originally thought. He looked to be in his mid-twenties.

Grapper sensed the scrutiny and whispered an explanation. 'You know, I 'ave to look like this or those fuckers would try to get me too. I should 'ave grown awt of this punk thing with the Pistols, but where there's a need . . .'

'I don't doubt the violence. I don't think any city is totally safe,' Miles said. 'They must be pretty unscrupulous around here. Steal your soul if it was up for grabs.'

Grapper lifted a cursory eyebrow. 'Yeah, well, that's another story. Anyway, sods the lot of 'em. They 'aven't learnt a bleedin' thing. Some of 'em still think Mussolini's a national bloody 'ero.' He lit another cigarette, 'Says it all, dunnit.'

Miles wondered if there might be more to this lout than met the eye. 'Still, Venice is beautiful and you've obviously got friends here.'

'Oh yeah, I like the people who run this bar – decoration's not up to much, though. Prefer modernist vibes meself, ya know, Bauhaus, Mackintosh. Don't go in much for Deco. These chairs gave me the inspiration for me barnet colour though, see . . .' He tugged at the bright green spikes.

'Yes I see,' said Miles, not seeing at all . 'How long have you lived here then?'

'Two years – I still don't know too much of the lingo. Too bleedin' difficult. I use sign language a lot. I came out here to get away – hated London after a bit. When Mum died there was no reason to stay there. I lived wiv 'er, see. She always wanted me to improve myself so I did a course at poly on art 'istory, then I came out 'ere – I work in the fish market now, though. Can't get a decent job the way I look and it suits me for the minute. I can tell yer the names of every fish in Italian, and quantities,' he said enthusiastically.

'Right, I see.' Miles was now more in the dark than ever. Their drinks arrived and were quickly drained, then Miles got up to leave. 'I'd better get moving. I've no idea what time my landlady locks up. Do you want to get together for a drink here tomorrow night? You know, one non-Italian to another.'

Grapper seemed eager. 'Yer all right, you are – yeah, that'd be great – see yer about ten thirty. I've got to do sommat before that.'

'Sure that's fine – see you tomorrow.' Miles shook Grapper by the hand and headed for the door. As an afterthought Grapper added:

'If yer can bloody find it that is.'

'You just watch me. I'll be like a native in no time.'

Grapper shook his head. 'I hope not,' he said. 'I bloody hope not.'

CHAPTER 3

His ordeal was over, but the aftermath proved hard to shake off and Miles had a sleepless night. The void between darkness and light, although only a few short hours, seemed to go on for days. Jet-lag was definitely taking its toll. He mulled things over: if it hadn't been for his unlikely saviour he could have been robbed or worse. Clearly, he thought, he was going to have to be very careful here. He turned over and thumped the pillow. It was no use, it was too hot to sleep, he had too many things on his mind. He stared at the ceiling and mentally changed gear, perusing all the things he found appealing. He was looking forward to his coming term at Cal Tech. It offered the best architectural course and he'd done well to get in. It had been a long time since he'd looked forward to anything. Maybe this trip hadn't been such a bad idea after all – it was giving him a fresh perspective already. He got up and took one of his books back to bed. He read more about this glorious city by the pink light of a bedside lamp with a fringed lampshade. This was one of his favourite books – Gore Vidal's pictorial view of some of the lesser-known Venetian treasures. He gazed at the beautifully photographed canals and found it hard to believe that those ribbons of stinking water outside were one and the same.

Finally, he managed to drift off to sleep just as dawn broke. Almost immediately, a cacophony of dustmen and traders started their boats and bellowed instructions outside his window. He opened his eyes and groaned. Unidentified objects clattered and banged, dogs barked and the sparrows and pigeons added their contribution to the din. He put a pillow over his head and thought, this is the real Venice: a noisy, dirty, smelly city with a maze of dark creeping alleyways that he would never be master of. He wondered if Grapper would teach him how to find his way around this labyrinth.

Miles rose around eleven. His morning passed pleasantly enough. After a breakfast of pastries and coffee, courtesy of

Giorgio no doubt, he set off in search of the textbook Venice, intending to take in as many of the sights as he could. He decided to look at St Mark's again, convinced that it would be far easier to find his way in daylight.

He reached the Accademia bridge and found it was seething with tourists. He pushed his way through the jostling crowd for a view of the length of the Grand Canal. It didn't disappoint. The city's main artery glistened in the dazzling sunlight. Gracious palazzos lined the water, their façades speaking volumes: of grandeur and abandoned dynasties. Like countless others before him, Miles leaned over the wooden railing and watched the gondolas ferrying the tourists away like ill-gotten gains. The gondoliers sang as they punted reminding him of Cambridge and that fateful summer's day at Grantchester. He closed his eyes. Was it really only a year ago? He pictured himself punting, the long pole wedging in the silt, Lisa laughing. The tearoom in the dappled orchard. He watched them finish their tea and climb onto the motorbike then snapped his eyes open as the memory threatened to take over again. The long scar on his right leg began to throb, demanding attention. He bent down and rubbed it. Time to move on, he thought.

Ignoring the nagging pain, he made his way over the bridge towards St Mark's, pausing for just a moment to study a beautiful white building surrounded by a large garden with elegant high walls. This was Palazzo Barbaro where Henry James and Byron had stayed when the creative juices dried. He envisaged them standing at the huge window, gazing at the view that had moved so many, collecting inspiration from the air like imaginary butterflies.

In the Campiello Santo Stefano, bright sunlight became hazy as a lone cloud softened the glare. The ochre-coloured buildings were neglected and worn. The squalor was a total contrast to the Grand Canal's well-preserved historic buildings. A young girl sat at the feet of a large bronze statue. On her outstretched hands half a dozen pigeons gently took the grain on offer. Hundreds more bobbed and cooed at her feet awaiting their turn. She threw her hands into the air, sending the privileged few away, and took handfuls of food from a bag. Her long ebony hair swung as she scattered it widely for them. She called softly to her children and they responded, cooing back to her in restful muted tones. Miles was mesmerized by her beauty and gentleness. He crouched down, pretending to tie his shoelace, and took a better look at her. He thought she was probably the most beautiful girl he had ever seen. Suddenly she looked up, aware that she was being watched. Shielding her pale eyes from the brilliant sun, she looked directly at Miles. He straightened and walked on, smiling as he passed her en route to the yellow sign which pointed the way to St Mark's.

The girl's eyes followed his retreating figure.

Miles ambled along, wondering if she would catch him up. He stopped before a shop window and looked at the Italian fashions on display. Armani and Valentino were out of his present financial reach. He eyed a calfskin suede jacket in pale brown, which would have looked stunning with his blonde hair and golden skin. The Amex card he'd sworn he'd never use burned a hole in his pocket. He wished he and his father could get along. Sometimes the dollar is mightier than anger.

'Beautiful, isn't it?' A soft lilting voice came from behind him. He looked beyond the jacket to the girl's reflection.

'Yes,' he said, holding her image in his gaze. 'I think you are too.'

'It is such a pity that men think all women will respond to flattery.' Her accent was charming.

'What other way is there to show appreciation?' Miles asked, surprised by her intelligent putdown.

'If you don't know then I am certainly not going to tell you.' She turned on her heel and walked away leaving him open-mouthed. Although he had little interest in the opposite sex these days, he was used to women falling over themselves to get to him. This was a new, more challenging twist.

He considered her arrogant and walked in the opposite direction, determined not to follow her. She had definitely aroused a sense of indignation and curiosity. The girl was not what he had expected to encounter here. He scuffed his shoes in the gutter. Was he such a bad judge of people? Why had he assumed someone who cared about birds would be a pushover? He walked without any real sense of direction and suddenly found himself in St Mark's.

Thousands of pigeons scuttled away from the hordes of tourists. As he walked among them they strutted around like grey-suited businessmen in the rush hour. Two little girls in identical outfits crouched down to feed the throng milling around them. The birds were better off here being fed by innocence than in a farmer's oven.

Once again, despite Carole's warning about prices, he needed sustenance and made his way over to the Café Florian. At an empty table in the plush red interior, he studied the beautifully painted panels of half-naked women with flowing tresses and pictured the girl he'd just met. By the time he got the bill for his consolatory beer, the cost so stunned him that he forgot all about her.

He walked into the heart of the square and viewed the cloisters from a distance. It had been described as the Drawing Room of Europe. Ivory-coloured awnings flapped in a slight breeze like elegant curtains at its windows. The Campanile bells began to ring, filling the air with a timeless, solemn sound. The pigeons suddenly took flight, as though startled by the loud pealing which they must have lived with all their short lives. The air felt suddenly compressed, expectant. Miles thought of the folk tale that suggested the pigeons only took wing and flew to the mainland when they were about to die. Was it the angel of death that had disturbed them and not the familiar bells? He watched them wheeling above him and thought them lucky. He had been close enough to death to feel its cool breath on his face. He knew with all his heart that he never wanted to come that close again – not until his time had really come.

To escape the heat, Miles wandered aimlessly through the cool marbled interior of the Correr Museum. His pale denim shirt clung to his chest. Pulling distractedly at it, he viewed magnificent works by Tintoretto and Carpaccio. His appreciation of their labours was marred by a sudden tiredness that made his limbs feel heavy. He sat down for a moment on the attendant's vacant chair and closed his eyes. He was still unable to stand for lengthy periods – his leg would probably never regain its original athletic strength. He listened to the tourists' hushed voices discussing the exhibition in a variety of languages. French, Spanish and English were being spoken simultaneously. The women's high heels clicked delicately on the marble – the sound was compressed, almost phased. The overall effect was a tranquil one and Miles felt tempted to ignore protocol and drift off. The demons of guilt never invaded his daylight sleep. Instead he stood up and looked at his watch – an hour to go before siesta.

He appraised the remaining room of paintings casually without really taking them in, until one particular artist penetrated the constraints of his tiredness. Antonio Canova was indeed a magician. His figures were somehow alive with passion – a passion that communicated openly, captivating those who heard its subtle whispers. The drawing which spoke to Miles in low seductive tones was of a young girl who appeared immensely saddened. Her delicate face cried out for the touch of reassurance. Dark liquid eyes of charcoal suggested that, with the certain knowledge someone cared, her suffering would be eased. Miles instinctively reached out to her, like drawn to like, then he stood back. If only she were real, if only a soulmate could be there to lessen his own terrible burden.

For the first time in his young life, he envied his father's wealth. The access it gave to locked doors of priceless possessions was now suddenly desirable. At that moment he would have truly given anything to own the drawing.

After a while he tore himself away to view other works by the same artist. Nothing moved him quite as much until, by a grandiose picture window overlooking the crowded square below, he came upon a strange sculpture in a glass case. This was Canova's masterpiece in miniature, an ominous pyramid fashioned in grey marble. Miles took a closer look. Three mourners followed the sinister hooded figure into a dark rectangular entrance; two impassive angels, guardians to the tomb, cast their eyes solemnly to their sandalled feet. Was it mandatory, this avoidance of direct eye contact with the tearful bemoaning of the followers? Were the angels party to some dread secret of the afterlife? Who suffers the most pain when the reaper raises the fateful scythe to take what is rightfully his – is it better to mourn or be mourned? His mind was filled with questions to which there was no mortal answer.

The milling, snap-happy crowd below him carried on with their banal preoccupations. Around five hundred peasants a day had been lost during the time of the Venetian plague. Miles calculated roughly that it would have taken a mere four days to wipe out every tourist below him.

When his exhaustion passed, he headed for his temporary home, finding his way back easily by following the yellow Accademia signs. In no time at all he was crossing the now-deserted Campiello Santo Stefano once more. He looked over at the bronze statue hopefully. The girl and her pigeons had long since left. He wondered if she too was indulging in the traditional siesta. He pictured her between cool white sheets, her black hair fanning out on the pillow, restlessly turning her head in troubled sleep. It amazed him that she had come so easily to mind again. He pushed the image away and quickened his step to escape the stifling humidity.

Katerina welcomed him with a glass of lemonade.

'It's like a blast furnace out there.' Miles downed the drink gratefully in one.

She chuckled. 'You think this bad, skinny, you wait. August worse – much worse.'

'Well, thanks a lot,' he said. 'I'm going to lie down now before I expire.'

Katerina looked at him as a mother would her child, then she wiped her sweaty palms on the dirty apron loosely tied around her ample waist. 'You want tea or I wake you at dinnertime?'

Miles suppressed a yawn. 'Oh, dinnertime please. I've got to lie down – I feel like I swam the Atlantic.'

His landlady laughed raucously and clutched her aching sides. She dabbed at her eyes with a floral print sleeve. 'Silly Skinny couldn't even swim the Grand Canal.'

Miles was bemused by the insult. He wondered if he should put her straight. His bedroom shelves were lined with high diving and swimming medals. As her laughter rang out from the salon he decided to let her have her fun.

The merest hint of a breeze worked its way through the closed shutters, nudging the cream net curtains as Miles drifted into a gentle doze. The sparrows were the only audible sounds of life in the sleepy street. They chattered incessantly but couldn't keep him from dropping off.

Gradually he began to dream of a white sand beach. Above the sound of the waves, he and Lisa listened to a piano playing softly in the distance. They watched the seagulls wheeling above them. Lisa turned to say something to him only it wasn't her – it was the ebony-haired girl from the square and he wasn't lying on sand – the ground was cobbled, uncomfortable. The girl crouched down, like the little girls he had seen earlier that day, and threw a handful of crumbs into the air. From his prone position Miles watched the startled birds take flight – they flew higher and higher, their shapes becoming blurred, the grey of their wings turning to black in the twilight. From behind a cloud a watery moon appeared, casting silvery strands of light on the now blackened shapes. He watched their metamorphosis with interest. They merged into a seething mass transformed, as if by magic, into a threatening cloud of bats. The dark airborne rodents multiplied in the pewter sky until there were thousands of them. Unexpectedly in attack formation, they turned and swooped towards him, squealing in high pitched voices. The girl's delighted laughter woke him instantly.

Miles snapped his eyes open and sat up with a jolt. He looked nervously around the room, then leaned back against the cast iron headboard and fought for breath. He had felt he was being slowly suffocated.

In a tiny squalid room, no more than nine feet square, Grapper sat on the narrow window ledge and observed the large spider-scuttling across the floor. He stood up slowly and walked towards it; his large Doc Marten boots seemed a likely instrument of execution. The spider stilled itself, sensing danger. Grapper bent down and with a surprising gentleness stretched his hand onto the grimy floor. 'Come on, yer know yer've got yer dinner coming', he commanded. The spider obligingly crawled onto Grapper's hand. He placed it on a rickety table. On the red and white chequered vinyl cloth, next to a half-empty milk bottle, a jar of diluted honey housed several dead flies. Grapper carefully extracted them and shook them to remove any excess liquid. He deposited them charitably before the waiting spider.

'Yer getting too lazy to make a bleeding web, ain't ya,' he goaded. The spider rubbed its forelegs together indifferently. Grapper took a slab of bread, buttered it lavishly and joined the insect in its meal. It was always nicer to eat in company. As he chewed thoughtfully a hazy vision appeared in his mind's eye. His saliva dried instantly – he swallowed hard and closed his eyes to get a better fix on the oblique message. The tingling in his limbs became a fire, his head lolled from side to side, his breathing grew laboured as unwelcome arms wrapped themselves tightly around him. His enlightenment was so abrupt he cried out in surprise. With the gory tableau set before him like a demonic Nativity, his new friend appeared, smiling naïvely at those who bore deadly gifts.

That night, Miles wanted to get dinner over with quickly. The conversation was unbelievably stilted and, as he toyed with Giorgio's tortellini, he wished he were going out every night. Broken English batted back and forth like an ill-matched game of tennis as the Germans struggled to convey their impression of this beautiful city. In the absence of words they resorted to mimes which looked like a strange game of charades. Miles wondered what an outsider would make of it all as he watched Herr Breitenbach trying to mime the domes of the Basilica.

Eventually, Miles excused himself and read in his room. Adventurous as he was, he decided not to explore. Last night's escapade had shaken him. No. Better to stay on safe ground. A large clock in the hall struck ten o'clock and dull chimes carried through the hallway. He closed his book and, although it was early, headed for El Souk. The barmaids would keep him amused until Grapper arrived.

Once there he felt more out of place than he had done with Grapper. Bella or Anna (he wasn't sure which was which) looked him up and down from behind the bar. He sat on one of the high stools and ate some nuts, ignoring the appraisal in her dark eyes. He asked for a beer.

'You meet Grapper later, no?' she asked as she reached up to take a glass down from the rack above her head.

He noticed her rounded breasts straining against the pale blue cotton of her T-shirt. 'Yes . . .' he said without meeting her eyes. 'He's an unusual person, isn't he?'

The voluptuous barmaid frowned at the words and he suddenly realized her English was probably restricted to bar-speak. She shrugged and gave him his beer with a smile. He smiled back and walked over to the table he had shared with his new friend last night. Several couples huddled together – the darkened ambience seemed to encourage borderline intimacy. They were dressed in ripped jeans and leather jackets – bearable in an air-conditioned room, but he wondered how on earth they stood it in the heat outside. Sipping his beer thoughtfully, he watched them and couldn't help thinking of Lisa. They had often been taken for brother and sister, their colouring was so similar. She'd been so vibrant and alive before the accident. He shuddered in remembrance and tried to close his mind to the assault on his senses that accompanied these thoughts: the smell of burning rubber, Lisa's body flying through the air in slow motion, the sound of her screams and the searing pain he knew he would never forget.

He opened his eyes just as Grapper walked through the door. Bella did her hip-wiggling routine at him – he kissed her as only a lover would and she motioned to Miles's table. Grapper walked over, grinning from ear to ear. 'You all right with that beer, mate, or do ya want anovver one?' he asked politely.

Miles shook his head. 'No, I'm fine. You get what you want though . . . I'm buying.' He seemed pensive.

'Nah, you ain't buyin', this one's on me. Give us a Scotch and annover beer, Bella, ya dozy cow.' He sat down abruptly and turned to Miles. 'You know she doesn't understand a bloody word I say – suits me fine.'

Miles gave a half-hearted smile. 'I described you as unusual and she looked at me like I was from Mars.'

'Dozy cow. She's all right, though, know what I mean?' Grapper winked knowingly.

'Yeah, I can imagine.' Miles felt a schoolboy affinity in their mutual appreciation of Bella's indisputable charms.

'Yer got a girl then?' Grapper asked.

'I did have – not now though.' Miles took a swig of beer and cast his gaze into its clear golden hue. He had a haunted look like a wanderer searching for some lost part of himself. Grapper watched him compassionately. He waited for what seemed to both of them like an eternity, then stared into the smoked glass mirror behind them and spoke in comforting tones:

'I get the impression everything ain't right with yer. Well, yer know what they say about time healing old wounds.'

Miles looked up and saw a serenity in the eyes of his companion which any self-respecting priest would have been proud of. 'I have a good reason to be sad,' he said, pensively.

Grapper twirled the beer mat round and round. 'Listen mate, everybody who's lost sommat or someone thinks they have a reason for self-pity, but they don't 'ave a real reason, they just wanna feel sorry for themselves. I felt that way when Mum died – it was a good excuse to do nothin'. All I can tell yer is the past is soon forgotten.' What he actually meant was the recent past soon becomes a whisper in your memory instead of a scream of anguish. Miles thought it was useless to try and argue the toss with him.

'I'm sure you're right, but this is a bit different . . . ' he said somewhat defensively. 'I have a greater reason than most, you know.'

'Do yer wanna talk about it?' Grapper asked, instinctively knowing the answer.

Miles took another comforting swig of beer. 'It's really hard to talk about it without . . .' He paused. 'This holiday is more of an emotional sabbatical than anything else; my parents thought it would take my mind off things. You see, there was an accident and someone I really cared for didn't make it through, she's in a coma.' He swallowed hard and held back the tears. 'She's been that way for almost a year. It was all so damned stupid – it should never have happened.' He stared at the glass.

'That's pretty tough, but yer know there's certain things in life we can't control – it's useless to even try,' Grapper said knowingly. He fiddled with the chains on his jacket. A heavy silence enveloped them making the atmosphere strangely tense – like a room after a heated argument between two people who really love each other. Grapper wondered for a moment whether this tragedy had anything to do with the ghastly image of his new friend which had appeared so alarmingly to him in his room.

Miles felt his emotional state was ruining what was left of a perfectly good evening so be bucked himself up and said: 'Well that's enough about my problems, let's drink to something more cheerful – like sex, drugs and rock and roll.' He raised his glass, smilingly tersely.

His companion groaned. 'You've got a hell of a lot to learn about what a bruiser like me thinks is a good time. The only one that qualifies out of that lot is sex, mate, and plenty of it.'

They laughed and Miles raised his glass again; 'Let's drink to sex then.'

'And friends,' Grapper added. 'Absent and new.'

CHAPTER 4

A week passed pleasantly as Miles embarked on the usual round of sightseeing trips: The Scuola Grande di San Rocco with its fifty-seven varieties of Tintoretto, the huge church of Santa Maria Gloriosa dei Frari, the Rialto bridge and along the Mercerie where he window shopped; he saw the Ca' d'Oro and the Palazzo Loredan-Vendramin-Calergi, where Wagner died. With all these sorties the route to St Mark's became very familiar. He felt quite superior when his confident manner occasionally prompted other tourists to ask him the way. Exploration of lesser-known territory was limited to daylight forays or night-time excursions with Grapper as his guide. The sights and smells filled his senses; his mind, while otherwise occupied, was less prone to reminiscences and unpleasant nightmares. As the heat intensified, the city was plagued by a strain of gigantic mosquitos which mercilessly dive-bombed their unwilling hosts. Miles had delicate skin and provided a virtual banquet for them. Angry lumps appeared on his exposed flesh. They burned and itched constantly. He wore socks to cover his feet and a thin long-sleeved shirt, but somehow the hungry managed to detect a way in for their main meal of the day. He sat alone at a waterside restaurant. Under attack again, he swore and slapped the side of his neck.

'From Florida,' the waiter said knowledgeably as he sawed the clammy air with his hand.

'I don't care where they come from, I just wish to God they'd stop biting me. Miles wiped a bloodied corpse from his hand with a pink napkin. The waiter shrugged dispassionately and, resuming his train of thought, gazed out into the night. Miles turned back to his omelette and the guidebook propped up against a large black pepper mill. His enjoyment of the trip had been impaired a little by the oppressive heat which bore down on everyone, making even the most placid seem irritable. The élite had long since escape to the Lido where the sea breezes made the atmosphere a good deal more clement.

Miles toyed idly with his meal, lifting the melted cheese from the eggs. Light glistened on pale yellow strands. He pushed the plate away and sighed; it was no use, he had no appetite, it was too hot. Last night, he had wisely decided to cut his trip short by two weeks – Florence would be a good deal cooler. Although he knew it was sensible, this decision now weighed heavily on his mind. He had fallen hook, line and proverbial sinker for the charms of this beautiful city and despite the jostling tourists, the evident vulgarity and this unbearable humidity, in his heart of hearts he wanted to stay.

His thoughts turned to Grapper and he wondered if they would stay in touch after he left. They'd become quite close. There was something very special about him, something different – he couldn't put his finger on it but it was there. Would they have bonded under differing circumstances? He really couldn't tell. Venice was a huge melting pot of tourists and refugees from banality. They were, from all classes and races, lumped together on one large island, tolerant yet wary of each other. He looked up to summon the waiter and noticed the girl from the square was engaged in conversation with him. She spoke to him in softened tones observing Miles as her question was answered. Then she nodded and walked over to his table. Her manner couldn't have been more direct – she looked into his eyes and asked if she could join him. Her head inclined slightly as she awaited an answer, her body language emulating a small bird awaiting titbits. Miles motioned to the vacant chair.

'Grazie,' she said softly, 'It is very hot, no?' She picked up the oversized menu and fanned her face.

'Yes, molto caldo,' Miles answered in Italian and wondered if she recognized him.

'Do you live in Venice?' he asked casually.

She sighed with slight exasperation and fanned herself a little faster. 'You know I do – you saw me with the birds in the Campiello Santo Stefano.' She was triumphant in her recognition. 'No more flattery tonight, eh?'

'Not if you don't want it. Anyway, you could have just as easily been a tourist feeding those pigeons.' For some reason he felt like an errant schoolboy caught outside the girls' changing-room windows.

'They do not take the same care as I do. You cannot feed them with just anything.' She signalled the waiter who came obediently to her side, and asked for two cappuccinos, assuming Miles wanted the same as her. He watched her and said nothing. She was even more beautiful this close. Her face was heart-shaped, slightly elongated; high cheekbones made her look more South American than Italian. In stark contrast to her dusky complexion, her eyes were a piercing blue; set within the coffee background the effect was stunning. Her silken hair was the darkest ebony. She wore it carelessly wound on the crown of her head, small curls escaping around her neck and face. It seemed to be held in place with only a sharp wooden stick which looked more like a weapon than a hairdressing aid. Her eyes twinkled as she observed his bemused expression.

'The stick is for protection,' she said in justification. 'The gangs you know – they are very bad. Venice is like any other city at night. If I am walking alone I feel safer with protection.' Miles laughed, picturing this slight girl giving a hooligan the fright of his life. 'I have good Maize too, you know.' Once again she put her head on one side like an inquisitive sparrow.

He bit his tongue, not daring to laugh, 'You mean Mace.'

'Si, si, Maace . . .' she mispronounced the word in an effort to correct herself.

'What's your name?' he asked as their cappuccinos arrived.

'Daniela Riaggi,' she said extending her hand. 'I am pleased to meet you.' (She pronounced her last name with a rolling 'r' and a soft 'g'.)

He took her hand gently, resisting the urge to kiss it. It was slender, an artist's hand. 'Miles Hanson, I'm pleased to meet you too. You have beautiful hands. Are you a painter?' he asked.

She took a spoonful of froth from the cup and licked it delicately. 'I thought you said there would not be any flattery tonight.'

Smiling, Miles copied her and thought her strange – with every other girl he'd known it was a definite pre-requisite to seduction. But then he hadn't seduced anyone for a long time – perhaps he was out of practice. As they talked enthusiastically over the coffee, fragments of his dream of Daniela nagged at the back of his mind. He put it down to a subconscious fear of involvement and let the conversation flow on. When he remarked on her excellent English, she told him she had lived in London until five years ago. Her mother spoke both languages at home so she was almost fluent in both. Now she lived in the San Lio district with her grandmother who was seventy-four and who sounded, from her very descriptive accounts, like a stubborn old goat.

Daniela also told Miles that she worked in one of the many boutiques by day and studied in the evenings. When he asked what she was studying she became secretive. 'In time I tell you, if I decide I like you,' she said slyly.

'Don't you know whether you like me or not?'

'I think I do.' She gave him a sidelong glance. 'Will you walk with me for a little while? Maybe that would help me to decide.'

'I'd like that. You can show me the sights I haven't seen,' he said suggestively as he drained the remaining coffee from his cup.

She waved to the waiter, 'Il conto, Vincenzo.' Her voice carried across the now empty restaurant. Miles thought for a moment she was being insulting then he realized she'd asked for the bill. His Italian stretched to three or four phrases of thanks or requests. He paid and they walked from the latticework terrace out into the night. Redundant gondolas bobbed violently as the water bus moored noisily by the swaying pontoon, disgorging a milling throng onto the jetty. Miles looked across the lagoon to the entrance of the Grand Canal. The illuminated white façade of the wedding-cake church of Santa Maria della Salute was a breathtaking sight. The starry night sky prompted the sudden urge to suggest a gondola ride. Fearing it would appear crass and touristy to a native, he dismissed the idea and followed Daniela's striding lead in the direction of St Mark's. As they walked she spoke of Soho and how it was very like Venice at night. He stopped in his tracks for a moment.

'I guess so, but what the hell was a nice girl like you doing in a garbage dump like Soho? It's a pretty suspect place.' She frowned. Her English might have been excellent but American was another matter. As he explained what he meant, images of porn shops and rent boys came into his mind. Daniela told him her mother had been an exotic dancer, they had lived above the shop as it were.

'So she was a dancer?' His tone said it all.

'It was erotic but she was an artiste, not an ordinary striptease person, if that's what you're thinking,' Daniela said petulantly.

'I'm sure she was great.' He sensed her pride. 'Anyway, she

must have been quite something to have given birth to someone as special as you.'

Daniela placed her hands on her slender hips and smiled knowingly. 'Well, in time, we will see if I am special or not. I know many things – things that would surprise you. I had the best teacher there was in my mother.'

'She must have taught you to look out for yourself in Soho – it's not exactly Anne of Green Gables country.' He suddenly noticed her skirt was very short. Her long brown legs deserved to be shown off but despite his admiring glance he couldn't help wondering whether it would be a mistake to take things any further. Her sexuality had undoubtedly been on display for more than the likes of him.

'Who is Anne Green, someone you know?' She leaned over the stone parapet of the bridge. The subsequent view left little to the imagination.

'I can see I may have to teach you some things, for all you know about nightlife,' Miles murmured appreciatively.

Daniela turned, rested her elbows on the stone and looked at him quizzically. Her gold-coloured silk vest revealed gleaming taut muscles and rounded breasts. In a tantalizing instant her expression suggested an awareness of her body that radiated the pent-up sexuality of an alley cat. Miles stared at her as she said: 'The night in such a city as this is an experience – it belongs to the young, to those of us that seek adventure – something different, maybe even dangerous.'

She walked away, leaving him momentarily lost for words. 'Are you dangerous, Daniela?' he called after her in a hesitant tone.

She turned to face him, locking his gaze in her black widow's stare.

'That depends on a great many things,' she purred. 'What you want to know is, am I going to be dangerous to you?'

Miles studied her with lecherous excitement welling up in him and thanked God the pharmacies stayed open late. If she was going to be dangerous to him, he was going to enjoy every damn minute of it.

'If you're worried about him why don't you tell him the truth?'

Grapper downed the Scotch in Fabrizio's apartment and shrugged: 'It's not the sort of thing yer talk about unless yer want people to think yer bonkers. Anyway ya know me – I like to keep everyfing under me 'air.'

Fabrizio, a rotund little man with an eye for women who loved Grapper like a brother because he had driven a London taxi and Grapper's accent reminded him of the good times, chuckled. 'With hair like that it is a miracle anything stays, no?'

'Very funny,' Grapper twirled the glass in his hands. 'Give us anovver Scotch, mate – I need it.'

His friend poured another Black and White and asked, 'How much of the picture have you got this time?'

Grapper took a gulp and looked concerned. 'Not enough, mate, that's the bleedin' trouble. All I know is Miles is walking into a viper's nest and you know me – I 'ate fuckin' snakes. If I'm gonna keep him out of trouble, I ain't gonna like it much, that I can tell yer.'

Daniela and Miles sauntered down the darkened streets on the way to her apartment, chatting happily with each other like best friends walking home from school. Miles gave her a slightly fabricated image of his background. Wealth either made false friends or frightened people off. He made it sound middle-class and comfortable, as opposed to a life which would not have been out of place in a Scott Fitzgerald novel.

After about fifteen minutes they came to the alley where Daniela lived. Mouldering rubbish was piled outside each of the shadowy doorways, neglected washing hung on the line above his head, pitifully thin cats cowered in doorways – this was nothing short of a Venetian ghetto.

The alley was a dead end. Daniela stopped before an enormous blackened door which ominously guarded against uninvited entry to the inner sanctum beyond. The rotting studded oak portico was but a few feet from a crumbling lichen-covered stone landing stage which had been partially eroded by the murky canal. The size of the entrance suggested it had once been far more than just another house in a slum.

'This is where I live . . . it was once a palace of the doges,' Daniela remarked somewhat proudly.

'Once,' Miles said with more than a hint of snobbery in his tone.

She extracted a bunch of keys from the depths of a large leather bag and jiggled one of them in the mortice lock. With a protesting groan the heavy door opened, revealing a musty-smelling expanse of pitch black beyond. Daniela snapped on a dim light. Miles could just make out a pammet stone floor – some discarded rotting furniture was lying on its side in a pool of water left from high tide. Directly opposite, another huge oak door virtually hung off its hinges. The mere size of the place suggested it had once been quite imposing. As they walked into the centre of the room, Miles could see two large double doors leading onto the canal. 'Fit for a king and his entourage,' Miles said. His voice rang out in the echoing darkness. A bright orange hosepipe hung on the wall just by the door.

'What's that for?' he asked.

Daniela, who was looking for another key, followed his finger. 'The flooding – this part of Venice floods if there is heavy weather. Once, the water came up to here on me.' She held the flat of her hand against her chest.

Miles imagined peasants wading through this once great hall to a ducal audience with dirty water weighing them down, their heavy clothes billowing like a galleon under full sail.

'At one time all of Venice would have come to this place to ask favours of the doge,' Daniela said as though reading his thoughts. 'It is sad to think of it as it must have been. Come on, let us go upstairs.'

The next door led onto a grand staircase. Remnants of pale frescos with their ice-cream pastels adorned the walls. The stairs were inlaid with an intricate marble mosaic. Miles had to admit it probably had been very beautiful once. Now this faded grandeur did appear sad; a tragic architectural princess reduced to the filth and desperation of a bag lady.

After three flights of stairs they reached the door to Daniela's apartment. 'Here we are then,' she whispered, looking him in the eye suggestively.

She opened the door quietly and turned on the light.

Miles was surprised by the antique opulence within the room. The furniture looked ornate – Renaissance: large period portraits, which he assumed were ancestral, hung on the silk-covered walls, the tasteful colour scheme was a muted grape and the palest of blues and a large crystal chandelier hung in the centre of the room. The family's affluence seemed wildly out of place in an area made over to such obvious squalor and poverty.

Daniela led him down a long hall into her bedroom. Her rebellion against tradition was evident in the abrupt change in ambience.

A cream four-poster bed hung with white silk curtains dominated the centre of the sparsely furnished room. Huge portraits of James Dean and Jim Morrison took precedence over grim-faced relatives. The room was strewn with feminine clutter. Daniela was either very untidy or constantly in a hurry.

She opened the drawer of her bow-fronted dressing table and took out three tall white candles and a joss stick. With the solemnity of a religious ritual, she lit the candles in turn and placed the joss stick in a small china container. Holding it in the flame of the match, she inhaled its musky fragrance.

'White candles bring white light,' she said matter-of-factly.

Miles walked around the room expectantly. 'And black candles bring dark light, I suppose – if there is such a thing.'

She said nothing but a knowing smile hovered on her lips as she took a bottle of Southern Comfort from the hand-painted linen press she used as a wardrobe. 'I hope you like this drink.' She held it out to him.

Miles squinted at the label. Without his glasses, reading from a distance was a little difficult. 'Oh good, nectar of the gods. I'm glad to see you've got taste.'

'In some things, yes,' she said, filling their glasses. 'Make yourself comfortable – the bed is the coolest place. There's a fan in the left-hand corner – why don't you turn it on while I put on some music.'

Miles tentatively parted the white curtains and lay down. 'You must be into sixties' stuff with all these posters of Morrison. I'm more of a Hendrix freak myself,' he said as he turned on the fan. It whirred to life. Silken drapes billowed out like a gentle tropical wind filling ocean sails. The cloying heat became cool night air.

Daniela fiddled with the cassette player. 'My mother gave me the posters and some records. I do not have many of my own.'

'I feel like the Sheikh of Araby,' Miles joked. 'Do you sleep like this every night?'

I could not sleep any other way; the silk is to keep the mosquitos out.'

'You're lucky to have this – I feel like a leper I've been bitten so many times.' He scratched one absently.

'I have some very good cream. I will get it for you.'

Miles closed his eyes as the strains of Jefferson Airplane's 'White Rabbit' began, and imagined her rubbing the cream in. It had been a long time since he'd felt the touch of a girl. The image in his head grew in intensity. He heard ice chink into glasses as Grace Slick intoned, '. . . and you just ate some kind of mushroom . . . and it's gone right to your head . . . to your head.' The rhythm quickened, as the music reached its drug-induced crescendo and the gossamer drapes at the foot of the bed parted on cue. Daniela stood facing him holding the two filled glasses. She was totally naked.

'I think it's time we got to know one another better,' she said, holding out his drink. Miles reached for it and opened his mouth to say something. No sound came – he was rendered speechless by her lack of inhibitions. He took a gulp and thanked God for the pharmacy. He'd been stupid on more than one occasion but this time he wasn't going to take any chances. Now he needed to loosen up. He drank the honeyed liquid virtually in one.

Daniela made no obvious move. She stood at the foot of the bed sipping her drink with a deliberateness that inflamed him even more. He didn't reach for her; they simply stayed still, like animals eyeing each other before the kill, each trying to gauge the depth of the other's need.

Eventually, Daniela drained her glass and placed it on the marble floor. She stretched her spine, her taut body gleaming in the candlelight, then very slowly she began to crawl up the bed on all fours. Hovering over his groin, she breathed heavily and pulled up his shirt pausing for what seemed like a lifetime. Finally, she tugged at the buttons of his 501s with sharp, almost feline teeth. Miles submitted with a mixture of desire and discomfort. He gazed at the gathered ceiling of the four-poster bed, allowing her to exploit him with the delicious expectancy of her game. He could feel a heated throbbing in his groin. He wanted to rip his flies open, releasing the unbearable pressure into her hands before it exploded of its own accord.

Daniela delighted in his torment. She raised her head slightly to look at him. 'If you look over to the candles you'll see something you may want.' Her voice tore the moment of premature ejaculation from him. Saved from embarrassment, he pulled himself up onto his elbows and looked beyond her nakedness to the candles gently flickering on the dressing table. He held his breath and stared with longing into the ornate gilt mirror which had been tilted with absolute precision to give him a soft-focus reflection of her beautiful behind. She raised it slightly and gyrated, in an attempt to entice his remaining self-control away. It worked like a charm. He pulled her to him and kissed her furiously as she tore at this clothes.

He was drowning, caught up by her, taken once more above the water where he could breathe, desperate for a passion she covered him with like a net, a soft clinging net.

Somewhere down the hall he heard a clock softly chime 4 am. Miles would have to stay until dawn; there wasn't a hope in hell of him finding his way back in the dark. He gazed at the sleeping angel beside him – her breathing was light and slightly irregular, like a baby's. He studied her face in the flickering half-light and thought she looked just as he had imagined she would in sleep. Innocent, untouched. Small beads of perspiration lined her high forehead, her tousled hair fanned the pillow, her limbs were strewn on top of the thin sheet as though, like him, she had been thrashing the air, the victim of an evil dream.

He thought of the unopened contraceptive packet in his jeans and felt angry with himself for allowing his passion to obliterate his common sense. But then he could be forgiven after all this time, couldn't he? The door to his emotional and physical needs had been firmly closed after Lisa's accident – no one had been able to get close to him. But Daniela had been different. Something about her defied resistance, or was it just that he was finally ready for a little action?

Daniela stirred slightly in her sleep and moaned under her breath as she had done earlier. Miles touched her hair, tenderly pushing it back from her delicate face. For a moment he wished she would never awaken, then he could go on looking at her. The ache in his groin soon put paid to thoughts of eternal stillness. The need to urinate was becoming uncomfortable. He wondered if movement in the hall would awaken her grandmother. Daniela had said she was a very heavy sleeper, but all he needed now was to be discovered, the guilty intruder. In a Catholic community his crime was second to none.

His need was greater than the fear so he padded silently into the hall. With a start, he realized that he had absolutely no idea where the bathroom was and furtively glanced at the four doors leading from the hall. The door to the living room was easy to identify, so that left a choice of three. Virtually taking his life in his hands, he turned the large brass door handle on the first door, thinking it would be logical to have a bathroom next to the bedroom. He peered into the darkness - he could just make out the outline of a hand-basin. Fumbling for the light switch he snapped it on. Stockings hung over the shower rail and the tiny bathroom was littered with what seemed to be every conceivable beauty aid on the market.

He urinated noisily; with a full bladder it was impossible for him to be quieter. He didn't flush - better to play safe. He switched out the light before opening the door and stubbed his toe. Hoping wildly he almost fell onto the cold marble floor. He leaned against the door for support and rubbed his toe for a moment until the pain subsided, then he opened the door a crack to identify his escape route back to the bedroom. As he closed the bathroom door behind him, an old woman in a white nightdress appeared. She peered into the light at Miles's nakedness but didn't speak. Miles froze, fully expecting she would scream or have a heart attack. However, she remained silent, still, gazing robotically through him as though he wasn't there at all. Then she turned and walked through the open door into what he assumed was her room.

He remained rooted to the spot for a few seconds more then, dripping with nervous perspiration, he fumbled his way back into bed. Daniela didn't stir. He felt shaken. He was going to make a run for it as soon as it was light. He looked down at her. Maybe he shouldn't see her again. Better to leave this as a wonderful memory, no complications, none of the searching questions that lovers always ask sooner or later.

He dozed for a few minutes at a time, waking suddenly, convinced he'd slept for hours. He watched the shutters for signs of light with heavy eyelids that scanned the length and breadth of the mullioned window before closing again.

At last salvation arrived within a few greying strands which cast spidery patterns onto the faces of Daniela's sixties icons. He moved as slowly as possible so as not to disturb her and dressed quickly. He put his hand on the door and then turned to take a last look. He couldn't leave her with a typically masculine brushoff. Wham, bam, thank you mam. Hurriedly, he scribbled a brief message on one of Katerina's cards. 'Meet me later, Café Florian – 12, love, Miles. PS Your grandmother woke up but I don't think she saw me.' He placed the card gently on the pillow and blew Daniela's beautiful sleeping form a kiss. Then he walked away, a free man.

Or so he thought.

Grapper watched the naked light swinging slowly backwards and forwards – the pendulum of poverty gauging his distress.

'I wish you'd help us out, Ma,' he pleaded with thin air.

Heavy silence and the dying strains of night taunted his child-like need for company. He sighed and placed his head in his hands. Searching the darker regions of his hitherto unwanted gifts, he looked for an obvious way to quell this current desperation. Beads of sweat broke out on his forehead, dripping evidence of psychic frustration. Why had be been singled out from the babies queuing for special favours? He would rather have had any gift but this one. Why couldn't he have been an artist or a musician. A healer, he could have handled that, but this – this black tunnel that dragged his subconscious kicking and screaming into the depths of oblivion to help out some stupid bugger that didn't deserve his help! Not that Miles was like that, but the lengths he had to go to were barely worth the effort. Grapper tried to focus again.

'Give us a clue, Ma, for fuck's sake . . .'

The oppression of solitude coursed through him – despite his plea he was still very much alone. Then gently, with the waft of lily of the valley that always signified he was in her company, her unseen hand began to turn the pages of the Bible by his side. Flicking through, she stopped when she found what she was looking for.

Miles sauntered across a deserted St Mark's square. The early morning air was virginal, uncorrupted by the clawing heat of the fierce sun – it was almost pleasant. The vulgar traders were not yet open for business so he had the entire place to himself. Save for the strutting, cooing pigeons that pecked around his feet, he could see no visible signs of life. For once he felt on top of the world. He took an upturned chair from one of the café's lifeless tables, sat down and inhaled the expectancy of this misty dawn. It had rained during the night and the paving stones were still wet. He gazed at the beauty around him and felt truly a part of it. It was as though this one night of passion had restored his equilibrium. He felt balanced, recharged, alive. He closed his eyes and held his fingers to his mouth; he could still smell her heady fragrance on him.

Suddenly a loud pealing from the Campanile disturbed his private thoughts. He glanced across the square towards the sound of solemnity and was unmoved by its doleful tone. Unmoved that was, until a wave of discomfort suddenly washed over him. The air around him stilled even more and he felt as though something foul had permeated his innermost self.

Daniela stirred and smiled. Stretching her long limbs, she opened her eyes, then picked up her lover's note. Placing it to her lips she breathed deeply, breathing in his innocence, breathing in the feel of his skin, of his body held so rigidly against her own, inhaling his strengths and his weaknesses, inhaling the boy and the man, inhaling the very essence of him that must be destroyed if she was to achieve her goal.

CHAPTER 5

Although it was just after five in the morning, Katerina busied herself with preparations for the evening meal by chopping onions vigorously. A faint ray of sunlight peeked through the withering vine outside the kitchen window. She wiped her streaming eyes on the hem of her apron and shredded the slivers with dextrous precision until they were just translucent veins. It made her contented to look after people and she hummed a folk tune from childhood as the blackened coffee percolator brewed the first batch of the day.

In the last two hours she had cleaned the public rooms, washed the linen which was now heaped in a red plastic basket waiting to be hung out to dry, laid the dining table for breakfast with pale green china, watered the few yellowing plants she possessed, and brushed and set her fine grey hair with a few tiny pin-curls. This was her routine. For the last forty years or so she'd been unable to sleep past 3 am. When she had been in her twenties, these precious hours of sleeplessness had been idled away as she tossed and turned. Now she had a business to run and it suited her well – these tasks would have taken twice as long with her guests under her feet demanding more coffee or directions to the gallerie.

Miles closed the front door as quietly as he could and tiptoed into the hall. He had one foot on the bottom stair when Katerina came out of the kitchen. Wiping her hands on the apron from which she was inseparable, she squinted at him in the half-light – he looked utterly exhausted.

'So Skinny has been out all night like a tomcat.' Her tone was mildly accusing but she was smiling.

Miles sat down on the bottom stair and guiltily pushed the uncombed hair from his face.

'I didn't think anyone would be up at this hour.' He looked at his watch. 'Are you usually up this early?'

'Come, have a coffee with me and I will tell you what I have done already – maybe you will also tell Katy what you have been doing.' She gave him an affectionate poke and went back into the kitchen with an endearing chuckle. Miles wanted nothing more than to crawl into bed but the aroma of fresh coffee was irresistible. He followed Katerina into her inner sanctum.

The enormous kitchen was very much her domain and guests entered uninvited at their peril. A large antique table, which Miles thought was as big as their pool table back home, stood in the middle of the room. A bleached wooden rack draped with damp chequered teacloths hung from the ceiling. Vast pans lined the walls. A gilt-framed Madonna and child hung over the huge blackened stove and Miles wondered if Katerina needed divine assistance with her culinary efforts. The inevitable string of garlic, which no well-dressed Italian kitchen would be without, and a few cured sausages hung on the larder door. The walls were a pale ochre, stained in places by years of acrid smoke, and the colossal stone sink had probably bathed many a child.

Katerina poured coffee from the percolator and added milk from a china jug. She placed the cup before Miles, sat down and placed her hands expectantly together, awaiting enlightenment.

'Well, Skinny,' she said as Miles drank gratefully, 'you 'ave 'ad a good time, no? I can see in your face something good 'as 'appened. Your cheeks 'ave colour now.' She leaned over and pinched one for good measure.

Miles peered at her over the rim of his cup. She didn't miss a trick this woman. 'Well, yes, I did meet a girl and, er . . . Let's just say I had an interesting evening.'

'Evening,' she mocked. 'You had an interesting night, no? I know I am right so you might as well tell me everythink. I would like to 'ear what 'appened. Now I am old there is no love for me so it is good to 'ear about such things from young ones.'

Miles felt weak with fatigue. Usually, he was inclined to secrecy about affairs of the heart, but he sat with this surrogate grandmother and breathlessly filled her in on his encounter with Daniela. Katerina rested her head wistfully on her hand like a young girl and listened to his impassioned flow with envy. She could remember all too well how the first flicker of infatuation warmed your heart before consuming you with a searing heat that made you long for release. She watched his tired eyes sparkle at the mention of the girl's name, heard his tone grow hushed as he spoke of her beauty, his body language became almost languid as he relived the passion while speaking of lesser moments in their affair. Miles didn't express his deeper reservations; he simply enthused until his eyelids began to droop. Eventually Katerina took pity on him and so, relieved of duty, he dragged himself up to bed.

Early morning sunlight filtered across the solemn faces of the icons who gazed impassively down at the young hopeful. He would soon become more of a man than he had dreamed possible.

Miles removed his clothes with a painful slowness. His head felt heavy, the beginnings of a headache pulsed in his temples. He rubbed them and looked at his bloodshot eyes in the mirror. He certainly looked as though he'd had a night of it. He collapsed onto the bed with a groan and turned his face into the pillow to escape the light which peeked through the closed shutters. For some reason he felt distinctly uneasy. The joy of last night's union with Daniela was now little more than an afterthought. The unfamiliar hung over him and he suddenly longed for home. He wondered if he was really ready for the outside world and thought his vulnerability might be evident to these new friends, a throbbing blemish on the fresh face of youth. But it was his skull that bore a scar, not his brain. He should be capable of rationalizing these fears. Why was he afraid? What was he afraid of? There had to be a reasonable explanation for it.

How quickly Miles had forgotten that just a short while ago a mere staircase had seemed like a ravine. He had stood there shaking, convinced he would fall. His sense of balance had been destroyed by the jarring of his equilibrium. The ability he had now to fend for himself was only a product of careful medical and Dianetic treatment.

He thumped the pillow and tried to sleep. He was just drifting off when something abruptly woke him again. He snapped his eyes open and looked nervously around the room. There was nothing there. When he closed his eyes again Lisa's face wavered in his mind's eye. Her expression, questioning and doleful, asked him why. Miles banished her by praying – something he hadn't done for years. When he had finished, he took down the wooden crucifix that hung above his bed and placed it beneath his pillow like a boy waiting for the tooth fairy. He felt easier and instantly fell asleep. It was to be a long deep sleep, undisturbed by noises in the street, undisturbed by bad dreams.

Grapper dozed fitfully in Bella's arms. His body twitched slightly and the sudden movement woke Bella instantly. She stretched lazily and pulled his troubled head onto her breast as she would a child who had been allowed into her bed. He was dreaming of home. In the dream his mother stood at the garden gate of their little terraced house and waited for his return from school. He appeared at the end of the road and ran enthusiastically the rest of the way; grey socks around his ankles, satchel flying. As he drew nearer he noticed Miles was standing next to her. They both smiled at him.

'Had a good day dear?' his mother asked.

'Yeah,' Grapper panted. 'What's 'e doing 'ere, Ma?'

'I'm going to give him some tea. Miles wants to stay here with me.'

'But he can't do that . . .' He frowned with childish displeasure.

'Why not, dear? He'll like it here, he knows some of our friends.'

Grapper looked down and found his sandals were now Doc Martens. Suddenly he was an adult – ridiculous in short trousers and grubby blazer. When he looked again Miles and his mother had disappeared along with the street. Now he was standing in a menacing wasteland, a vast barren landscape with one lifeless tree, a skeletal image against a huge darkening sky.

He became agitated and jerked again in his sleep. 'I'll 'ave to walk 'ome naw,' he muttered aloud. Bella, now half asleep, stroked his temple distractedly as he trudged across the sodden terrain. His feet grew unbearably heavy, as though iron weights were attached to them. The mud sucked them in and he had to use all his strength to keep going. Then he gave in to the exhaustion and collapsed in the boglike substance that closed over him.

Now he was falling, falling through the air that whistled like a distant kettle in his ears. He braced himself for contact with the ground but there was no sickening thud, no splintering of bone, only a curious suspension as though someone were cradling him in their arms. He gazed up at his rescuer; his mother's eyes glistened with recent tears. 'You must help him, Charlie. Look,' she said softly. Grapper looked down and saw Miles had not been saved from the fall as he had been – his crumpled body lay below him on the foreign earth.

He awoke with a start and sat bolt upright.

'Are you okay?' Bella asked.

He was shivering a little with the memory. 'Yeah, I just 'ad a bad dream that's all – go back to sleep, baby.' He stroked her hair and she snuggled into the crook of his muscular arm and closed her eyes.

'Dozy cow,' he whispered, gazing down at her with affection. As her breathing became more regular he was wide awake. Something was going on. Whether Miles thought he was a nutter or not he was going to do the Tarot for him the first chance he got. But that wouldn't tell him everything he wanted to know – it never did. No, if he was going to find out what was going on he would have to resort to other methods. Without disturbing Bella, he lit a cigarette, leaned back against the headboard and began to formulate a plan of action.

CHAPTER 6

Miles bolted out of bed at 11.30, showered for two minutes, grabbed a pastry and hurried off to meet Daniela. It was a beautiful day and as he walked along, nibbling at the icing, he felt the curtain of trepidation had at last been lifted. It was good to be alive after all. He paused on the Accademia bridge for a moment. The water glistened with tiny pearls of light. The dry heat was already fierce – his shirt was damp in places. He walked on and thought about the turquoise majesty of the pool back home with its rather over-the-top Grecian pillars. What he wouldn't give to be lying by that pool now with a long cool drink listening to the gentle sounds of the fountain on the upper lawn and the rustling of the cedar tree's branches. The fantasy went on; he imagined his body caressed by a light breeze, Daniela by his side, oiled and gleaming. He sighed. Well, that wasn't to be. Instead he was going to an over-priced café for a ham and cheese sandwich that would probably cost him as much as two tickets to a Yankees game.

When he arrived at St Mark's, the square was positively teeming with tourists. He scanned them and wondered where on earth they had all come from. They were like ants swarming to the Basilica as though it were a pile of spilt sugar. He opted for a banquette inside the café by one of the many open doors. Here he was pleased to find a draft of cooler air brushed his face. When the orchestra struck up the opening chords of 'Granada' he wished he'd gone further inside. This time he ordered coffee instead of beer and put on his Valentino tortoiseshell reading glasses. As there was no sign of Daniela, he read the pompous leaflet on the Florian's history. In 1720 it had been open twenty-four hours a day. The prices must have been more in keeping with everyone's pocket then or they would have gone bankrupt. Finally, the waiter arrived with a complex brass object precariously perched on a delicate white china cup edged with gilt.

'This isn't going to last me very long. You'd better bring me another,' Miles said as he scrutinized the tiny cup with a typically American lack of diplomacy.

'Sir, allow me to explain,' the waiter took on the tone of an overstretched schoolmaster. ''Ere we 'ave 'ot water, you lift this like so and pour a little onto the grounds.' He lifted the lid of the brass receptacle and demonstrated. 'You see, you now 'ave plenty coffee.'

'Thank you, I see now.' Miles felt duly reeducated. The waiter muttered something under his breath and walked away. Miles took a tentative sip and looked across the square – Daniela was flying towards him, dispersing pigeons and tourists en route. She sat down breathlessly:

'I am sorry to be late. This stupid woman came into the shop just as I was leaving. She picked a dress two sizes too small – I told her she would never get into it, I tell her it is a fantasia,' Daniela waved her hands, 'She says I am wrong, tries it on and of course it was all ripped – at the back. Then she refused to pay for it.'

'What did you do?' Miles asked smiling.

'I made the old bitch pay for it – what do you expect?' She raised her dark eyebrows, surprised he doubted her authority in the situation.

'I wouldn't expect anything less from you. Hello.' He kissed her forehead. 'Coffee?'

'Si, I'm dying, and water please. Did you miss me?'

'I haven't really had time to miss you. I only left you a couple of hours ago.'

'Six hours ago – that is half a day,' she interjected.

'Okay, okay, six hours but, yes, since you're asking I did miss you a little.'

'You went so early, I am a very heavy sleeper so I did not wake when you left. I thought perhaps you had been frightened away.'

'Yeah, listen, I'm really sorry about that unfortunate business with your grandmother, I hope she didn't butt your behind when you got up.' Daniela looked puzzled. He explained. 'You know, I said she sounded like an old goat.'

She didn't seem to appreciate the joke. A shadow passed between them, and Daniela looked suddenly agitated.

'What exactly did she say to you when you saw her?'

Miles grimaced as he took a swig of coffee and got a mouthful of dregs. 'Well that's the weird thing. She didn't say a word – didn't ask who I was, nothing – she just looked at me like I wasn't there. She's not half-blind or anything, is she?'

'No,' Daniela said through slightly gritted teeth. 'She is certainly not blind.'

Miles sensed he'd said something wrong and fiddled with his tiny brass spoon. 'What shall we do today?' he asked hopefully.

She sipped her drink vacantly for a moment.

'Hello, you still in there?' Miles waved a hand before her face.

'Yes I am in here,' Daniela said irritably. She thought he looked like a small boy who has just broken his mother's favourite vase. Outwardly she softened, inwardly she was still disturbed about something. 'Will you come to meet me later? I have a secret to share with you.'

'Yes, of course. I love secrets.' He pushed a few tendrils of hair behind her ear then kissed it and whispered, 'Where shall I meet you then?'

Daniela pulled a note from her pocket. 'I have written down the address and time here. We will meet at five o'clock in the Campiello Santo Stefano. You know it. It is the place where you saw me with the pigeons.'

'Sounds good to me.' Miles took the note and pushed it down into the pocket of his jeans.

'Now I will finish my coffee and then I have to go – there is something I must do with the old goat, as you call her, today.'

Miles glanced at his watch. 'It's only 12.30 – do you really have to go right now?'

Daniela drained her cup and got up to leave. 'You forget you are in Italy now. Our eating habits are very different from yours. We eat at twelve usually, then we siesta until three or four at least.'

Miles stood up. 'I'm not sure about eating that early but I like the sleeping part. Can't I come too?' he said jokily.

'No, you cannot.' She pulled his head down and kissed him. 'I will see you later . . . you be good,' she whispered. As she released him, Miles noticed Carole, the courier he'd met at the airport, standing behind her.

'Well, you didn't waste much time, did you Miles, cheating on me already!' Carole winked at him.

Daniela wheeled around and scowled menacingly at her. 'And just who the hell are you, lady?'

Miles put a calming hand on Daniela's shoulder:

'Daniela, this is Carole. She's the courier who helped me . . . I told you about her, remember?'

'I think I can guess how she helped you,' Daniela said petulantly.

Carole tried to relieve the mounting tension. 'Very funny. I'm not even a friend yet – Miles and I hardly know each other, really.' She smiled half-heartedly at this cauldron of jealousy bubbling before her.

Daniela narrowed her eyes. 'That's an old story. I'll see you later, Miles. If you can tear yourself away, that is.' Without a backward glance she flounced out of the restaurant and marched across the square with a thundercloud of fury above her head. Carole waited respectfully until she was out of sight before sitting down.

'Christ you've got yourself a live one there, Miles,' she said.

'Yeah, she seemed agitated by you, didn't she.' Miles looked unconcerned.

'Agitated? I've seen tigers at feeding time with better manners.'

'Seems I might have caught a tiger by the tail then.'

'Looks very much like it to me. Anyway that's enough about her. How are you getting on at old Katy's?'

'She's one in a million, isn't she?'

'Definitely. Anyway, the world's only big enough for one Katy.'

Miles noticed Carole's eyes had a mischievous twinkle. 'How's Thomson?' he asked.

'Thomson, that company needs a rocket up its backside. I've had more mix-ups this season than a Robochef.'

Miles looked puzzled. 'Company? What company? And what's a Robochef?'

'A mixing machine, you know, for cooking – don't you know anything?'

'Well, I obviously don't know anything about cooking. Sorry, I thought Thomson was your boyfriend.'

Carole shook her head slightly and smiled. 'You wally. Thomson's the company I work for.' She pushed her blonde hair back from her pretty face.

'Have you got one then?' Miles asked casually.

'One what, a boyfriend?'

He nodded.

'The only males I get to go out with are like those unruly northern tourists out there waiting to cause havoc in some of the better places Venice has to offer.' She glanced at her watch. 'Christ, look at the time. I've got to go.'

'See you around perhaps?' He looked hopeful.

'Yeah, if you're unlucky!' Carole pulled a large pole with a yellow flag attached to it from the umbrella stand. 'If you see this waving around above their greasy heads you'll know it's me. Bye.'

Miles watched her take command of the gaggle of tourists waiting patiently outside the café. Holding the yellow flag aloft she herded them with sheepdog-like precision towards the Basilica. He smiled and ordered his sandwich and a beer. When it arrived he chewed thoughtfully. Carole had handled Daniela's jealous streak with great diplomacy. It obviously didn't take much to inflame Daniela's typically Italian temper – she'd behaved appallingly. Miles couldn't fathom her overreaction. What had provoked her? As Carole had pointed out, they hardly knew each other. He put it down to teenage possessiveness and searched his Baedeker for something to while away the afternoon.

Daniela's shadowy presence vigilantly observed Carole and her charges. She kept herself well hidden behind a side gate in a tiny chapel to the right of the Basilica's main entrance. A few white candles flickered with prayers for the departed. Her face emerged behind them, then disappeared like a ghostly hologram. Carole sensed something and looked over. She hunched her shoulders, protecting herself from the unseen, and carried on with her tour feeling mildly queasy. She took a pristine handkerchief from her navy bag and dabbed at her face. The room began to sway so she sank onto a pew. One of the 'greasy northerners' asked if she was all right.

'Yes, I'm okay, just a bit hot, that's all,' she said. Taking a deep breath, Carole moved on leaving the handkerchief behind on the velvet-covered rail. Daniela moved stealthily from the shadows and lifted the white cotton square as though it were contaminated. Then, changing tack, she held it to her face, inhaling Carole's floral perfume which was so unlike her own musk. This would serve her purpose well. She smiled with malevolence, certain she could control these disruptive influences. With the earlier darkness banished she clutched her treasure and scanned the golden glory of the Basilica, observing Carole's movements like a pretty kestrel watching a vole, curious when driven by instinct.

After a short nap, Miles spent an hour wandering aimlessly through the Gallerie dell'Accademia. He felt his total lack of concentration was an injustice to the exhibition and gave up. The brilliant afternoon sunlight highlighted shafts of grey dust in the air. They streaked across the garish colours of Gauguin's life's work like pale iron bars imprisoning his black faces. Once outside, Miles bought an ice-cream and sat down to kill a little time. As he savoured the cassata with its pink and green candy, he watched the gondoliers' rather drunken manoeuvres. Too much chianti at lunch, he suspected. They were like overgrown children in aqueous bumper cars. As he observed these greasy emissaries of Venetian life with amusement, he felt quite good. A gondola rocked alarmingly, almost depositing a mammoth woman into the foul water and Miles, unable to control himself, laughed aloud. As he wiped away tears of mirth he wished his mother could have seen this. They were very much from the same mould and shared the same taste in most things. She'd been a great support to him and he suddenly missed her dreadfully. He decided to send her a tacky postcard.

A chattering mill of Jamaican tourists in brightly-coloured summer clothes passed by him. The women wore headdresses and made a living Rousseau collage. Only a parrot was needed to complete the picture. Their gaudiness stood out from the hazy subtlety of the resplendent cityscape beyond.

Miles shaded his eyes. The sun had lowered. He looked at his watch. It was almost five. He made for the Campiello Santo Stefano and his rendezvous with Daniela. What was this secret she wanted to share with him? Well, whatever it was, it could make the last few days of his stay more interesting. He found the dilapidated building easily, using Daniela's untidy map as a reference, and waited for her in the shade of a large muted yellow building with dark green shutters and flaking plaster. He looked around the neglected square. It seemed criminal to him that these wonderful buildings had been allowed to fall into such a state of disrepair. Litter drifted silently across the cobblestones as two lean dogs rooted around in the mess at the base of the statue foraging for canine treasure.

From beyond an open window, directly above him, someone played a piano softly. Miles closed his eyes and listened. Within a few bars a soprano voice had taken the melody over. She sang 'O Mia Bambina Cara'. Miles's impression of opera was one of fat women with blonde plaits voluminously emptying their lungs whilst cymbals crashed and trumpets blared. This was very different – it was gentle, lilting. The voice soared like a skylark. Miles's ignorance about musical interpretation did not impair his ability to feel. The beauty of the piece made him want to cry. Its tenuous emotion conveyed a greater understanding, floating away, untouched, pure, far beyond the reach of human corruption. The aria took him to another place: to summer meadows, soft winds, pastel hues, bullrush seeds making their lazy way to pastures new, escaping like lover's sighs then drifting on across an azure sky. He didn't want to leave this place of tranquillity and kept his eyes tightly closed when the music ended. At the sound of Daniela's voice he opened them and looked up. She was leaning out of the open window. Her hair was loose, and gleamed in the sunlight.

'I am pleased to see you appreciate what I do,' she called out.

Miles looked up at her, astonished. 'You don't mean to tell me that was you singing?'

To leave him in no doubt she began an unaccompanied version of the aria, much to the delight of passers-by. When they applauded spontaneously Miles felt he would burst with pride. She modestly withdrew and after a few brief moments he heard her bounding down the stairs. He hugged her tightly. 'You really are wonderful,' he whispered, meaning every word.

'That's what Lorenzetto tells me, but I don't believe it. I have a long way to go yet before I will be as good as I want to be.'

'Why didn't you tell me you could sing like that? I couldn't believe it was you.' Miles pushed the wedge of hair from his eyes.

'I told you if I like you then I will tell you what I am studying.'

He took hold of her tiny shoulders and gazed, totally ensnared, into her liquid eyes. 'I'm glad you shared this with me,' he whispered. 'I'm so proud of you.'

'Then you will do something for me,' she said casually.

'If you'll repeat your performance – anything.'

'I will sing that piece again, of course,' she goaded, 'But there is another I would like you to hear – it is more powerful, more beautiful. I want to sing it for you in a special place.'

'Tell me more. I'm intrigued.'

'Not now. The day after tomorrow, Saturday. We will meet here at three o'clock. I will take you somewhere fascinating and then . . . well, we will see.' Daniela's eyes shone with treacherous anticipation of her game.

'What do you mean, I'm not going to see you before then? What about tonight?'

'Tonight I cannot see you, I have obligations, there is something I must do. But Saturday will be much better. You will see.' She pulled his face to hers and kissed him passionately, pulling away before he could reciprocate, leaving him wanting more.

Miles shielded his eyes from the sun and watched her walk away. He could scarcely believe it. God, she had talent as well as beauty; she had it all, except, except what? He told himself his reservations were misplaced but somewhere in the back of his mind an element of doubt would go on prodding away at him. There was something about Daniela he would never be sure about. Still he thought, did it really matter? He doubted they would stay in touch when he moved on. His parents would have been amused by her. He decided to call in on Grapper at the bar tonight. It would be good to have someone to talk to and perhaps share his feelings with. Maybe he could throw some light on it all – maybe.

Daniela was thrilled. Now all she had to do was ensure Miles was not distracted from her lead in any way. She clutched her music to her breast with excitement. Soon, all she desired would be hers. A pity her gain would be another's loss. But then was not all of life about sacrifice, of some kind or another.

CHAPTER 7

On his way back to the pensione Miles stopped at the largest of the souvenir stands to buy some postcards. He studied the vulgar wares with interest. There were the inevitable model gondolas and red cheeked gigolos in striped vests, plastic replicas of the famous winged lions, alabaster Madonnas slightly askance on their tiny pedestals and black gondolier's hats with red and white braid. Miles tried one on and raise the hopes of the rotund little souvenir-seller.

'Signore, may I say that looks wonderful. It is very cheap too – only ten thousand lire. Please, see for yourself.' He tilted the mirror so Miles could get a better look.

'Don't listen to a word he says – it looks bleedin' terrible. Anyway yer can get one for five thousand by the Rialto.'

Miles spun around. 'Grapper, hi! I was going to call you about getting together tonight.'

The chubby little man shook his fist at Grapper and punched him playfully on the shoulder. 'You dog, you 'ave just cost me a lot of money.'

Miles put the hat down. 'I wasn't going to buy this. I just want some postcards.'

Grapper laughed. 'This is me mate Fabrizio, the best crook in Venice. He can get more money out of stupid tourists than anyone I know. Fab, this is Miles, I told you about him.'

Fabrizio held out his hand. 'Please not so much of a crook and the tourists are not so stupid, eh!' He shook Miles's hand vigorously. 'So you are unlucky – you know my friend Grapper.'

Miles took out some money. 'I'm pretty glad I met him actually. Things could have been a bit more complicated for me if I hadn't.'

Fabrizio shot his friend a knowing look as Miles selected his postcards. He paid for them. 'I've got to run. I'll see you at the bar around ten if you like.'

Grapper put a hand on his friend's shoulder. 'Sure, mate, that'd be great – about ten.'

Miles walked away studying his purchases and Grapper looked worriedly after him as a parent might a child on its first unaccompanied errand. Fabrizio shrugged, sensing his concern.

'Maybe tonight you tell him, eh! I think you should spill the jelly.'

Grapper kept staring after Miles. 'Beans, Fab,' he said. It's spill the beans.'

'Mom, What can I say about this place that hasn't already been said. Having a great time. I've met some really interesting people. Next stop Florence, leaving in a day or so. Will call, much love, Miles.' He placed the postcard with the others he had written and went down to dinner. Sadly, the quality of the company and the food hadn't changed. It was Thursday, so tonight they were having chicken cacciatore with a glutinous sauce and oily fried potatoes with rosemary. Lost in thought, he played with his vegetable soup, oblivious to the prattling of the German girls. He had more important things on his mind.

'Miles, you are not eating.' Katy's voice cut across their girlish chitchat like an intercepting torpedo. 'It is not good?'

He looked up apologetically. 'No, it's great, Sorry. I was thinking.'

'Too much thinking not good. Ve leave tomorrow, Skinny, you should talk to us more. Greta looked down at the pale orange liquid congealing in her plate.

Miles cheered up. 'What a pity you're leaving and we haven't had a chance to get to know one another.' he said relieved by the news of their departure.

'Perhaps ve could go for goodbye drink?'

'Sorry, no can do. I've got to go somewhere later on.'

Katerina chipped in. 'You two will be wanting to 'ave an early night – your train leaves at eight does it not, Herr Breitenbach?'

Their father nodded and pushed his plate forward. Miles grinned at Katerina and spooned the lukewarm soup rapidly into his mouth. The girls frowned.

After dinner empty farewells were exchanged. Greta pressed a piece of paper into his hand. 'If you come to Munich you vill call us on this number, yes?' Her tone sounded more like a Nazi command than a casual invitation.

'Sure, of course. I'll definitely look you up,' he lied.

'Vell, ve vill go to bed then as there is nothing else to do,' Greta sulked. 'Goodbye then, Skinny.' She kissed him on both cheeks.

'Auf wiedersehen,' he said politely.

Eva peered at him coyly from beneath her spiky fringe and emulated her sister. 'Behave yourself,' he whispered in her ear, thinking if they got the chance that's exactly what they wouldn't do.

Outside the night air had cooled a little and Miles was glad to be away from the slightly cloying atmosphere of the pensione. At El Souk, to his surprise, Grapper wasn't at their usual table. Instead he had hidden himself away in a darkened corner of the room. He was nursing a Scotch. Bella took the top from a beer and handed it to Miles as he walked in. He joined his friend, took a swig, wiped his mouth and said: 'I'm really glad you could make it tonight. There's something I need to chew over with you.'

Grapper sipped his Scotch. 'Yeah, there's sommat I've gotta tell you an' all.'

With their heads slightly bowed, they avoided eye contact. Confessions were easier that way. Acquaintances make comfortable confidants – they rarely analyse and when they do you can tell yourself they don't know you well enough to give advice worth taking. These acquaintances soon realized how little they knew of each other. Egged on by more alcohol, their deeper feelings emerged tentatively like moles who run blindly across a trap-ridden lawn.

Grapper spilled the jelly, as Fabrizio had put it, but kept the more alarming truths to himself. He spoke in lurid detail of his tortured childhood. He had soon found out that he and his mother were different from other people. At school he had been mercilessly teased about the trances that sometimes led to blackouts, until he found a profitable use for his gifts. The older boys placed his racing bets with pocket money and the profits kept most of his class in enough chocolate to feed a small army. He was then considered something of a hero. When he became terrorized by the visions, his mother's clairvoyance helped him to understand. She said he'd been blessed, but he considered it a curse. 'I think of meself as a freak so it doesn't matter to me what I look like,' he said. 'Freak on the outside, freak on the inside.'

Miles listened attentively but didn't really know what to make of it. Gradually, he came around to speaking of his own nightmares. They had plagued him since the accident – detailed, vivid, terrifying dreams that haunted him for days afterwards. He told Grapper of his hopes for Lisa's recovery, his recent unease and, of course, Daniela.

'Will yer let me do a reading for yer?' Grapper asked. 'I think it may help.'

Miles looked sceptical. 'What sort of reading?'

Grapper took a carved box from the seat beside him. Inside was a deck of elaborate cards. 'Tarot,' he said. 'You've 'eard of it, ain't ya?'

'Sure I've heard of it, but I don't believe in any of it. All this New Age garbage that people are getting so caught up in. Not for me thanks.'

Grapper held out the deck. 'Just shuffle these and trust me, will yer.'

Miles reluctantly took the cards. 'You know me, I'll try anything once,' he said with false bravura.

Grapper frowned, 'Yeah, that's what worries me.'

'How long do I have to keep shuffling for?' Miles nervously shifted the cards around in his clammy hands.

Grapper took another swig of Scotch. 'They'll tell yer when – just keep going until yer feel like stopping.'

Almost as soon as he said this, Miles wanted to put them down. His hands were tingling – he rubbed them. Grapper lit a cigarette, placed it in his mouth and spread nine cards in a semi-circle. 'This is the quick version,' he said. 'I just wanna look at the immediate stuff. The past ain't that relevant. Well – not right now anyway.'

'They certainly don't hang around, do they. I didn't shuffle them for long,' Miles watched Grapper with interest.

He turned over the first card – the Fool. 'Very appropriate,' Grapper said.

'Should I be insulted? I presume that's me.'

'Yeah. But it don't mean what you think. Grapper took another card from the pack and laid it face down across the Fool, then he turned a card to its right – the Queen of Cups – the next one along was the Hanged Man. 'This means someone you love is disabled in some way – that's obviously Lisa.'

Miles looked unconvinced. 'Sheer fluke,' he said.

Grapper turned the card to the left of the Fool – the High Priestess. 'Well, well,' he said. 'What a surprise.' He turned the next one – the Devil. Satisfied, he leaned back in the chair and inhaled on the cigarette. 'Well, that just about says it all, mate. The Devil represents pride, ambition and lust.'

Miles looked suddenly nervous. 'What else does it say?'

Grapper ground out the cigarette. 'This girl is going to bring you nothing but bleedin' trouble. She's very dark, very powerful. She's got a lot of tricks up 'er sleeve.'

He turned the card which had earlier been placed face down across the Fool. The dancing skeleton of death held his scythe aloft, ready to strike.

'Well I guess there's no need to ask what that means.'

Grapper looked at this innocent intensely, his earring glinted in the half-light. He leaned forward. 'It doesn't necessarily mean what you think it does. But one thing I do know.'

Miles finished his beer. Thoughts of the unused condom flashed through his mind. Could that be the trouble? He felt beads of sweat forming on his temples. 'What do you know?' he asked.

'If you've got any sense in yer 'ead you'll stay away from this bitch. There are more things in heaven and earth, mate – more than you could imagine – even worse things than you've seen in those dreams of yours.'

Katerina was reading a book by the light of her red fringed lampshade. The pink glow softened her features as she peered at the text with a large magnifying glass. Her little salon was cluttered but comfortable. There were two moth-eaten chairs with lace covers on the arms, a few plant stands, and in the window a square table draped with a burgundy velvet cloth. Miles saw the light under the door and went in to say goodnight. She offered him a nightcap and he jumped at the chance – his nerves needed steadying a little.

'Thanks for helping me out back there with the girls.'

'I could tell you did not want to go out with them. When Greta asked you – your face was like this.' Katerina wrinkled her nose simulating acute distaste.

'Was it really that obvious?'

'Yes, Skinny, very obvious. This friend you go out with – who is he?'

'I met him on my first night here. Some mad tramp tried to mug me, but he stopped him – it was pretty frightening at the time. He's a really unusual guy.' Miles picked at the lace on the arm of the chair. Grapper's revelations had made him feel uneasy again.

'In what way he is, unusual?'

'I'm not sure you'd understand. He's some kind of psychic, I think.'

Katerina sighed. 'You think I do not know about such things. I 'ave gypsy blood, these ways are well known to us.' Her massive chest doubled with pride.

'Oh, sorry I didn't mean . . .' His voice trailed away. 'Well, anyway, he told me some things and I'm not quite sure what to make of them.'

'Do you trust him?' she asked.

'Well, yes I do but . . .'

'Then you should not 'ave fear. If you trust, then trust with your heart – that is all that matters.'

'I don't think I'm a very good judge right now, not since the accident, anyway.' He paused.

Katerina folded her hands in her lap. 'What is this accident?'

'It's still pretty difficult for me to talk about it, but . . . I think I'd like to tell you.' Miles felt slightly exposed and looked uncomfortably around the room, taking in the delicate china figures and silver framed photos.

'I am listening. I do not sleep much these days – so we 'ave all the time you want. Maybe I can 'elp a little.'

Miles cleared his throat nervously. 'It happened last summer. My girlfriend and I went to Cambridge, in England. Her brother's at university there. Well, he lent us his motorbike so we could go into the countryside. I can handle a bike pretty well but . . .' His hands began to shake a little at the memory. 'This stupid dog ran out in front of us. I tried to avoid hitting it and the bike went right out from under me. I just couldn't control it.'

He gripped the arm of the chair. Katerina remained silent.

'The thing is we weren't wearing crash helmets – it was so hot we took them off. I was injured. I've got this skull fracture.

Lisa came off much worse. It was really bad . . . she went into a coma two days later and she's still that way now.' The tears he'd withheld now ran freely down his young face. 'It's my fault, I lost control. I should have killed the stupid dog. She'd be all right now.' His shoulders heaved with silent sobs.

Katerina prised herself from the depths of her armchair and perched like an enormous Buddha by his side. She had seen enough of life to know it rarely gives, only takes away. She made soothing noises and stroked his hair.

'It was not your fault. You did what you thought was right. It was the hand of God that caused this accident, not the hand of Skinny.'

'I'm sorry, I don't know why I'm telling you all this. The trouble is the hand of God, as you call it, seems to be playing with me. I keep having these nightmares sometimes when I'm wide awake.'

His sage shook her head knowingly. 'If God took away the thing that you loved then he gave you something in return for your suffering.'

Miles looked blank, confused by her understanding of something which was foreign territory to him.

'Come and sit by me. We will have a nice drink and I will tell you a story about my life. It will help you. You will see there are worse things in the world.' Katerina stretched her weary body and poured two large brandies from the dusty crystal decanter. Miles took his and sat on the floor at her feet. He sipped thoughtfully in the dull pink glow. The air outside remained oppressively still. A dog barked as she began.

'I am sure when you came here you believed I was of Russian descent.'

'Well sure, I mean your accent and the borscht and everything, I assumed that, yes,' he said.

'It suits me that people believe this, so I do not say anything different. I am Slovene – Yugoslavian.'

'I don't understand. Why would you want to conceal your nationality?'

Katerina's full lips curled at the edges in a wry smile. 'You are such a child. Have patience, I will tell you.' She took a long drink to steady herself. She had not spoken of these things for years. Although Miles didn't know it, this was an honour.

'During the war my country was divided between Germany and Italy. They were animals stripping a rotting corpse. My family were very poor peasants, working the land was all we knew. Like many of our kind we were ignorant about war. When the Fascisti came we did not know what to expect. There were terrible stories but we were sure if we stayed out of the way, they would do us no harm. We knew nothing of Fascism and the evils of Mussolini and Hitler.'

She stared into space. Her expression reflected nothing of the agony to come.

'When the Ladislav came to our village they asked questions about the partisans, Jews, and gypsies who were in hiding. They did not get the answers they wanted. They began first to shoot the old men, then they raped and killed the women and sent the children away ... It was to teach the villagers a lesson, you see. We were afraid. You cannot imagine such fear.'

Fine beads of perspiration lined her brow. She mopped it with her sleeve.

'My father had gypsy blood – only one half, but it was enough. One day, when the burja wind moaned like a widow, they came for us. Our neighbour told the Italians because he did not want to be shot. He had betrayed us and they rounded us up like cattle. All of us. We were terrified, but my father said they would treat us well if we worked hard for them. At that time, Hitler's gas ovens were just a rumour, no one really believed. But his evil spread like a carpet of blood over all the occupied countries and we were not to escape it. We were taken to a concentration camp on the island of Ran. It was a terrible place.'

She took a sip of brandy to steady her nerves, then continued in an automaton's voice. 'When we got there you cannot imagine such terror. Hundreds of tents for people to live in, the sick walked only with death on their shoulders – they were living skeletons. My parents were very afraid we would be separated but they put us in a tent together. Soon we learned that the many shots we heard were executions. Many people died each day. They were starved, executed, tortured ... Their only crime was breathing. I was twelve years old. I knew nothing but our village. It was the most terrible experience.' She gulped more brandy. 'They gave us one mouthful of bread a day. How I longed for the pogaca my mother had made. On Sunday four spoonfuls of a thin soup. It was really like 'ot water but we were glad of it. I am sure they meant to starve us to death to save their precious bullets. My brother Drago and I became very ill – my father stole a knife from a kitchen guard to dig in the ground for worms and grubs to eat. He risked his life so we would have insects to eat.'

Miles tried in vain to conceal his disgust.

'You think that is bad, but we were dying of starvation. That is why I am as I am now. I said to myself in that terrible place, if I ever got out I would be fat, big as a 'ouse.' She drained her glass. 'So my mother, Franciska, she was beautiful woman you know.' She took down one of the tarnished silver frames. Miles looked at the young couple in traditional wedding dress who smiled with the knowledge that their lives were ahead of them. The tiny photo was badly damaged but the girl's beauty shone through the cracks.

'One night, I lie awake pretending to be asleep and I hear her and my father speaking of a dangerous plan. She will go to the guards and give herself to them, and they will let us escape. My parents were afraid if we became more sick they would send us to the children's hospital.'

'Wouldn't that have been better for you?' Miles asked innocently.

Her face registered a mere flicker of the burning emotion within. 'Better, you think this would be better? This hospital was the worst place of all – they left the little ones to die. They starved the children to death. This we knew because one of our women was sent to nurse them. Nurse them, ha!' she said incredulously. 'These poor little ones had no medicine, they died for nothing, without help, without love.' She wiped away an angry tear. 'Your children will not know such suffering. Now maybe you understand why my mother and father were desperate for Drago and I not to be sent there. So, this night, my mother is leaving the tent to look for a guard who would help her. Some of these pigs preferred a woman to give herself willingly than to rape. My father watched her go – he was dying inside. He waited a few minutes and then I saw him take the knife from under his blanket - oh, da, they gave us one blanket each but we slept on the cold earth.' Katerina took an amber rosary from the pocket of her apron and clutched it until her knuckles turned white. 'I did not find out until later what 'ad 'appened that night. My mother, she crept to the guard's hut. One of them came upon her and called two others. They had been drinking. They decided to 'ave an 'orrible bet. They bet on 'ow many minutes it would take to choke her to death. They raped her and then one of them forced himself into her mouth while another pig held her nose closed and her jaw open to stop her breathing.' Katy was no longer able to stem the flow of tears – it took her a moment to compose herself as Miles shook his head with disbelief. 'My father saw them cheering and laughing while she died. He could not help himself. He ran to them with the knife and in a rage he stabbed them all again and again. They were no match for his strength. When the heart is ripped open the body it is strong.' She wiped her eyes again.

'God I'm so sorry.' Miles held her hand feeling the gesture was inadequate. His own troubles receded. Katerina told him to refill their glasses and continued. 'Then when he had killed them all, Papa stabbed himself. Another guard saw this terrible crime 'appen but he was too afraid to try and stop them. I 'eard Papa's cry and ran out of the tent to try and find my parents. This guard caught me and took me away from their bodies. I was screaming – he told me to be quiet or I would be shot. I led him back to the tent where Drago was sleeping. It was easy to see 'ow ill we were. He said we would be taken to the mainland to the hospital the next day. I was afraid of him, but now that my parents were dead it was up to me to look after my little brother. The next day this guard, he came to take us away. We were very afraid. He put us in the boat with other sick little ones and when we reached the mainland he sat with us in the lorry and gave us some food. The others were too sick to eat – they were dying. Soon he tells the driver that he wants to urinate so the truck stops. He 'elps us down and tells us to keep quiet. He leads us into the wood and says we must climb a tree and stay there until somebody comes. We were very weak but we managed to do as he said. We saw him fire two shots into the air. At the time I did not know why. We stayed up there for hours – you cannot believe how frightened we were. Drago cried all the time. I was afraid someone would hear. I did not know who was meant to be coming. Later we saw some men on horses below us. They were partisans, two of them were from our village. I called out . . . These men kept us safe for a time and took us with them.'

Her face was now drained of colour as she concluded her story. 'Eventually we were captured again but these Italians were kinder men. They took us to an orphanage near Parma. Drago was very ill and he died of typhus. I worked with the nuns, caring for the other children and then we learned that this place was to become a prisoner-of-war camp for English soldiers. I was taken in by someone in the village to clean 'ouse in return for a bed in the barn and some food. I learned Italian quickly. Soon the soldiers came to set up the camp and I go to watch them putting up barbed wire and turning a place of safety into a prison. I was at first sad and then I see the guard, the one who 'ad 'elped me. It is two years since he has seen me and at first he does not recognize me. I 'ad grown much bigger here.' She patted her huge chest. 'He comes over and gives me a cigarette. I was good-looking then – we talk and he cannot believe I am the same girl he saved. He tells me the shots were to make the driver think he 'ad killed us when we try to escape. I told him I would never forget he saved my life. We started to go out together, to see American movies which I liked a lot. In 1943 there was Armistice and the camp is not needed. So I find he is to move on and I am unhappy. Apart from him I was alone, you see. So we got married and he promised to send for me. I never doubted him. He was a Venetian, they do not think of themselves as Italian – he hated the evil things they had done. We agreed to keep certain things secret from his family when we came here. My reason for living was to be with the man I loved, I did not mind living among pigs. He was the most gentle man I ever knew in my life. He did not often laugh, he cared too much about the past, but when he did everybody laughed with him – he died twenty years ago and I made our home a pensione.'

'That's quite a story, but I still don't understand why you pretended to be Russian.' Miles was still curious.

'After the war many Nazi criminals were punished for what they had done. The Italians got away with things very bad - just as bad as the Nazis. Many Italians knew what 'ad 'appened in the occupied countries. They would 'ave thought I was a traitor to live among the killers of my people. If they 'ad known I was a Slovene gypsy they would spit on me.' Her brow furrowed. 'But now I will tell you why I 'ave chosen to speak of this. Each soul knows its own pain, and that pain is great.' She placed her hand upon his head. 'You must try to understand that life exists only in the shadow of death. In New York and London they ate in fine restaurants with their furs and diamonds. Some of them knew of the death camps, others did not, but when they could not buy eggs or butter for their families they thought this was terrible. If they had seen what I 'ave seen . . .' Her voice trembled as she digressed, then she came to the point: 'You must never again believe you were responsible for what 'appened to your girl. The men who laugh as they kill and torture, they are the ones who will meet their fate at the hand of God – not you.'

Miles suddenly understood and felt grateful to her. Her deeply lined face showed the anguish and suffering. Sadness hung in the air like a dark cloud, penetrating, damp. He felt suddenly cold. She stroked his hair wearily. 'Now it is two o'clock and you must go to bed.'

'All right. Listen, thanks for telling me. It can't have been easy.' He wanted to say more but couldn't.

'This is true – it was not easy. But now perhaps you do not feel so bad.'

Miles kissed her flushed cheek. When he reached the door Katerina spoke his name for once. 'And Miles . . .'

'Yes, Katy?' He turned.

'Say your prayers and give thanks for the things you 'ave – thank God for the love and safety of your family and friends.'

He gazed at her mournful features in the dull pink glow. 'I will,' he said softly. 'After tonight you can be sure I will.'

He lay awake and went over Katerina's heart-rending story. Everyone knew of Hitler's genocide but it seemed the madness had spread much further. Himmler had furniture made from human bone, babies' heads had been smashed against walls and now this. Miles imagined the heaped bodies of Dachau and Belsen and wondered what Katerina had left out. The images made him feel sick. His head was throbbing – he took a dihyracodine because it was the only drug that worked. It would make him feel like hell tomorrow. He groped beneath the pillow for the crucifix – it was still there. Katerina had made his bed that morning but she left his comfort where she found it. This tragic woman knew only too well how little protection there was from the demons that invaded the unconscious mind.

He muttered his prayers with a grim determination, praying for forgiveness and for Lisa's recovery. Forgive us our trespasses as we forgive those who trespass against us. His father's crime now seemed trivial and unimportant. So Miles had found him in bed with his secretary – so what. There were far worse things, as Katy had said. As he burrowed down into the bed he decided he was leaving on Sunday. Whatever else he did he was going to book that train ticket tomorrow. It was definitely time to move on.

Daniela had other ideas. Morrison sang 'L.A. Woman' as she knelt on her bedroom floor and wrapped the six black candles in the swathes of midnight blue velvet with a gentility reserved for newborns. Her smile was satisfied. 'Now everything is ready for us.' The hall clock chimed a reminder. She placed her hands on the wall and began:

'Desa dea metto in tera,
scongiuro il cielo et la terra,
il vivo passa . . .'

When she had said this five times she went into the hall. 'Buona notte, grandmamma,' she whispered at the closed kitchen door. Her step was light with expectancy as she flew down the stairs into the damp night air, clutching a piece of paper with the address of her appointment. Daniela was very late but it did not matter because they were not expecting her.

CHAPTER 8

Katerina tapped on her guest's bedroom door. In her free hand was a lukewarm cup of tea, a morning-after-the-night-before gesture. Their intimacy had been more revealing than any sexual encounter and both were feeling the after effects. Miles gradually woke up, convinced he was somewhere else. 'Come in,' he groaned. Katerina padded across the room and placed the tea on his bedside table. He raised his head, which hammered with the sudden movement. 'God, I fell like hell. What time is it? He squinted at his landlady.

'It is almost twelve. You 'ave slept for a good while I thought you would want to be woken up. In 'alf an 'our I will make you something to eat. We are alone now.'

Miles sipped the tea and tried not to grimace. 'When are your next lot arriving?'

Katerina opened one set of shutters revealing a beautiful day. 'They do not come until Monday, so we will be alone until you leave. I will be very sorry when you go. Now, you 'ave a nice shower and come down for some food.'

The last thing he felt like was food. His stomach churned at the thought. The drugs always made him feel weak but they killed the pain so he had to take them. When she left the room he drifted in and out of sleep for a few minutes. Then, reluctantly, he got up, showered and joined her for a lunch of cheese and flat brown bread. They talked casually. Neither of them wanted to awaken the sleeping beast of their tragic disclosures. Finally, Miles thanked her for the meal he hadn't wanted and went into the hall to telephone his mother.

'I can't hear you very well – can you hear me?' Miles raised his voice above the crackles, and it carried along the empty hallway.

'Yes darling, I can hear you.' Celia sounded delighted. 'How are you finding glorious Venice?'

'With great difficulty,' he joked.

'You mean you're getting hopelessly lost like we did the first time – poor baby.' His mother laughed softly, then studied the barely noticeable fine lines in the mirror and imagined ravines.

'It takes a little getting used to, but it's been wonderful – I'm leaving for Florence on Sunday.'

She made a mental note to make an appointment with her surgeon. 'Oh, you'll love Florence, darling. It will be much cooler there, I expect. How's your money holding out?'

'So far so good – are you okay?'

'Yeah, I'm doing fine, sweetheart. Don't you give me another thought now, you just have a good time.'

He took a deep breath. 'How's Dad?'

'Well let's just say he's being his usual self.' Her tone was considered.

'Yeah I can imagine . . . give him my love, will you?'

The line sounded dead, Miles shook the receiver. 'Mom, are you there?' he shouted above the grating static.

'I can just hear you, darling. Are you sure you're all right? You sound a little strange – has your head been bad again? You've got your pills.'

'Yeah, honest, couldn't be better. I'm fine.' He knew she was surprised by this display of affection for his father. 'I've got to run – this is costing a small fortune. I've sent you a postcard . . . I'll call from Florence. Bye.'

Miles put down the receiver and picked up the train timetable. The 1.15 seemed the best bet. He felt sure his last night with Daniela would be memorable enough to warrant a late start the next day. Despite Grapper's warning signals, he had to see her one last time.

Daniela bobbed respectfully before the white-clothed altar in the little church of San Teodoro. One or two women were muttering desperate prayers. She walked towards the elaborate mahogany confessional. Neither of them looked up. The small choir rehearsed a Benedictine Mass which resounded celestially through the stone recesses. Daniela listened for a moment, soothed by the heavenly strains of interwoven descants. She closed her eyes. A fist slammed into a woman's face. Ten angry voices chanted as the woman was dragged screaming through the church: Stregoneria, stregoneria, stregoneria. She opened her eyes and rubbed her slender shoulders. The priest entered the darkened booth and indicated his willingness to listen. She followed, sat down, and bent her lace-covered head. 'Father, forgive me for I have sinned,' she whispered slyly.

The priest suppressed a yawn. 'How have you sinned, my child?' He scratched his left ankle without interest, presupposing her reply would be the usual sorry tale of a battle lost against repressed teenage sexuality.

'I have done something to cause another person great pain.' Her features were tightly drawn by the memory. 'I have done something terrible for which I am ashamed, Father.'

The priest felt the tiny hairs on the nape of his neck prickling. He sensed this confession needed his attention and sat up, listening intently. Daniela whispered the murderous detail of her crime in a childlike voice that sought forgiveness for a mischievous deed. But she had not just been naughty – she had killed, with pleasure. Sweating profusely, the priest considered his position carefully, then gave her a penance and wiped her disclosure from his brow and his mind.

Daniela drew her elongated fingers across the damp skin of her chest, making the sign of an inverted cross. 'Thank you Father,' she said. 'I feel much better now.'

Bella was drying glasses when Miles walked into the bar. He scanned the tables. There was no sign of Grapper. She reached up and took down a glass. 'He is not 'ere today – he is working – the Pescheria.' Miles shrugged. Bella picked up a beer and held it aloft. 'You want?' she asked.

'No thanks, I'd better be going. I just wanted to see if he could meet me later tonight. I'm leaving, Sunday.' He didn't know the Italian for Sunday.'

'It is not possible tonight – my famiglia, Treviso. Tonight we go to Treviso.' She was inclined to possessiveness.

'Tomorrow then, domani. Lunchtime. Tell him I'll meet him here about one, a l'una. Okay?' He wondered if she understood.

'Si, capisco. Domani.' It appeared she did.

Slightly disappointed, Miles walked the sunlit streets and wondered what to do with himself. The stifling heat closed around his throbbing temples. His head still felt muzzy. He pulled a street map from the back pocket of his jeans and tried to locate the Splendide, Carole's hotel. The schedule was tight for the next two days and he couldn't possibly leave without saying goodbye, so tonight was their only chance. He hoped she would have a drink with him – he enjoyed her company.

He walked through the labyrinth gazing up at a crack of blue sky between the red tiled roofs. Perhaps a gondola ride would be better. Why not?

The striped-vested gondoliers descended on him like a group of vultures as he approached the landing stage.

'Si, si, Signore, you get good price – very good price.' They attempted to entice him and hurriedly placed straw boaters upon their oily heads.

Doubting their sexual preference, he wisely selected the eldest of them who looked about seventy – too old for any slimy advances. He had enough problems without lewd suggestions from a bum bandit. Miles settled back into the red heart-shaped seat of the gleaming black boat. The old gondolier turned and sullenly asked if he wanted music. 'How much extra?' He was now accustomed to Venetian greed.

'Ten thousand lire.' The would-be entertainer had a take-it-or-leave-it attitude. Miles nodded and he lurched into a surprisingly good rendition of 'Santa Lucia' in a rich deep baritone.

He closed his eyes and listened to the evocative sounds: the amateur operatic singing, pigeons cooing softly above him, the gentle lapping of murky waters gradually eroding the crumbling, irreplaceable architecture like a rat gnawing away at Eve's apple. All this was the Venice he had expected to find – today at least he was not disappointed.

After a few balmy minutes they arrived at the hotel's flower-covered entrance. He thanked the gondolier by tipping him generously and made his way into the cool of the wood-panelled foyer. He asked for Carole and was informed by the haughty concierge that she had not arrived today. The concierge seemed rather exasperated by her absence. Miles asked for her home address and was pointedly informed that the hotel could not divulge personal information. Was she due in later today? Yes, of course, she came every day, except Sunday and tomorrow was Saturday, transfer day, and there would be chaos if she was still sick – well, the concierge assumed she was sick because she was normally very reliable.

Miles asked for a pen and stationery. His note said he was

leaving on Sunday and would like to see her for a drink tonight, if she was up to it. He scribbled Katy's telephone number on the cream-coloured paper, then sealed the envelope and handed it to the concierge who eyed him suspiciously. 'For your trouble.' Miles gave him a 2000-lire note. The raffish hireling studied it from behind his steel half-moon glasses. If Miles had given him gold he would almost certainly have bitten it to determine its authenticity.

CHAPTER 9

In the darkened salon Katerina settled into her threadbare armchair. Siesta time. The grief of her past had reared its ugly head again, taking up residence in her troubled mind like a filthy squatter, unwelcome, soiling her newfound peace. She snuffled and grunted in her sleep and began to dream about the war-torn village of her childhood.

A rickety cart laboriously bumped along the pitted track. Her childish figure stared at the desolate countryside. The bare trees and scorched earth bore the scars of a raging battle which had mercilessly consumed the scenery she loved. She turned to the driver, a peasant with a dirty face who spat into the mud every twenty yards or so. 'Where are we going?' Her voice was small, frightened. The peasant stared ahead to the distant figure who straddled the track. His back was turned. The half-light picked out the colours of his Italian uniform. The soldier's stance, feet wide apart, hands firmly clasped behind his back, was dictatorial. Katerina was afraid.

The mules pulled against the reins. The driver raised his arm and sent the whip whistling onto their skeletal backs. 'Don't make them go on ...' she cried out in alarm. 'We 'ave to go back now ...'

Katerina screamed at the driver and tugged on his sleeve. He drove the mules on, ignoring her cries.

'Please take me back.' Her voice trembled with fear. The mules reluctantly carried their burden closer and closer to the unknown soldier. Then suddenly they reared and whinnied with fear, their nostrils flared, spirals of breath hung in the frosty air. She tried to jump from the cart but couldn't move. She flailed her arms and struggled as a fly tries in vain to free itself from a sticky, poisonous substance.

'Go back now – turn around!' She screamed hysterically at the peasant, pummelling his arms in a desperate attempt to make him respond. Suddenly, as though waking from a deep trance, the driver slowly turned to face her.

Dark eyes stared blankly from a mutilated face. The blood congealed in dark lumps on his torn flesh, making recognition impossible – impossible for anyone other than Katerina. With a long-forgotten terror she gazed upon her disfigured father and cried out.

Directly ahead of them the soldier turned and smiled knowingly. Her cries became screams that woke her and Miles, who was dozing above her. Katerina clutched her chest to soothe her distressed heart. It was only a dream; she wasn't really in that terrible place. The nightmare was over. Yes, it was only a dream.

Miles woke up with a start. Had he heard screams? It must have been a dream. He peered at the clock. It was just after six. He stretched lazily and swung his long legs onto the floor. Running his fingers through damp hair, he covered his eyes for a moment with his hands. The darkness was almost meditative. The headache was worse. He wondered if Carole had called yet. He splashed his face with lukewarm water and peered into the chipped mirror. He looked drained, tired. Maybe he had been overdoing it a bit. He poured a glass of water and sat on the edge of the high bed. It was two hours until dinner. He climbed back between the slightly damp sheets and burrowed down. The pounding receded slightly so Miles drifted off again.

An inky shadow had broken away from the snake pit below the earth and settled beneath this little house. Here it could feed on the deepest fears of the two inhabitants. It seethed and probed their unguarded sleep still further, grasping their subconscious with icy fingers that squeezed and squeezed until they cried out.

Miles dreamed of Daniela again. A hazy vision emerged in muted colours. He watched, an unseen voyeur in the shadows of a grandiose marbled room. Daniela made languorous circles with her naked body. She waltzed around something that flickered. The light danced. He couldn't quite make out what it was. A fire, no – too fragmented. Suddenly there were more people, hazy, unclear. They danced with her. She sang to them. The room began to turn and then spun like a top. He tossed his head, fearfully aware, at least in his subconscious, that he didn't want to be there.

When he woke again it was just after eight. The distant clatter of pans suggested dinner must be imminent. Miles dressed quickly. He felt hungry now. Downstairs he checked the message pad. Carole still hadn't called. Miles presumed she was still sick, or otherwise engaged.

The neighbour banged angrily on the door. The telephone had rung every half hour for the last four hours. He was sick to death of the constant disruption. He swore and muttered vague obscenities. She had to be in there; his wife hadn't seen her leave for work. And his wife watched everyone come and go. In fact that was all she did these days. Sit and stare, and knit jackets for the bambini. The many bambini. His grandchildren – they were always in need of something. A new this, a new that. He banged on the door again. No response. He went back down to his own apartment to telephone the landlord. If they got in they could pull out that cursed phone – or at least take it off the hook.

Grapper grimaced as Bella held up a tie she had bought. 'I ain't wearing that, for a start.' She pleaded with him. Didn't he want to make a good impression on her family? Grapper couldn't see what possible difference it would make to his appearance. He didn't need a tie, he needed a miracle. They'd probably faint with shock when they saw him. Not their idea of a good Catholic boy – not that it really mattered. They weren't going to get married or anything. Or was that it? Was that what she wanted? He put on a checked seersucker jacket. A Paul Smith. It had cost him a fortune. If that didn't impress them nothing would. Well it had green in it. It matched his hair. He was at least coordinated.

Fabrizio handed Grapper the keys to his precious Fiat. 'You take good care of my Bianca,' he said. 'All you Engleesh drive like crazy people.'

'Don't worry, mate, I'll treat her like a real lady. Ta for lending her. I'll have 'er home by eleven, don't worry, Pappa.

Fabrizio raised one eyebrow, then laughed a deep-throated

pot-bellied laugh. ''Ow is your friend with the problem?' Grapper was walking out of the door. He turned.

'I dunno. Miles wanted to see me tonight. Bella said 'e's leaving on Sunday. I'm gonna see 'im at lunchtime tomorrow. I just 'ope 'e stays out of trouble till then.'

Fabrizio shrugged. 'Maybe you should tell 'im the whole ball grass.'

'I give up with you, Fab. It's ball game. The expression is ball game.'

'Well, whatever. I think it is better if you say.'

'We'll see. Right now I've got Bella's lot to sort out. I can tell yer I'd rather be boozing with Miles then giving 'er parents the fright of their lives. They'll probably never forgive 'er.'

Fabrizio studied his friend's plumage and nodded. Then he beamed. 'Eh! What is it you say – never judge a book by its paper.'

Grapper shook his head and went back to the girl with the flaming curls who was waiting impatiently for him with her hands on her generous hips.

Miles and Katerina ate their meal in virtual silence. Miles made vague attempts at conversation but after a few sentences it came to nothing. The silence dominated. Eventually Katerina cleared away the plates, with Miles helping her. He was prepared to dry up, but she shooed him away. 'No, you look tired. Go to bed.' He left her to it – he did feel suddenly tired. In truth she wanted to be alone with her thoughts.

Later, unable to sleep, Miles read J.D. Salinger and found it hard to concentrate. He was surprised Carole hadn't called. Perhaps she would tomorrow. For some reason he felt concerned for her. He wished he'd got her home number. That way he would at least have been able to say goodbye. He decided to telephone the hotel again tomorrow.

No sooner had the thought entered his mind than it was plucked from him by the shadow. Of course, unfortunately, he would forget.

Katerina also tried to read and found it impossible. Her eyes watered with tiredness. She rubbed them and gazed mournfully at the empty chair facing her. If only Mario were still here. She was so lonely. As was often the case when these feelings dominated her, she talked to him in her head. She spoke of both the trivial and the profound events of the last week, asked questions and imagined she heard her husband's answers and told him how much she loved him. Soon, she said aloud, soon they would be together again. And how she longed for the day with all her heart.

The shadow heard her.

Although it was after ten the landlord went to Flat D, 127 Calle del Fruttarol, at the insistence of one of his tenants. A telephone constantly ringing. No, that did not seem like a good reason to drag him away from a poker game early. If he had not lost so much money he would have denied the request.

He rang the bell of Flat B. Michele opened the door in a grubby vest. He had more body hair than a gorilla. His head, however, had not been blessed. He seemed grateful to the landlord for coming to his rescue. They knocked on the door to Carole's apartment. First gently, then loudly. No answer. The phone rang again. The landlord opened the door with his key. Michele went to the phone and pulled out the plug with a little too much force. He looked at the bare wires, surprised. The landlord clicked his tongue and told him he would have to pay for the repairs. Michele didn't care – at least now he'd get some peace. The landlord sniffed – a bad smell. No, a foul smell. He walked down the hall and opened the bathroom door. It wasn't coming from there. He opened the door to the bedroom, looked inside and threw up his triple Scotches onto the pale pink lino. Michele followed his pointing finger, then he threw up too.

Miles bit into the toasted ham and cheese sandwich and chewed thoughtfully. Grapper continued with his story of last night's fiasco with Bella's parents. Initially the mother had cried and the father had crossed himself. The atmosphere had been dreadful at first, but once they gave him the benefit of the doubt it was all smiles. As Fabrizio had so eloquently put it: 'Never judge a book by its paper.' Miles listened to Grapper's tale of woe and thought it extremely funny. So Bella had marriage in mind. Hence the visit – hence Grapper's sudden depression. 'I can't get married. I'm too young to die.'

Miles wiped his mouth with a rough paper napkin. 'How old are you, anyway?'

'Thirty next month. Too bleedin' young to settle down, that's for sure.'

Miles thought he looked much younger. 'Just take it easy with her. I don't think she can expect you to bite the bullet just yet.'

Grapper gazed pensively into the froth on his fresh beer. 'Well I tell yer, mate, there's sommat brewing back there. Anyway, talkin' about biting the bullet, you're a fine one to talk. That Daniela. Remember I told yer, she's trouble.'

'I can take care of myself, you know. Anyway, what's one last time between friends? She was pretty hot. I give her at least a nine. I don't think I can pass it up. My self-control isn't that good.'

Grapper felt a sudden chill. 'Well, if you do manage to keep yer pecker clean I'll be 'ere after ten – we've got to 'ave at least a couple of drinks to wish yer well in Florence. Beautiful place that is. You'll love it.'

'Yeah, I'm looking forward to it. It's so hot here I can't wait.'

'Don't expect miracles. It won't be that much cooler, but I'm sure it'll be better for yer.' He thought, 'In more ways than on,' but didn't say it.

Miles looked at his watch. It was twenty to three. 'I'll have to get going in a minute, but look, if I don't make it back here tonight, will you come to the station to see me off? Bring Bella if you want.'

Someone was dancing on Grapper's grave with hobnailed boots on and he hoped with all his heart that Miles would make it to the bar later that night. At least that way he'd be safe. He agreed to the sendoff if it didn't pan out that way. They arranged to meet at the pensione in good time for his train and Miles stood up to leave. He was slightly unsteady on his feet. 'I knew I shouldn't have had those beers. These new drugs are really strong!'

'Whatever yer taking they ain't dolly mixtures or bleedin' M & M's, are they? Yer not supposed to mix drink wiv 'em.'

'No, I know. But when have you known me do what I was supposed to?'

Grapper bit his tongue. That's what he was afraid of – Miles's gung-ho attitude. He knew that absolutely no amount of reiteration about the dangers was going to make a blind bit of difference. Best to let him go his own way.

'Well, see you tomorrow if I don't see you later on.' Miles walked somewhat uncertainly to the door.

'See ya, mate.' Grapper watched him go and for a split second wondered if he should try and stop him. If only he could get a decent fix on what was in store he might be more convincing. But then, like dire warnings of seismic activity, such disclosures were rarely believed. The Californians still lived on the San Andreas fault, didn't they? Like others of his kind he'd seen an aerial view of imminent disaster. The jagged crack in the terrain. An artery splitting open, a slashed vein that would drown the golden people in rivers of their own blood.

He wondered what it would take to make Miles understand that the Richter needle was shaking in his case – only gently, but that was enough. Enough to make this psychic extremely nervous.

Daniela sauntered down the marble stairs of the apartment building. The promise of fulfilment put a spring in her step and the moisture of sexual desire on her lips. When she reached the floor below a door opened and a feeble voice called out from the shuttered darkness beyond. 'Is that you, Daniela?'

'Yes, it's me, Signora Guindini. Is everything all right?' There was more than a hint of irritation in her voice.

'I am a little concerned. Your grandmother does not answer the door. Is her arthritis bad again? I did not hear her call out to me as she usually does.'

'She sleeps a great deal at the moment. I am sure when she is better she will ask to see you.'

The wizened neighbour looked unconvinced. 'Oh well, be sure and tell her I asked after her health. Off you go then.'

'Ciao.' Daniela bolted down the stairs. Her elegant suede pumps slipped on the freshly washed marble. She cursed and descended a little slower. She'd have to make up the time. She couldn't be late – not today of all days.

Miles stood beneath the green shuttered window of the building in the Campiello Santo Stefano. This time there was no musical accompaniment to his vigil. He sat on the step for a moment. The square was empty – silent as the proverbial grave. The siesta was still in full swing. Bored, he scuffed his shoes in the thick layer of dust on the cobbles. A stray dog cocked its leg on the side of the building, then wandered over in search of titbits. 'Sorry, fella, I've got nothing to give you.' He reached out to pet the mangy dog, then thought better of it. It was probably covered with fleas. He scratched a mosquito bite.

Daniela walked towards him and the dog ran off. They were alone. Solemn bells tolled the hour. She broke into a leggy run. He held her close, breathing in the perfume of her lustrous hair. 'How's my little genius today then?' he whispered.

'I am fine.' She pulled away from his strong hold and gazed up at him, sure of herself yet uncertain of his desire for her. 'Come on. I have much to tell you and time is short.' She took his hand.

'I have quite a lot to tell you too.' Miles wished for just a moment that he could extend his stay.

'Here, you can carry this for me.' Daniela handed him the flight bag.

'God, what have you got in here? This is a dead weight!'

'I'm sure you can manage. Now come on, Miles . . .' She walked ahead towards the Accademia bridge.

'Where are we going?' He called after her.

'It's a surprise.'

They walked over the bridge and like countless lovers before them paused for a moment to kiss. 'Tell me where we're going.' He bit her ear. She giggled like a schoolgirl, giving him a false sense of importance.

'First a drink and then the surprise. Now let's go – we are wasting precious time.'

Daniela led him through the virtually empty back streets then stopped at the ivy-covered entrance to her favourite restaurant. 'This will be our first stop.' She announced this fact casually.

Miles stepped inside and surveyed the scene. The restaurant was small and seemed rather cosy. Several couples lingered over late lunches – sambuca and seemingly endless coffees. The tables were covered with red-and-white-chequered vinyl cloths, rivers of wax ran down the inevitable Chianti bottles. It was the ultimate guidebook idyll, almost a cliché with its semi-open air atmosphere. A vine clung to the glass ceiling; small multi-coloured lanterns hung precariously from its gnarled branches.

They sat down. A huge sweaty man lumbered towards them

with his arms outstretched. He kissed Daniela furtively on both cheeks and they talked avidly. Miles couldn't understand what they were saying but it was obviously of some importance. The proprietor bowed his head at her tiny frame – she was dwarfed by his immense stature.

Eventually Daniela remembered her manners and introduced the two men. They eyed each other with mild displeasure. 'You are taking care of my little Daniela?' The man looked vague, troubled about something. Miles managed a smile. 'I think she is taking care of me.' He noticed the man had a glazed expression as though his thoughts were elsewhere.

He grunted and trudged away. A gaunt woman was standing by the espresso machine. She glared at her husband then gave Daniela a withering look. Daniela nodded in acknowledgement and turned away.

'Do you know these people well?' Miles asked innocently.

Daniela pushed dark tendrils of hair from her face. 'I do some waitress work for them sometimes.' She sighed and cast her eyes heavenwards. 'Franco. Well, he is not quite right – up here.' She tapped her temple.

'What a pity.' Miles had thought there was something slightly different about him.

'Anyway, it does not matter.' She seemed anxious to change the subject. 'Tonight is very special . . . after midnight it is my birthday.'

'Why didn't you tell me? I would have bought you something.' Miles beamed. 'Happy birthday for tomorrow.' He leaned across the grimy table and kissed her mouth.

'I think you will agree that birthdays are special. So I hope you will do something for me.'

'You got it. Name your poison.' He wondered what she would ask for.

She raised one eyebrow. 'Poison? Why poison? This is a strange thing to say.'

'I didn't mean literally – it's just an expression. It means you can have anything you like.'

'You will stay the night with me then?'

The sun danced through the vine, creating golden highlights in his hair. 'What a horrible sacrifice to ask of me.' He managed to look serious but his eyes twinkled.

She smiled wryly. 'Sacrifice, not quite . . . but what I have in mind – well, let us just say it is an unusual request.'

'Sounds intriguing.' Miles still found the scenario amusing. No warning bells tinkled in the breeze she stirred up.

'Tell me – have you been to the Ca' Rezzonico yet?'

'Christ, you've just reminded me – I was saving it till last. With all the arrangements I had to make for leaving I forgot all about it.'

'Leaving?' Her eyes clouded over.

'I . . . I . . . was going to tell you later – I'm leaving for Florence tomorrow.' He felt unnecessarily guilty. As though she had caught him out.

Daniela bit her bottom lip. 'Then it is right that you should help me tonight. I promise it will be the most exciting thing that has ever happened to you.'

'How could I possibly refuse an invitation like that? Tell me more.'

At that moment the lumbering Franco arrived with two glasses of white wine. He placed them before the couple and gazed lovingly down at Daniela.

'Grazie, Franco.' She was irritated by the interruption. She didn't look up so he lurched away again.

Miles eyed the wine and knew he shouldn't really drink it. He was only just feeling better after the beer that had hit his system like a truck. He took a sip and leaned back in his chair. 'So come on. Tell me more, I'm dying to know.' A smile flickered on her lips. The coloured lanterns above them quivered.

'Not here. When we get to the museum I will tell you everything.'

She sipped her wine and eyed his athletic body. He was wearing his palest denim shirt and jeans. With tanned skin and golden hair he looked stunning and she considered herself lucky the package was this appealing. Her task was going to be highly enjoyable. Impatient to move on, Miles drained his glass a little too quickly. 'I can't wait to hear what you've got in mind. I'm going to use the men's room first.' He stood up. 'Which way?'

Daniela pointed to a staircase. 'It is up there. I will pay and wait for you outside.' He protested, but she insisted.

As Miles turned and headed for the staircase Franco nodded

knowingly to Daniela. For a brief moment she didn't acknowledge him. Then she rewarded him with an affectionate look. He felt satisfied. Daniela lifted the bag and reached into the front pocket. She pulled out a large bundle of 50,000-lire notes and placed it by the Chianti bottle. A rather drunken man eyed the exchange between the pair and thought she had bought the most expensive wine on the list.

Miles pushed open the toilet door. A loose tap dripped into the dirty sink. He looked disdainfully at the pine-clad walls and the pale blue linoleum floor which curled at the corners exposing the filth beneath. No expense spared for customer comfort, he said under his breath. Whilst urinating, he studied a faded poster of a half-naked Bruce Lee which had been thoughtfully placed above the low level cistern. He wondered if there was more to Franco than met the eye.

Grapper sat in a darkened corner of the bar and waited for Bella to finish her shift. A few regulars chatted amiably to her as she dried glasses. Grapper didn't want to join in. He had far more important things on his mind. Things that needed his utmost concentration. He closed his eyes and tried to get a fix on Miles's whereabouts. A slight buzzing in his ears told him the trance was beginning. A hazy vision appeared. A bare-chested Chinese was holding a small brightly-coloured lantern at arm's length. Angered by his apparent lack of psychic ability, he dispelled the image of Bruce Lee and tried again.

Miles nodded politely to Franco as he returned. Franco sniffed and blew his nose. 'Outside,' he said.

Daniela was leaning over a small lichen-covered stone wall. She gazed thoughtfully into the filthy canal. Miles put his arms around her waist and kissed her downy neck. 'Shall we go then? He seemed enthusiastic, a child hurrying the parent to an outing. She straightened and turned to him smiling.

'Yes Miles. We will go now.'

He picked up the inordinately heavy bag and walked with his free hand in hers.

'Do you know very much about the Ca' Rezzonico?' she asked.

'Ah the Ca' Rezzonico,' Miles said authoritatively. 'Built by Baldassare Longena, main man of Venetian baroque. It was originally owned by the Pesaro family and got sold to the Rezzonicos in seventeen fifty-something. It was also owned by Browning. It had to be turned into a museum after the then owners ran into financial trouble in the nineteen thirties. It's meant to be one of the most fantastic palazzos in all of Venice. Shall I go on?' He seemed pleased with himself.

Daniela groaned and laughed. 'No, please, enough. You have obviously done your studies.' They continued on past a few weary tourists. The jaunty locals, refreshed from their rest, returned to open the shuttered shops. Laden barges made their way up the narrow canal with doubtful cargos. The bargees hailed one another in raucous tones. Most of them were related.

Miles and Daniela crossed the tiny bridge that led to their destination. They passed the deserted garden and stopped in front of the dark green doors of the museum.

'I'll pay for this. After all, it is your birthday in a few hours.' He reached into the pocket of his jeans as they walked through the tiny terrace to the ticket office.

The woman dishing out tickets didn't look up. An open book by her side seemed far more worthy of attention than the person she was serving. They passed through the glass doors and climbed the huge staircase. The masonry was wonderfully intricate and Miles seemed in awe of the craftsmanship. However, nothing could have prepared him for the pure unadulterated splendour of the main ballroom. Its ambience was quite simply the most magnificent he had encountered. 'Wow, this is incredible,' he breathed in a long sigh.

'Beautiful, isn't it?' Daniela murmured. She gazed up at the ornately decorated rococo chambers within the ceiling. Two huge crystal and gilt chandeliers hung like suspended Christmas trees. This elaborate decoration had kept a small army of craftsmen employed for many years. The ethereal beauty, texture and light within this great baroque room was an absolute joy to behold.

'It's the most wonderful room I've ever seen.' Miles inhaled the atmosphere.

The monstrous and the wild culminated in the rococo passions of Brustolon; the ebony and the gilt, the vast figures of Hercules and Cerberus. The intricate elements of this vast stage closed around the two lone figures moving slowly in wonder around its inner sanctum like a vast suffocating shroud. This was the room Miles had dreamed of where Daniela danced around a flame.

Unfortunately, he didn't remember.

CHAPTER 10

Grapper raised his wrist and pointed to his Mickey Mouse watch. Time to leave. A slobbering Frenchman was trying out a new come-on in a baffling mixture of French and Italian. Bella hardly understood a word but the sentiment struck home. She was seething. 'Mon mari. Il m'attend là-bas,' she said tersely. The Frenchman looked over at Grapper and did a double take. He downed his drink and left, seemingly in a hurry all of a sudden.

'So I'm yer husband now, am I?' Grapper teased as they made for the bridge.

She answered in her native tongue. 'Sorry. I had to say something good. He was really trying it on with me.'

Grapper understood some Italian but stubbornly spoke only English. An Englishman abroad. 'Well, they're all gonna try it on, darlin'. You're a live one, ain't yer.'

'Alive? Yes of course I am alive.' She didn't understand him at all sometimes.

'Never mind, it don't matter. Come on, dozy. Let's go 'ome.'

Hordes of tourists jostled at the foot of the Accademia bridge. Grapper looked hopefully over to Fabrizio's stand. It was still closed. He was of course sleeping, his dormouse wife cuddling up to his rounded belly. Grapper felt hungry and asked if Bella wanted an ice-cream. She seemed to be consuming it in great quantities just lately. If she carried on at this alarming rate she'd end up like her mother. God forbid.

'Si, grazie. Mocha with plenty nuts.' Her English made him smile. He kissed her damp forehead. 'You sit 'ere, babe. You look tired.' She nodded and sat down on the wooden seat, raising her face in homage to the fierce sun. He joined the queue.

'Grapper, how you are?' The girl filling cups with flavoured ice looked pleased to see him.

'Hi. Getting there, just about. Give us one of those lemon ones and a mocha dolce with nuts, will yer.'

'You do not seem so 'appy today.' The girl shovelled the ice around.

'Me? It's a beautiful day. I've got a beautiful girl, a few hours to meself. Ain't got a care in the world really.' Still smiling he turned around. What he saw almost made him drop the cups.

An old woman was sitting next to his amore. She wore a hooded cloak which wafted around her wizened face as though she were in a draught. The apparition locked him in her gaze and shook her head. Then she curled her lips. A chilling smile, blackened teeth, a friendly gesture? He didn't think so.

'Holy fuck.'

Bella crossed herself and looked around to see if anyone had heard him. She frowned at his rigid stance.

The woman pointed in the direction whence they had come.

'What is it? Do yer want me to go back there? What?'

The sage remained mute.

'Go back – why we go back?' Bella still seated and blissfully unaware was puzzled.

'Na, not you baby. Come on, let's go.'

He took his eyes from the spectre for a split second. When he looked again she had gone. He cursed and walked away. Bella caught him up. 'Did yer see anyone back there?'

'Anyone. Who exactly?

'An old woman . . . sitting next to you.'

Bella shaded the sun from her eyes and stared at him.

'I saw no one, I was alone there. I don't understand.' Confused, she licked the now melting ice-cream.

'It don't matter. I thought there was . . . Never mind.'

They walked on in silence. Grapper sucked on the lemon ice and hunted for a vague truth. Sometimes it came easily to him sometimes not. Okay, so Miles was in some kind of danger. What did this stranger in his camp of strays have to do with it? Often random souls popped into his subconscious like nosy neighbours, but he'd never seen one in the flesh before. What did she want? He was sure he'd seen her before. But where?

From behind the curtain that shielded the living from the departed, his mother emerged. He felt her presence. Then she was so close he could smell her – lily of the valley by Yardley.

He reached out in his mind, probing for reassurance. 'What's going on, Ma? Where is Miles? Do you know what's going on?' He felt a slight breeze on his face. Warm intimate breath. Mrs Rice had a word in her son's ear. 'Belloti.'

'What in God's name does Belloti mean?' He spoke aloud. Bella, who was lost in thought, jumped. The smell of perfume grew stronger. His mother's disembodied voice more insistent. 'Think, Charlie,' she said. 'Belloti.'

Bella sniffed first the air and then her boyfriend's shirt. This was something she had not noticed before – a cologne that smelt of flowers. Could this be why English men were considered less macho than their Italian cousins? Perfume of poofs. She made a mental note to buy him some Missoni.

Daniela and Miles strolled through the museum's spectacular rooms. As was her intention he was beguiled by his surroundings, seduced by the breathtaking palazzo. The cryptic purpose of their visit was now almost forgotten. His eyes danced along the gallery. Daniela led the way, moving him slowly toward her target. They climbed the stairs to the second floor.

In the majestic Hall of Paintings, Miles studied an oil, transfixed by weatherbeaten features that expressed suffering and great hardship. The old woman contemplated her lot in life from beneath the folds of a crude hooded cloak.

'Let's go on to the balcony for a moment.' Daniela was growing impatient.

The huge mullioned windows overlooking the Grand Canal at the end of the grandiose room were open, revealing an ornate stone balcony beyond.

Here they were out of earshot of the lazy guard. In his light slumber, balding head resting on his chest, he resembled an oversized pigeon.

The gallery's only other occupants, a middle-aged couple, moved to the next room. The air was still. The lovers contemplated the water traffic below.

'Are you going to tell me now what this is all about?' Miles broke the silence first.

Daniela stared at the water. The first deceptive sentence poured from her slightly pouting lips like honey.

'You know how much our time together has meant to me, don't you Miles?'

He watched a water bus pass by, crammed with tourists tightly packed like sardines. 'It's meant a lot to me too – of course.' He wondered what was coming next.

She touched his cheek. 'You have been very patient with me. I will explain now what is on my mind. For many years I have had a childish dream – a dream that has meant more to me than anything else in the world. When I met you I knew that dream would be more special with someone to share it with. I hope you will not let me down.' Her eyes shone with convincing tears.

Miles watched her, saying nothing.

'When I was younger I was sent here to live with my grandmother. My mother taught me that because I could sing I was special – she told me whatever else happened in my life I would always have that gift and nobody could take it away from me. My Grandmamma didn't agree. She said I was vain and stupid and made me study hard. I could not play like other children. I hated her. When I was twelve I was brought to this place and fell in love with it just as you have done. I decided, one day, when I am a great opera singer, I will sing in the great ballroom.' She looked determined.

Miles wondered were on earth this was leading. 'I'm not sure why you're telling me this.'

'I will be eighteen at midnight tonight and tomorrow I run away from Venice ... I am going to London. It is better for me there. I will see Mamma. At least she understands me. Anyway, I have brought with me the things I need to make my dream come true.' She glanced over her shoulder to make sure no one was listening. 'Through there is a hiding place. A good hiding place. You and I can stay until it is dark. Then we can have a spectacular adventure. I have brought food, music and wine. We do not need anything else. We have each other. Think of it – what a place to spend our last night together! I will sing not only for myself but for you. I cannot tell you how much this all means to me.'

Miles had to admit it sounded tempting. 'Sounds like you've got it all worked out.'

'Afterwards we will hide until morning. When they open the doors we will walk out like we just came in. At ten o'clock big parties come here. Schools and students, they will not realize we are not part of their group. It is a great plan, no?'

This was of course a criminal action, but it had the desired effect on Miles's enthusiasm for adventure.

'I can't believe you thought all this up by yourself. If it really is possible. God, imagine a whole night in this place with it all to ourselves . . .' He rose to the scam until a modicum of sense surfaced. 'But wait a minute – they must have complicated alarms and things . . .'

Daniela sensed victory. 'Alarms, yes – complicated, no. They have only alarms on the first-floor windows and doors. There are no sensors in the rooms. If we tried to take anything from the walls maybe something rings, but there are no movement sensors. We do not try to get in from the outside so nobody will know we are here.'

'What about a guard? They must have some form of protection,' Miles asked excitedly. 'Wait a goddamn minute – what am I saying? How the hell do you know about room sensors and things? I mean, we have them at home, but how do you know so much about it?'

She sighed. 'I know what I have to know. There is a night guard. The restaurant where I took you . . . Franco, well, it is his cousin who is on this duty. Franco told me he slips away at eleven to see his woman, on Saturdays. Franco says he stays until sometimes early morning.

'How can you be so sure?' Miles asked.

'I am sure.' She was giving the performance of her life. Utterly convincing. She wiped a trickle of sweat from her glistening collarbone. 'Think of it, Miles. This incredible place all to ourselves. Of course, if you are afraid . . .'

He stared at her and wondered for just a moment. Then he took the bait. 'No, I'm not afraid. So today is Saturday. The guard's gonna sneak off. Just one thing. We couldn't put any lights on. How will we see?'

Daniela smiled a half smile. 'That is very simple, Miles. Tonight la luna is good to us. There will be a full moon.'

Katerina groped along the wall for the light switch. The damp weaved into her nostrils, an odour which stirred unwanted memories. She edged with care down the slimy steps that had taken her loved one then pushed her weight against the door. It gave way. Petrified wood rasped on stone.

The light bulb, caked with years of grime, was hopelessly dim, inadequate. She could just make out the outline of the trunk – this was to be its final resting place. She'd rather have burnt the lot. The memories of childhood had remained buried. Now she cursed them for rising like poisonous algae on a stagnant pond, consuming hope. She struggled to pull the trunk from the recess. The rusted clasp was hard to prise open but Katerina persevered. Beneath the mementoes of her husband's dark past she found what she was looking for – his photograph album. A thick layer of dust rose in a choking cloud around her face. The half light made authentication impossible. Katerina would have to pollute her sanctuary still further. Reluctantly she tucked the disintegrating book under her arm as the reception bell rang above her. Startled, she looked up. She wasn't expecting anyone.

As Katerina heaved her weary frame up the cellar steps, the shadow breathed a little more rapidly.

It was now ten minutes to closing time. Daniela took Miles through a series of anterooms to a small simulated bedroom. The glossy brochure referred to it as 'The Alcove'.

No one witnessed their progress. They reached their destination undetected.

'Well, this is it. This is where we will hide.' Daniela motioned to a beautiful silken bed which dominated centre stage. This tiny elaborate room was a perfect eighteenth-century reproduction. The walls were covered with country scenes of reclining nymphs and shepherds in a watery blue. The bed-cover was a golden silk damask, there were intricate pale blue and gilt paintings on the ivory bedhead. This was a long-lost period elegance.

'The decor's exquisite, but you can't mean to tell me we're going to hide in here?' Miles exclaimed in hushed tones.

'Of course. It is not a problem to hide here. Look.'

Daniela stepped lightly onto the dais and lifted the silken bed-cover to reveal a more than adequate space beneath. The bed was merely a flimsy frame. A deception.

'I see what you mean,' Miles whispered. 'But how long do we have to stay under there?'

She looked at her watch. 'It is now five o'clock – this means we have to hide until eleven or so.'

'Jesus, that's six hours. I'll never manage to keep quiet for that long.'

I cannot remember. Do you make noise when you are sleeping?'

'What do you mean, do I snore? No. Why?'

'Then we are going to be all right. I took two of my Grandmamma's pills to help with the sleeping. It will put us out for at least five or maybe six hours.'

'You've thought of everything, haven't you.' He sounded excited. No caution ensued. That had been her intention. The spell had worked beautifully. Daniela smiled. 'Of course. Now quickly, let's hide.' She pushed the flight bag beneath the bed then crouched down and held the bed-cover aside in a final act of deadly seduction. 'Well, Miles, are you going to stay here with me?'

She knew the answer.

'Just you try and stop me.' He stepped up to the bed and placed an accepting kiss on her slightly flushed cheek. Then he crawled into the dark recess.

Daniela hurriedly joined him.

He moved over to make room for his lover. She dragged the bag noiselessly through the fine dust layer to her side and drew back the edge of the bed-cover to let in more light. Miles propped himself up on one elbow and watched her. 'You're incredible,' he whispered. She placed a finger to her lips and rummaged for the small bottle of water and silver pillbox. With dextrous precision she took one pill between thumb and forefinger, as though it were an entomologist's specimen, and placed it on her tongue. She gulped some water and handed Miles another. For a split second he wondered what effect it would have when mixed with dihydracodine and hesitated. Well, he was here now. This was illegal – he was in pretty deep – so he might as well go the whole hog. He placed the white pill onto his tongue – it tasted bitter. She handed him the water. Water of life. Amniotic fluid. Birth of a victim. He took a gulp and swallowed hard.

Daniela placed a large bundle of soft velvet behind their heads. It served as a pillow for them both. She placed his hand on her breast and closed her eyes. 'Sleep well. And if you dream, I hope you dream of me.'

'I'm sure I will,' he murmured drowsily.

Another mistaken assumption.

Katerina rubbed her eyes as they adjusted to the light. Two men paced slowly through her hall. 'Can I help you?' she asked innocently.

'You are Signora Fratanelli?' the smaller of the two asked in Italian.

She answered in English.

'Da, that is me. Do you need a room?' She placed the photograph album on the counter and picked up a registration card.

'Thank you, but . . . alas, no. You have a Signor Miles Hanson staying with you, I believe.' The tall elegant man scrutinized the icons. His hands were clasped behind his back, his fingers entwined.

'That is so. Why do you ask this?'

'Is he here now?' He kept his back turned.

Katerina considered him rude. 'No he is not 'ere. Who are you anyway?' she demanded crossly.

He turned and offered his hand. 'I am sorry, Signora. I did not wish to offend. It is simply the paintings. They took me by surprise – beautiful examples of their type. I am Inspector Marcello Cappitta, and this – he motioned to the younger man – is Sergeant Gianelli.'

Gingerly she took his hand and shook it. He was quite the most elegant man she'd ever seen. Six feet or more, thick dark hair slightly greying at the temples; a designer suit that must have cost a small fortune and of course a glowing tan. Gleaming bronze skin, chiselled cheekbones. A strong jaw. A real man. Her anger abruptly subsided. If only she were twenty years younger and at least five stone lighter. She still had an eye for beauty. 'Please, please to come through. We will be more comfortable in here.' She led them into the little salon patting her hair into place.

'Thank you, Signora. You are most kind.' The inspector moved with the taut grace of a big cat.

Katy flopped into her worn armchair. 'Please to sit down,' she said. The sergeant moved towards the other chair.

'Thank you, but I prefer to stand.' Marcello took up position before her fireplace. Here he would obtain the optimum view of her expression when he delivered his blow.

'Signora Fratanelli, has the Signor Hanson mentioned a young lady to you? Her name is Carole Davis.' He pulled a box of black Sobranies from his inside pocket. 'Permesso?' He held up a cigarette.

'Yes, please go ahead.' She hated cigarette smoke.

'Carole the English girl. She gave Miles my address – he needed somewhere to stay.'

The inspector blew a perfect frivolous smoke ring into the air. 'How long has the Signor Hanson been staying with you, Signora?'

She thought for a moment. 'Two weeks perhaps. I cannot remember exactly when he arrived.'

'May I ask, how well did you know Carole Davis?' He flicked ash casually into one of her delicate porcelain ashtrays.

'Not very well. She was giving me some customers when her hotel was overbooked. She is a nice girl, no? What do you want with her?'

Marcello inhaled deeply. 'Was, Signora ... She *was* a nice girl.'

Katerina held her breath. 'What is this you are saying? What do you mean – was a nice girl? I am not understanding you.'

Marcello nodded to his sergeant who continued with Katerina's enlightenment: 'We found the Signorina Davis's body in the early hours of this morning. Her throat had been cut and I am afraid she was horribly mutilated. Do you understand? She is dead, Signora.'

Katerina gripped the worn arm of her chair and theatrically put her hand to her throat. 'Dead! Such a young one ... my God.' In a fleeting moment the reason for their visit came to her. 'You cannot believe Miles did this thing? He is a sweet boy. He would 'arm no one. Never would he do such a thing as this.' Their unspoken accusation horrified her.

The inspector pulled on the Sobranie. 'Signora, at this time we have to question everybody who knew the girl. When will he return?'

'I do not know that ... and I do not know where he is. He could be anywhere in Venice.'

Marcello studied her clutter for a moment, picking up a small figurine. 'Then as you are so sure of your guest I take it you will not mind telephoning us when he returns.'

'Da, da. As soon as he comes back I will telephone you.' She felt relieved. Maybe she could get him away from here. He was innocent. Didn't the poor boy have enough trouble? She had to help him.

'You will of course ensure that he does not leave before we have questioned him? I would have to hold you responsible if he managed to disappear before we conclude our investigation.' He turned to face her. Katerina seemed uncomfortable with the voice of authority. Strains of the past.

'Da, of course.' She mopped her brow. The policeman's amber eyes narrowed. He undoubtedly meant business. She prised herself from the chair and went to the small safe, taking out Miles's passport. He had given it to her in accordance with regulations and hadn't asked for it back yet. 'Would you like to take this, inspector? Perhaps then you can be sure he will not leave.' She sought deliverance from responsibility. All temptation removed.

Marcello waved a dismissive hand. 'Please, Signora, that will not be necessary. I am sure you can be trusted to do the right thing.'

As Katerina showed them out Gianelli handed her a small printed card. She promised to telephone them in due course and closed the door firmly behind them. The enormity of the situation dawned. In the kitchen with a comforting cup of tea she told herself this had absolutely nothing to do with her young guest. Very much a case of being in the wrong place at the wrong time. Was he courting disaster? No. As she had said he was a dear sweet boy who had not brought these things upon himself. After all, he had done nothing conscious to cause one near-fatal accident and a murder now, had he?

Miles drifted off in Daniela's warm embrace. He mused. Strange how life turned up the unexpected when you were content with routine. This had been an adventure to end all adventures. Lisa seemed so far away now. Two short months ago he'd bolted from the cinema where he and Josh had gone to see *Platoon*. When they used Barber's Adagio virtually throughout it overwhelmed him. He'd felt such a fool blubbing in the foyer. Distraught at the injustice of it all. Lisa had introduced him to that piece and many others. Weaned him off rock, given him a subtle education in the classics she so loved. Eternally the romantic. He pushed her memory away like debris. That was then, this is now. Here he was – up to tricks again. A new lease on life. And some.

As he dozed a nagging thought pushed its way through. What would Grapper think when he didn't show up at the bar? Well, he'd guess he was getting his rocks off for a start. Something was back there – something Grapper had said. He couldn't remember. Anyway, this criminal activity would impress his friend. He was a rebel himself.

Warning signals, held back by the cocktail of chemicals whirring through his bloodstream, remained dormant. His sensibility struggled with a demon in his brain. This dark cloying spell overpowered everything in its path. It would have ultimate control. Daniela had made sure of that.

CHAPTER 11

In an untidy bedroom with rosebud wallpaper, a shrine to the Madonna, and peach silk scarves draped over the bedside light, Grapper slept soundly, as always, after lovemaking. Despite constantly worrying about his friend, there had been momentary solace. Bella's body was swelling in places. He'd thought it was water retention. She knew differently.

Bella pulled the sheet over her 'ostrich' and placed a maternal hand on her stomach. He'd notice soon – she had to be brave and tell him. What would he say? Did he love her enough to marry her? She crossed herself, muttering an express prayer for divine intervention, then rose to prepare for the evening shift. It was just after seven. She pulled on the fuchsia polyester robe and wondered if she should wake him. He had so many things on his mind these days. The strange embryonic ball in her bed, curled like a baby, unguarded, vulnerable, looked so peaceful she let him sleep on. Like father, like son. She hoped it would be a boy. A girl would be too much trouble. Especially if she took after her mother.

Grapper dreamed of an African plain. A group of nuns surrounded him with outstretched arms. 'Look, but don't touch.' Mother Superior had spoken. 'He must be saved for our Lord.' The nuns swayed hungrily, their rosaries swinging back and forth. Religious pendulums. Grapper protested violently. The nuns advanced. Now they were naked hags. Sagging flesh hung like empty pouches, empty breasts, empty hearts. He screamed and ran; past rows of men who nodded silently and a resplendent cardinal who said 'Stregoneria my son' knowledgeably; past a cloaked old woman with blackened teeth who smiled.

In the far distance, through a wavering heat haze, he could just make out a tent. Several men laughed and toasted their efforts. He stumbled towards them, calling for help. He drew nearer. The men were in uniform. One stood head and shoulders above the rest.

Grapper collapsed with exhaustion at their feet, pressing his face into the coarse sand. He heard them discussing his plight in Italian and turned to the soldiers. The taller man held something over Grapper which dripped rhythmically on to his face. He squinted and wiped away the stream. Then looked at his hand – it was covered in blood. Two freshly severed black heads drained their life source onto Grapper's face.

He woke up screaming.

Miles was disorientated. Where was he? His head pounded like a hammer. It was pitch black. He wanted to sneeze suddenly, dust. Now he remembered: Daniela, the museum. God he'd really done it this time. He wondered how long he'd slept and reached out for her. The space next to him was empty.

Miles moved out from under the bed, risking discovery. His body felt like lead. He stood up uncertainly and grasped his temples. God it hurt. Must be the drugs, he thought. He steadied himself and brushed the dirt from his clothes. The alcove was quite dark but he could just make out the rooms beyond. Stepping from the dais he walked through the antechamber which had a narrow picture window. He peered at his watch in the half light. It was twenty past eleven. Miles couldn't believe he'd slept for that long. What was it Daniela had said about the guard and his mistress?

His brain was now candy floss.

From somewhere below him, music played and jogged his redundant memory. It came to him not so much in a flash, more a glimmer. Eleven. The guard was going to leave at eleven. He pushed dishevelled hair from his face and made for the vast hall of paintings.

He crept into the gallery which was now glowing with eerie light. Daniela had been right. There was a full moon. It blazed through the huge mullioned windows, flooding everything with a beautiful silver light. The marble floor became calm water, stilled by an unseen force. Ghostly faces, reflections from the paintings stared up at him.

He edged along the gallery. When he reached the entrance to the stairwell the music grew louder, beckoning, drawing him to its source. He moved slowly down the stairs to the grand ballroom.

Daniela was playing 'Riders On The Storm' by The Doors. One of her mother's all-time favourites. Quite appropriate really.

Miles crept through the imposing portico then made his way through several smaller rooms to the ballroom. The scene before him caused a sharp intake of breath.

This room did not face the Grand Canal and the full moon. Within the enormous rococo splendour, its gilt and marble glistening, Daniela had supplemented pale strands of light with candles. Six black candles – each one at least a foot tall. They formed a large circle and Daniela now sat cross-legged in the centre. Her ebony hair draping her shoulders like a gleaming curtain. Her head bent as she prepared something with a look of intense concentration on her heart-shaped face. She wore their pillow – a full-length midnight blue velvet cloak which fanned out around her.

She looked up.

'Miles,' she said softly. 'Come and join the party.'

In the bar Grapper gloomily hogged a darkened recess and turned his glass slowly round and round. He went over the clues he'd assimilated. It was hopeless. He couldn't get a fix for love or money. Where was the stupid fucker? He'd telephoned Katerina just after 10.30 and envisioned a big old woman chewing thoughtfully on a parmesan rind as she listened, but what use was that?

Grapper gave her a message to pass on: he'd be at the bar until twelve if Miles came back and still wanted to see him. Of course he wouldn't come.

He gripped the glass. Fat lot of good he was as a psychic. Useless, utterly useless. He closed his eyes and sighed deeply. Surreal moments from the dream drifted in and out of his mind. Bella brought him a fresh Scotch and sat down. He opened one eye. She put a hand on his forehead.

'Okay?' she asked.

'Yeah, I'm fine, just tired.'

Bella shrugged and walked away. She knew better than to hang around when he wasn't in a talkative mood. When Fabrizio came in she warned him off. He ordered a drink and glanced over to his friend, concerned.

Grapper looked at his watch. 11.30. Miles had to be with her.

He couldn't just sit here on his arse and let the worst happen. It may be pointless but he had to go looking for him. He drained his glass in one and went up to the other two people he cared about.

'I'm off Bella, I'll see yer at 'ome.' He clapped a hand on the little man's shoulder. 'Fab, I'm glad yer 'ere, mate. Do you know what ''stregoneria'' means in English?'

Fabrizio thought for a moment. 'Nasty, Wizard of Oz,' he said.

Grapper frowned. 'No jokes, Fab, not now,' he said tersely.

'Okay. It mean . . . witchcraft.'

Miles entered the circle with scenes from *Rosemary's Baby* running through his mind. Hardly the teddy-bears' picnic. For some reason he wasn't in the least bit alarmed.

He sat down cross-legged as she was. 'Jesus, I slept like a log. I feel like someone drove a truck though my head,' he said. 'How do you feel?'

She touched his face. 'Me? I feel fine. I have something that will help with your head. First we eat. Are you hungry now?' She tried to gauge the depth of the spell. Was it wearing off? Time for a top-up?

'Well, not really. These heads always make me feel a bit sick but food generally helps. What have you brought?'

Daniela stepped outside the circle and rummaged in the seemingly bottomless flightbag. She took out a plastic carrier bag with bread, some foil-wrapped parcels, a bottle of white wine and some paper cups.

'No wonder that bag was so damn heavy. You've thought of everything.'

'Almost – there is also this.' She held up the fruits of her labours. A joint of cannabis.

'You brought dope with you as well! That should help the headache.'

'That is what I was thinking. Impressed?' she asked coquettishly.

Daniela had to be sure Miles wasn't in full control of his faculties. That wouldn't do. Wouldn't do at all.

'You never fail to impress me. Come on, let's light that thing. Forget the food for a minute. We'll feel more like it after a joint anyway.'

'We should feel like a lot of things after this.' Daniela leaned over one of candles to light the joint, exposing gleaming flesh. She inhaled deeply. 'Why don't you open the wine?'

He watched her. Caution, deeply buried, stirred like dead leaves by a breeze, momentarily brought to life, rustling somewhere in his subconscious. If he drank on top of the drugs ... No, they should have worn off by now. Just one perhaps. Should be all right.

'Where's the corkscrew?'

'I'll get it.' Daniela stood up and handed Miles the joint.

When she reached into the bag he heard the faint chink of metal. Unperturbed, he studied her music set-up. A Walkman had been attached to two small speakers. 'Pretty smart, this set-up with the Walkman.' He dragged on the joint and felt instantly relaxed from the hit.

'I had to use something I could conceal easily. We would not have been allowed in here with the blasting ghettos. It's strictly forbidden.'

Miles burst out laughing and almost choked on the acrid smoke.

She was annoyed. 'What is so funny?'

'You, that's what's funny. You were close – they're called ghetto-blasters. But your version would make a great name for a heavy metal band.

She didn't like being laughed at and swished her cloak angrily. An inner voice said: 'Calm down – don't rush. There is plenty of time.'

Miles handed her the joint and took the corkscrew. 'You shouldn't be so tetchy. It's all right to laugh at yourself from time to time, you know.'

She stared into the shadows.

'All right. I'm sorry I spoke.' He pulled out the cork. 'Look, in five minutes it'll be your birthday and everybody knows it's bad luck to be unhappy on your birthday, so just lighten up. Let's have some fun, shall we? After all, that's what we're here for.'

The glowering became a dazzling smile. A cloud lifted from the sun.

'Of course you are right. I have a lot of things planned for us ...' She pulled on the joint. 'First a toast and then I will sing before we eat. I cannot sing afterwards – things get stuck in my throat.' She stretched her swan-like neck.

'Sounds good to me. I'm curious about something, though . . .'

'What's that?' She handed back the joint.

'How come you didn't choose La Fenice as the setting for your dream? Surely an opera house would have been more relevant.' He inhaled.

'Perhaps. But a little clichéd, don't you think? Besides, I like to be different.'

'You're certainly that,' he said, exhaling.

'You are different too, and secretive. I know so little about you and you know so much about me. I don't think it's fair, do you?'

He looked down at the floor, then passed the joint again. They looked like overgrown kids playing pass the parcel. 'It's probably better this way. If you knew the whole story you wouldn't like me as much.'

She inhaled again. 'You sound very sure.' The smoke made her eyes water a little. They glistened in the light.

'I am, believe me.'

'I think you should tell me at least one secret. Something you have told no one else.' The joint was low as she held it out. He shook his head.

'That's not easy. Let's see. Well, I used to wish I didn't exist. I was going to kill myself when I was about fourteen.'

'What made you want to do that?'

'I decided that life was a bitch and I was better off without it. There was some trouble at school. I was so dumb. I had a real problem separating reality from fantasy. I've always thought my imagination had the edge over the everyday shit.'

'What changed your mind?'

'I was afraid my friends would think I'd taken the coward's way out.'

She ground out the joint on the floor. 'And what are you afraid of now?'

'Of being shut away in a dark place where there's no light, like I was before.'

'Who shut you in?'

'I did – I was trapped inside my own mind. Anyway, this

conversation's getting doomy. We're here to have fun, remember? I can't wait to hear you sing again. This really is a fantastic setting.' He babbled on, unaware of her mood. 'I'm sure it's gonna be the experience of a lifetime. It'll really be something to tell my crazy friends about back home. Josh thinks he's the one that has all the adventures. He's done some insane things. Anyway, I doubt if they'll believe me . . .' He poured the wine and handed her a paper cup. 'You know, champagne and crystal would have been far more appropriate. If I'd known I would have come prepared.' He took his grandfather's gold watch from a back pocket. 'This has got a second hand so we won't miss the moment.'

Daniela gazed enviously down at the watch and felt a stronger presence. This she had to have. Later.

Miles began the countdown to midnight. Somewhere outside in a Venice that stretched wearily, its streets almost empty, distant bells chimed the hour. 'This is it,' he said jubilantly. 'Happy birthday! Here's to the most beautiful, talented person I know.'

He raised his cup.

Daniela gazed in to the darkness outside their circle.

'Here's to us,' she said, raising her wine to the shadow.

'To us.' Miles took a sip then kissed her hungrily. She responded despite herself. Their kiss grew more urgent. She pulled away. 'Not yet, please,' she whispered as his passion grew. 'If you get me hot I will never be able to sing.' Her breath was warm on his cheek.

'All right. I want to hear you but don't be too long.' He released her.

Daniela placed a new tape in the Walkman and still crouching said: 'Now my dream has come true and I am so happy. Thank you for sharing this with me.'

He was glad he had contributed in some way.

She picked up the thought and smiled to herself – he'd never know how much. She flounced over to the huge windows at the far end of her marbled stage. 'When I say, start the tape,' she called out.

Miles crouched by the Walkman. Understandably, excitement welled up in him.

She breathed deeply to prepare herself. 'Now start the tape,' she said. He obliged.

Puccini's 'Vissi D'Arte' filled the great room. Miles stared up at the painted architecture as Daniela soared with the aria, her voice carried by acoustics that accentuated her finest moment. This haunting melody gave vitality to dead rooms. Breathing new life. A glorious communion. She sang of her darkest hour, of desertion by the Heavenly Father in whom she had trusted.

Of course Miles did not know what she was singing but the effect was devastating. The ballroom glowed replete with light and sound. Gargantuan gods within the rococo ceiling looked down smiling. Ah, the folly of youth.

Daniela's voice caressed and aroused Miles to a point of ecstasy as she stood rigidly, face proudly raised. Beauty born of pain into a writhing pit from which there could be no escape. Her gaze intensified with the words. Torrential black hair cascaded down her back, gleaming ropes that would embrace her victim, holding him fast until his skin became clammy, cold, dead.

He thought Daniela had been right again – this was the most exciting moment of his life. The aria gathered momentum, and when she reached the highest note she cast the cloak aside with a sweeping gesture. Then she flung her arms wide. Miles caught his breath. She was completely naked.

He applauded wildly as Daniela walked the length of the incredible room, dragging the cloak theatrically behind her. 'I don't know what to say.' His voice rang out. 'That was absolutely incredible.'

She smiled. 'It could have been better. It is not quite the right key. It will take years before my voice is mature. But as long as you enjoyed it. That is all that matters.'

He pulled her close. Should she take him now, she wondered. Perhaps it would be better to prolong this sensuous game for just a little while longer. After all, she had earned her fun. He showered her neck and shoulders with passionate kisses, unable to contain himself for a moment longer. She was kneeling now and leaned her head back. The ebony chains quivered. He misread her pleasure and probed for moistened treasure. 'Not yet Miles, please,' she whispered intently.

The joint had sharpened their senses – each moment became a delicious torture. 'I can't wait – I want you now, Daniela . . .' Miles gently bit her earlobe, then kissed her collarbone. She pulled his head to her face.

'Stop, please . . .' she said girlishly 'If you want me you're going to have to find me.

'I have found you and I want you now.' His skin felt on fire.

'Look, I will make a deal with you.' She sounded resolute. 'We are going to play hide and seek.'

Miles kissed her shoulder distractedly. 'Mmmm . . .'

'When you find me we will make love. It is my birthday and I get to make the rules.'

He sighed with exasperation. 'All right. What do I have to do?'

'Miles, don't sound so sad. You will find me. There are not so many places to hide.'

'You're kidding. This place is huge, I'll never find you. Unless you want to be found, that is.' He tickled her playfully.

She pushed him away, impatient. 'You must go back to our hiding place. Take off all your clothes and count to one hundred. That does not give me that much time now, does it?' she taunted.

'Oh I get it, a nudist game. Great, I'm all for that. I warn you I'll sniff you out sooner or later.'

'I'm sure you will. Now go on.' She pushed him playfully towards the stairs.

As Miles climbed to the second floor, someone breathed heavily behind him. He wheeled around. 'Daniela . . .' whispered. There was nobody there.

In the bedroom he hummed to himself as he pulled off his clothes, then dropped them on the floor. Naked apart from his shorts, he moved through the anterooms counting as instructed.

The empty halls amplified his furtive whispers as he counted. He cocked his head listening for barefoot steps but all he heard was distant water traffic. He moved towards the stairwell counting all the time. 'Fifty-three, fifty-four, fifty-five. What the hell, sixty-four, sixty-five . . .'

'No cheating,' whispered an educated male voice.

'Who's there?' Miles stopped dead in his tracks and wheeled around again. The vast room was completely empty, as before. He shuddered and chided his imagination. The dope must have been stronger than he thought.

He resumed the game, edging all the time down the gallery. As he passed before the painting of the hooded old woman he stopped for a second. The shimmering moonlight made her eyes appear wet with tears. He reached up to touch the picture and then remembered the alarms.

He walked away.

A single droplet fell from her face onto the silvery floor.

'Coming, ready or not!' Miles bounded through the rooms to the ballroom. 'Come out, come out wherever you are' he whispered as he searched the hallowed regions of the Salon de Brustolon.

Contented, Daniela settled herself in her hiding place, a black widow waiting for the mate she would devour. When it suited her. She leaned back against the faded red velvet seat of the gilt sedan chair and smiled to herself. 'Come and get me, Miles,' she murmured as she ran her finger along the master's blade. 'I'm ready for you now.'

Grapper angrily pounded the length of the Rialto bridge and raced through narrow alleys that led to St Mark's and the Correr museum. His thoughts were of the apparition who'd appeared to him earlier that day. A familiar face. He cocked his head, like Pavlov's dog. Conditioning stirred. He'd seen the old woman somewhere before, somewhere around the Correr. He dashed from a side street into the square. A few stray tourists looked on. No pigeons rose up. They were sleeping.

In the far right-hand corner of the cloisters, Grapper lent against the doors of his destination. Coughing loudly he banged his chest and scrutinized the poster opposite advertising yet another museum. The old woman's hooded face had a slight tear across her left cheek. The inscription however was undamaged. It read: 'Portrait of an old woman, by Belloti. The Ca' Rezzonico.'

Miles padded through the baroque expanse and heard a muffled noise. He turned abruptly but saw nothing. Then he felt suddenly nervous. Was someone else in there with them? Maybe the guard hadn't left at all but was watching them. Getting his kicks before calling the police.

He dismissed such thoughts and made his way through the salon to the long portego. In the far corner was a black gondola cover. Miles tiptoed across the room and peered into the dark recess hopefully. The canvas was suspended by a fragile frame. The space below was empty.

'Shit.' He cursed, frustrated.

'Temper temper . . .' Daniela taunted from her hiding place.

He turned and saw the sedan. Why was he so stupid? Miles wrenched open the fragile door with a cry of 'Gotcha!'

Daniela squealed as Miles pounced on her. 'Now you're mine,' he said. Ignoring her muffled giggles, he showered her face and neck with pleading kisses. The dope mingled with the sleeping pill and the wine. He felt languid, almost drowsy. He kissed a skilful line to her breast and took a small brown nipple between his teeth, biting her gently. She submitted to the sensation, aroused by him. He knelt suddenly, moving his head between her legs. Initial teasings became gradually more urgent. Her hand moved away from the knife by her side to his head. As she ran her fingers through his tousled hair, her worshipper devoured her like a starving man falling on a banquet; all thoughts of AIDS banished by desire, need. His hands grasped her tiny waist as she moaned with pleasure.

The worn velvet ripped slightly as Miles pushed Daniela harder against the fragile wood. Neither of them were aware of the brutal hands that reached for her through the curtained window. The hands twisted. Her slender neck snapped like a twig. A single cry, which Miles mistook for ecstasy, left her dying lips. As a thin line of blood trickled from her open mouth, Miles exploded with an animal cry at her feet.

The brutal hands receded with their owner. Unseen.

Miles rested his head on Daniela's thigh for a moment. The shadows breathed in unison with him. He whispered his gratitude. 'That was wonderful . . .' He kissed her inner thigh and gazed up at her.

Daniela's head lolled grotesquely. Dull eyes stared blankly at him.

'Daniela, stop clowning . . .' He shook her gently. She didn't respond.

Miles pulled himself to his feet and placed a questioning hand under her chin. He saw the blood – it didn't register in his numbed brain. Then suddenly he realized. 'No, please God, no . . .' His torment echoed through the vast rooms.

God had nothing to do with it.

He held her lifeless body. Tears flowed freely as he rocked her to and fro in his arms, pressing her flaccid head into his chest.

Unable to move, Miles stayed rigid for what seemed hours. In fact it was only minutes. Dazed, confused, not believing, he stroked her hair and whispered to her, 'It will be all right . . .' When she refused to come alive he pulled her from the litter, laying her down on the cold marble.

Daniela's ritual knife clattered onto the floor by her side. The unexpected noise made him jump. He wiped away tears and gazed at the strange curved weapon. What could she want with this? In the dim light he could see a dark rim on the blade. He ran his finger along its sinister length. The blood had congealed but it was still moist – fresh.

CHAPTER 12

A gondolier sang 'My Way' on his way home as Grapper ran past engrossed lovers on the Accademia bridge. They viewed this flying green menace with mild curiosity. He cursed the limitations of his extraordinary ability. What was the point in the gift of precognition if you were too fucking stupid to translate the meaning? The painting of the old woman burned in his mind. He paused to catch his breath, leaning against a clammy stone wall. His strategically ripped T-shirt clung to his back like a leech. He was out of condition. Should get more exercise.

His laboured steps echoed through the labyrinth as he ran on, jumping over black rubbish bags, adrenalin pumping. He turned a corner. The bundle of rags extended a leg from the dank cavity in the stone.

Grapper swore as he fell. A strong arm grabbed his wrist. He pulled away: 'Luigi, yer stupid fucker – what did I tell yer?' He shook his fist angrily in the tramp's face and ran on.

Miles felt dizzy. The room began to turn slowly. He felt sure he was going to pass out and sank to his knees. The faintness subsided but his head throbbed. He picked up the golden curved ritual knife and stared at it, raw nerve ends jangled. What was happening? He caressed Daniela's cheek with a trembling hand. It was still warm. Hard to believe she was really dead. Her neck was obviously broken. How? Dazed, Miles stared at her lifeless body with deep sadness and like a helpless child began to cry. From somewhere within him the sobs of grief came not only for Daniela, but for Lisa, for himself, in fact for everything that had gone so horribly wrong.

The shadows looked on, lamented and sighed. Suddenly, above his heartbreaking sobs, a loud metallic noise raped the sound of mourning from supposedly unoccupied depths below.

Miles stopped crying and raised his head. An animal instinct took over. Danger. There was definitely someone in there with him. He had to get away. He gazed at his lifeless lover. He couldn't leave her like this.

Miles hurried to the ballroom for Daniela's discarded cloak.

The black candles still flickered, casting a pale light up into the elaborate ceiling, into the faces of Brustolon's gigantic figures who stared down dispassionately.

Miles lifted the cloak and longingly caressed its soft folds. Her musky fragrance still clung to the silk lining. His eyes filled with tears. He just couldn't believe she was gone. Burying his face in the velvet, he wept again. Then metal crashed onto metal. The sound was clearly coming from below him. He crept back to his lover's temporary resting place.

Crouching beside Daniela's spent body, now little more than a husk, Miles wiped away his semen with the hem of the cloak. Covering her, he muttered a prayer, then placed a final kiss on her now cooling lips and pulled the fabric over her face. 'Goodbye. I think I loved you,' he whispered, hoping somehow she heard him.

He ran to the dark staircase, listening all the time for further evidence that he wasn't alone. Intense pain pulsed in his temples, sweat ran freely from every pore. Instinct took over, the will to survive fuelling him. 'Gotta get out,' he whispered furtively as he backed slowly along the wall. He craned his neck around the stairwell – no visible signs of life. The staircase was dark, the stone cold. He edged up the stairs and told himself there had to be a way out. The alarm system must be switched on. How the hell was he going to escape?

He made it to the Hall of Paintings. The moonlight seemed brighter. The room still looked empty. He stayed close to the wall without touching it and reached the next chamber. The anterooms were almost totally submerged in darkness. He moved through the panelled halls to the alcove and his clothes. Partial salvation.

Miles sat on the bed with his head in his hands and began to shake with delayed shock. He rocked to and fro muttering desperately to himself: 'Jesus. Think, Goddamn it. He tried to be rational. It couldn't be the guard in there with him – Daniela had said he wasn't due back until much later. But Daniela was dead.

He went to the anteroom window. Tall glass doors overlooked a small enclosed quadrangle – some renovations were taking place. Miles could just make out a cement mixer and some sacks of building materials. If only they'd left a ladder in place.

Miles rested his head defeatedly on the glass. There had to be a solution.

A guiding light glowed suddenly from under the candy floss. 'That's it,' he whispered excitedly.

Daniela's words floated back to him. 'There are alarms on the doors and the first-floor windows.' Did that mean the second-floor windows weren't alarmed? He hoped to God she was right. It was a miracle this had happened in Venice.

The drugs were now beginning to wear off. A degree of sensibility emerged from behind nebulous chemical clouds.

He ran through the vast room to the enormous mullioned doors which overlooked the Grand Canal. They were flanked by two smaller windows. Miles dragged a chair noisily to the left-hand window and studied the length of the frame – he couldn't see any wires. He prayed he was right and tentatively pulled back the large bolt at its base, expecting to hear the clanging alarms which would give him away.

He pushed the window open and waited for a cacophony that didn't come. The night air brushed his burning forehead. A whisper of promise. Astonished by the silence, he leaned out of the open window. Not daring to hope, he judged the distance from the balcony to the water. No more then eighty feet – he could make it. He'd dived from greater heights than this in competition. The stone balustrade now presented a viable means of escape.

Miles had read somewhere that the Grand Canal was only seven feet deep at low tide. Did a full moon mean low tide or high? He'd have to take the risk either way.

Panicked into a fast getaway, he was about to step onto the window ledge when he remembered his clothes and wallet had been left on the silk-covered bed. He could hardly run back to Katerina's in his shorts. Better figure something out. He scanned the length of the Canal. It seemed free from water traffic. He hoped it would stay that way until he'd made his escape. How was he going to keep his clothes dry?

A small boat moored directly below him, a little to the right, bobbed with hope. Over here. He saw it. Now if he put his clothes in Daniela's flight bag and threw it into the boat they'd stay dry. He could swim around the corner to the side street and dress himself in a doorway. It was after one o'clock, and the streets should be empty. He ran back for his clothes and placed them on the chair in readiness. Now all he had to do was get that bag.

As he edged down the stairs he tried not to think about Daniela. He muttered to himself, determined to get out. Stay alive.

Miles felt the comfort of stone against his back as he crept to the next entrance, listening constantly. He heard nothing but his own seemingly thunderous heartbeat and craned his neck into the room. It looked empty.

He ran into the portego. The gilt litter taunted, glowing in the moonlight. He made himself look over to Daniela's body.

It wasn't there. Someone had moved it.

If he had been reasonably in control up until now, the certain knowledge that an intruder had moved her body caused a total loss of bladder control. Warm urine trickled down his leg. 'Christ,' he said and urinated into the corner. He had no choice.

The gate-crasher breathed heavily behind him. Miles could smell garlic. Terrified, he wheeled around. Once again there was nobody there.

'Get a grip,' he told himself as he ran into the ballroom.

The exquisite stage had been thoughtfully set for their tragedy.

Daniela's ominous candles still flickered as Miles stood there shivering. Goose pimples rose on his clammy flesh. He was stunned - couldn't believe his eyes.

Her naked body gleamed in the candlelight, all respectability removed. She had been serenely laid out in the heart of the circle; eyes closed, arms crossed over her chest, fingers curled around the ritual knife that rested upon her breast.

Miles recited his twelve times table aloud to focus his mind as he crept past the demonic circle to get the bag. He glanced anxiously around the vast room chanting desperately, afraid for his life. He grasped the handles. A loud noise. The clattering sounded as though below him metal objects were being hurled onto the floor. Whoever was in there, they were otherwise occupied. This was his chance.

He raced up the stairs to the second floor. Breathless with fear, he pounded down the gallery, all the time glancing behind him. He got to the chair and ripped off his wet shorts. As he stuffed his clothes into the flight bag, his watch fell from the pocket of his jeans onto the marble with a loud noise that echoed through the room. He picked it up, rammed it into the bag and glanced to the far doorway. He heard footsteps. Someone was coming.

Miles zipped the bag closed and stepped onto the window ledge. Echoing footsteps grew louder, the intruder drew nearer. He jumped onto the balcony and looked down. It seemed a long way. No time for last-minute nerves.

He tossed the bag into the tiny bobbing boat. It landed with a dull thud. The intruder had now broken into a run. Miles looked back.

Franco was running down the length of the gallery with Daniela's cloak billowing out behind him. Tears streamed down his demented face. He brandished her knife and shouted, 'You killed her . . . my Daniela . . .'

He only had a few short yards to go as Miles stepped onto the balustrade. He raised his arms and with an arching grace dived into the murkiness. As he hit the filthy water he sliced through, arching horizontally, narrowly avoiding a blow from the bottom. Something grazed his thigh, then he bobbed up in a matter of seconds. He spat out the foul water and glanced up at the museum's open window. He could just make out a shadowy form slowly closing the aperture. He swam to the boat and hauled himself up, collapsing onto the wooden floor. It took him a few moments to catch his breath then he reached for the flight bag. A launch approached. He ducked.

When it had passed by Miles lowered himself into the water and swam one-handed to the landing stage with the flight bag held above his head. He struggled onto the green lichen-covered step, almost slipping; then, crouching like a naked tribesman, he edged along the museum's elegant white wall to the doorway. At the dark green doors he listened for Franco. All seemed quiet.

Shivering, he took out his clothes and pulled them onto his wet body. They stuck to him like glue. He tugged hard at his jeans and struggled with the fly buttons. Then he tried to close the bag. The zip was stuck fast. He was about to toss it into the narrow canal which ran along the side street when something changed his mind.

Miles gazed tearfully at the only evidence he had of Daniela's existence and couldn't part with her things. He ran blindly along the dimly-lit alley like a successful mugger clutching his spoils. Which way should he go? He dared not stop. Franco might be following. He wiped the sweat from his forehead and turned the corner, colliding headlong with an oncoming runner. The breath was painfully knocked from him as he fell onto the damp cobblestones.

Miles clutched his stomach and looked up, half-expecting to find himself at the mercy of some attacker or other.

Grapper's illustrious plumage glowed like a fluorescent beacon. He hauled Miles up by the shoulders. 'Thank fucking God,' he said. 'Miles, what 'ave yer been up to?'

CHAPTER 13

Unable to speak, Miles shivered like a child towelled after swimming as Grapper parentally brushed the dirt from his clothes. Relief came in waves. Large tears coursed down his flushed cheeks. His shoulders heaved.

'Come on, mate. We'd better get yer 'ome to a warm bed and a stiff drink – thank God yer all right.' Grapper took his arm, picked up the flight bag and they headed for the relative safety of Katerina's.

Neither one spoke for a while. Miles wanted to feel safe, but kept glancing nervously behind him. Grapper too was concerned, but something else gnawed at him. He hadn't used his psychometric technique for a long time but the gift was by no means dormant. Raised veins in his left arm pulsed, demanding attention. What the hell had Miles got in this bag?

Katerina sat in the big armchair and sipped her nightly brandy – one of the few pleasures left to her. Rosy features, highlighted by a red glow from the fringed lampshade, softened her look of depression. But the troubles of a heartless world had settled upon her shoulders and would be there until she achieved release from the fetters of her memories.

A battered radiogram played a worn Schubert recording. The music took her in familiar arms and soothed her cares for a moment. She closed her eyes and tried to blot out unwanted images.

Still, the mildewed photograph album now rested on her table in the window – so unwelcome in the peace of her closing years. How she had cried and demanded its destruction when she discovered it amongst her husband's castoffs. Beneath moth-eaten suits and shoes that pinched, this gruesome evidence had nestled for years, unnoticed like a tumour. But Mario had insisted, it must be kept, to show the world how inhumane man could be to fellow man. Emphatically he'd told her they could not burn it. One day those monsters would be brought to justice as God intended.

The memory angered her. God! And what use was He? He who gazed helplessly upon the face of suffering. Who brought only pain and grief and allowed you respite only to taunt you again. Forget, yes. But for how long? A month, a year? Certainly not a lifetime. Only a short while.

Until the day he died, Mario had been obsessed with the notion he would eventually be punished. Punished for deeds he had carried out under orders. His religion dictated that no one escaped justice. Where there was none in life there would be penance in death. The trial had made him very ill and he'd never fully recovered.

But now when she pictured him the doleful eyes were bright again, his pallor banished by the afterlife. No, God did not blame him any more. He could rest easy.

However, her time for peace had not come yet. Now she must gaze once more upon the faces of these oppressors. She had to be sure. If only it were a coincidence. If only she was mistaken. But she knew. The devil she hated had found a way to poison another young life, reaching out to take him as he had so many others. Perhaps, if she were right, she could do something to help. The truth had come too late for Mario, but now she was strong.

The spectre of their past had always remained one step ahead. Always just out of reach, defying abolition, waving the blood-stained banner of Fascism in their faces. There would be no escape while this accursed memory crawled from the rotting framework of a coffin she wished to lay to rest – once and for all.

As she thought of Miles, her heart became constricted. Her young guest was in trouble now and she had to help him as she had been helped so long ago.

Miles pushed the front door open as quietly as possible and went to switch on the hall light. 'No, don't turn it on. You'll wake everyone up,' Grapper hissed. They crept through the dark hall to the staircase.

Katerina opened her door and switched on the light. 'Who's there?' she squinted into the glow. Grapper's plumage bobbed towards the stairs. Her shock rendered Miles invisible. She thought she was being burgled. The silence was shattered by an ear-splitting shriek.

'It's all right, Katy, he's my friend,' Miles called out.

'Such a fright you are giving me, Miles.' She patted her wildly palpitating heart, saying, be calm please. 'Where you 'ave been? What you 'ave been doing, for heaven's sake? You are in big trouble, Skinny. Come now, you will both sit down and tell me what goes on.'

Grapper shrugged and followed her into the salon.

Miles collapsed into the chair trembling with relief. Katy quickly poured them brandies and handed them round. Grapper thanked her and introduced himself.

'Did he meet you, then? What you 'ave been doing to him?' Katy stroked Miles's hair as though he were a baby with a delicate skull.

Grapper took a long gulp of the brandy. 'Naw, 'e didn't make it. I think 'e'd better tell ya what's going on. I'd like to know what's going on meself.'

Miles gulped at the brandy and steadied himself. 'Thanks for this.' He glanced up at Katrina. 'Jesus, I'm sorry I've been so much trouble to you both.'

Grapper grinned at his new charge. 'Don't be daft, mate, this is exciting . . . you've got yourself into a right mess. Well I'm 'ere to keep yer out of trouble, so don't give it anovver thought.'

Katerina studied his green spikes. 'So you will protect him from the carabinieri, will you?'

'The police? What the fuck do they wan't wiv 'im?'

'Please not to use such language.' She crossed herself.

'Sorry! But what do they want Miles for?' He sniffed.

Katerina ignored the question and parked herself with some difficulty on the threadbare arm of Miles's chair.

'Miles, you are going to 'ave to be very brave. You remember Carole the English girl?'

He took another steadying gulp of brandy. 'Of course I remember her. Why? Did she telephone? I left her this number.'

'She is dead, Miles. They say she was murdered. I am so sorry.' She touched his arm.

He stared into the dim red glow of the lamp, transfixed, seemingly not registering the facts. 'One more casualty to add to my list then,' he muttered.

Katerina frowned and looked to Grapper for an explanation. He shrugged. He didn't understand either.

'Miles, the carabinieri believe you killed this girl, I think. You are in trouble now. Do you understand?'

Miles remained silent, robotic. He squeezed the glass in his hand until it broke. Katerina jumped. He didn't seem to notice. Grapper waved a hand before his taut features. There was no response.

'E must be in shock. We'd better get him up to bed. Can you make some tea with lots of sugar?'

While Katerina made the tea as instructed, Grapper tenderly bandaged his friend's hand. The cut wasn't too bad. 'Yer a silly bugger,' he chided. Miles stared ahead at nothing. Grapper sat him down and pulled off his trainers.

Katerina came in with the tea. 'How he is now?' she asked. Grapper shrugged. She viewed this strange man with newfound affection. 'You are very kind, although your hair – it is a little frightening to people like me, no!' She placed the floral china cup on the bedside table.

'I think it scares most people, but that's the general idea.' He pulled Miles's shirt over his head.

'You will stay until the morning, when he is perhaps better?' Katy asked.

'Sure, don't worry, I ain't going anywhere. I'll be 'ere if 'e needs me . . . stupid bugger. Sorry.' He apologized for the umpteenth profanity.

'It does not matter.' Katy opened the door. 'I am sure I will get used to it – goodnight.'

'Night.' He put the cup to Miles's mouth and tried to make him drink. Miles turned his head away.

'Don't want it eh! Well let's get you into bed then.'

As Grapper tucked him in Miles fell asleep with a deep frown lining his forehead. His friend took off his Doc Martens and lay down fully clothed, by Miles's side.

He turned to face his charge. What was going on in that mind of his? And what the hell had he been doing in the museum? How did he get in for a start? Questions bred like flies and buzzed around in his head. Exhausted by it all, he closed his eyes and decided: whatever was going on, the morning would shed new light on it all.

Keeping his eyes closed he placed a cool palm on Miles's moist forehead to gauge his distress. He drew a blank. 'All quiet on the western front,' he whispered. Relieved of duty, he felt able to sleep. The fact that Bella was still waiting for him at her flat completely slipped his mind.

Katerina turned the mildewed cover of the album and felt sick. She took her magnifying glass and studied the tragic contents that turned her face ashen.

Three soldiers stood before the gallows beneath a bleak winter sky. Two of them beamed proudly as though the dangling bodies were a row of freshly caught game, their expressions utterly devoid of compassion or human decency. Mario gazed sheepishly at her from the grisly scene as though he were saying, 'This has nothing to do with me. You know that, don't you?'

To Mario's left a tall thin man smiled wryly. On his right her leering devil taunted from this fading memento. There could be no doubt in her mind now – this sadist had found another way to bring her pain. Crossing the very boundaries of hell, clawing his way to renewed existence. Permeating the very air she breathed with his foulness. She must do whatever she could to save Miles from this evil. His bloodline was depraved, corrupt.

She flicked through the newspaper cuttings and hurriedly scanned the report in question, looking for the connection. She gripped the rosary in her pocket. So, she had been right about the name. Then God help them all.

Daniela's flight bag lay forgotten on the reception counter where Grapper had left it. Her belongings held the key to the past and the future. Only one of them would have the courage to open the door to unspeakable evils. And he would need not only inner strength, but the protection of whatever forces he could muster. He dared not doubt himself now – or his seemingly dubious gifts.

CHAPTER 14

A young woman's low heels clicked on the marble as she walked the length of a seemingly endless mahogany panelled room. Dawn filtered through the acacia tree like fingers gently probing. Strands of light shimmered on the walls.

Before a priceless Tintoretto, a man sat at an ornately carved desk. Sixteenth-century. Patina-blackened with age. His pate glowed in the light from a crystal chandelier which hung directly above him. He was thinking. The telephone rang. The sound interrupted his train of thought. His ringed hand picked up the receiver.

'Pronto.'

'We will go ahead with our ridotta as planned.'

'In Mantua?'

'No, time is limited. Treviso – the fourteenth.'

'Do I assume our little problem has been eliminated?'

'I've taken care of it.'

'And the boy.'

'That problem we will leave to our friends.'

The man replaced the receiver and leaned back in his high-backed velvet chair. He placed his hands together, contented now.

'We are ready for you now, Monsignore.'

The nun waited patiently as the man covered his pate with a red skullcap.

As Miles slept like a baby Grapper dreamed of one. His mother handed him a plate of Marmite soldiers and poured inky tea from a chipped earthenware teapot. She was bouncing a round-faced baby on her knee, beaming with grandmotherly pride. 'Isn't 'e luverly, Charlie?'

She cooed to the pink-cheeked infant who gripped her finger with surprising strength, ''E's got a good grip. Just like you as a nipper.' The baby gurgled. A little cherub.

Grapper reached out to take the baby from her arms. Its tiny face became wizened. It began to cry. 'What's the matter, fella?'

'He probably don't like your 'air. You'll 'ave to change it. You're a dad now. You'd better act like one.' His mother jogged the baby up and down. It stopped crying abruptly and pulled at her crystal beads.

When he awoke, Miles was moaning in his sleep. Talking gibberish.

Grapper shook him roughly. 'Wake up, yer dreaming. Come on, mate. Wake up.' There was no response. He slapped the side of Miles's face lightly and tried again.

Miles snapped his eyes open. He stared up at Grapper, confused. 'What are you doing here? Where am I?' He tried to lift his head. It felt unbearably heavy. 'Christ, it hurts.' He flopped down onto the pillow again.

'Do you want some tea or something?'

'No, just water, thanks.'

His friend handed him a glass. Miles took a long drink then said: 'You didn't answer my question. What are you doing here? I . . . Oh my God.' Now he remembered.

Grapper didn't want to rush him. He let him take his time, saying nothing, twiddling his earring.

Fragmented detail poured into his friend's mind. Last night. The museum. Daniela. Her singing. She was dead. He closed his eyes and swallowed hard. Then Franco. The dive. The nightmare came flooding back. If only it had been a dream. But it wasn't. It had happened.

'Do you want to tell me about it?'

Miles kept his eyes closed. 'Not just yet. Can you give me a little time?'

'What about a coffee then?'

Miles nodded.

Grapper went to the window. Best to let in some light even if it wasn't the light he wanted. Sparrows chattered, normal life continued outside, unhindered.

'Can you leave them closed?' Miles's voice sounded small, weak.

'Sure.' He drew the shutters together and left the room, closing the door quietly behind him.

In the kitchen Grapper sat at Katerina's table and shelled peas for her while she made coffee. For the first time in years she'd slept until eight. A miracle. 'So what do you think 'appened to him last night?'

'God only knows.' He popped a pod and for some obscure reason thought of the old Bird's Eye advert. '. . . and the peas went pop.'

'Perhaps later he will tell you something. Food may make him feel better.'

Grapper doubted it. He handed her the colander.

'There you go, all done.'

'Thank you. Do you think we should telephone for a doctor?'

'Let's just see how 'e goes, shall we? I'll take this up to 'im.'

'Then you come back and have something yourself.'

'Ta. I am a bit 'ungry.'

He trod the stairs with a coffee in one hand and a plate of chocolate slugs, as he called them, in the other. These were small conical pastries dusted with icing sugar, somewhere between bread and cake. They were warm and smelled wonderful.

'Look what I've got.' Grapper said as he walked into the darkened room. Miles still had his eyes closed. He put the cup and plate on the bedside table. 'Miles,' he whispered. 'Breakfast . . .'

Miles didn't answer. He was out for the count. Grapper shook him again. Unbeknown to him Miles had taken another painkiller. Little chance he'd wake now.

Grapper picked up the plate and shrugged. Taking a bite of the slug, he chewed thoughtfully and gazed unblinking at the bottle of drugs. He picked it up. 'I wonder,' he said. Then, still chewing, he went downstairs for a second helping.

Inspector Marcello gazed down at the beautiful body neatly laid out on the cold, impersonal marble floor. Daniela would soon be transferred from one sheet of marble to another. Rivers of wax ran from the circle surrounding her like extended talons. 'Such a waste of young life,' he murmured. His eyes moved like sensual fingers over her pale nakedness.

Gianelli led the sobbing cleaning woman from the vast rooms into the humid air outside. They leaned against the low stone wall. He supported her weight as she sobbed into a lace handkerchief and prayed to the Virgin for deliverance from evil.

With a quiet assurance, Gianelli extracted the core detail. Normally the night guard let her in, she said between sobs. Today she had used her key to open the outer door but when she rang the bell inside nobody came. Then she'd tried the other doors. They were open. No alarm system. Inside she had found the bodies. A tragedy. How could this happen here? She began to howl. Gianelli took her back inside and sat her down.

Marcello watched impassively as a colleague from forensics pulled on thin plastic gloves which were little more than a membrane. He turned Daniela over and felt the snapped vertebrae. 'It looks an interesting break. I'll give you a report as soon as I can.'

'This black wax suggests some kind of ritual, but this is not a ritual killing. It's puzzling. What about the other two victims?' Marcello asked, taking out his packet of Sobranies. 'Can you determine the cause of death?'

'Please don't smoke now.' Soldati was emphatic. That was half Marcello's problem. No respect for the dead. Been on the job too long. 'The guard had his throat cut – with this I shouldn't wonder.' He held a plastic bag aloft.

Marcello took it from him and examined the large golden ritual knife. 'Is this a dagger I see before me?' he said jovially in English.

Soldati shook his head disapprovingly.

Marcello sighed. 'You have no sense of humour, my friend. The symbols on the knife are interesting. I'll look them up. What about the other man upstairs – cause of death?' He returned the bag to it's rightful place with the other evidence.

'Same as the girl. Broken neck obviously.' Soldati returned Daniela's body to a more respectable position and zipped up the black body bag. The sound rang out intrusively. A final statement.

Brustolon's wild imagination observed through the curious eyes of his gigantic figures. High above the scene, they hovered mutely. Now they were more than just painted gods. They were harbingers.

Marcello looked up at the ornate ceiling then studied his fingernails. 'Our friend was upstairs, by a window. Killed before a getaway perhaps. But the question is, exactly what did they get away with? It appears nothing is missing. It's all very curious.' Marcello always thought aloud when perplexed.

Soldati knew this and didn't comment on the question. 'The other victim's neck would have taken far greater force to break.

There are substantial bruises on his throat which indicate he was also half strangled but eventually his vertebrae – well they were simply cracked, like a nut. Whoever did this, his strength was incredible. The victim had a neck like a bull.' He stood up and stretched his back. It made a series of dull clicking noises.

'You really should see a chiropractor for your lumbar problem. I know an excellent man.' Marcello delicately removed a piece of stray tobacco from his tongue. 'I knew our poor fool upstairs. I will tell Signora Vercini myself. His death is a great pity. I quite liked his restaurant. She may well have to close it now.'

As several men nervously paced through the room with the museum's director, looking for damage they hoped they wouldn't find, Gianelli hurried over to his boss. He was clutching a small card.

'I think I've discovered something important.' He was excited, like a boy who has just discovered his first earthworm. 'When we found the girl's clothes – this was in the pocket of her jeans.'

Marcello perched elegant reading glasses on the end of his nose and read the note Miles had written to Daniela, asking her to meet him at Florian's café just days before. He tapped the card with a long forefinger. 'This is curious. Our American friend is now connected with at least two of our murder victims. I think it is time we heard what he has to say. Make sure they dust everything the director will allow for fingerprints. Tell them to start with the windows and doors. We can only assume that as the alarm system was tampered with they got in somewhere. Tell Brazzi I want a full report by this afternoon. In the meantime you and I will see if our American has come home to roost.'

As Miles thrashed violently, his arms flailing, screaming incoherently, a fat white-haired doctor administered an injection with some difficulty. He rubbed Miles's arm with a small square of tissue impregnated with strong antiseptic and said in English: 'This will calm him down. It is strong tranquillizer. He sleep now five maybe seex hours.'

Grapper mopped the patient's forehead with a damp face cloth.

Katerina looked tired. 'Thank you, Antonio. It was good of you to come so soon. We were very worried when he started to scream. We could not make him stop.'

The doctor turned to Grapper. ''E was in deep shock. And

those drugs 'e 'as with 'im. They are very strong. No more for three days. It is easy to take too many. Then lights go out. Unconscious.'

Grapper looked up. 'Thanks, doc, I'll 'ang on to 'em for a while.'

The doctor nodded and left, certain that, despite Grapper's alarming appearance, he could be trusted.

Katerina showed him out.

In the kitchen she and Grapper discussed Miles's condition while she prepared a late lunch. The doorbell jangled. She sighed. Who was it now?

She went to answer the door wiping her hands on her apron (a souvenir from Pisa showing the leaning tower).

Marcello took her hand in both of his. 'Signora, forgive this intrusion. But we assumed that your guest must have returned by now.'

Gianelli nodded a mute greeting.

'Buongiorno, Inspector.' Her stomach churned. She managed a half smile. 'Please come in.'

They stepped into the hall. 'So, Signora. We have come to question Signor Hanson. The mountain has come to Mohammed, as it were.'

Katerina didn't understand the oblique joke. She looked tense.

'I am afraid that will not be possible today. Miles is in very bad way. Il doctore 'as only just left. He could 'ave told you. The shock of the English girl's death 'as made him very ill. A bad fever and he was delirious. My doctor has given him a very strong sedative. He will not wake for hours. Tonight, if there is no improvement, I am sure he will be taken to the ospedale for observation. So you can see it is impossible.'

Marcello looked hungrily towards the staircase. 'You will not mind if I see for myself?' He smiled knowingly, a predator's smile.

Katerina knew there was no alternative and led the inspector upstairs.

The shutters were now slightly open. Bright sunlight played hide and seek in the lace curtains. Spidery shadows crept across Miles's angelic features. His blonde hair fanned the pillow in shining golden strands. He looked a picture of innocence. Pure, untouched.

'He looks like an angel, does he not, Signora?' There was more than a hint of irony in Marcello's tone. 'Who would believe that such an angel could be avenging. An angel of death perhaps?'

Katerina said nothing. Her lips were tightly clamped. Her expression conveyed a determined maternal protectiveness.

Marcello was beaten. But only for the moment. Reluctantly he retreated. As they descended the staircase, he asked Katerina what time Miles had come home. Her heart beat a little faster. To buy time she collapsed abruptly on the nearest step. 'Are you unwell, Signora?' Marcello bent over her huge frame.

She dramatized a little, panting. 'Si, I 'ave a weak 'eart. You know Inspector, at my age, life is not so easy to bear. Unfortunately, there is always some pain.'

'We are none of us getting any younger.' He helped her up then, struggling with her bulk, and supported her on a rather precarious journey down the stairs. Gianelli turned away and put a hand to his mouth, hiding a smile.

Grapper listened from the kitchen as Katerina asked Marcello to help her into the salon. She would have to sit down now for a while. Grapper crept into the hall and took up a position near the open door.

The two men lowered her with some difficulty into the worn old armchair.

Marcello waited patiently for her to recover, then gently asked his question again. Katerina was about to answer when Grapper came bounding into the room like an over-friendly Great Dane. 'Sorry. I didn't know you 'ad company.'

Gianelli's jaw dropped. Marcello raised one eyebrow. 'Well. It is my strange friend from the market. I am surprised to find you here.'

'I 'eard there was a bit of bother. I can tell yer, mate, Miles has got nothing to do with it,' Grapper flopped into a vacant chair and splayed out his feet. Muscular tattooed arms adorned with studded manacles protruded menacingly from the torn black T-shirt.

Not unwisely, Marcello considered switching his investigations from the angel asleep upstairs to the hooligan now displaying his aggression like a territorial cockatoo. He lit a Sobranie.

Grapper fancied a fag but didn't want to light one in case it was misconstrued. He wasn't nervous, just uptight. Marcello's reputation preceded him. His drug busts were almost legendary. The junkies called him 'The Nose'. It was rumoured he could sniff out cocaine from a hundred paces. Better than a dog – more accurate but more expensive to keep.

'Now, Signora, I will ask you once again – at what time did Signor Hanson return here last night?' He blew a lazy smoke ring into the air.

'That's a good 'un. I wish I could do that,' Grapper interjected before Katerina could answer.

Marcello raised an eyebrow in disapproval. His expression said: If you don't mind.

Katerina bit her bottom lip. 'I do not know at what time he was returning. I think it was quite late.' She turned to Grapper. Her expression asked for rescue. 'Grapper, do you know what time you brought 'im home?'

'Sure. About 12.30.' Grapper pulled on his gum, elongating it to a sticky six inches or so from his mouth. He looked at it for a moment then distractedly chewed it back to its rightful place.

Marcello looked disgusted. 'So, Signor Hanson was with you?' He sounded congenial but his eyes were cold.

Grapper sighed. 'E was wiv me from nine o'clock until twelve-fifteenish. He got a bit drunk so I brought him 'ome. After Katerina told him about the girl who was killed, he went into shock so we called the doctor. I haven't been 'ome yet because I wanted to stay wiv 'im.'

'I presume you will supply witnesses to this fact.'

'Sure. We was at a bar called El Souk – do yer know it?'

Grapper knew damn well he knew it. The bar had been busted enough times.

'Yes, I am familiar with the place. In the meantime you will, I am sure, read in the papers later today of three deaths discovered early this morning at the museo, the Ca' Rezzonico. I would very much like to know if any of these names mean anything to either of you.' Marcello nodded to Gianelli who read the names from his notebook.

Neither Franco's name nor the guards registered with them. However, at the mention of Daniela's surname a flicker of recognition crossed Katerina's face. She suppressed the urge to cross herself as she had done before when Miles had first mentioned it. Colour drained from her face.

Grapper spoke up, drawing Marcello's curiosity from Katerina's obvious distress. 'Miles mentioned 'er to me, Daniela Riaggi I mean. I think 'e spent the afternoon at the museum with 'er. I know 'e's taken her out a couple of times.' His mind raced with possibilities. He knew Miles had been at the Ca' Rezzonico. He'd got to cover for any fingerprints they might find there. He thanked God for Ed McBain.

'Are you certain of this?' Marcello sensed a cover-up.

'Yeah, Miles told me 'e was going to meet her in the afternoon. 'E wanted to see the Rezzonico before 'e left. I ain't lying, yer know.'

'That is very helpful.' Now he was sure Grapper was covering. 'As we are unable to question Signor Hanson just now, we will return later this evening. I am sure by then he will be feeling better.' He walked to the door. Katerina struggled to rise. 'Please, do not trouble yourself, Signora. I'm sure our young friend here can see me out.'

Grapper stood up.

'There is just one more thing. In the meantime I would like the name and telephone number of your doctor. It will be better if I can be here when he makes the next examination.'

Grapper wrote down the number, as dictated by Katerina, on one of her little cards, and handed it to Marcello. He was studying the blue and silver flight bag which still lay on the reception counter. 'Who does this belong to?'

'It's mine, Inspector. I told you, I'm going to stay here until Miles is better – if that's all right by you?' He looked sullen.

Marcello distinctly remembered Grapper saying he hadn't been home. This was curious. 'I am quite sure he will greatly appreciate your company. Well, until this evening.' He stepped into the glaring sunlight and reached into his inside pocket for his sunglasses.

'You know Miles ain't done nothin', Inspector.' Grapper sounded earnest.

Marcello placed expensive Valentino sunglasses on his Romanesque nose. 'Unfortunately for him, my friend, that is not for you to decide.' He turned on his heel without another word.

Foreboding hung in the air like a bad smell. Grapper ignored it and put his head around the salon door. 'All right to use the phone?' he asked.

Katerina looked drained. She waved her hand dismissively. 'Yes, of course.'

Her mahogany clock ticked loudly as Grapper listened to the ringing tone. Beads of sweat formed on his high forehead. 'Come on, come on,' he said impatiently. Finally a sleepy voice answered.

'Bella, luv, it's me.'

At first she was relieved he'd called. She'd waited up half the night. Then she realized. The bastard had been out all night. She let rip.

Grapper held the receiver at arm's length as Italian profanities spewed forth. He tried to interject. 'Listen to me Bella, listen. I was with Miles. 'E's in a lot of trouble. We've got to help him . . .'

Bella started to cry. Her delicate condition was making her even more emotional than usual.

He sighed and muttered endearments. When she had calmed down he instructed her laboriously in Italian and English. 'Listen to me, Bella. The carabinieri will come. You must say Miles and I were drinking in the bar from nine o'clock until twelve. Hai capito . . . Bella, hai capito? E' molto importante.

His tone frightened her, but tearfully Bella said she understood and asked when he was coming home.

'Soon baby, soon. Listen, who was in the bar last night?'

'A few friends – it was quiet. Grapper, come home now? There is something I want to tell you,' she sniffed, feeling sorry for herself.

'Darlin', I'll be home as soon as I can. Look, just phone Fab and anyone else you know who'll lie for us. Remember to say they saw me and Miles . . . at the bar, va bene? He repeated himself in dreadful Italian to be sure she understood and gave her Katerina's number in case she needed to reach him.

During the heated conversation, Katerina had come into the hall and was now perched like a redundant Sumo wrestler on the stairs. Her big elbows rested on her knees as she listened to him struggling. He replaced the receiver with a deep sigh. 'I'm not a hundred per cent sure she understood, but I've done me best.'

'Perhaps you should go home until the police come back this evening.' Katerina hoped he wouldn't leave her alone.

'No can do. If the police go round to question 'er and find me there they'll put two and two together. I would 'ave 'ad time to corroborate my story now, wouldn't I?'

'It seems you know a lot about these things.'

Grapper chewed thoughtfully on the flavourless gum.

'I love detective stories, dunn I?'

She pulled herself up. Miles is very lucky boy to 'ave friend like you.' A fleeting smile swept across her face, then a sudden realization. There had been three more deaths. Where would it end? 'Miles is still in danger, isn't he?' she said intuitively.

Grapper gazed at her and took a deep breath. 'Yes. There's a lot going on that I don't understand. But like you say – Miles is lucky he's got me to keep an eye on 'im. Now, how about some grub?'

Katerina was in charge again. Someone needed looking after. This would take her mind off things. She swept a mottled hand through black and silver hair and shuffled into the kitchen. 'I am glad to make a nice lunch now. Plenty of good food will make us feel better, you'll see.'

Grapper was about to follow her when something pulled at him – the flight bag spoke of half truths. Later on he'd take a look inside. Right now food was far more important. More important even than a potentially deadly process of discovery.

CHAPTER 15

In a dilapidated palazzo near Treviso which rose up from the cornfields like a vast monument, strangely out of place, the only building on the horizon, an old woman dressed entirely in black, apart from a white apron, prepared for the visitors. Everything must be ready in good time. She kneaded dough with gnarled, liver-spotted hands, slapping it down on the floured table. A faint white cloud rose up, obscuring her face for a moment.

Outside a lazy dog slept under a tree in the courtyard. Within the loggia chickens ran freely. They hadn't laid for two days. A small white goat, tethered to a rusty standpipe, bleated its distress. Separated from its mother, it called to her. She bucked and kicked at the rotting wood of the small pen. She tried to jump the high wire fence and cut herself. Several other goats looked on sympathetically. They had also suffered like this. Her efforts were in vain. She would never see her kid again.

Marcello leafed through the file. In the hall raised voices bellowed instructions. There hadn't been a multiple murder here since '78. The place was in uproar. He wasn't distracted. He perused fragments of the investigation. At least he'd seen the American boy now. If Soldati was right about the strength it would have taken he couldn't possibly have killed Vercini. But what of the girls? What of Carole Davis and Daniela Riaggi? They were a different matter altogether. And the English cockatoo. Where did he fit into the overall picture? He was lying. But why? What was he hiding?

He doodled absent-mindedly on a large blank pad. Wrote down their names. Linked them with chains studded with barbs. What tied them together? There had to be a link.

The name Riaggi struck an ominous chord. He'd heard that name somewhere before. A court case – he vaguely remembered. And the landlady at the pensione, she'd looked upset when Gianelli spoke the name. His pencil lead snapped with the force of his frustration. He opened the metal jaws of the sharpener.

His telephone rang. He stopped turning the handle and answered it.

Gianelli sounded excited. 'I'm at the girl's apartment. You'd better come and see for yourself, sir. We've found another body,' he said.

Marcello took the pencil out of the sharpener, leaned back in his chair and placed his feet languorously on the antique desk. He said he would be there in around fifteen minutes, took down the address, then put the pencil in his mouth and bit on it thoughtfully.

The police launch sped from the lagoon into the Grand Canal, the heat abolished by the cool stream of air. Marcello should have been sipping Martinis by the Cipriani's aquamarine pool with a Vivaldi cello concerto soothing his troubled mind. Instead he was about to make an important discovery. He turned. The distant lagoon sparkled as though the hand of God had scattered precious jewels upon its glassy surface. He took a deep cleansing breath.

He loved Lombardy, but Venice had its own special place in his heart. Never was its iridescent splendour more breathtaking than in sunlight. On days like this, with a fresh challenge pumping adrenalin, he felt lucky.

The policeman who was driving shouted above the roar of the engine: 'We'll have to walk part of the way. There's no way I can get the launch past the Calle del Fruttarol. It's too narrow.'

The idea of a walk appealed to Marcello even though that area was rundown and the stench would be much worse. For all the years he'd lived in Venice he still found the smell occasionally turned his stomach.

When they arrived, he stepped gracefully from the moving launch and strode towards Daniela's apartment. His overweight officer had some difficulty keeping up. In the Calle del Fruttarol the mephitis was a mixture of rotting rubbish and stagnant water. He stopped abruptly, extracted a white silk handkerchief from his breast pocket and held it to his face to abate the foul air.

Washing hung overhead and dripped onto his suit. He hoped it wouldn't stain.

At the end of the alley, they came to a huge oak door. The

subordinate rang Daniela's security bell and they entered the dank stone entrance hall. It was still, bar the sound of dripping water. A loud buzzer sounded, giving access to the inner sanctum. Climbing the stairs, Marcello studied the fading frescos. 'This was probably once very beautiful,' he said.

The officer looked as though he might expire at any moment. He nodded, unable to speak.

'It is a pity that we do not take greater care of our heritage.'

The fat man panted his agreement. A door opened slightly. The woman peered at them as they ascended the next flight of stairs.

Gianelli opened Daniela's front door. Inside it was a hive of activity. Soldati barked instructions as a man took photographs with a large flash. Marcello walked through the hall as Gianelli babbled, 'We had to break in. The neighbour said she hasn't seen the girl's grandmother for over a month. Apparently whenever she asked after her Daniela Riaggi said she was too ill to see anyone. If the girl went out the neighbour came up and rang the bell. There was never an answer so she assumed the old woman was asleep. Apparently she was bedridden with arthritis.'

Marcello stared into the small kitchen at the frozen body quickly thawing in a pool of water. 'You found her like this?' he asked incredulously.

'When we found the place was empty we searched. She was in the deep freeze, sir.' The sergeant crossed himself at the notion of such a vile resting place.

'We've got to get her out of here fast, Marcello. The stench will suffocate us all.' Soldati issued hurried instructions to his assistant.

'Such a death.' Marcello stared at the frozen body. 'This family is obviously not vegetarian.'

'Spare me your jokes, Marcello,' Soldati turned away. 'I'd say she's been dead weeks – maybe even months. You'll have my report by tomorrow.' He closed his case and rushed from the apartment.

How could this be? Marcello frowned. In his note, the boy had said he'd seen Daniela's grandmother. As the old woman thawed in the oppressive heat, an unbelievable smell pervaded everything. Gianelli wanted to gag. Marcello gave his instructions quickly. 'When you've disinfected the place see what you can find. Try and find out where the other family members are. We'll have to notify them. Someone will have to identify her.'

Heavily sedated, Miles dreamed of home. A wonderful summer's day. Miffi played on the lawn and barked for the ball in Miles's hand, demanding it to be thrown. Smoke spiralled from the barbecue, filling the air with the scent of charcoal and meat. He could smell it in his sleep. His mouth began to water.

Miles raised a hand to his eyes to shield them from the bright sun and looked over at Lisa. She lay on a sun lounger, her oiled body gleaming. She stretched up, worshipping the sun god. His parents looked happy for once. They handed out drinks to all his friends. Josh was there and Piers, Danny and Spike, Valerie and Kate, even Grapper and Bella. They clinked champagne glasses and laughed politely at his father's jokes.

Daniela threw open the French windows. She was dressed in diaphanous white chiffon which floated on the warm summer breeze. She glided among the guests, greeting them one by one as though they were long-lost friends. 'Darling,' she intoned falsely. An old woman observed her from an old-fashioned Bath chair. She looked extremely fragile. Her hands were deformed, twisted like petrified wood. Miles recognized Daniela's grandmother instantly.

She manoeuvred her chair towards a man he didn't know. Small and balding, he wore uniform. Franco was with him. The men sipped champagne then raised their glasses to Miles in a silent toast.

The long bright green lawn sloped gently down to the Hansons' Grecian swimming pool. Daniela danced among the guests as though she were floating on air. 'Let's all have a swim,' she said in a sing-song voice as she drifted over to her grandmother. Daniela started to push her along. Then she stopped and said: 'No wait. I have a better idea. Let's not swim – just Grandmamma. We'll all watch.' With a violent shove she sent the bath chair careering down the grass slope.

Miles jumped up and ran after it. Miffi barked excitedly at his heels. He called out as the chair toppled into the water. He pulled frantically at his shoes and clothes, then ran to the edge of the pool. He heard someone calling his name and looked behind him. Grapper ran towards him. He was waving a large stick.

Miles prepared to dive into the crystal blue water. He must save the old woman. She flailed her arms helplessly. He felt a hand on his arm. 'Look before yer leap, Miles.' Grapper reached out to the water with the stick and tapped it. Miles looked down. The pool had frozen over. The old lady peered at them from beneath the ice.

Miles's eyelids twitched in his sleep. Grapper felt his head. It was warm but not hot. He dabbed it with the face cloth and left the room.

Katerina was washing salad at the kitchen sink.

'I don't think an earthquake would wake 'im up.'

She turned to Grapper. 'The sedative – it must be very strong.'

'How long till food?' Grapper asked.

'It is ready now. You are hungry, yes? Don't worry, I have made enough for four like you.' She put the limp lettuce into a wooden bowl and tossed it with the other ingredients. 'Come along. Let's eat.'

She shuffled to the dining room. Grapper followed.

On the large dining table, she had laid out platters of prosciutto and assorted Italian cheeses, bread and a bottle of white wine.

Grapper was pleased. He needed a drink. 'This looks great,' he said enthusiastically.

They fell on the food and talked between mouthfuls, discussing Miles. They pondered his visit to the museum with Daniela. Neither could work out how he had come to be there so late. Both wondered how Miles had escaped. Grapper said they must find out what was in the bag. Katerina was reluctant – it was an invasion of privacy. Grapper insisted. They had to try and find out more. After all, he was now an accessory. He almost had a right.

The air outside the little pensione was still, oppressive as ever. The vine wilted even more. The inanimate Cupid, still resting his hand on his hip, stared through the dining-room windows at the inhabitants, seeming to envy them. An outsider looking in.

When they'd finished eating, Grapper checked on Miles again, then he picked up Daniela's flight bag and joined Katerina in the salon. She was slumped in her armchair. She looked drained.

'Perhaps ya should go up and lie down. I can take care of this by meself, yer know.'

Katerina looked sorely tempted for a moment, but instead urged him to hurry up. She felt just as much a part of all this as he was. Her pride was misplaced.

He unzipped the bag and unceremoniously tipped the contents into a large eclectic pile. Katerina gazed at the potpourri of objects. Grapper laid them out like mysterious ingredients. There were several cassette tapes, a small plastic water bottle, a wallet containing travellers' cheques and ten crisp sterling fifty-pound notes; there was a red key to a locker, number 119B, three pairs of underpants and two silk T-shirts, a plane ticket in her name for London and then Paris and a small dagger in a leather sheath. There was also a letter written to someone on bright pink stationery and lastly a very worn leatherbound book with a faded pentacle etched in patchy gold leaf on its cover.

Grapper picked it up and felt an unmistakable current reaching out to him. With shaking hands he leafed through it. It was filled with spidery handwriting. Copies of grotesque medieval engravings of torture had been pasted onto the yellowing pages. There were notes on methodology and spells. He recognized the metre but he couldn't translate. Fascinated, he turned another page and came upon a poem in English which he read aloud to Katerina.

'Unto the night from whence he came, I offered up a child's refrain,
And dying cry soon brought the sound, of cloven hoof on frosted ground,
With nostrils flared and blazing eyes, all power he epitomized,
Depriving human hearts of love, anointing evil prayers with blood,
And bade me follow to the edge of darkness where he made a pledge,
To show me all the wondrous things that stemmed from my imaginings,
And gazing down the wish reversed, within the depths all things perverse,
So what is mind if man is blind, to all the torments of the mind.
Mary Whitely. Salem, 1867.'

Katerina didn't understand what it meant. Grapper was left in little doubt. Now they were getting somewhere. It was pretty obvious to him now that Daniela had fancied herself as some kind of witch. He felt almost relieved. Perhaps that was all there was to it.

He turned to the last section. A large black and white photograph had been strategically placed under the heading 'Invocation and Metamorphosis'.

Katerina stared horrified at the photograph in Grapper's hand. Her heart raced. The image clearly terrified her. She had been right all along.

'What the fuck is all this?' He gaped at the two uniformed men. The taller of the two held three severed African heads by their remaining clumps of hair. Obviously proud of himself, he grinned like a repugnantly overgrown child with a bunch of champion conkers. Grapper turned the photograph over and read the inscription: 'Belloti massacre. Abyssinia, August 1936.'

CHAPTER 16

Marcello studied the evidence littering his mahogany desk. The fading newspaper cuttings told of the Belloti trial in Milano in '58. Now he remembered why the name Riaggi had seemed familiar. Amongst the cuttings were several military photographs of executions. He turned to Gianelli.

'You said these were found behind the old lady's wardrobe?' Marcello dispassionately picked up a magnifying glass and studied one of the more gruesome deaths at closer quarters.

'Yes, sir, they were fairly well hidden - in a hole in the wall. We noticed a join in the wallpaper. We also found these bills amongst her papers.' Gianelli handed Marcello several invoices on expensive paper. 'They appear to be for psychiatric treatment by a doctor named De Chesaris.'

Marcello looked at the dates and subject. 'Well, it seems Daniela Riaggi consulted the good doctor once a week. That would be a very expensive undertaking for someone with a minor mental problem.' He placed his hands together. Contemplation. Gianelli looked out of the open window.

After a few minutes, Marcello imparted a conclusion to his subordinate. 'I believe the girl was seriously disturbed. Tell me, were all her clothes intact? For instance, were there gaps in the hanging space or empty hangers that would suggest she had taken clothes?'

'Yes there were empty hangers and some of the small drawers were empty.'

'Did you find anything of value in the apartment - money, jewellery, a passport, anything of this nature?'

Gianelli considered for a moment. 'No. Now I think about it we found no valuables at all, I didn't think it strange at the time.' He made a futile attempt to intercept Marcello's train of thought. 'Do you think they were robbed?'

The epitome of elegance leaned back in his equally elegant chair, sighed heavily and delivered the goods in a matter-of-fact tone. 'No, they were not robbed, Gianelli. It is now quite obvious to me that Daniela Riaggi has been in psychoanalysis for some time. We need look no further for her grandmother's murderer. It is my belief that she smothered her in a psychotic frenzy. Then took everything of value to sell. She was quite obviously intending to escape before the discovery was made. Hence the refrigeration of the body.'

Gianelli wiped his brow with a grubby handkerchief and stared at Marcello with admiration.

He replaced the lid of the shoebox and stretched. 'The problem I have now concerns our beautiful museum. The question is not so much how did she come to be there, but who was there with her? Have you discovered the old woman's next of kin?'

Gianelli consulted his notes. 'Yes. There's a widowed sister-in-law who lives near Mantova and also – and this is interesting – Franco Vercini.'

Grapper watched Katerina's huge frame rocking to and fro. She sobbed hysterically and shook her head, not wanting to believe. Grapper had tried to comfort her and failed. She whispered first in her native tongue then in Italian. He managed to decipher one or two virtually incoherent sentences: 'Now he has found me. No escape. Not true. I cannot believe it.'

Grapper crouched by her and held her hand. 'Katy, what is it? Why can't ya tell me what's wrong with yer?' He squeezed her hand.

'Belloti,' she whined. 'Grapper, he has found me.' Tears of despair coursed down her ashen face.

'I don't understand. What d'yer mean he's found yer?' he asked softly.

Katerina pointed to the photograph album on her table.

'Read for yourself. Go on, look at it. Perhaps then you will understand.' She dabbed her eyes and took the rosary from the pocket of her apron. She gripped it tightly.

Grapper sat at the table and stared beyond the lace-curtained window. Sunlight glimmered in contrast to the cloying, grief-stricken atmosphere within, daring it to exist on a day like today. The street outside bustled with normality. Grapper wished with all his heart that he were normal, a porter with a fat wife and umpteen kids perhaps. At that moment he would rather have been anywhere but there.

When his mother had given the name Belloti it had enabled him to find Miles. That obviously hadn't been all she meant by it. This was often the way it was. He knew all too well that seemingly obvious spiritual clues needed the deepest thought processes to extract the hidden meaning. Riddles cast by a mighty hand, his mother called them.

He had dreamt of the soldier with the severed heads. Maybe he wasn't such a bad psychic after all.

He opened the album and went deeper into the maze. There were several military scenes. Executions. Pretty gruesome. He was flicking through them without really paying attention when he came upon a hanging scene. Wasted bodies dangled from a high gallows beneath the bleak winter sky. Of the three soldiers in the foreground, one took his breath away. The man leered with obscene pleasure.

Grapper felt as though he'd been punched in the stomach. The air seemed thin. This was the same soldier he'd just seen with the severed heads in Daniela's photograph. It was Belloti.

On the beautiful island of Giorgio San Maggiore, in an elegant white building, Marcello and Gianelli waited in the pale grey patients' waiting room of the psychiatrist's office. Art prints adorned the walls, the Deco lighting was dimmed, air-conditioning hummed. The atmosphere was restful.

Tired of waiting, Marcello stood up and paced like an animal unused to confinement. Gianelli fiddled with the metal rings of his notepad, opening and closing them until he caught his finger and uttered a tiny cry. As he shook the pinched finger vigorously, a well-heeled beauty graciously asked them to enter the inner sanctum. Marcello held her gaze for a moment, then strode into the room as though he owned it. The secretary watched his rear appreciatively as he approached their host. The man didn't get up.

'Inspector. I was sorry to hear of Daniela Riaggi's death. A tragedy.' The psychiatrist motioned to two black leather chairs placed before his enormous oak desk. 'She was an unusual girl. Quite a talent, you know.' He leaned back in the high leather chair and placed his hands together. Assured. Territorial. 'What can I do for you?' he asked.

'In your opinion, was your patient capable of murder, doctor? Do I call you Doctor, incidentally?' Marcello viewed him with sharp analytical eyes.

The doctor wore a pale grey double-breasted suit which was an almost perfect match for the coordinated office interior. His gaunt face was elongated with a high, intelligent forehead and prominent cheekbones. His complexion was rather pallid, like wax. He was probably pushing seventy but looked younger. Longish white hair curled over his collar.

De Chesaris thought for a moment then smiled. Deeper lines appeared at the corners of cold grey eyes. He leaned forward slightly.

'Certainly is the answer to both questions, Inspector. Daniela Riaggi was a paranoid schizophrenic with distinctly psychotic tendencies. She was most certainly capable of murder – and a great deal more, I suspect.'

Marcello felt good. He had been right. As usual. He launched into a series of questions.

De Chesaris imparted the facts in a rather patronizing tone normally reserved for calming nervous patients. Daniela had been brought to him for treatment from the age of thirteen. Her mother was unable to look after the child due to her unfortunate imprisonment in England.

When Marcello attempted to obtain the exact circumstances of this imprisonment, the doctor simply waved a dismissive hand and continued. He told them the reason for his treatment of the child: within a year whilst in her grandmother's care, Luisa Riaggi had witnessed several wilful acts which gave her cause for concern. She was afraid that the child might have inherited undesirable family traits.

'What kind of family traits?' Marcello asked, pulling the Sobranies from his jacket pocket. His eyes wandered around the room. The black leather armless couch looked extremely inviting. He had a sudden urge to lie down.

'Of course I assumed you knew at least some of the facts, Inspector.' De Chesaris seemed surprised by Marcello's lack of knowledge.

'May I?' Marcello held the Sobranie packet aloft then, after a nod of approval, lit one and inhaled deeply. 'I'm afraid I don't understand, Doctor. What exactly am I supposed to know?'

'Simply, Inspector, that Daniela Riaggi is the granddaughter of the infamous General Belloti.'

This Marcello knew, but he hadn't made a connection with psychosis. The Belloti case had been quite famous in its day. He had been assigned, as a young sergeant, to Belloti's wife for protection. She had adopted her maiden name Riaggi in an attempt to avoid the press. There had been death threats from those who believed the verdict to be unfair.

'I was assigned to his wife when I was in Mantova, you know. The family received one or two death threats from extremists.'

The Doctor opened the buff-coloured folder before him and smiled. 'Only one or two threats? You surprise me, Inspector.'

'So is this what you meant by family traits. Do you think Daniela inherited his psychosis?'

'Inspector, to understand that you must first understand the mind of the man we are dealing with. I treated him for five years after the war. He was addicted to power, almost a megalomaniac. Belloti was the worst kind of sadist – an absolute monster. I am no expert on genetics but I know that unfortunately this kind of mental disorder can be hereditary. His children have definitely suffered.'

Marcello went back one step in his mind. 'So forgive me for the assumption, but am I right in thinking you believe he was guilty of war crimes? I know he was exonerated but our wonderful judicial system has been wrong before,' he said with more than a hint of sarcasm.

'My dear Inspector, of course he was guilty. At that time the military powers had the blood of our occupied countries still fresh on their hands. They could not possibly convict a decorated general on supposedly circumstantial evidence,' he said incredulously. 'The extradition order was virtually laughed out of court.' He opened a thick file.

'You said his children hadn't escaped the madness.'

'I did not say madness, Inspector. Disturbed, perhaps, but then I believe there are reasons for that which I prefer not to go into. I mentioned Daniela's mother had been imprisoned. For murder.'

Marcello leaned forward.

'Antonella Riaggi ran away from home at eighteen. Luisa knew her daughter was pregnant but they could not find her. She had gone to England and apparently worked in Soho. Years later she murdered her lover when she found him trying to molest Daniela. She stabbed him. I have a report here.' He shuffled the papers. 'Yes, here it is. She stabbed him eighty-two times. The police found evidence of witchcraft in her apartment. There had apparently been several black masses held there. The neighbours reported to the police that they had heard what the English described as ''strange goings on''.' His smile was enigmatic.

Marcello visualized the remains of the black candle wax found in the museum and pulled his silk tie down further. 'You seem to know a great deal about this family's history, doctor.'

'I have made it my business to know, Inspector. Do you wish me to continue?'

Marcello nodded, trying not to show eagerness.

'Daniela's mother had, I believe, an erotic striptease act which encompassed elements of devil worship. Rather enterprising, I thought. This of course explained the objects for black masses they discovered.'

Marcello listened intently. Gianelli looked distracted.

'At first her lawyer pleaded insanity. However, painstaking analysis proved she was quite sane. I was informed they tried for a crime of passion. A laughable notion, it was quite simply murder in cold blood. Eventually the defence saw to it that the plea was changed to manslaughter. This of course gave her certain privileges within her sentencing. She was given ten years only. Understandable under the circumstances, don't you think? Daniela was initially placed in the care of the English authorities until Luisa Riaggi came to bring her home.'

'Was Daniela aware of all this family history?'

'Of course witnessing such a brutal murder at a young age had a profound emotional effect on her. I suspect that had a great deal more to do with her psychosis than any rogue genetic strain, but it is almost impossible to tell. If you are referring to Belloti's crimes, her grandmother made certain she knew all the facts. She subjected Daniela to constant lectures about Belloti's sadism. She meant well. She was undoubtedly trying to frighten the child into having a rigid moral conscience. Luisa Riaggi was obsessive. With a husband like hers, who can blame her? In a misguided way she was trying to protect Daniela – to arrest the hand of fate, as it were.'

'Surely, as you said, it wasn't a foregone conclusion that Belloti's sadism would be automatically inherited?' Lines of sweat formed on Marcello's brow.

'That will never be clear. I was asked to monitor Daniela's progress. She suffered hallucinations as a result of her grandmother's nightmarish tales.'

Marcello hurriedly ground out the cigarette, which was now close to burning him. 'Can I ask you to elaborate on that?' he asked pointedly.

'The child suffered traumatic hallucinations by association. It is my belief she wanted only to be loved. But I digress. The child believed she was frequently visited by a demon or devil that took her grandfather's form.' He inclined his head.

'That doesn't sound unreasonable, after all she'd been through.'

The air-conditioning hummed as the atmosphere in the elegant office tightened around him.

'No it is not unreasonable at all. In fact it is an entirely logical explanation. However, Belloti died in 1984 just before Daniela arrived in Venice. She did not know what he looked like yet she described him perfectly to me. It is possible she had seen the photographs her mother took with her but I doubt it. She described him to me as an old man, yet the photographs were taken when he was young.'

Marcello frowned. 'Yes, I see that is strange.'

De Chesaris continued. 'These photographs inadvertently caused Belloti's death. You see, he killed himself when the paparazzi ran a series of rather damning articles after his daughter's imprisonment. The scandal was all too much for him. The police had put two and two together when they found the rather grotesque items which Antonella had stolen from his collection. The fool should have burnt them but he couldn't part with them. It is rumoured he even distributed some of them among his senior officers. It's a miracle none of them surfaced around the time of the trial.'

Marcello sighed deeply. 'We found photographs like that hidden in the Riaggi apartment. So he was definitely guilty then?'

De Chesaris leaned forward and pressed a buzzer on his digital telephone. 'I have already said so. Now if you will excuse me, Inspector. I have an important conference to go to and Mestre will soon be impossible. I swear the rush hour now starts at three in the afternoon.'

'Yes, the congestion is ridiculous.' Marcello felt the downy hairs on the nape of his neck rise as the secretary came in. She smiled invitingly to him. Her auburn hair gleamed in the sunlight. Her long legs were bare, tempting. Marcello stood up to leave. 'Thank you very much, Doctor, you have been a great help to the investigation. There is one more thing I would like to ask, however.'

'Certainly, Inspector, ask whatever you wish.' De Chesaris closed the file before him and began to write on its cover.

'How did Belloti kill himself?' Marcello hovered, awaiting an answer.

De Chesaris, didn't look up, but carried on writing. 'He shot himself in the head before an ancestral painting in our beautiful museum the Ca' Rezzonico. I am pleased to say his brains avoided the painting. Even a monster can appreciate great works of art, Inspector.'

CHAPTER 17

Grapper stared out of the open window at the empty street. Tension throbbed in his neck. He rubbed it slowly. He felt depressed by the thought that he belonged to a different tribe, not to that breed that exists in ignorance of a parallel world. He was a pack horse for their journey. Carrying a burden, a burden of knowledge so deep it burrowed into his soul like a small animal with sharp claws, tearing at his heart, demanding he listen to its chattering, incessant language, a language few others understood.

He glanced over to Katerina. She had some answers to the searching questions burning in his mind, but he'd have to wait. Her eyes were tightly closed. She looked half asleep. Her forehead was creased into a slight frown.

Grapper turned his attention to Daniela's sinister pile of tricks. He fingered the objects for a moment and tuned in, using his psychometric gifts. He picked up a cassette tape. Daniela's spidery handwriting was on the label. He read aloud: 'Puccini and Verdi'.

On Katerina's dusty sideboard he saw a small cassette player. Her stereo had only a radio and record player. She had bought this for the occasional cassettes Giorgio (he of the pasta and pastries) made for her of Venetian music. Scarlatti and Albinoni were her favourites.

Grapper knew he should wait until she woke up but he had felt something – the tapes were important. He couldn't be sure why but he had to find out. He was definitely on the right track. With a growing sense of anticipation he inserted the tape and pressed Play.

Quiet conversation took place between a man and girl. Instructions. He cocked his head, barely translating. Then a piano began to play softly, and as if by magic, the purest shimmering of a soprano's voice took up the melody and set it free. The textures were velvety. Not his cup of tea but he had to admit it was beautiful.

Katerina opened her eyes and struggled to sit up. The music was arrested by a hollow tapping sound. A male voice bellowed, 'Molto legato, Daniela!'

Grapper and Katerina looked at one another, each wondering if they had heard correctly.

In the peaceful atmosphere of the room above, Miles became suspended in a fragile state, half-way between sleeping and waking, between fantasy and reality. His sleep grew shallow with the distant sounds of interruption. Something ethereal took hold of him. It wasn't a pleasant feeling. He was being smothered, he could feel hot breath on his face. Invisible hands leaned on his chest, pressing him into the bed. He couldn't wake up. The hands pressed more, he must dream on. And so he slipped back into the other world where Daniela ran through a field of cornflowers with her ebony hair floating on the wind. She laughed as she ran, teasing in a sing-song voice, 'You can't catch me, you can't catch me.'

Bright blue flowers bowed their heads as she dashed through their midst, paying silent homage to her memory.

Miles watched her running down the hill. In the far distance, peasant workers scythed the waving corn. Women gathering the fallen lengths stopped for a moment and looked towards him. A pretty young girl in a floral dress with a headscarf wrapped around her head waved to him enthusiastically as though he had returned from far away. He waved back although he did not recognize the young, slim Katerina.

He ran after Daniela's scampering figure, calling out to her to wait. She stopped for a moment and shaded her eyes from the bright sunlight. Then she scurried on like a fawn dancing in dappled light. Young, free, alive.

Miles ran faster and caught up with her at the base of a large oak tree. He leaned against its gnarled trunk, gasping for breath.

'You need to have more exercise if you want to run faster, and you have to run very fast to catch me. Now I am air. Touch me if you don't believe it.' She lay down on the soft mottled earth and reached up for him.

'Don't lie there. You might not be able to get up again.' Miles was afraid.

Daniela ignored him and began to hum. The humming became singing. Her Puccini aria rose on the air like a host of butterflies.

Miles became more agitated. He pulled at her slender arms as soft earth collapsed beneath her languor. As she was swallowed up her voice grew muted.

Miles tried desperately to prevent her from being dragged into the bowels of the earth, crying out as her hand was cruelly pulled from his. Then he heard raucous laughter, mocking, obscene. He looked to its source.

A tall uniformed man stood proudly with his hands on his hips. His head was thrown back with pleasure at Miles's distress.

Miles marched towards him, demanding he stop. As he drew nearer the man stopped laughing. Then he realized his tormentor was not human.

He woke abruptly and sat bolt upright. Sweat poured from him. For a split second he was comforted by the knowledge that it had just been another crazy dream. His head pounded. He felt sick. His tongue was furred. He took a sip of water and leaned his head back. But one part of the dream was true. Daniela was dead and it was probably his fault. If he hadn't agreed to the scam maybe she'd still be alive.

He began to sob unashamedly. Misery hooded over him in waves that consumed all pride.

Suddenly, from below, the gentle strains of a piano wafted toward him. Then he heard it. Daniela's voice, high, pure, granting him one last audience before she was lost to him forever. 'Daniela?' he whispered. Maybe she wasn't dead after all. Maybe it had all been just a bad dream.

He threw the bedclothes aside and pulled on a T-shirt. It barely covered his nakedness. He raced out of the room taking the stairs two at a time despite the frailty of his drugged condition.

Grapper and Katerina were listening intently to Daniela's rehearsal tape. The beauty of her voice astounded them both. Grapper was about to comment when the door burst open and Miles came careering into the room. 'Where is she?' he asked.

He ran to the window, his head darted quickly from side to side, like a dog eagerly expecting its dead master to walk in at any moment.

Grapper got up from his chair and stopped the tape abruptly. A judgemental silence hung in the air. Miles bowed his head.

His friend came to him, placing caring hands on heaving shoulders. 'Come on, mate, let's sit down, shall we?' He looked down. 'I think we'd better make yer decent first.'

After Miles had been given the shorts he'd discarded in his sleep, he sipped hot sweet tea that Grapper had made for him.

'Yer know Ma always used to say there wasn't anything in life that couldn't be solved over a good cup of tea.' Miles managed a half smile. 'Mind you, the Italians don't know 'ow to make tea and neither do your lot. They never boil the bleedin' water. Disgusting.' Miles sipped shakily.

Katerina looked on, saddened, unable to comment, no torch-light to shine in the darkness. Her pain had subsided years ago but now here it was again, throbbing, aching. Like a man whose leg has been amputated and believes the wound is still there, very real, just below a knee that no longer exists, she too had lost a part of herself but was unable to come to terms with the truth. Her eyes watered. But surely her distress had been surpassed by this young man's dilemma? Now she must not think of herself. Only of him. She spoke up, 'Silly Skinny, what a mess is all of this. Will you try to 'ave a little food maybe?'

He felt slightly better. 'If it wouldn't be too much trouble,' he said softly. He turned to Grapper: 'I feel like I've done thirteen rounds with Sugar Ray Leonard.'

Katerina smiled. 'Nothing is too much trouble for you, Skinny. I only 'ave to heat it. You must not expect to feel so great after the drugs. The doctor gave you a strong injection. Don't you remember?' He shook his head. She eased herself with a grunt from the armchair. 'Well never mind. You will feel better when you 'ave eaten. I will leave you two alone, da.'

Miles watched her leave over the rim of his china cup.

'Can you tell us what 'appened last night, mate? The police have been back 'ere looking for yer. Sommat's really cookin'.'

Miles put the cup back in its delicate floral-patterned saucer and swallowed hard. He filled Grapper in on his incredible adventure, quelling the emotion when he spoke of Daniela's death. He was ashamed of his grief.

Grapper listened, nodding occasionally but saying nothing. Miles left out a good deal of important detail, but felt inclined to talk about Daniela's black candles.

His friend needed no enlightenment on that subject.

'Then I ran into you literally. The rest you know.' Miles finished his story and picked up the cup. The tea was cold. He grimaced and put it down.

'The police told us about the three bodies at the museum.' Grapper watched the blonde hair falling over Miles's face and thought how vulnerable he looked.

'What do you mean three bodies? Daniela and I were the only ones there apart from Franco the head case.'

Grapper wondered how much more Miles could handle. He jumped in anyway. 'The security guard didn't leave the museum. 'E's dead too. Apparently 'is throat was cut.'

Miles was horrified. 'But that's impossible. She told me he was going to see his mistress. She said we'd be alone there.'

'Look, mate, what she told yer and what 'appened are two different things.'

Miles could scarcely believe it. 'You said there were three bodies. Who was the third?'

'Your loony friend Franco.'

Colour drained from Miles's face as Katerina entered the room with a steaming bowl of soup on a tray. 'That's impossible unless . . .' His voice trailed.

'Unless what?' Grapper asked as Katerina placed the tray on Miles's lap.

'Unless there really was someone else there with us.'

Miles eyed the steaming soup.

Grapper felt his mother close by. She had something to add. She was agitated. That was unusual for her. He closed his eyes for a moment. When he opened them again, Miles was eating and seemed much better. 'So what are we going to do?'

Grapper stood up. 'We'll figure it out. Now eat yer bloody soup. I've got to bleed me rat.' Miles looked puzzled. 'That means take a leak to you,' he said and bobbed out of the room.

Marcello eyed the vast pile of books cluttering his desk with dread. He had absolutely no belief in all this stuff. Witchcraft, demonology, the paranormal. As far as he was concerned it was a load of complete balls, dreamed up by madmen to exploit the weak.

Venice, it seemed, had quite a history when it came to witchcraft. But he didn't believe Daniela's antics were anything other than childish games that had gotten out of hand. She was obviously deranged but he knew she was incapable of Franco's murder, even in a psychotic rage. Soldati had said it would have taken exceptional strength to kill him in the way he'd been murdered.

He loaded the books into an Armani carrier bag and buzzed Gianelli. He should have concluded his undoubtedly inefficient questioning of the staff at the Hotel Splendide.

Minutes later his sergeant sat down wearily and wiped the sweat from his forehead with a grubby handkerchief.

Marcello leaned back in his chair. 'Well what have you found out? Anything of interest?'

'The concierge told me that a girl fitting Daniela Riaggi's description had been asking for Carole Davis's home address on the afternoon before we found her body.'

'Well that is certainly interesting,' Marcello intoned. 'And did the concierge give it to her?'

'Eventually, yes, sir. He told her it was against company policy to give out home addresses. Daniela, if it was her, told him she was her cousin from England. She made such a scene that the poor man gave her the details to make her leave the hotel. She must have been a pretty good actress.'

Marcello picked up his telephone and pressed two buttons. 'Have we had the forensic report on Carole Davis back yet?' He paused, awaiting an answer, then listened intently, punctuating the one-sided conversation with thoughtful mm's. Finally he said. 'I see, fine. Send the report up to me, would you.'

'Well, it would appear that I was correct. The wound on Signora Davis's throat matches exactly the blade of the ritual knife which killed the night guard at the museum. What is your deduction given these astonishing facts?' Marcello closed his desk drawer and waited patiently for Gianelli to answer.

Gianelli felt as though he were back at school. He racked his brains then spoke up reluctantly. 'Is it possible that the knife belonged to Daniela Riaggi and that perhaps ...' he paused, fearing ridicule.

'Yes go on. Please continue.' Marcello tapped his fingers rhythmically on the desk.

Gianelli cleared his throat. 'Is it possible then that Daniela murdered Carole Davis by slitting her throat?'

Marcello applauded quietly. 'Well done. Riaggi's fingerprints were found all over the apartment. Now all we need to do is find out who killed her and Vercini. Do you have any further theories on these murders?'

'No idea, sir.'

'Ah well, Rome was not built in a day, was it? Now I am going to see Maria Vercini. I will meet you at the pensione at, say, seven o'clock. You said the doctor intends to see Hanson then?'

Gianelli nodded.

'Well, we will have to see whether he is well enough to talk to us. Let us hope for his sake that his alibi checks out. Zanchi will overheat if I haven't found our killer by the time he leaves for his sabbatical at that great palazzo of his. He's invited me to Treviso next week, you know. I feel privileged.'

He placed the last book into the bag.

Gianelli walked to the door then turned. 'Oh, sir. You've reminded me of something. The old woman's sister-in-law, who lives in Mantova – apparently she's not there at the moment. She is also in Treviso.'

Grapper rushed into the tiny cloakroom and locked the door hurriedly behind him. He sat down abruptly on the closed toilet seat, shut his eyes and began to rock to and fro with a slightly pained expression – the opening stages of his psychic trance.

'Ma,' he whispered softly, hoping she was still around. He waited for a few seconds then called her name again.

Slowly through the wavering strands of light shimmering in his mind's eye, she appeared, smiling serenely, chubby arms outstretched. An ethereal welcome.

'I don't understand. What can you tell me?' he asked. Mrs Rice said nothing but just went on smiling stubbornly. The time would come, in a moment. She didn't want to be rushed.

A tingling in his limbs grew stronger as he drifted deeper and deeper into the trance. The sensation was like falling from a high building knowing your body would land gently on the softest bed of down feathers. Fear, then trust.

He watched her raise a finger to her lips as her hair became pressed to her face. Her lilac print dress began to flap as though it were being blown around her by a bracing sea breeze. He smelled the invigorating concoction of ozone and salt and inhaled deeply, welcoming the fresh air.

She reached into her pocket and pulled out something shiny. Grapper reached for it in his mind but she shook her head and stepped back, denying him enlightenment. The wind picked up and he felt suddenly uneasy. It always came, this point of no return. But then she always brought him back. After all it wasn't his time – not yet anyway.

Keeping her left hand tightly closed, she extracted a pale pink scarf from her right pocket and, with a magician's flourish, shook it out. He gasped as it became a pink bird with bright blue flashes emblazoned across its wings. With a vitriolic cry, the bird flew through the air across his line of vision in a circular flight pattern, then came to rest on his mother's right shoulder.

'What the ...?' Grapper cried out, but his expletives were interrupted by a loud squawk. The bird bobbed up and down and began to chant. 'The moving finger writes ... the moving writes.'

Grapper snapped his jaw shut in surprise as the bird burst into song. 'London bridge is falling down, falling down, falling down, London bridge is falling down, Antonella. Antonella has the key, has the key, has the key ...' It repeated the little song once more, to be sure Grapper had heard it correctly. Then it disappeared.

He pulled on the earring distractedly. This was a good one. For the moment he didn't have a clue what it meant.

Mrs Rice unclenched her left hand and held the shining object at arm's length. The wind lulled, the dangling object swayed gently, hypnotically.

Grapper squinted at the object and moved toward it. It was a gold watch on a chain. His mother arrested the movement and beckoned to her son. He took a closer look. One word was inscribed upon it: 'Necromancy.'

That was entirely logical. So that had been Daniela's little game. Perhaps that was how the three of them had died. But spirits could not harm the living with their own hands – only their thoughts.

As though reading his mind his mother spoke three words to him as a parting gift:

'He is alive.'

CHAPTER 18

Early evening sunshine warmed Marcello's body. He strode along purposefully, shirt sleeves rolled up, designer jacket thrown casually over his broad shoulder. He climbed the wooden steps to the Accademia bridge two at a time, feeling momentarily at peace with the world. He was on his way to the Trattoria Vesuvius to question Franco's widow.

A few giggling students passed by and he observed them with a wry smile as they ambled along, brown arms tightly wound around each other, engrossed in their chatter, oblivious to everyone and everything around them.

Marcello did not envy their youthful lack of responsibilities. He had craved the supremacy of middle-aged status since his early twenties. Power suited him. He wore it proudly on his lapel, as a faded war hero displays medals for valour. He too had been brave at times. More in affairs of the heart than on the battlefield. The scars were still there but they didn't show, not outwardly anyway.

As he walked on, his intellect wrestled with the facts, twisting them into a submissive conclusion. Of course they defied him. This was no ordinary case. He suspected a minefield lurked beneath the obvious.

Like an ominous spectre dancing one step ahead of him, the intricacies of truth would remain just out of reach.

These murders undoubtedly had a distinct pattern to them, but how were they related? What was he missing? Something important. He struggled to place a logical finger on the pulse of homicide and couldn't find it.

His thoughts turned to Alessandro De Chesaris. His disclosures had been invaluable, but he too was hiding something. He pictured him. Congenial, intelligent and yet . . . Those steel grey eyes reminded him of someone, or rather something. A Burmese cat with eyes that burned into your skull. It continually brought rats and mice into the apartment, depositing them on his pristine linen pillow while he slept. Misguided tokens of affection.

Still deep in thought, he reached the ivy-covered entrance of his destination. He rang the bell, which tolled solemnly outside closed doors. No business today. The owner is dead.

After a few moments, the door was opened by a young girl. 'I am here to see Signora Vercini.' Marcello spoke softly, sensing the aftermath of bereavement within.

He followed the girl inside and sat down at one of the rickety tables. He placed the bag of books on the chair next to him and glanced up at the ceiling. Tiny multi-coloured lanterns quivered slightly, coaxed by a faint breeze which also stirred yellowing leaves on the withering vine.

The silence seemed strangely out of place – no pans clattered, there was no whoosh of the cappuccino machine, no gentle hum of conversation. He sighed. A pity. He drummed his fingers on the chequered vinyl for the comfort of sound.

After a few minutes the girl returned.

'The Signora will be with you in a moment, Inspector. Can I get you something while you wait – a little pasta perhaps?'

It was after six. He realized he felt hungry and was about to accept enthusiastically when a sense of tact intervened. It would be disrespectful to question a widow whilst demolishing a plateful of her delicious fettucine.

'Thank you, no. Perhaps an espresso.' He winked at the girl who smiled back sheepishly.

'Of course, anything for you, Inspector,' she said, walking away with the merest hint of a wiggle.

Flirtation from one so young amused him. He smiled to himself.

At that moment, Maria Vercini appeared from a doorway at the rear of the restaurant. As befitted a recent widow, she was dressed entirely in black. Her pale face was tear-stained.

Marcello immediately rose and kissed her lightly on both cheeks. 'Maria. I am so very sorry. What can I say?'

She bowed her head and sat down wearily opposite him.

'How anyone could want to hurt him I do not understand,' she said quietly.

'Did Franco have any enemies that you knew of, Maria?'

She answered not that she knew of, then took out a lace

handkerchief and dabbed red-rimmed eyes. She twisted the lace around her bony fingers as the girl arrived with the espresso.

He took a sip of the bitter liquid. 'Why was Franco at the Ca' Rezzonico last night? Do you know?'

'He often went there. He has a morbid fascination with that place. He particularly liked to go there at night with my cousin Guido, who was the night guard at the museum. Franco often kept him company during the night shift. Thank God Guido had no children.' She crossed herself in memoriam. 'What I do not understand is what Daniela was doing there? Four deaths in our family. I can scarcely believe it. It is so terrible.' She sobbed quietly into the damp lace.

Marcello raised his eyes from the rim of the cup. 'Maria, you said Franco had a morbid fascination with the Ca' Rezzonico. I know it is difficult for you, but could you tell me what you meant by that?'

Maria's watery eyes clouded over like an overcast sky.

'I will tell you, Marcello. It can do no harm now he is dead. Poor fool. Five years ago, my Franco killed his father in that museum. He had a good enough reason – that maniac deserved to die.' She clenched her fist with repressed anger.

Marcello took another sip, trying not to register his astonishment. 'I'm sorry, Maria, I do not understand,' he said gently.

'That is the reason why Franco had such a morbid fascination with the museum. It is not so difficult to understand. My Franco suffered and his pain made him mad. His father deserved everything that came to him. I am only sorry he did not suffer as Franco suffered. It was a long overdue vengeance.' She clasped her hands tightly together at the painful memories and muttered a blessing to herself.

A wave of recognition crossed Marcello's face, an unwelcome shadow waiting in the wings of his psyche. He could almost feel cold fingers tracing the outline of his forehead. He swallowed hard. 'I must ask you, Maria. Who was Franco's father?' He already knew the answer.

'Vercini is my name. We could not have hoped for a successful restaurant business if it had become known that General Belloti was Franco's father. I'm sure you remember why.'

Marcello sighed. Of course, De Chesaris had mentioned children in the plural. 'So Daniela was your niece. Again I am sorry.'

'Please don't be on my account. I hated the little bitch. Franco was completely under her spell. He would have done anything for her. God knows what she asked him to do in the museum,' she said tersely.

Maria had mentioned four deaths in the family. She had obviously had a visit about Franco's mother, and identified the body. He thanked her for her co-operation and asked about Luisa Riaggi's sister-in-law, who was now in Treviso. Maria looked as though she might spit on the floor. Evidently this woman was also disliked intensely. He changed the subject and asked her about Belloti's murder. 'How did Franco murder Belloti? Can you tell me?'

Maria raised her downcast eyes and looked at him with steely determination. 'Oh yes, I know how he did it – he shot him in the head with his own gun. It was easy to make it look like suicide.'

Marcello wondered if forensics had checked the bullet trajectory properly.

Maria continued: 'It was a very simple matter to stage the suicide. Franco's sister, Antonella, had stolen photographs from the old bastard. There was an exposé in the British press about his war crimes. He was virtually suicidal anyway. Franco just helped him on his way.'

Marcello raised a troubled eyebrow. 'Franco succeeded very well. I was told only today that Belloti had committed suicide.' He swilled the now lukewarm coffee around in the cup. 'Tell me,' he said, 'how exactly did he escape from the museum without being held as a suspect? The police would have questioned everyone who was there at the time of the death. I unfortunately did not come here until '85, as you know. All this was before my time.'

Maria answered, 'He did not get away. He hid himself until it was safe to come out. Franco knew how long it would take the guard to reach the room where Belloti had been shot. He had time to hide.'

'Where did he hide? I don't recall any obvious hiding places in the Ca' Rezzonico.'

Maria rubbed her forehead wearily. 'On the second floor there is an alcove. He hid there, beneath the bed – it was the obvious place. No one knew he was there. He left no fingerprints on the gun, so they assumed it was suicide. Later that night, when the police had gone, Guido let him out of the museum.'

Marcello thought that for such an obvious fool, Franco had planned this murder extremely well. He deduced that it was almost certainly beyond his capabilities. Maria had helped him but of course he would never be able to prove that. She was a clever woman. He stood up to leave. 'Thank you, Maria. I won't keep you any longer. I know all this has been a terrible strain on you.'

She supported her weight on the chair. He helped her up and she took his arm as they walked to the door. 'It has been a very great strain. You are right. I think now the financial pressure will be even greater. The funeral expenses will be enormous, and I still have all Franco's most recent psychiatric bills to pay.'

His temples pulsed. 'Psychiatric bills?' he enquired casually, sensing he was walking on eggshells.

Maria sighed heavily. 'Yes, I told you, Franco was quite mad. After Belloti's death he had terrible nightmares. He was a child trapped in a man's body, you see. I had to do all I could to help him. He was my husband,' she said emphatically.

'Of course I understand. May I ask who was Franco's psychiatrist?' Once again he was afraid he knew the answer.

Maria glowed with a sudden reverence. 'He had the best money could buy, an expert in his field,' she said. 'Alessandro De Chesaris.'

In the ochre-coloured palazzo near Treviso, the old woman carefully set the medieval oak table in the enormous dining hall. Everything must be exactly right.

She muttered to herself as she polished. She was glad Lugrezia was ill. This was her chance for recognition. A ridotta was only an informal gathering. But perhaps, if they were pleased with her, she might finally be granted a permanent position. After all these years she felt she deserved it.

She laid out the cutlery. It was an unusual service. Gold with jet handles. Silver was unacceptable. Then she placed one glass and one pewter goblet by each setting and sprinkled salt around the base. There were thirteen places.

Suddenly she heard a rapping sound from the room above. Someone was banging on the floor impatiently.

'All right, I'm coming,' she muttered.

She pulled herself up the magnificent marble staircase. The banging continued. She couldn't hurry. Her joints were stiff.

At the end of the long hall she entered a large room where another old woman in a white nightdress lay in bed. The shutters were open, pink light flooded the room. The walls were covered with ancestral miniatures dating from the fifteenth century.

'Lucia, I am so hot, please sponge me down, and I need some water quickly . . .' the sick woman rasped. Her throat sounded dry.

Lucia went to the sink and filled a jug, then poured some into a glass although she knew it wasn't really safe to drink. She held the invalid's head, as her friend drank thirstily. When Lugrezia had finished, she wet a facecloth with cool water and opened the woman's nightdress.

As Lucia Belloti sponged Lugrezia's sagging flesh, she gasped when she came upon a black half-sunburst tattooed just above her left breast.

'So Lugrezia,' she said. 'They finally gave you the mark.'

The old woman chuckled and coughed. There was a glint in her dark eyes. 'Would you have me die unbaptised, Lucia? Surely even you would not begrudge me that comfort.'

CHAPTER 19

Alone in the Vercinis' restaurant kitchen under harsh fluorescent lighting, Marcello gripped the telephone receiver and studied his reflection in the stainless steel work surface. He looked tense, drawn.

'Pronto,' Gianelli answered cheerfully.

'Gianelli, you took your time. Look I want you to go to El Souk before you meet me. Check out the American boy's alibi. When you come to the pensione bring someone for night surveillance . . . and for God's sake make sure it's anyone but Brazzi.'

He hung up abruptly. Time was too short for explanations. He reached into his jacket and took out the pale grey printed card. He dialled and listened to the ringing tone, certain the office would now be closed. It was after six. He looked up at the grease stains on the ceiling and cursed. 'Be there,' he whispered edgily on the sixth ring.

A female voice answered. She sounded breathless. 'Pronto, De Chesaris surgery . . .'

'Good evening. I'm sorry to telephone so late, Signorina. This is Inspector Marcello.' His intonation almost purred.

'Inspector, I was just leaving.' The secretary arched her back and glanced at the clock. She didn't have time for this. She was already late for the pick-up.

'I would very much like to take you to dinner tomorrow night . . . if you are free, that is?' He sounded assured. A turn-down simply wasn't on the cards.

Alicia looked at her long pink nails. 'What a surprise. Of course, I'd love to.'

'I thought perhaps Poste Vecie. I know it's a little touristy, but we can eat outside. It is very pleasant. Say we meet at eight – would that suit you?'

'That sounds wonderful, Inspector . . . ' Alicia, assured of her attractiveness, had known he would call. She was pleased he hadn't asked to see her tonight. That would have been out of the question.

'Please call me Luciano. You are . . .?'

'Alicia, and now I must go. Until tomorrow.' She hung up and made a dash for the door thinking she'd never make it on time.

Marcello replaced the receiver. The young girl was waiting to let him out. She unbolted the door, suggestively revealing her bare midriff.

On the threshold he turned and flashed her a dazzling smile. However, he was distracted, his mind already plotting a course for the following evening's deception, a deception which was necessary if he was to gain vital unauthorized access. Into De Chesaris's office.

In Katerina's normally peaceful salon, in an atmosphere that almost crackled with tension, Grapper held the bright pink envelope aloft. 'Now we'll see what's going on,' he remarked excitedly to his two confused companions. He read out the name and address: 'Antonella Riaggi, Holloway Prison, London N7, England.' (The pink bird in his trance had sung London Bridge and added Antonella at the end instead of 'my fair lady.' Same number of syllables.)

'Clever old Ma – now we'll see what she was on about.' He ripped open the envelope. Eager eyes scanned the pink writing paper. 'Shit, it's in Italian. Katy, can you translate this fer us?' He handed her the flimsy writing paper.

'I will try my best. Let me see now.' Katerina squinted at the paper and picked up her magnifying glass.

'I'm almost afraid to ask what's going on.' Miles was eyeing the scene warily. He felt like hell and needed to lie down. But he had to stay, had to find out what was happening.

'Hang on a minute,' Grapper hissed at him. 'I don't know meself yet.'

Katerina read aloud, 'Mamma, I am pleased to say we are getting closer. The . . .' She paused. 'I've never seen this word before. I think it says ''Grimoire''.'

'It's okay, I know what that means. Go on,' Grapper said tersely.

She continued, 'The Grimoire you sent has been a great help. The task is not easy but tonight I think my goal will be achieved. After my admission tomorrow, I am to be driven to Milano where

I will catch the plane to Paris. By the time the discovery is made I will be long gone. After the audition with Madame Aquarone, I am coming to see you. The Adeptus Major says my acceptance is guaranteed. That will show those idiots on the committee here who turned me down.

'I hope they are treating you well. If the Conservatoire accepts me, I will begin next term. So you see, I will be able to spend some time with you. I hope that pleases you.' Katerina took off her glasses and rubbed her eyes. One glance at Grapper's stony features made her realize she should go on.

'I have some money from the sale of the jewels but I had to give Franco half of it, so it will not last long.

'I cannot tell you how glad I am that after tomorrow I will be free of all of them. I know this is what you want too. You should not be afraid for me, I am stronger than they think. When they have given me what I want, I will deprive them, just as you did. They are fools to think they can contain me – I will be as free as you were. I have only one regret, Mamma – that the beautiful American boy I met has to be the one. It is a great pity, I really like him. But, as you know, there is no other way. Katerina put the paper down and sighed deeply. 'Then she says, "See you soon and goodbye." That is all.'

Grapper unwrapped a piece of chewing gum and thoughtfully put it in his mouth.

Miles stared at his hands, disbelieving. 'So she really was going to kill me,' he whispered.

His friend spoke wisely through the gum. 'She didn't want to kill yer, mate . . . She 'ad to kill. There's a difference.'

'Oh yeah, and what exactly is that?' Miles said angrily.

'I don't know meself yet. But there's a lot more to it than we think. I need some time to figure it all out. That knife you told me about. You said it had some strange symbols on it.' He rummaged in the flight bag.

'Yes, I suppose she was planning to kill me with it. Is that what you're thinking?'

Grapper handed Miles the sheathed dagger. 'Take a look at that – is it similar? I mean, were the symbols like these?'

Miles studied the dagger. The pentangles were inscribed. 'I can't be sure, but they look the same.'

'Did she say anythin' that might give us a clue why she was

involved in black magic? Judging by 'er book, she took it pretty seriously – this wasn't a prank.'

Miles grit his teeth, he'd believed everything she said. What a fool he'd been.

'Everything she said was a lie, so even if she had admitted it I wouldn't have been any the wiser. I said she had these black candles, well I never dreamed she was going to perform some fucking ritual, with me as a sacrificial lamb . . .' His voice seemed to hang in the air. 'The thing is, at the time it didn't register at all. I mean, I stayed in the museum with her, we could easily have been caught, then there was the dope, all these risks, it was crazy – all of it. I must have been mad.'

Grapper shrugged. 'No mate, not mad, just infatuated. I don't think you could 'elp yourself. She did one or two things to influence you that way.'

'Like what exactly,' Miles shouted.

Katerina flinched at the raised voices but remained silent.

Grapper opened Daniela's book and flicked through until he found what he was looking for. Solemnly, he handed the book to Katerina. 'Can you do the honours again fer us?'

Once again Katerina read aloud. 'With five fingers on the wall, each represents a devil and will ensure the victim is consumed with passion and loses all sense of reason, recite this incantation five times.'

Miles frowned as Katerina translated the spell. 'I don't believe a word of this crap,' he said. 'There has to be a logical explanation for all this.'

Grapper took out his gum and rolled it into a tiny grey moistened ball between thumb and forefinger. 'Okay, calm down. I've got a theory but I need more time. You said she could sing, right?' The atmosphere tightened as they neared some long-awaited grains of truth.

'Sure, you've heard her. How could someone with such an incredible talent be an out-and-out killer?' Miles was flushed with anger. He stood up hesitantly and paced the room. His steps were laboured.

Grapper thought for a moment. 'Left 'n' right brain', he said matter-of-factly. 'She used 'er right brain, that's the creative side, to sing. And the left brain, that's the administrative side, to kill. Simple as that.' He pulled on his earring.

Miles looked far from comforted. 'I've heard the theory. But how the hell do you know so much about it – you're hardly neurosurgeon material,' he sneered.

Grapper felt sorely tempted to tell this septic tank a thing or two about Holistics but decided ignorance was probably bliss under these complicated circumstances. Grapper explained that when his mother had her stroke, she could neither move her limbs on the right side nor speak coherently. However, as her right brain was unaffected, she could sing entire songs. 'That's 'ow I communicated with 'er until she died.'

Miles felt suddenly ashamed of his unwarranted anger towards the strange Londoner who had shown him nothing but kindness, caring for him with a consideration that went far beyond mere acquaintanceship. He shouldn't be taking his frustrations out on him. 'I'm sorry, Grapper. I didn't mean to doubt you. It's just . . . well, I'm a bit edgy, that's all.'

'We're all a bit edgy, ain't we Katy?'

Katerina looked half asleep. She blinked and turned to face him.

'I think now, it is time I tell you both what I know of all these troubles. In the album you will find newspaper cuttings. Please – you will both read them, now.'

Grapper and Miles studied the cuttings. Most were in Italian. Some later ones, in English, reported on Belloti's trial, the war crimes and his exoneration. The report on Antonella's conviction for murder showed the new evidence which had been discovered. The photographs depicting torture and execution said it all.

Katerina spoke in a low voice that came from another time. A time of suffering. She spoke of the terror, how the Jews and gypsies were considered little more than sewage to be flushed from humanity, poisonous debris to be swept away. She spoke of her husband's kindness, how he was tortured by nightmares but believed, one day, they could finally commit these evils to memory. This of course was not to be. Her voice cracked a little: 'Imagine – we go out to eat one day and, in a restaurant, we see this monster, who we know is guilty of unspeakable crimes. Eating and drinking, laughing, without a care in the world. Mario pulled this bastard to the ground punching and kicking, screaming like a banshee. I was terrified for him. I got him away. He wanted to go to the police with evidence we had.' She looked up at Grapper with watery eyes. 'You have seen this evidence.'

Grapper nodded, unable to speak. He felt the writhing live wires were about to come together in one almighty bang.

Katerina wiped her eyes. 'When Mario went to the cellar to get those photographs – he fell.' Tears she could no longer control coursed down her flushed cheeks. 'His neck was broken in an instant. Thank God he did not suffer. We had both suffered enough.' Her shoulders heaved. It took her a moment to regain her composure. She wiped her eyes on her sleeve and took out her rosary for protection, comfort. This was an inadequate crutch, but she felt able to continue. 'But that is not what I want to tell you. Later, in those English articles, the truth was told and Belloti killed himself. There was some justice after all. But what is important is the name in those newspapers – Riaggi. Daniela was this devil's granddaughter. Now you know.'

Miles looked horrified. 'You mean to tell me that the sadist who tortured and killed all those people in the camp was Daniela's grandfather? No, I don't believe it. The name is just a coincidence. It can't be the same family.'

Katerina gripped the rosary tighter. 'Skinny, listen to me. When you come home and tell me about the girl, Daniela Riaggi, I too think it is impossible – I think no it is not the same family. Then when you are sick last night and we look in her bag, we find the photograph of Belloti and I know I am right. Now, he has come back to bring me more pain. Perhaps I did not escape my fate after all. . .' She buried her face in her apron.

Grapper spoke sternly. 'I think you'd better believe it, Miles. Besides, this article is about her mother Antonella. It says she killed her lover. That's how they found the evidence,' he said solemnly. 'That must be why she's in Holloway. Anyway, that's not the 'alf of it. Look, it even mentions witchcraft. Katerina, when you saw this guy in the restaurant and Mario attacked him, did he lose anything? I know it's a lot to ask of yer, but can you remember?'

Katerina sniffed and gave him a determined look. 'I remember like it was yesterday. It was wintertime. He lost a glove.'

Grapper sighed. 'This is going to take some time to sort out. But I've got some ideas. After the doc's been I'll 'ave to get 'ome.' Mickey Mouse said it was twenty past six. 'Those cops will be back 'ere soon. We'd better get sorted.'

Miles gazed distractedly at the photographs, trying to force together ill-fitting pieces of an incredible puzzle. 'I've been having these really weird dreams lately. Today I dreamed about this guy. I'm sure this is the same man . . .'

Grapper looked at the photograph and sighed. 'I 'ad a dream about 'im too.' He walked over to Katerina and showed her the picture of the man with the severed heads.

'I presume this is Belloti.'

Katerina forced herself to look.

Grapper was pointing to the tall thin soldier with gaunt features.

'No,' she said. 'That is not him. Belloti is the short man, there. I do not know who that is. I 'ave never seen him before.'

The gilt clock on Katerina's mantelpiece chimed a single delicate strike. Half past six. Three exhausted people ignored it. Incredible circumstances hovered, a dark winged creature they feared would consume them. Each was afraid – for differing reasons.

Grapper's voice broke the silence. 'It's getting late. We've got to get our story straight for PC Plod.'

Miles sighed. 'They're bound to want to take me in. I know you covered for me but the Inspector doesn't sound like an idiot to me – and what if they want to fingerprint me? My prints have got to be all over the sedan chair – and the windows.'

Grapper offered Miles a stick of gum. 'You let me worry about that. I've got to buy more time. Right, now 'ere's the plan. You're sick, right. We'll get yer back into bed . . . ever done any actin'?'

Miles took the gum and unwrapped it. 'Well, a bit. Nothing much really. I played Hamlet in high school.' He couldn't fathom what Grapper had in mind.

'You're a bleedin' professional then, mate. 'Ere's the gameplan. We've told you about Daniela's murder and it's more than yer can take emotionally. That's what we'll tell old doc. We'll give yer a fever – you thrash about a bit when 'e comes to examine yer. We'll say yer've been like that all afternoon.' Grapper tweaked his earring again. ' 'E's bound to give yer another sedative – then the cops can't take yer in fer questioning, can they?'

Miles was bemused. 'Sure, I can do all that with no trouble. But how the hell are you gonna give me a fever?'

'Oldest trick in the book, mate. Katy, you've got an 'ot water bottle, ain't yer?'

She had been listening intently to the plan but was far from certain it would work. 'Da, da,' she said wearily, pulling herself up. 'I will get it now for you.'

'Great, ta.' He smiled at his conspirator, 'Oldest trick in the book this is. I used to put mine on me forehead to bunk off school.' He called after Katerina, 'While yer there, I don't suppose you'd make us a cuppa, would yer.'

Katerina sighed. 'What is this cuppa?'

Grapper winked. 'A cup of tea, of course . . . wiv boiled water,' he added.

She nodded and shuffled away with painstaking tiredness.

Miles looked at Daniela's flight bag. 'What are you going to do with that? If the police find it we'll be in trouble.'

'You leave all that to me and don't worry. Now come on, let's get yer into bed.' Grapper heaved Miles out of the chair. He looked drained.

'Grapper, if you're going to destroy her things, do you think I could have something? I'd like some small thing to remember her by.'

Grapper frowned. 'Yer a glutton for bleedin' punishment, you are. Don't yer realize how dangerous that could be? If the police ever found yer with it . . .'

'It could be something she gave me – the tape, for instance.'

Grapper went to the sideboard and salvaged the rehearsal tape. 'Don't say I didn't warn yer,' he said, waving it tauntingly before Miles's harrowed features.

Miles took the tape and caressed it for a moment. Daniela had planned to kill him in cold blood but he would never let go of her memory. And if this was to be all he had left of her, then so be it. His infatuation was clearly here to stay. He closed his eyes and pictured her as she was. Piercing eyes, cascading black hair, translucent skin, arms outstretched – living, deadly. He jumped as Grapper took his arm. They climbed the stairs with Grapper supporting his friend's now very weak body.

'I guess those drugs the doc pumped into me had more of an effect than I thought. I felt fine for a while.'

'Well, if you get more of the same in a bit, you know what to do.' Grapper pulled Miles's arm further onto his broad shoulder.

'What should I do exactly?' the invalid asked hesitantly.

Grapper laughed. 'Just lie back and enjoy the trip, mate.'

Miles sank into the high bed with a groan. 'I feel like I've been hit by an eighteen-wheeler – that's a truck to you,' he said. Wearily, he closed his eyes. Blackness undulated around and through him.

Grapper looked around the room and clicked his tongue loudly. 'Well, if yer was 'it by a bleedin' truck it must 'ave come through the room first – look at this mess.'

Miles opened one eye and struggled to get up. Grapper pushed him back down and, although undomesticated, roughly gathered the clothes. He opened the large ornate mahogany wardrobe and took down a wire coat hanger. As he folded Miles's jeans, a bright gold chain dangling from the pocket caught his eye. He pulled out the antique watch and swung it back and forth, back and forth.

For a moment, mesmerized by the light that glinted into his eyes, he appeared curiously unworldly. He could feel a presence. Why hadn't he sensed this before? Or had he?

'Where d'ya get this? A gift from one of yer rich ancestors, was it?' His tone was casual – he knew the answer.

Miles opened his eyes and raised his head a few inches from the pillow. 'You mean my unusual watch? Grandfather left it to me. Go ahead, open it up. There's a really neat inscription inside. It's quite historic. You'll probably find it interesting – should appeal to your perverse nature.

Grapper dropped the clothes on to a chair and opened the watch case carefully. Miles was right, it was unusual, in more ways than one. It was running backwards. Although the inscription was in German, even he recognized the names. The presentation date didn't come as a surprise.

'I can't read this, mate – don't speak German.' He turned the watch over and over, staring at the ornate Magick symbol inscribed on the front.

Miles kept his eyes closed and spoke automatically. 'My grandfather commanded the Rainbow division. He took it as a souvenir from some hideaway in Bavaria – we've got some of Hitler's silverware too. Grandfather had a rainbow stamped over the Third Reich eagle as a symbol of victory – my mother wheels it out at important dinner parties.'

Grapper felt drained of energy as Miles translated: 'The watch is commemorative. Grandfather said it was presented to Hitler by this fanatical group called The Golden Dawn, to celebrate some art exhibition of theirs opening in Berlin. It says: '"Presented to Adolf Hitler in recognition, from the Great Beast".'

'I'll give yer one thing mate – you don't do things by fuckin' 'alves.' He walked towards the window and opened it. 'This was presented on the 6th of June 1936 – three sixes – number of the beast.'

Miles pulled himself up. 'So that's what the Great Beast means. Holy shit . . . Damien rides again.'

'You can joke if yer like. But this is going.' Grapper hurled the watch into the cloudy green water below, sending it to a putrid grave.

Miles leapt up in an act of sudden strength and grasped Grapper's arm forcefully. 'What the hell do you think you're doing? That was a family heirloom! It was damned valuable too,' he said angrily.

Grapper turned to face him. 'Valuable maybe, but to who? Think about it fer just a minute. Of all the tourists in Venice how did Daniela come to pick you? And what made yer choose Katerina's place out of all the hotels and pensiones yer could've stayed in? That precious watch of yours acted like a kind of magnet. Look, mate – I know it sounds incredible but yer've gotta believe me. That watch was bad karma.'

Miles slumped into the chair by the writing table and tried to grasp what his friend was telling him. He didn't doubt his ally had some experience of the Twilight Zone. He thought for a moment. Hadn't everything fallen apart after he'd taken possession of it two years ago. First his father's affair, then Lisa, the accident, now this bizarre turn of events. Despite his raging scepticism he had to admit it made sense. Distraught, he ran his fingers through his hair.

Grapper stared out of the open window, keeping an eye trained on the street for the doctor or Marcello.

Miles bent his head defeatedly. In a hesitant tone, he spoke of his troubles. Almost as the words left his mouth, a series of small forgotten household accidents flooded into his mind, and of course, although he didn't make the connection, there were the strange, lucid dreams.

Turning to the innocent, Grapper concluded his observations from the window. 'You think this is bad luck then d'yer . . . all these coincidences?'

'Sure. Just because the watch was owned by Hitler and he was an evil bastard, I didn't think any of that so-called evil was automatically going to rub off on me.'

Grapper lost his temper. He slammed his fist into the fragile window frame so hard that Miles thought it would surely splinter. 'Let me tell yer somethin', mate. Evil begets evil. He probably had direct access to something even I won't talk about. The Holocaust was the most effective penetration of our world by the Lower Astral ever experienced. It's all in Revelations. Yer should read it sometime. I've done some research and I could tell yer some unbelievable things about sadism and mass hypnosis that went on at that time. Do yer really think it was a fuckin' accident that genocide spread over virtually every occupied country during the war? All those blokes who bashed in kid's 'eads and then said their prayers at 'ome with their own kids. Do you really think that was just them being trigger 'appy – or temporary madness?' Miles shook his head. 'Well if you admit that sommat evil can exist en masse then you have to accept that bad energy can stay in one place or one object. Look, I 'ad a mate who bought a car with three sixes in the number plate. From the minute 'e got the bleedin' thing 'e 'ad terrible luck. I told 'im to get rid of it. The day before the bloke who was gonna buy it came to pick it up, me mate got killed outright in a car crash. Freak accident they called it. Accident my arse. And that was just a car with a dodgy number plate. What you've got there – well, I shouldn't 'ave to spell it out for yer.'

Miles watched early evening sunlight cast strange iridescent green shadows through Grapper's plumage, flickering across his strong features giving a surreal luminosity.

'So you mean to tell me that because the watch had three sixes on it, and it was owned by Hitler, I'm attracting evil?'

Grapper frowned. 'Like I said, yer don't do things by 'alves, mate. Yer must have been lighting up like a Belisha beacon. That watch belonged to someone much worse than 'itler. Someone who probably influenced 'im a lot – if not directly, at least indirectly. We all know 'e was interested in the occult.

It don't surprise me at all.' He reached into his pocket for some gum to help him think.

Miles felt suddenly confused. 'Well if it's not Hitler, who then?'

Grapper spat ceremoniously into the street below. 'Aleister Crowley – otherwise known as the Great Beast, that's who,' he said, popping the gum into Miles's now open mouth.

CHAPTER 20

Lucia Belloti stood at the upstairs window and watched. The light was changing, deepening; rose glow would soon become blood red. A mackerel sky swept towards the ochre palazzo, accusing fingers from the heavens, pointing toward a source. She inhaled, scented herbs, goat droppings, camphor on her fingers from Lugrezia's chest rub. She stretched brittle joints and yearned for her time to come. She was impatient now. Old age had become a burden.

The chickens were quiet in the loggia, the dog slept soundly by a sack of feed; there was momentary stillness as though the palazzo and its inhabitants were breathing slowly, waiting.

A trail of dust appeared at the end of the long, tree-lined drive. Black paintwork glinted in the dying rays of sunlight. The first had arrived. She took assiduous steps down the grand marbled staircase, a superfluous duchess, still resplendent in black silk, diamond and jet earrings glinting in the dappled half light that flooded through the portico, Lucia glanced into the dining room. Everything looked wonderful, almost too formal for a ridotta. She was pleased. A pity their sustenance would be inferior tonight. Her palate was unaccustomed to animal blood – it always gave her severe indigestion. It would be a poor substitute for the real thing.

Miles lay back in fragile repose, a towel-wrapped hot water bottle pressed against his forehead. 'What I don't understand,' he said weakly, 'is what this guy Crowley has to do with anything. So he was a black magician, so what?'

Grapper sat on the edge of the bed sipping his tea. 'Look, mate, to understand that you would 'ave to 'ave a bleedin' lecture on the occult, and I ain't gonna give it to yer.' He stood up and put the cup down on the bedside table. 'When we've got rid of the cops I'm going back to Bella's, poor cow's probably got the rolling-pin ready for me, anyway, I'll bring yer a book of mine. Yer might understand a bit more if yer read it.' He took the bottle from Miles's forehead just as the doorbell rang. 'Right, now remember – shake yer head about and mumble a lot.' He quickly unscrewed the bottle top and, dipping his fingers into the near boiling liquid, sprinkled a few droplets on to Miles' heated forehead for insurance.

'Ouch!' Miles cried out ungratefully.

His altruistic conspirator raised a finger to his lips and deposited the bottle at the bottom of the wardrobe, beneath discarded clothes and shoes. Katerina brought in the doctor who nodded and perched on the edge of the bed. His round face, steel-rimmed glasses and white hair gave him a caring, almost Dickensian, air. He opened his Gladstone bag and rummaged through its contents. Grapper winked at Katerina. Her face was ashen.

The doctor took the patient's temperature. Miles pushed the thermometer, rather dramatically, from his mouth and moaned incoherently. Then, sensing he was cooling rapidly, on the doctor's third attempt he kept it on his tongue for a moment and feigned sleep. The doctor prised open an eyelid and shone his pencil torch into Miles's eyeball. The amateur actor rolled his eyes as far back into his head as he could and resumed the moans. The doctor frowned at the thermometer and spoke to Katerina in Italian. 'He is marginally better, but he still has a very high temperature. Has he been vomiting at all?'

Grapper recognized the word from Bella's streams of abuse at drunken punters who were given to that particular activity on the doorstep of the bar. He shook his head from behind the doctor's back. 'No there has been none,' Katerina said collaboratively. 'I am afraid he 'ad another shock. Another friend was killed last night. For a while he seemed much better, so we told him about his friend's death. He was hysterical again straight away.'

The doctor took a limp wrist. 'It would have been much better to wait until he was fully recovered. Well, the pulse is strong. I will given him another sedative, a lesser dose this time, I think. I believe the police suspect him. I had a call from an Inspector Marcello. He should be here in a moment to hear my prognosis. He seems extremely anxious to question this young man.' He rooted through his bag again as the doorbell sounded. 'Ah, that is probably him now.'

Katerina glanced nervously into the upper hall.

Grapper went to answer the door, turning at the top of the staircase. The doctor was filling a syringe. Grapper went back and closed the bedroom door.

Marcello and Gianelli waited impatiently. Grapper could see their silhouettes, fidgeting beyond the stained-glass panels. He took a deep breath and opened the front door. 'Ah, Inspector, nice to see you. Please come in.' He bowed comically.

Marcello ignored the farce, 'Has the doctor arrived yet?' he asked pointedly.

'He's upstairs with the patient. I'll show yer.'

Marcello turned to Gianelli. 'You had better wait here for a moment, Sergeant.' He added in Italian, 'I'm sure our invalid would not appreciate too many visitors in his delicate condition.'

This sarcasm amused Gianelli somewhat. He plopped down on the only chair in the hall, next to the clock, and, still smiling, mopped his brow.

Marcello hoped to find the boy conscious. He needed to make some progress. He entered the room like a cheetah stalking a herd of impala, shook the doctor's hand, introducing himself, and scrutinized Miles from the foot of the bed.

'Well, doctor, how is our young patient?'

The doctor answered in Italian. 'Not exactly well, Inspector. I have administered another sedative so I'm afraid your questions will have to wait, at least until tomorrow.' The doctor closed his bag and addressed Katerina. 'If his condition changes at all please let me know. The mind can do strange things to the body in cases of extreme shock. Isn't that correct, Inspector?' He turned to Marcello.

Marcello perused Miles's chemically induced sleep and smiled despite his frustration. 'Absolutely, Doctor. Tell me, have you taken a blood sample?'

The doctor walked toward the door. 'No, I didn't feel it necessary. Why?'

'I will need a sample at some stage, that is all. As I cannot take it without the young man's permission, I could have determined his blood type from you.' Marcello opened the door. 'After you, Signora.' He gestured. Katerina looked relieved. Grapper's plan had worked.

Miles was now extremely drowsy and it was for real. He heard low voices coming from far away. He felt weak, vulnerable. He wished that he were in his own bed, in the comfort of familiarity. He wanted to wake up at home, and find this had all been just a bad dream.

In Katerina's salon, Marcello closed the door and filled Gianelli in on the irritating circumstances.

'It would appear our cuckoo is once again incapacitated. I want twenty-four-hour surveillance from our man outside. Tell him to radio anything suspicious – anything at all.'

Gianelli eyed his boss with a mixture of admiration and nervousness. 'Yes sir, I'll do it now.' He made for the door.

'No, you will not do it now,' Marcello hissed. 'We don't want these people to know they are under suspicion.'

'No sir, of course.' He sat down abruptly.

'And we do not sit down until we are asked – do we?'

The sergeant stood up again as Katerina and Grapper entered the little salon. In the glow of evening, particles of dust disturbed by Gianelli's ample rear drifted silently through the heavy air like minute insects.

Katerina feigned a kind of normality. 'Can I offer you something, coffee or perhaps a drink? Please to sit.' She motioned to the comfortable armchairs.

Marcello inhaled on his Sobranie. 'Thank you, Signora, that is most kind, but I must decline your hospitality. We will not impose on you any longer.' He ground out the cigarette in the delicate porcelain ashtray. 'You may be interested to know that I have reason to believe the Signor Hanson did not kill Carole Davis.'

Katerina crossed herself dramatically and muttered her relief to the saints. Grapper narrowed his eyes. A potent challenge. 'So yer ain't got no reason to suspect him of anything else then, 'ave yer Inspector?'

'Ah, if only everything in life were simple. There are several witnesses at the bar – El Souk – who seem to remember the two of you drinking there until the time you mentioned. However, until the investigation is concluded it would be better if your friend were to remain in Venice. It is unlikely, given his present condition, that he will be able to leave so I'm sure it will not inconvenience him.' He turned to Gianelli and waved a dismissive hand. 'Now, if you will excuse us. Thank you for your time, Signora. May I say you are looking extremely tired.

Perhaps you should rest. I am sure all of this has been a great strain.'

Katerina appreciated this sudden display of concern. 'Yes, I am a little tired. I will rest now – thank you.' She showed them out and turned to Grapper. He was grinning from ear to ear.

The two men stood on the warm pavement outside. A shadowy figure hovered in the doorway on the opposite side of the canal. Marcello nodded to the officer and removed his Armani jacket, throwing it casually over his shoulder. As he and Gianelli sauntered towards the bridge they discussed the case. Marcello hoped Soldati would throw a little light on the matter. The presence of witchcraft disturbed him enormously. He was not a believer in the paranormal and found the occult laughable. How could he probe the mind of a killer if he was unable to comprehend the motive? No doubt the textbooks would prove to be enlightening. He needed to tie these loose threads together somehow. He had at least two unsolved murders on his hands but the most pressing was one he felt he'd already solved – the old woman's. Daniela might well have killed her as he suspected, but he felt there was more to the motive than mere psychosis. He had a theory. 'Gianelli, when you searched the Riaggi apartment, did you see any writing implements by the old woman's bedside – paper, envelopes, pens? Did you find anything of this nature?'

Gianelli thought for a moment. 'No sir, I don't think so. I seem to remember there was a small tape-recorder – the type with a built-in microphone.'

Marcello breathed deeply, inhaling the growing scent of deduction. 'Ah, that makes infinite sense to me.'

Naturally the sergeant had no idea why. He didn't ask for enlightenment. It came anyway.

'A woman with crippling arthritis would not necessarily be able to write letters. She would either have to get someone to do it for her, or, if she were as independent-minded as I suspect she was, it is logical to assume she would tape her correspondence.' He stopped walking. 'Well, I'll leave you here. I need you to find me an expert on witchcraft. Judging by the complexities of the varying types I need a short-cut – and fast. The state archives would be a good place to start. Anyone studying would want to see the Inquisition records. Goodnight, Gianelli.'

Gianelli stared after him and shook his head. If he investigated a million cases, his mind would never be a match for his boss's. But maybe, if he stayed close enough, some of that genius might rub off. He mused. Marcello's intellect was so sharp it could slice a braesola.

As Marcello sauntered down the pretty street, the smell of garlic-enriched dinners, cooked by waiting women, wafted from the open windows; mingling with the stench from the narrow canal, it dominated his senses. He was starving. It would be bread and cheese tonight, but he'd make up for it tomorrow evening with a sumptuous meal at the Poste Vecie. His mouth watered at the thought – langoustine swimming in herb butter, followed by the speciality of the house, calamaretti col Pien. Delicious. What more could he ask for? A wonderful meal, the company of a beautiful woman and hopefully a series of important clues that would help to narrow the field. As he turned the corner someone stepped into his path.

The apparition smiled revealing hideously blackened teeth. Her cloak wafted around her. Time seemed to screech to a halt. Marcello couldn't breathe. He closed his eyes for a split second. When he opened them again she had gone.

Katerina and Grapper stood by her front door, 'Are you sure you don't mind if I go 'ome? I reckon 'e'll be all right until the morning. This is the number where I'll be. Give us a ring if yer need us. I'll come back tomorrow. You should get to bed. You look bleedin' exhausted.' Grapper opened the front door.

'I'll be all right, don't worry about me. I 'ave no guests until the day after tomorrow so I can rest for a day or two. This 'as been very bad day – very bad.'

He touched her shoulder caringly. It seemed so unfair that she should be dragged into all this. Fate had dealt her a pretty dirty hand. 'You get yourself to bed and remember, call if anything 'appens that worries yer – anything at all.'

He was extremely pensive as he walked down the little street to the bridge. Everything now made perfect sense to him. The watch, as he had said, had acted like a magnet, drawing Miles in. Poor bastard didn't stand a chance. He was convinced that

Miles had been allowed to escape from whoever had killed the others at the museum, but couldn't fathom the reason. He fully intended to use his gifts to find out more. Daniela was obviously a witch, so his recent dream of the nuns and the Cardinal who had told him so was even more important than he'd originally thought. He'd considered Belloti and his severed heads to be the most significant part – but there was obviously more to it.

In her letter, Daniela had mentioned the Adeptus. He was the leader – the high priest – the master. She was definitely part of a group. But how deeply in were they? He was going to have to do an awful lot of digging to suss it. And as for Crowley, what a turn-up! Actually holding something that belonged to the Great Beast. No wonder Miles had been besieged. He hoped the traumas were over. Somehow he doubted it.

When he arrived at Bella's apartment her front door was ajar. He imagined her poised behind it. A coiled spring, rolling-pin in hand. 'Bella darlin',' he enquired softly, pushing the door further open. The red-haired shrew, far from his mental image of a whirling dervish, was curled on a floor cushion like a fawn. She was dishevelled, crying. 'Hey what's all this in aid of?' He went to her side immediately.

Bella reached for him, as a child after a bad dream reaches for parental comfort. Large tears coursed down her cheeks. 'I'm so sorry. Ostrich, so sorry . . .' she said between sobs.

Grapper rocked her in his arms, kissed her hair, held her at arm's length. 'What's all this for? It's all right now, everything's all right.'

Bella wailed. 'No, you don't understand. It is not all right.'

'Well if you don't tell me I can't help. Come on, baby, what is it?' He stroked her flaming curls.

She explained how the police had come and questioned her and Anna. As luck would have it, Fabrizio was in the bar and backed them up. Also two other friends who had been, she thought, less convincing. She was worried the police would find out she was his girlfriend.

'That's no reason to get upset. You did great, honest.'

She clutched a disintegrating tissue and explained there was another, more serious reason why she was upset. She muttered a prayer and told him about the baby she was expecting, searching his stunned features for signals.

Grapper stood up and paced the tiny room angrily. 'A baby. A bleedin' baby . . . We can't even look after ourselves, let alone a baby,' he shouted.

Bella began to cry again.

Suddenly he remembered the last dream he'd had: afternoon tea, his mother holding a baby out to him. 'Yer never get it wrong, do yer,' he said to the damp patch on the ceiling. The light bulb quivered with silent mirth.

The fawn looked at him quizzically with doe-like eyes and sniffed.

'Well I suppose we'll just 'ave to get married, won't we? Thank God I'm a Catholic. The way I look might 'ave freaked 'em but your bleedin' parents would 'ave killed me if I was Protestant.'

Bella jumped up enthusiastically. 'Santa Maria!' she said, throwing her arms around him and showering his boyish face with hot kisses.

'What a day, what a bloody day,' he said, hugging her. 'All this an' now a sproglet on the cards.'

In a small bar, where nets hung from the ceiling and huge fish were preserved in glass cases for posterity, Marcello nursed a large brandy. His hands were still shaking slightly. The barman, a big bear of a man with a shark's tooth on a gold chain, a relic from his active years as a seaman, dried a glass and held it up to the strip light. It still looked grimy. 'You don't look yourself – is it another junkie murder or something more interesting? I have never seen you like this.'

Marcello drained his glass and coughed loudly. 'You know better than that, my friend. I can't tell you of course, but let's just say I've never experienced anything like it.' He drummed his fingers on the lemon and grey vinyl bar top. 'What have you got on the menu tonight? I don't feel like going home just yet.'

'Not much, Violetta's gone to her mother's. But I can heat some risotto from yesterday if you like.'

Marcello thanked him and stretched. He was dog-tired. He moved to another table and watched a game of chequers. An old man was beating the shit out of his teenage opponent. Marcello whispered something in the boy's ear. The old man looked annoyed. 'Marcello, if you want to play you wait, eh! I'm about to make 10,000 lire. Eat somewhere else.'

Marcello shrugged and obliged. Always one to step in, he hated to see the underdog beaten. His meal arrived in a chipped china dish. Its inky grey colour would have looked unappetizing to anyone but a Venetian. In fact it tasted far better than it looked. It was of course an improvement on bread and cheese – but it wasn't as good as Sarah's. For an English girl she'd made the best risotto he'd ever tasted. While he ate he thought about her. Svelte, fair, knowing hazel eyes which had flecks of green in them that glinted like minute emeralds. Not just a beauty, she had been highly intelligent too, with a first-class degree in philosophy. It would always remain a saddening mystery to him how someone with such a mind could become a hopeless addict: ravaged, taken from him by the only demon he knew how to fight – heroin.

Miles slept soundly as evening melted into night. Fragmented dreams permeated his subconscious, creating a fabric, half-memory, half-reality. Mostly he dreamed of Daniela. She danced and sang, naked then clothed; touching him sensually with her hands, and her psyche; invading, calling. 'Come to me, Miles. I am lonely. I need you.' And he responded, running after her, begging her to wait for him. He wanted to go with her, to exist in an afterlife where there was no pain, no loss, only a bright, flower-filled world, all sweet nectar and kisses.

The big hall clock chimed ten. Katerina was baking bread; turning out the high loaves one by one, banging tin on wood. She left them to cool and went through to the salon for a drink. Katerina doubted she would sleep at all tonight. Her mind was filled with anguish. She had contemplated asking Grapper to take Miles away. Perhaps then her troubles would cease. While Miles remained here, in her nest, she was in danger. She tried to rationalize. In danger, but from what? Belloti was dead, dead, dead. He could do her no harm. She must stop this nonsense, arrest this fear which crept up and tapped her on the shoulder – causing her heart to palpitate, her palms to grow sweaty. She poured a brandy, then ran her finger along a dust layer on the sideboard. There was going to be plenty to keep her occupied tomorrow. With new guests arriving the place must be spotless. She settled into the chair.

Now she was as good as alone, her normally secure, comfortable surroundings felt distinctly uncomfortable. As though someone or something had done something unspeakable – right here in this room.

In the Treviso palazzo, twelve sat down to eat. There were eight men and four women. The host recited grace – backwards of course, then congenial conversation took place in muted tones. They were catching up on the gossip. Later, everyone complemented Lucia on the meal. Wonderful – she had excelled herself. She beamed with pride. Then it was time for the toast. All stood and raised glasses to the diabolical Lord. They downed the warm sweet liquid with relish.

At the head of the table, their towering Adeptus Major sat down again. The others followed suit. He tapped his glass delicately with a knife three times.

'And now we come to business. As some of you may already know, our plans for Lugrezia's passage have to be changed. We had hoped for a fitting farewell. However, sadly that is not to be. A replacement has to be found for Daniela, Lucia's niece. Our host knows of a number of suitable candidates. But before he speaks I am sure you would all like to join me in congratulating our newest member of his recent promotion. It seems our last efforts were a great success. Join me in a toast if you would.'

Everyone rose again and turned. The Monsignore remained seated and smiled benevolently.

The Adeptus continued. 'And now I come to a rather more unpleasant matter. We have recently come under suspicion. If immediate action is not taken a path may lead to our door.'

Several members inhaled sharply.

'However, there is no cause for alarm. Fortunately, we are able to inflict some damage which should keep him from prying any further into our business at least for the time being.'

The others nodded and smiled knowingly.

'And now I will hand over to our honoured host who will tell us how we are to acquire our next unwilling subject.'

The fat man, with tomato splatters on his front, rose and scanned eager faces. 'In the old disused prison camp there are a group of squatters – junkies. They are filthy undesirables, but we can none of us afford to be particular at the moment. Besides, they are unlikely to be missed . . . my dog is being led from the trail, as we know, however we must be prepared for any eventuality.'

The assembled nodded, agreeing.

He glanced to the empty place at table. 'One of us is selecting a suitable candidate for tonight's ceremony as we speak. I am sure she will find it an easy procedure.' He took a small plastic packet from his pocket. 'They will do almost anything for this and there's plenty more to keep our brood mare from bolting. For those of you who indulge, please, help yourselves.'

CHAPTER 21

The ruinous façade of the prison building towered against a vermilion sky streaked with bright blue flashes. A lone figure gazed up at the weeds sprouting from the crumbling brickwork. Within the many broken windows of the upper floors, occasional fires glowed – lifelike eyes in a carcass.

Alicia wore a headscarf and dark glasses. An Italian Jackie Onassis, she picked her way through the long grass and weeds. Something stung her bare leg. She swore and rubbed the place vigorously, then walked on.

Within the huge gloomy interior, water dripped incessantly, in single drops, echoing through the vast emptiness. The place had an eerie, forgotten air, permanently stained with the aftermath of lives cruelly taken before their time. Alicia was neither moved nor afraid. She kicked at the rubbish and looked around for the staircase to the upper floors.

She gazed suspiciously at the long flight of stairs. The wood was rotting in places. It looked unsafe. She took off her shoes and tentatively placed her weight on the first step. It creaked but didn't give way. She tried the next and the next, ascending with extreme caution.

A rat poked its head over the top step and peered at her, its nose twitching. She had a phobia about rats. In her darkest nightmares they crawled all over her, gnawing away at living flesh. She screamed and grabbed the rail. It came away in her hand, and she almost tumbled to the floor below.

When Alicia reached the next landing safely, she brushed the dirt from the soles of her feet and peered toward a flickering light at the far end of a vast room which ran the entire length of the building. She put her shoes back on and made for the fire with a purposeful walk.

As she drew nearer, she could just make out several dark shapes, huddled together for warmth in a room so humid it was like a sauna. Must be cold turkey, she thought. A few threatening, shadowy forms stood by the wall. They watched her approach with dark staring eyes, saying nothing.

A boy who looked no older than fourteen was extracting the filth from beneath his nails with a small penknife that had been a gift from his father. The gentle greengrocer had long since given up looking for him. He believed he would come home in his own time. But it had been two years now and the boy was still here, perpetually cold, hungry; a helpless victim enslaved by harsh reality. He didn't look up as she approached. 'Got any money on you?' he asked.

'Why should I give you anything?' His directness irritated her.

'Makes no difference – we'll take it anyway.' His tone wasn't menacing, just resigned. He continued with his manicure.

Alicia ignored him for a moment and scanned the shapeless bundles. Long bare legs protruded from a large cardboard box.

The boy followed Alicia's gaze. 'She won't be any use to you.'

Alicia rummaged in her bag and took out a 10,000-lire note. 'That's all the cash I've got so don't even think about attacking me, right?' She sounded fierce.

He took it from her and shrugged. Then he placed it inside his boot and defiantly held out the knife to two older boys. They looked far too ill to take him on. Despite his lack of years, the boy was well developed. His forearms were strong from exercising on the rusty iron rings in the west wing.

Alicia lifted a cardboard flap in the girl's flimsy shelter. Her hair was filthy but she might be fair. Her skin was white enough. She slept with her mouth slightly open but uttered no sounds. It was difficult to determine her age – she could have been anywhere between thirteen and twenty-five. She was also painfully thin – not quite Alicia's ideal. She liked them rounded. Tenderly, she pushed knotted strands from the girl's face. She was pretty enough. 'Wake up now,' Alicia said, shaking her roughly.

The girl snapped her eyes open and was faced with her dishevelled reflection in Alicia's mirror glasses. She sat up and spat on the floor to her right. 'What do you want?' she demanded. Her voice was hard, almost harsh, a voice that belonged in a world of violence and deprivation.

In contrast, Alicia spoke softly, as though she were enticing a child to eat. 'I've brought you something nice.' She took a small plastic packet from her handbag.

The girl snatched it from her and greedily opened it with shaking hands. She dipped her finger into the white powder and licked it as though it were sherbet. 'This is no good to me – it's only coke. Haven't you got any smack?'

Alicia clicked her tongue. 'Ungrateful, aren't we. Yes, as a matter of fact I do have some. I haven't brought it with me though – it's at home. If you come with me you can have all the stuff you need. There's enough to put you into orbit for ... ' She paused. 'Mm ... weeks at least.'

The girl's eyes shone at the prospect. 'Got any cash?' she asked, scrutinizing the elegant, moneyed appearance of this fairy godmother.

Alicia turned. 'I gave the monkey over there my last note – this will serve your purpose.' She handed the girl a multicoloured straw which had been cut down to size.

The addict snatched it and placed one end in the powder and the other in her nose. With a filthy finger on the other nostril to hold it closed, she hoovered the entire contents of the bag in several long drawn-out sniffs. Alicia was astonished. There had been a gram at least in the packet, enough to give the average person a cardiac arrest if consumed in one go. The girl leaned her head back.

'Now I feel better – thanks.' She lit the stub of a cigarette and inhaled. 'What do I have to do for this stash of yours?'

The fairy godmother placed a firm hand on the girl's tiny breast and stroked it sensually. 'Let's just say I would like you to entertain me ... and a few of my friends.' The girl had closed her eyes. She bit her lower lip then opened one eye knowingly. 'Fine. But I've got to see if I fancy you first.

Alicia glanced at the boy. He was watching closely. It was risky but ... She took off her glasses. Pale green eyes glinted in the firelight. She unwound her silk scarf and shook out gleaming auburn curls.

The girl's look was hard. She leaned forward and pulled Alicia's blouse to one side, exposing her right breast – and her black sunburst tattoo. 'Very nice,' the girl murmured. 'And funky too.'

Alicia pushed her away. 'Not yet. You need a bath first.'

The girl laughed. 'Sure I wouldn't want to make you too dirty – not yet, anyway. When does the fun start?'

Alicia pulled her to her feet. 'Right now,' she said. 'Let's go, shall we?'

By the inadequate light of a solitary candle, Grapper sat at the tiny table in the corner of Bella's studio apartment, and pored over his textbooks like an overgrown schoolboy. Last-minute homework. He was wracked with worry. Miles had inadvertently opened a can of worms. Only they weren't so much worms as vipers. Somehow he'd got to close the lid again before it was too late.

His knowledge of the occult was pretty extensive but even he was at a loss. Where was Daniela coming from? The symbols on the dagger were half Hermetic but the influence wasn't Hermetic or Gnostic – where the path of worship led to higher wisdom. This was much more debased. The symbols were corrupt. Could it be straight witchcraft? There was certainly an ancient tradition here in Venice.

The Venetian witches of the sixteenth century had escaped, without exception, the grisly fate of their European counterparts. Not for them the horrors of torture or the barbecue. The Venetian church presided over inquisitorial proceedings like benevolent aunts at a tea party, ensuring that the few found guilty were sentenced merely to penance or, at worst, to a stint in the stocks of St Mark's. Of course the vengeful peasants, who had suffered misfortune as a result of laughable spells which inflicted gout or bad luck, took great delight in pelting the high-minded with putrid fruit and vegetables.

The élite Necromancers had been even more protected, and had largely evaded arrest altogether. They were tipped off in advance by their paymasters – priests who actually blessed them before their conjurations, to ensure a good spirit came on the scene and not just some stray demon. These so-called good spirits gave the names of future council members and provided knowledge which helped them to triumph over their enemies. Yes, they were a protected lot all right.

But the tradition of what Grapper considered to be harmless witchcraft had died out in the late seventeenth century. What he was dealing with here was diabolical witchcraft, Satanism, pure Dennis Wheatley country. There was no doubt in his mind that Daniela's Satanic leanings were born from some kind of group activity. Her mother had obviously been a member of some kind, so, as far as he was concerned, the source had to be the same. If Daniela wasn't yet an initiate she'd certainly been destined for it. Her reference to the audition at the Paris conservatoire had definite Faustian overtones. She must have promised them something in return. But what exactly?

He went over the facts again and again. When he felt he was getting nowhere fast, he tuned into the other channel for further education. His mother wasn't playing ball. She was otherwise engaged. Frustrated, he turned back to the books and studied the Key of Solomon. Daniela hadn't drawn even a rudimentary pentangle on the floor of the museum. She was either reluctant to deface the marble or inexperienced in the rules of conjuration. Maybe she hadn't intended to call anything up in the first place. Perhaps it was merely a sacrifice without purpose. This notion puzzled Grapper. It was highly unusual to sacrifice a human without the promise of reward. Was she simply a nutter? No, he couldn't swallow that either. She was a malevolent little bitch. She'd had something in mind all right. But what? The slender facts didn't really add up to anything meaty.

He sighed and closed the book, rubbing his eyes. Bella turned over and ground her teeth in her sleep. She threw the covers from her damp body on to the floor. Grapper sighed and went over to the bed. He gazed at her nakedness for a moment, considering himself lucky. She was so pretty, this little minx. He wondered what sort of mother she'd make. He felt suddenly excited about the baby. As the strain floated away for a brief moment, he covered her and kissed her lightly. Green spikes brushed the pillow.

Grapper decided to give up for now and join her. Dog-tired, he pulled off his boots. Please God let this ordeal be over soon, he thought. Deep down he knew that was impossible. Daniela had been a threat to Miles when she was living but psychically Grapper knew she was even more of a threat now she was dead.

No, he wasn't going to rest until he'd found out what she was up to. If she came near his friend again he'd wipe her out once and for all. Maybe then the dust would settle on all of their lives again. They'd certainly sleep easier – of that much he was certain.

Alicia's car bumped along the long dirt track that led to the palazzo. The girl, who had been sound asleep, woke up suddenly. Her body jerked with the movement. She held on to a strap which hung above the passenger door. 'Where are we now?' she asked.

'We've arrived.' Alicia turned into the circular drive in front of the imposing façade. A number of cars were parked down one side.

'Wow, this place is huge. Looks like there's a party going on. You must have money to burn.'

Alicia laughed. 'Not burn – just have a little fun with.'

She took the girl through the stately marble portico into the magnificent dining room. All conversation halted abruptly. The master of ceremonies stood up and extended his hand.

'Well Alicia, I see you have brought us a young guest.'

The girl took a half-eaten slice of black rye bread from his plate. Ignoring his extended hand she chewed and scanned her opulent surroundings. 'This is really neat,' she said with a full mouth.

De Chesaris nodded to his secretary, his Adeptus Minor. His look said, 'You've done well.' The others eyed the girl hungrily.

Alicia pushed her into the vacant place at table. 'Eat something now, then we'll put you into a nice hot bath.'

The girl seemed more pleased by the food than the prospect of the bath. She took a peach and ate it with relish. Nodding in turn, one by one the others retired to prepare themselves for her welcome party.

Lucia Belloti made the long ascent to her friend's bedroom. Lugrezia was propped up against several pillows.

'Good news, Lugrezia. Alicia has brought a girl. It will be tonight.'

Lugrezia sighed and quivered slightly with excitement like a young girl on her wedding day, nervous yet thrilled the moment had finally arrived. She had been waiting a long time for this. Now, tonight, her journey would be completed and a new life would begin. She could hardly wait.

Grapper snapped his eyes open. He had seen a fire, a campfire? Dark shrouded forms danced around it. When they discarded their cloaks their nakedness gleamed in the firelight. They'd chanted in muted tones, their bodies writhing, invoking evil. Somewhere a ritual was happening. Someone was about to die. He looked at the small clock by the bed. It was twenty to twelve. He wondered, should he telephone Katerina to make sure she and Miles were okay? It was late but he had to be sure.

'Pronto.' Katerina had been dozing. Grapper insisted she check on Miles. She didn't understand why he was concerned but she obliged anyway.

She shuffled down the hall and opened the door to his room. Everything seemed fine. Miles was sleeping soundly. She bent over him and listened to his breathing. With his eyes still closed, Miles spoke to her in a soft voice that didn't belong to him – in fluent Italian.

Alicia led the junkie, who was now replete with heroin, down and down an endless winding staircase into the cellars of the palazzo. She wore a white towelling robe. In stark contrast, Alicia was wearing full-length black. They entered the circular room where the faithful were gathered. On pewter metal stands, six black candles flickered. An old woman, dressed in a white gown, rested on an invalid bed next to a high draped altar at the head of an intricate pentangle which had been expertly painted on the floor.

De Chesaris was imposing in full regalia. This was his most favoured ritual. The passing of life from one form to another. He smiled at the girl. Her eyes were glazed, her pupils fully dilated. Alicia led her to the altar and took off her robe. The faithful hissed like snakes in a pit – a live shrew had been dropped among them.

Alicia moved the girl's body until her legs were draped, slightly apart, over the altar. De Chesaris stood by her. A semi-circle was formed and the chanting began, becoming more and more intense as the followers grew impatient. De Chesaris raised a hand, silencing them.

Kneeling he recited Mass, in reverse, and kissed the girl between the legs during moments when a priest would have kissed the altar. The Monsignore winced. This was the only part of the ceremony he was uncomfortable with. The Rosicrucian order he had believed he was being initiated into had malformed into this blatant excuse for devil worship. But of course he couldn't leave the order. That would be too dangerous.

As the powers of darkness were called upon, the chanting resumed. He went along with the frenzy as usual.

Once again De Chesaris silenced them. 'We the assembled open our hearts to the great god Pan. Let him fill us with his presence. I call upon him to accept the life of his servant Lugrezia. Let her be reborn in the afterlife. Let her walk among other great souls of darkness. Give her power in death. Power to do your will.' At this he fell to his knees and spoke in a voice so impassioned it sounded almost hysterical. 'We call upon you. Let the dead walk to avenge themselves. To wreak havoc on the living. Let the sun turn black. Let the world fall away to nothing to be reborn as your world, where evil reigns supreme and all that is holy is abolished forever, into that darkness where you have been imprisoned for so long. We call upon you to walk among us. Sow discord in the hearts of all who disbelieve.' There was an expectant atmosphere. Nothing happened.

He picked up the long ritual knife and blessed Lugrezia with a reversed sign of the cross. He bent over her. 'Have courage,' he whispered.

She nodded. 'I am ready.'

Alicia stood by with a chalice, held just beneath her neck. With a swift, sweeping movement, De Chesaris slit the old woman's throat. She gagged, choking, slipping away. As the blood flowed, Alicia caught her life source. The assembled hissed again, growing ever more impatient. The girl tried to get up, but was now hallucinating.

De Chesaris went to her with the chalice and made her drink. Dark rivers ran down her chin as she gagged. He took a long drink himself and handed the chalice to Alicia. He discarded his robe and gave the command for the others to do the same. Then he turned his attentions to the girl. His congregation passed this communion blood and watched as De Chesaris pounded into the girl, all the time chanting that this child would be given at birth to the powers of darkness, their gift to the dark forces to which they were eternally enslaved. Alicia observed, patiently awaiting her turn. When each of the men, bar the Monsignore, had violently taken the girl, the women fell on her. Alicia delighted in their multiple rape of this pathetic individual, who could only stare at the painted ceiling as hands abused her flesh. The men stood around and watched, their lust spent. The question of AIDS didn't enter their minds. They were the protected few. The Monsignore felt differently. He wasn't a true believer. That is why he always abstained.

Breathlessly, Katerina told Grapper what had happened. He said he's be right over and told her not to go into the room – no matter what she heard. He put down the receiver. Blood pounded in his ears like rhythmic fingers beating a warning drum roll.

Miles felt as though someone was inside him, clawing at his stomach, tearing tissue. He was freezing. Then he was burning. He opened his eyes. The room was turning. He tried to lift his head. Impossible. The effort made him cry out. A familiar voice whispered in his ear. Then it was inside his head. He held his temples and screamed. Pain seared through him like a comet. He called out. No one answered. He reached for the bedside light and managed to turn it on. A rose-coloured glow flooded the semi-darkness. A comfort. He turned his head to the open window. Lace curtains drifted into the room. He felt afraid of something unseen – a presence. The breeze increased. The feminine lilt taunted again. He could feel warm breath on his cheek. He called out to Katerina. Pain shot through him again. Why didn't she come? He tried to get up, struggling on to his elbows.

The table in the window shot across the room as though it had been moved by a very strong man at immense speed. He gasped and closed his eyes in terror. When he opened them again Daniela was standing at the foot of his bed. Her diaphanous image shimmered as though she was a heat haze. Her arms were outstretched, inviting.

His screams woke the policeman who was dozing lightly in a shop doorway across the street. He listened intently and took out his radio. When the screams stopped, he put it away again. Someone must have had a bad dream.

CHAPTER 22

In the place where pigeons walk and lions fly, Grapper entered the St Mark's Basilica. He stood by the door, an envious outsider, listening to the heavenly strains of the Palestrina Mass as though it were a conversation he would love to be part of yet knew he could never join. Although raised a Catholic, he was an ardent disbeliever and had no time for the manipulative constraints of the faith. His presence here was wildly hypocritical. But he had to get some help from somewhere – this was as good a place as any. He lit a thin white candle for his mother's restless spirit. She had found it difficult to settle in life – death was merely an extension of her inability to accept the inevitable.

The candle threw light on to his face, into penetrating eyes. His fair skin was even whiter than usual. He looked like death – ghostly, mournful, a spectre of the punk era, seriously out of place in the tiny side chapel. A few mothers raised their eyes and frowned. However, despite the intrusion, they continued to beg the Almighty's forgiveness – desperate mutterings, not to be interrupted.

Grapper knelt and prayed too, but to a different God. His was not the God of opulence, of over-the-top purple and gold, of exploitation of the weak. His was an all-seeing God who had given him a gift – a gift that he now cursed for its weakness. For the first time in his life he was afraid of it. Very afraid.

Fabrizio, seated outside the Café Quadri, waved enthusiastically to Grapper as he crossed the square sending pigeons up into the bright blue sky. It was an incredible morning, full of hope.

Grapper joined his friend at the table. Although it was only 10 am a beer had already been ordered for him. Dewy moisture trickled down the long glass. Grapper's throat felt dry. He picked up the beer and took a long drink before speaking. Then he passed pleasant conversation before Fabrizio finally intercepted the charade.

'Tell me about last night. I know you. This is very bad, no?'

Grapper looked at his fat friend with steely eyes, hardened by the memory. 'Sure it's bad enough. Miles is lucky to be alive, that's all.'

'What 'appened then? You said ... you said the girl came back. It is not possible, surely.'

Grapper took another drink. 'Oh, it's possible all right.'

'So 'ow come 'e's not dead now, the Americano? If she wants him. Why she not take heem?'

'That's the problem, Fab. I don't know. Anyway I've blessed the room with holy water now. There are Communion wafers in the corners of his bedroom and on the threshold. That will hold 'er off. She can't get to 'im now. As far as I'm concerned it's over. All we have to do is get Miles off the hook with the police and get him the fuck away from here. Tomorrow at the latest.'

Fabrizio nodded. It sounded like Grapper had the situation under control. 'So, what you want me to do?'

'You'll have to make a sworn statement – that yer saw me and Miles in the bar. Marcello said the alibi checks out but if I know 'im 'e's bound to want written proof from ya – and a few of the others.'

Fabrizio shrugged. 'That is no problem. Anything for you, my friend.'

Grapper drained his glass. 'What about the others?'

Fabrizio beamed with pride. 'Please, you will leave this to me. I will round them up like cows and make them bark like dogs, eh!'

Grapper managed a smile. 'Right, that's great.' He glanced at his watch. 'I've got to go. You should be on the stall, shouldn't yer?'

Fabrizio signalled the waiter. 'Not today. My little Claudia she is – 'ow you say – minding the ship.'

In a beautiful building attached to the magnificent church of Santo Agostino, which overlooks the Grand Canal, Marcello stood in a huge mahogany-panelled room with his hands clasped idly behind his back. He studied the priceless Tintoretto. His fingers entwined and flexed alternately. He sighed in deepest appreciation of this masterpiece. The thought crossed his mind, that the painting was far beyond the reach of a mere Monsignore.

A token of someone's gratitude? Connections? Perhaps. At the far end of the room a door opened and a man entered the room. Greying hair suggested he was in his mid-fifties. Of average height, he was quite good-looking in a holy sort of way; clad in black with a bright purple sash around his waist, his air was serene yet authoritative. He extended his hand.

Marcello took a few steps towards him. 'Monsignore, thank you for seeing me at such short notice. I hope this isn't an inconvenience?' He took the man's hand. It felt cold.

The Monsignore sat down at his beautiful desk. 'This is not an inconvenience at all. Please sit down, Inspector. I see you are an art lover.' He leaned forward attentively.

'Of course. I have made it my business to acquire as much cultural knowledge as I can. Only a fool would live in this great city and not be seduced by its many treasures.' The analogy of a man without knowledge in Venice being akin to a eunuch in a harem came to mind, but, remembering whose company he was in, he kept the joke to himself.

The Monsignore took his obvious cultural bent as a statement of intelligence. 'Now, what exactly do you wish to know, Inspector?'

'I am here because it is said you are a great authority on witchcraft and matters of the occult.'

The Monsignore smiled wryly. 'That is very flattering. A great authority? Alas, I think not. However, I do know a great deal about the subject.'

Marcello took the ritual dagger from a large black leather bag. 'This is a murder weapon. There are strange symbols inscribed upon it. The script appears to be Arabic. I wonder – could you try to identify them for me?'

The Monsignore took the dagger and studied it for a brief moment, turning it over and over in composed hands. 'Well, this is very simple, Inspector. The script is Hebrew. What you have here is a Sephirotic Tree. This is of Cabbalist origin. The Cabbalists believe it is possible for the living to unite with God – that one does not have to die to reach the microcosm. To avoid contact with demons, the Cabbalist must have knowledge of words of power which will paralyse evil spirits and compel the angels to open their gates, thus ensuring a safe transition.'

Marcello looked confused. This wasn't what he had been

expecting to hear. 'Forgive me, Monsignore, but your analysis does not give me the impression that these symbols are in any way linked to witchcraft – in fact, it sounds quite spiritual.'

The Monsignore handed back the knife. 'Yes indeed, the tradition is extremely spiritual. But you see, that is what puzzles me. What you have here is an enigma, Inspector. The Tree is not strictly legitimate.'

Marcello studied it, none the wiser. 'In what way is it – not legitimate?'

'The Sephirotic Tree on that dagger is in reverse. Whoever this obscenity belongs to, they are far more concerned with the passage into death than life.'

Miles gazed at the open window and longed for a breath of fresh air. But the air was still now, no longer breathing. His skin felt clammy. He leaned over and took a sip of water. His head throbbed, he was desperate for a painkiller. But Grapper had taken them away and wouldn't let him have any more. Even after what had happened last night – at a time when he most needed them. No matter, tomorrow he'd get them back. Tomorrow he would be far away from this place. He'd had enough of Venice to last him a lifetime. Whatever Grapper implied, he knew what he'd seen was real. It was no hallucination. His friend could try and explain it away with talk of the aftereffects of sedatives but he knew damned well what he'd seen. Daniela had been right there – in his room. Alive again. She had come for him. She wanted him.

The ample remains of his breakfast lay on a tray at the end of the bed. Grapper munched on a cold croissant, frowned, and spread it with preserve from a tiny glass pot. Jam for individuals. Greengage. He didn't like it much but he was starving. 'So do yer see what I'm getting at? I know you thought you saw 'er, but I'm telling yer, mate, it was just the drugs.'

Miles continued to stare out of the window. Sighing for freedom. 'I know what I saw. I've told you. She was here. I'll grant you it was only for a few minutes . . . but she was here, damn it. She wanted something.'

Grapper knew bloody well she did. 'Look. The sooner we get yer away from 'ere the better. I'm going to buy yer train ticket this afternoon. If I'm right Marcello can't keep you 'ere without some special dispensation. We won't give 'im time to get it. Yer'll be long gone by the time 'e sorts himself out. Remember what I told yer about the times when we were at the bar. Don't fuck up. And remember to tell 'im you went to the Ca' Rezzonico – in case 'e brings a fingerprinting kit wiv 'im. That way yer'll be covered. Got it?'

Miles nodded. 'Sure. We were at the bar from nine until just after midnight. I got drunk. Then you brought me home.'

Grapper handed Miles a brown paper packet. 'Here's the book I was telling yer about. Read it later. I'm going to hide it until after Marcello's been. I wouldn't want him to get the wrong idea about yer.'

Miles took out the book and read the title aloud. '*The Devil and All his Works.* Good, this should be quite educational. It may even have some startling theories about ghosts that don't exist,' he said sarcastically.

Grapper took the book, ignoring his tone, and went to the wardrobe. 'Yeah, there's a lot of stuff in it you should find interesting.' He pushed it beneath the clothes. The hot-water bottle was still there. 'I'm sure ya think yer right about Daniela's ghost, but I'm telling yer it's all in yer 'ead.'

Miles looked over at the writing table. It was back in its rightful place. That he certainly hadn't imagined.

'I've got to go and do some work. I was meant to be at the market at eight. Slippery Ed's gonna kill me.'

Miles took another drink. 'Who's slippery Ed?'

'Eduardo the eel man. I call 'im that 'cause they're 'is favourite – I think it's 'cause 'e likes to chop 'em up while they're still alive. 'E says it makes 'em taste better.'

Miles felt sick again. He sighed. 'Give me a break – get lost. I'll see you later.'

Grapper closed the door and went downstairs. Away from his friend's scrutiny, his expression said it all. He looked totally drained.

Katerina was on her hands and knees scrubbing the hall floor. She straightened painfully as he came down the stairs. 'Where you go now?' she asked. Her head was full of questions. She was desperate to find out what last night had been about. She had been terrified.

'I'm going to work, but don't worry, I'll be back later on

tonight. Just keep an eye on 'im. Everything should be all right now. Don't move those Communion wafers, will yer. And for God's sake don't get 'em wet.'

Katerina looked to the thin line of white rice paper littering her doorstep like virginal confetti, the aftermath of a union definitely not made in heaven. 'I will take care,' she said. 'I put the bag of the girl's in the cellar. But later, we will burn everything, yes . . . and Mario's book.'

Grapper smiled at her. 'Yeah. We'll get rid of all this crap and then I'll go through every room in the house – to cleanse it. I think from now on everything's going to be okay. I promise.' He kissed the top of her head.

She wiped her furrowed brow, brush in hand. Water dripped on to her dress. 'Okay, I will see you later. You come for dinner maybe?'

He walked out of the front door and turned. 'Yeah, that'd be great. Now try not to worry. I've taken care of everything. Yer safe now.'

With a deep sigh, Grapper closed the door and wished he could be as sure in his heart as he sounded.

In a small square, lined with shops and cafés all bustling with pre-lunchtime activity, Marcello and Gianelli sat outside a bar drinking citron pressé and espresso. Marcello's toasted sandwich was half-eaten. Gianelli, who had devoured his at the speed of light, eyed it hungrily. Marcello pushed it toward him and spoke of their leads, which barely amounted to anything, in a fashion which implied he was merely thinking aloud. Now the American boy could not be regarded as a true suspect, they had precisely nothing. Marcello flatly refused to believe the presence of the occult in this case was anything other than a red herring – a dead end in the maze. But then he had seen something, with his own sceptical eyes. Something that couldn't be explained away. Something that had frightened him. Gianelli of course knew nothing of this ethereal experience. Marcello wouldn't dream of imparting this waking nightmare. He wanted to keep his sergeant's respect.

He issued instructions for the next round of interviews and told Gianelli he was going back to see the Monsignore as agreed. The Monsignore had said he needed to consult the Corpus Hermeticum, a Cabbalist bible, in order to determine the meaning behind the perverse Tree of Life inscribed on the murder weapon. He'd told Marcello it would be a lengthy process.

'Shall I relieve our man on surveillance duty?' Gianelli asked casually. 'We don't really need to keep it up now, do we sir? I mean, if the boy is no longer under suspicion . . .'

Marcello drained his glass and put on his sunglasses. 'I want round-the-clock surveillance until I tell you otherwise. Get someone else on the case right away. Who's next in line?'

'I'm afraid it's Brazzi, sir.'

Marcello groaned. 'Well, if that idiot can keep his eyes open for more than five minutes at a time, we might stand a chance of knowing precisely when our cuckoo plans to leave the nest.'

Marcello trudged up the stairs to his apartment. At his front door, he dropped the heavy bag of reference books on the floor and rummaged for his keys. Much to his frustration, he had found the Monsignore was unable to keep their appointment. He had been curtly informed that he would have to return tomorrow by a nun who had definitely missed her vocation in life; she would have been far more usefully employed in the army keeping barbarians in line. So, he'd stocked up with his own variations on the occult theme from the library. He was planning some intense research of his own.

As the door swung open, the smell of polish mingled with another, less pleasant odour that stank like a urinal. He was about to step over the threshold when he saw it. A pale greeny grey mound that looked like vomit and urine mixed. He put a hand to his mouth and wondered what the hell his cleaning woman was doing. Had she been unwell? Surely not, she would have cleaned it up. He took a large step over the mound and, unaware of the danger, found it merely puzzling.

In his open-plan kitchen he ran the taps into a bucket and gazed distractedly into the elegant sea-green living room. It had an excellent view of the Rialto bridge through large picture windows which led on to a balcony. He switched off the taps and added toilet cleaner. It seemed appropriate – he wondered what it would do to the parquet. Then he heard it. A muffled sound, coming from the bedroom. Someone was in his apartment.

He crept down the hall and listened outside his bedroom. A

rustling noise. Then it stopped. He pushed open the door but stayed hidden. He couldn't see anyone. He leapt into the room. The intruder was ready for him. A reproduction Tiffany lamp crashed on to his skull. He fell to the floor.

The woman dashed through the hall and almost slipped in the substance she had left there earlier. She cursed her stupidity. Now she would have to ask for a cleansing spell. The Adeptus would not be pleased.

Marcello groaned and felt his skull. There was no blood, just a huge lump. He'd been lucky the lamp hadn't broken. It could have been much worse. He stood up carefully and surveyed the damage to the room, expecting things to be missing. Nothing seemed out of place ... except his bed wasn't quite right. ... What had they have been looking for? He went to the bathroom and wet a facecloth. Holding it firmly against the lump, he went back into the bedroom. His head was pounding. He pulled back the sheets. There was nothing there. On turning the mattress, he found a neat flap had been carefully cut from the material. He pulled it back and stuck his hand inside.

From within the springs, he pulled black feathers, a mound of pink wax, and two tiny bones. He felt a little further and found a small round object. He withdrew his hand and looked.

It was a tiny fragile skull – an animal's, perhaps? Or an infant's.

The junkie threw herself against the walls of the padded room, tearing at her hair, mauling her skin. Deep gouges bled profusely in torn flesh. She screamed at the top of her voice. 'If you don't let me out now I'll kill you the first chance I get.' Her arms flailed violently as she flung her fragile body against the padded door.

Lucia opened the grill. 'You're not going anywhere, my lady. Just relax and calm down. If you're very good we'll give you something to help you sleep. If not – well, I think you know what will happen.'

The girl tried a different tack. 'Please, I'm in so much pain. I need something, a little coke maybe ... anything, just give me something, for God's sake. Even in rehab they give you something ...'

Lucia shook her head. 'Now that wouldn't do – wouldn't do at all. If I give in and you are pregnant, that muck you inject might harm the baby – and you wouldn't want that now, would you?'

'Marcello, it's Soldati. You sound half-asleep. Did I disturb you?' He was delighted at the notion of catching Marcello asleep on the job for once. 'It is a little late for siesta.'

Marcello had in fact lain down after taking two painkillers for his head. 'Let's just say I had a visitor.'

Soldati grinned. 'Extra-curricular activity, eh!'

'Unfortunately no. Someone hit me over the head with a very expensive lamp. Thank God it wasn't an original.'

'A burglary – are you all right? You should be examined, you're probably concussed – there may even be a fracture. Did they get away with much?'

'No. I'm not sure it was a burglary. They left things as opposed to taking. Can you send someone to check this place over? We may find something. Certainly one or two of these objects are – well, let's just say they're interesting.'

'Of course, I'll be there in about an hour. Don't touch anything and lie still. I rang because I thought you might be interested to know that we have the results on Luisa Riaggi's autopsy.'

Marcello grinned. 'You mean to tell me there's at least one woman you've managed to thaw out, Soldati.'

'Very amusing,' the pathologist said drolly. 'As I said, I have the results. Our victim died from asphyxiation, approximately four weeks ago.'

Marcello was puzzled, thought of Miles's note and stretched. 'Thank you for coming back to me so soon. When will you have the results on the girl?'

'It will have to wait until tomorrow. I'm afraid we're really backed up here. However, the cause of death is very straightforward. Her neck was broken, so pretty, like a tiny bird's ...' Soldati drifted into thought, picturing Daniela's nakedness, beautiful against cold steel, her blood washing away as though she were merely meat, without a soul, tragically ceasing to exist. Normally his work had little effect on his emotions but, somehow, she was different.

'Are you still there?' Marcello interrupted his train of thought.

Soldati returned to the land of the living. 'Yes, sorry. We took a vaginal swab. You'll be pleased to know there was a trace of semen. I should be able to give you a blood type tomorrow. I'll take a look at your head later but I'm sure it's been damaged for some time. It would explain your warped sense of humour.'

Marcello smiled as he hung up. He stood up with some difficulty. An express train was screaming through his brain.

The strange objects littered his glass coffee table. He picked up the tiny skull and fingered it. He was no expert but was left in no doubt that these things were in some way meant to bring about his destruction. He was obviously close. But to what exactly? Marcello dropped the articles into a plastic bag and went to do the job he had been putting off. Before cleaning up the foul mess on his inner doorstep, he took a spoonful and placed it into a plastic bag for Soldati. He didn't really need an analysis. He'd come across this mess many a time in a junkie's hellhole. It was the skull he wanted to know more about.

Miles flicked through Mr Wheatley's anthology. He appeared to have covered every conceivable aspect of the occult imaginable. However Miles wasn't particularly interested in his far-reaching account of Eastern and Western occultist tradition. He restricted himself to background information on Crowley, who was of extreme interest. After all, he had owned something that reputedly once belonged to him. Then, burrowing down under the sheets, he turned to a section entitled 'Of Apparitions'.

Tale after tale of spirits, both good and malicious, washed over him with little effect. He was an intelligent, rational person – surely a logical explanation existed for everything paranormal? At the very end of the section, Wheatley spoke of elementals who are born from evil thoughts and endeavour to maintain a life of their own. Wide-eyed, he read the last few sentences, muttering aloud: 'Normally they are invisible; but they are often seen by chronic alcoholics and drug-takers, on whom they feed as a spiritual parasite.'

CHAPTER 23

While Miles found a justification of sorts in Wheatley's anthology, Marcello was engrossed in a book on the Cabbalist traditions of the Rosicrucian order, who had links with Freemasonry. The doorbell rang. Momentarily distracted, he stood up too quickly. His head swam. He gasped and rubbed his head. Steadying himself, he took faltering steps down the hall. Soldati stood on the threshold with a younger man. Marcello asked them to come inside. The vile mess on the doorstep had now been cleared away. A faint smell of disinfectant still lingered.

Soldati followed him into the elegant living room. A bookcase ran down the entire length of one wall. The low-level sofas were ivory leather. Two tall black pyramids looked like modern sculptures that would not have been out of place in a Milanese art gallery. They were in fact part of Marcello's precious hi-fi system.

Soldati let out a long sigh. 'My my, your salary must be astronomical – to afford such a place like this. It's wonderful. I had no idea you had such immaculate taste.'

Marcello collapsed onto the sofa. 'I'm afraid you're wrong. I have good taste, yes, but alas not a fantastic salary. This apartment belonged to my wife's parents. When they died it was left to her. I took it as part of my divorce settlement.'

Soldati perched on the edge of the sofa and opened a black bag. He took out a pencil torch. 'You don't know how lucky you are, Marcello. Now, follow my finger with your eyes.' He held out his index finger and moved it up and down and from left to right. Marcello followed it with ease. 'Now fix your eye on something to your left and hold it very still.' Marcello obliged. The scientist examined the back of the eye, then put away the torch.

'It's as I thought – mild concussion. Are you in much pain?'

'A little, but it's not too bad. I have some painkillers left over from an operation for an impacted wisdom tooth. Perhaps I should take them? Paracetamol didn't do a thing.'

'That depends on what they are.'

Marcello reached for the tiny brown bottle. 'These are what he prescribed – I was in agony for weeks.'

Soldati read the label. 'These are the strongest you can get. Only take one – and no more than one. They'll knock you out otherwise. And don't drink alcohol. I know all about your excesses.'

Marcello bowed to the voice of authority and led the two men into his bedroom. They searched for clues but found nothing. They took fingerprints which Soldati guessed would only be Marcello's or his cleaning lady's.

'They certainly knew what they were doing,' he said as they walked from the bedroom into the living room.

Marcello sat down and took the sinister artefacts from the bag. 'I don't doubt that,' he said.

Soldati studied the bones. 'These look like animal bones, from a rabbit or a cat possibly.' He picked up the tiny skull and fingered it lightly, respectful of its fragility. 'This, on the other hand, is not from an animal. I'll need to do some tests, but I'm pretty sure it's human – from an infant; no more than two or three months old. Look, there is a hole where the skull had no time to close.'

Miles, propped up in bed with a tray on his lap, tucked into veal piccata. He was suddenly ravenous. He talked to Grapper, who had eaten earlier with Katerina, between mouthfuls. 'So it says in that book of yours that these "elementals" can feed off people. They can be brought into being just by someone having malicious thoughts. Maybe – and it's just a possibility – but maybe Daniela was taken over by one of these things, er, spirits.'

Grapper eyed his friend. He was certainly no fool. 'Yeah . . . of course it's possible, but I told yer, it was probably just the drugs makin' yer 'allucinate. The doc didn't give yer no more when he came today, did 'e?'

Miles shook his head.

'Well then, it should be out of yer bloodstream by now. And besides, I've protected yer room and I've put stuff by the front door. There's no way she could get to yer again – even if what yer saw was real.'

Miles put down his knife and fork. 'I'm telling you it was definitely real. Besides, in the book it says that these elementals can be seen by alcoholics – or drug users. In a way that's exactly what I was.'

This was of course very close to the truth. Grapper felt he had to divert Miles from this course. 'Look, even if the book is right ... there's no way yer gonna be bothered again. I'm coming back later – I'm gonna sleep on the floor wiv yer – so she'll 'ave to get past me first.'

Miles resumed eating and felt almost sorry he was about to acquire an unwanted bodyguard. He was fascinated by what had happened to him. Daniela's vision had enticed him to never-never-land. Part of him wanted to go with her, to see if it really existed. He was haunted not only by an infatuation that refused to die, but by intense curiosity.

No longer hungry, he put down his knife and fork.

''Ave yer finished then?' Grapper asked. Miles nodded. 'Right, I'm off. I'll be back about eleven. Now remember yer gonna be fine,' he grinned and spoke with a pseudo-American accent. 'At 6 am tomorrow. You're out of here, bud. History, right!'

Miles resumed his studies with Dennis Wheatley. 'Right. And if I'm asleep when you come back, for Christ's sake don't wake me. Sounds like we're going to have an early start in the morning.'

Marcello poured milk into a long glass and took a drink. He spat into the sink. It was sour. But it had only been bought that day. He checked the other carton – it was the same. He put a finger into the butter and tasted – it too was rancid. In fact, all the dairy products in his fridge were off. He checked the temperature. It was fine. It couldn't have blown a fuse – the light was still on. This was curious. The telephone rang. Distracted, he went into the living room and picked up the receiver.

The Monsignore at least had the decency to telephone after standing him up. 'I'm so sorry I wasn't available when you called to see me. It's bad news, I'm afraid. I have been unable to identify the true origin of your bizarre Tree of Death, as you call it. However, I will continue to research.'

'Thank you for calling. I've been doing some research of my own. Of course I bow to your knowledge but the Rosicrucian order sounds interesting. I'm convinced there may be a secular element in these murders.'

The Monsignore remained silent. Marcello took the silence to be mute agreement. 'I wonder if I could presume on you for a moment – I found some rather disturbing items in my apartment earlier today.'

Marcello described the objects and the mess on his doorstep. The Monsignore sounded as though he were considering the facts. Then he spoke. 'What you have in your apartment, Inspector, is known as ''fatture''. Fantastic as it may sound, these items, left by a witch, are meant to bring about illness or sometimes even death. In our Archivio dello Stato there are several accounts of victims turning prematurely black after death from one of these spells. Tell me, Inspector, did you tread in the substance on your doorstep?'

'Fortunately no, although I flatly refuse to believe that stepping in a pile of vomit would bring about my immediate downfall. A colleague has taken away the objects for further analysis. I hope to know more tomorrow. Well, I will wait to hear more from you. Once again thank you, Monsignore.'

Marcello did not attribute the sour milk to the presence of a witch. He replaced the receiver and glanced at the clock. It was half past seven. He had half an hour before going to meet Alicia. His head felt like a thunderstorm was raging inside. The humidity didn't help, a storm was also brewing outside. He picked up the bottle of pills and tipped one into his hand, doubting it would work. He swallowed anyway. Anything was better that this headache – he didn't want anything to spoil his evening. He had been without female company for far too long.

The Monsignore picked up the telephone and dialled. The recipient of his call answered, sounding annoyed by the interruption.

'De Chesaris, forgive the intrusion. I thought you might like to know your plan has failed miserably. Zalchi's dog, as he calls him, is still very much on the trail, and – if I may make an assumption – if you do not take immediate action, he will soon be snarling at our heels.'

CHAPTER 24

Miles frantically rummaged through his clothes, tossing them aside when they didn't yield what he was searching for. He was in agony. His head felt as though it were being compressed in a vice. He had some emergency spares somewhere. Finally, in his denim jacket pocket, top right, he found a tiny paper packet. He tipped the contents into his shaking hand. Eureka! Two dihydracodine. Thank God. He swallowed them rapidly with a gulp of water and got back into bed. He shut out the light. A film of red swam before him, threatening, pulsating. He prayed for release from this damned pain, for sleep, peace.

Katerina sank back in the chair, exhausted from her labours. The house was now spotless, expunged of neglect from top to bottom. She could clean the visible dirt, but what of the invisible? That would have to be left to Grapper's doubtlessly capable hands. She tried to relax. Her solitude was both a blessing and a curse. The disturbing events of the last few days had made her edgy. It unnerved her to be alone now - even in daylight. But Grapper had told her everything was going to be all right. Of course she believed in him. What possible choice did she have? Besides, tomorrow Miles would leave for Florence and her life would become her own again. Thoughtfully she sipped a dark full-bodied red wine that warmed her chilled bones. Yet almost at the precise moment she contemplated the restoration of peace to her troubled domain, something drew her attention to the table by the window. Her husband Mario's photograph album, which had been returned to the cellar along with Daniela's flight bag, was somehow now back in the room - on her table - demanding attention. It was open.

Fear gripped her pounding heart, squeezing, constricting. She obeyed a silent command and shuffled to the table, peering at the album with a sidelong look. Within the familiar confines of grey and white, wasted bodies dangled, suspended in their agony: Mario gazed at her once more, sheepish with innocence.

She sensed his presence. Smelled him. He was close to her. Very close. With spectral urgency his handwriting appeared as if by perverse magic on the page, scrawling diagonally across the scene – urgent, informative.

Shaking uncontrollably, she gazed at the words. 'We were three!'

Her stressed aorta palpitated wildly, urging her to calm herself. She had suddenly realized a half-forgotten truth. Her terrifying dream of childhood had not been of Belloti. The devil she had seen was this tall, gaunt soldier who smiled wryly – the very man that Miles and Grapper had also dreamed of. The man she'd said she had never seen before.

Marcello felt mildly queasy as he walked across the little wooden bridge to the Poste Vecie restaurant. Quaint carriage lanterns glowed invitingly in the twilight, welcoming him to this rather clichéd setting for his investigation. He bowed his head and descended into the low-ceilinged vestibule. Stefano, the maître d'hôtel, beamed at him as though he were a long-lost relative. He treated most of his regular customers this way.

'Luciano . . .' he said warmly. 'This is indeed an honour.' He kissed him on both cheeks and led him into the quaint restaurant. When he didn't continue on to the terrace, Marcello seemed disappointed.

'What's this, Stefano? No al fresco tonight?'

The little man sawed the air theatrically. 'You must be crazy, Luciano. Do you think I would put my customers outside when there is a terrible forecast? I think we will have much rain tonight. Can you not feel the thunder in the air? Besides, I have given you the best table inside . . . here by the fireplace.' He pulled back the chair for Marcello, who smiled and sat down. As the napkin was placed in his lap with a flourish he glanced at the huge seventeenth-century stone fireplace which dominated, centre stage. He'd always wanted one like this for his living room. He surveyed the scene idly as Stefano summoned the waiter. Several couples were engrossed in each other, locking their gaze over flickering candlelight.

'Yes sir, what can I get you?' An effeminate waiter broke Marcello's momentary and somewhat uncharacteristic envy of the couples' intimacy.

He looked up. 'I'll have my usual, I think,' he said, picking up the menu. 'A campari soda.'

Grapper sat at the bar, chatting idly with a few of his friends. He felt almost light-hearted. He'd earned a moment's respite from the intensity of Miles's troubles. He laughed away his fears with superficial appreciation of Fabrizio's dreadful jokes. Someone offered him another drink. He wanted to keep his wits about him but agreed readily, driven by a depression no one sensed. He downed the Scotch in one go and ordered another triple. As the alcohol took over, he became the life and soul. Ever the clown, appearing the fool. Yet those who knew him well saw through the façade. Bella glanced nervously at Fabrizio. It was unlike her man to drink like this. Something was very wrong.

Alicia, confident that she looked absolutely stunning, dispensed with formality and kissed Marcello's suntanned cheek. He studied her appreciatively. She had taken great care over her appearance tonight. It showed. Dark brown hair, gleaming with recent auburn highlights, was pinned in a neat chignon; her lithe figure was captivating in an impossibly tight skirt suit with large padded shoulders. The muted sage green complimented her skin tone beautifully. She sat down, removing a gold and green scarf which had been loosely thrown over one shoulder. Placing it carefully on the back of her chair, she turned to face Marcello and flashed him a dazzling smile. Huge gold earrings reflected a glimmer of candlelight and sent it twinkling across the table to him.

'You look beautiful, Alicia.' Marcello sounded sincere because he was. 'What can I get you to drink?'

Alicia glanced up at the waiter, who was now hovering on cue. 'A Bellini, please.' She opened her clutch bag on her lap and extracted her cigarettes. 'Do you mind?' she asked politely.

'Not at all,' he said. In truth he hated anyone smoking before dinner. Very uncivilized.

She lit the cigarette herself, before he could get to his lighter, and exhaled to her left. Then she gazed deeply into Marcello's hazel eyes. He was almost impossibly handsome. He had to be married. A man like him must have at least one wife and one mistress. For a woman in her late thirties the options weren't particularly plentiful – at least she had a shot at both camps. She suddenly remembered why she was here and launched into mindless conversation, attempting to extract as much detail as she could about Marcello's personal life. Feigning interest.

He of course was guarded and sidestepped her questions, answering with questions of his own. However, he took care not to appear cold; she had to be manipulated a little. He must get into that office.

And so they danced cautiously around one another while an invisible wall kept conversational intimacy at bay. The waiter brought their order. Alicia seemed pleased by her choice of scallops and bacon. Marcello toyed with his langoustines, his appetite now dormant.

During the meal their small talk couldn't conceal a strong attraction. Eventually the moment came for Marcello to make his move, albeit a professional one. He was about to jump in when the heavens opened. Torrential rain pounded on the tiled roof and cascaded into the tiny strip of water outside.

Alicia smiled. 'I love the rain, don't you? It's so refreshing to walk in, especially at night. So romantic, don't you think?' Her voice held more than a hint of promise. Marcello perused a mental image – peeling off her wet clothes before a roaring fire in true Hollywood style. Romantic – perhaps. Also arousing. The thought gave him an immediate erection. He considered postponing his use of her in favour of another sport.

Stefano descended on their table, rudely breaking the mood. He tapped greying hair knowledgeably with his forefinger. 'You see, Luciano. I know what is best . . . listen to that rain. There will be a mother of storms tonight. Now, coffee for you, Signora?' He cleared away Alicia's plate of unfinished formaggio. The rapid dispersal of her carefully constructed ambience irritated her. She demanded an espresso in a strained voice.

Marcello asked for the same and got down to business. 'So Alicia . . .' He took her hand gently. 'What can you tell me about our friend De Chesaris?'

Miles blinked and opened his eyes. The pain was still there but it had diminished considerably. His bedroom was dark. It must be late. He tried to lift his head – it hammered mercilessly. He got the message and let it flop back on to the pillow. His mouth was dry, his tongue furred. He reached out for the glass of water by the bed. Suddenly, his hand began to shake uncontrollably. The glass fell on to the floor. He swore – what the hell was the matter with him now? His right arm felt like a lead weight. He needed a drink. He called out for Katerina, expecting the sound of doors opening, footsteps. There was only silence.

'Katy!' he called again – louder this time.

Downstairs, in the darkened gloom of the little salon, a motionless Katerina appeared to be sleeping. She was slumped in the armchair with her husband's faded photograph, the one she talked to when she was lonely, resting on her breast.

She didn't stir when Miles called out to her. Even the loud crash of his bedside table falling onto the floor failed to wake her.

Brazzi, the officer on surveillance duty who had also been dozing in a large doorway on the opposite side of the narrow canal, woke up with a start. Heavy rain partially drowned out Miles's cries from behind the open window. Brazzi put his head on one side listening. Had someone been calling? All seemed quiet now. He looked at his watch. Two hours to go until relief. What a night. He moved further into the doorway for increased shelter, took out his neatly folded newspaper and, with half an eye on the building, scanned the football results.

Grapper was now returning from the verge of a drunken stupor. Bella placed another inky espresso before him and urged him to drink it. She told him in heated Italian that he'd better sober up or she wasn't going to let him through the door.

He sipped the coffee, which was like warm glue. 'I'm gonna walk you 'ome then I've to spend the night with Miles. Didn't I tell yer?'

Fabrizio raised his eyes heavenwards and stepped down from the bar – out of harm's way. Bella's face was a picture of pent-up rage, as she demanded to know who he was sleeping with in a raised voice that amused the bar's other occupants.

Grapper was in no mood for this. 'Come on I'll take yer 'ome now,' he muttered tersely.

She took her powder-blue angora sweater from an iron hook on the door to the kitchen. She still had an hour left of her shift-time. Anna told her not to worry – she would cover for her. Just this once.

Once outside Bella let rip. Grapper walked ahead, ignoring her jealous accusations. Her tantrum fell on deaf ears. She'd calm down – eventually.

Bella trotted along behind him, screaming abuse. Grapper mused that it was he who worked on a fish stall – not her. Perhaps they should swap jobs. She could certainly drum up custom with that voice – probably from Milan. What was he letting himself in for by marrying this shrew? When the penny dropped that she was getting nowhere fast she turned on the waterworks. This of course had the desired effect. She looked a sorry mess, bedraggled, stained by tears and rain. He pulled her into a shop doorway. At first she resisted his comforting arms, pummelling his chest with frustration – frustrated more by her unfounded suspicions than his seeming indifference. He kissed her roughly and, as usual, she gave in, melting against him. As she pulled up his shirt, all other thoughts and obligations became obscured by his desire for her. It would keep. He'd just have to be a bit late.

Alicia stretched out her bare legs in the speeding water taxi. She looked smug. This time everything would go according to plan. She'd make sure of that. She couldn't afford another stupid mistake. But she wanted to have some fun with Marcello before De Chesaris got his way. He might consider himself all-powerful but she had learned a few tricks from the Magus herself. Besides, she'd earned this one. She lit another cigarette and inhaled deeply, gazing at Marcello with purposeful eyes that intimated she meant business.

Marcello, who had been watching her with interest, spoke above the roar of the engine. 'Something is obviously amusing you, Alicia – you look like an exotic cat who has just successfully spilled the cream . . .'

'Do I?' she said, thinking to herself that if she got her way, that was exactly what she was going to have. Spilled cream of the tastiest kind.

Their taxi came to a halt outside the elegant façade of De Chesaris's office building on the island of San Giorgio Maggiore. Marcello leapt from the launch while it was still moving and extended his hand. Alicia threw the lighted cigarette into the water and took his support.

'Adding to the pollution? Shame on you,' Marcello chided.

Unsure if this was a sarcastic joke or a true reprimand, Alicia didn't comment. As Marcello extracted a note from his wallet, she rummaged through her leather clutch bag for a large bunch of keys. Marcello paid the driver and took a giant step into the recess to escape the thunderous rain. She struggled with the keys, trying to find the right one. He took them from her gently and opened the door. 'Thank you,' she said as they stepped into a dimly lit hallway.

'Shall we go up?' he asked, pulling back the intricate cast-iron lift doors. Alicia stepped into the lift and hummed to herself as he wrenched the doors shut with a loud metallic clang. She pressed the fifth-floor button and leaned against the wall for support as the lift juddered into action.

Marcello observed her intense look of unrepressed lust and pressed the emergency button. The lift came to an abrupt halt. Somewhere in the building a bell jangled. There was no one there to hear it. Without a word, he went to her and, taking her face in sensual hands, locked her in his gaze for an agonizing moment. Then he kissed her with all the conviction and hunger one would expect from a man who hadn't made love for three months. She responded greedily, almost violently. He pulled at her jacket – she tore it from herself. He moved her silk shirt aside and kissed her collarbone descending toward her right breast. She smelled musky, almost animalistic. He pulled her breast to his mouth and noticed she had a black sunburst tattoo. He found this amusing and asked her what it was.

'You'll find out in a moment,' she said as she sank down his taut body. She undid his belt, then his fly – he tried to protest – this wasn't how it was meant to be, he was usually the one in control – but the flesh was definitely weak. He submitted, certain he could contain himself. With sensuous, expert precision Alicia slowly dragged a climax from him. He gasped, angry with himself – he was normally able to hold back. He'd wanted to give her a good time first.

Alicia wiped her mouth and looked up at him. 'Traditio Mystica,' she whispered.

He stroked her hair, his eyes were closed. 'Mmm?' he murmured.

She stood up and rearranged her clothing. 'That's what the tattoo means – Traditio Mystica.'

Miles placed his bare feet on the worn carpet. He had no idea how long he'd dozed for. Why hadn't anyone come when he called? Perhaps Katerina was out. The room was now very dark. It must be late. Grapper should be here soon. Light from the street filtered through the lace. Outside, thunderous rain filled the canal, swelling it by several inches. Sometimes these summer storms caused minor floods. The rain sounded as though it was here to stay.

He stood up uncertainly, then, holding the back of the chair for support he turned on the standard lamp. His room was in disarray; the bedside table lay overturned, his things were strewn over the carpet. Fragments of glass from the broken water bottle spread over a dark wet patch. Drops of water still glistened on his reading glasses. Daniela's cassette, all Miles had left of her, was saturated.

Miles knelt, wincing as tiny shreds pierced his skin. He picked up the tape, at first fingering it gently; then he tore the membrane from its housing in long ribbons. Even this memory had been cruelly stripped from him. He buried his face in his hands. Why had he come here? Was he cursed, singled out, a plaything of malicious gods? Were they up there laughing? Placing bets on whether or not he would go mad? At this moment he felt he could. Why not have a breakdown – maybe then he would be left alone.

He rocked for solace, close to the edge, muttering, 'Why?' over and over again. An unanswerable question. Then gradually he heard it. A familiar sound. As though some unseen force had heard him and decided to respond. Light, wavering strains from a delicate high soprano drifted down the alleys, across the tiny bridges, down the street and through his open window. The haunting sound floated above the rain and the rumbling of distant thunder, calling to him. He raised his head. Was he imagining this? He got up painfully and went to the window, leaning into the warm shower of raindrops.

The beautiful aria, strangely amplified by the compression in the air from the approaching storm, filled the empty backstreets. The atmosphere crackled with natural and unnatural tension as his chanteuse floated toward the pensione, displaying her wares, a perverse wandering minstrel. But she could not perform within. No, the way was barred. Her audience would have to come to her.

Miles watched the spectral cloaked figure approaching over the little bridge. Her enticing melody was meant only for his ears, beyond normal human hearing.

She stood for a moment, allowing him a closer look.

He felt strangely resigned as she turned, inviting him to come to her with outstretched arms. Ebony hair gleamed in the dim light against ivory translucent skin. A smile hovered on blood-red lips, shimmering, enigmatic.

Miles rushed with new-found strength to his waiting clothes, overjoyed because she had come back for him.

Alicia and Marcello stood at the picture window in De Chesaris's office and watched the storm raging over the lagoon. A bright pink fork streaked across the sky, a pyrotechnic finger. Nature's fireworks. Marcello turned on the light.

'You know, it does not matter how many times I see this phenomenon, it always makes me feel privileged to live here. Our summer storms are quite the most spectacular I have ever seen.'

Alicia went to a large black cabinet and opened it, revealing an array of elegant crystal glasses and decanters. She took a cut-glass bulb from the whisky decanter with a delicate chink. 'I expect you'd like a drink.'

Marcello eyed the reel-to-reel tape recorder and the extensive rows of tapes. 'Thank you, but no. I have to keep a clear head if I am to find what I am looking for. Perhaps later on.' He winked at her suggestively.

She smiled. If only he knew that later on he wouldn't be capable of anything. She poured herself a stiff measure. 'Damn, I'll have to get some ice. I can't drink this stuff without it.'

'Does De Chesaris have a particular cataloguing system for these tapes?' he asked.

'The session tapes? Yes, they are filed by initials and date . . . quite simple really,' she said, walking towards the door.

Marcello tried the desk drawers, all of which opened bar one. 'Do you have a key to this drawer?' he asked.

'No. Only De Chesaris has a key. Why?'

Marcello ignored the question. 'Is there a safe here?'

Alicia laughed. 'Not that I know of. De Chesaris keeps nothing of value here - nothing except his ego, that is.' She went to fetch the ice.

Marcello rooted through the desk. There were several copies of client bills and one or two case notes on recent sessions. He read a recent report on a patient which was written in psycho-speak. Jargon. Impossible to decipher. He scanned the tapes, hoping to find some evidence that might shed new light on Daniela's mental state. He could find nothing that related to her but one label read 'FCV 23/5/90'.

He took the tape out of its box and threaded it skilfully on to the machine. He pressed Play. The tape spun round slowly. De Chesaris's dulcet tones identified the session.

'Subject: Franco Vercini . . . the twenty-third of May. Further regression.'

Marcello sat at the desk and listened to De Chesaris talking Franco into a hypnotic state. Once satisfied the patient was completely under his influence, he began. 'Now Franco . . .' he said soothingly, 'you are eight today. What are you doing at this moment?'

Marcello heard a series of snuffles.

'I'm coming home from school.' Franco's voice was childlike.

'That's nice, isn't it Franco? Today is your birthday, you're going to have a party, aren't you?'

Franco began to cry.

'Why are you crying? You want it to be your birthday, don't you? There are bound to be presents.' De Chesaris was positively brimming with sugary concern.

Franco sniffed. 'No, I don't want it to be my birthday,' he said emphatically.

'Why not? All little boys like birthdays.'

Franco began to scream hysterically in a high-pitched voice. 'No, I don't want to go . . . Pappa will be there . . . don't want to go!' He sounded as though he really was having an eight-year-old's tantrum.

De Chesaris tapped loudly three times. 'Now you are no longer

Franco. You are Paolo, you are grown and you are very angry . . .' he said sternly.

The deep guttural voice took Marcello completely by surprise. 'What the fuck do you want, arsehole?' it rasped.

De Chesaris seemed unperturbed by this abrupt change in character. 'I apologise for disturbing you, Paolo. I only wanted to talk . . .'

'I know why you want me to talk to you . . .' The menacingly raucous laugh gave Marcello the chills. It was a tone he was all too familiar with.

'Who do you want me to carve up this time, arsehole?'

Alicia walked in with the ice bucket just as the tape went blank. Marcello swore and wound it on. He pressed Play again. Nothing.

Hurriedly he grabbed a large curved paper knife and drove it into the locked desk drawer.

Alicia watched him with mild amusement. She wondered if she should tell him he was getting warm.

He forced the drawer open and rummaged through reports which were obviously meant for no one's eyes but De Chesaris's. The patients were all women. Some had been admitted to a mental home – Clinica di San Patrizio, in Treviso. It appeared from the headed notepaper that De Chesaris was on the board. This didn't surprise Marcello at all.

Alicia stepped up to the bookcase and pressed a minute concealed button. 'I think this may be of more help to you, Marcello.' The bookshelves slid back, revealing another, hidden library of a less professional kind. Psychology textbooks bowed to a more primitive form of mental manipulation. Ritualistic rape of the mind. These huge leather volumes looked hundreds of years old. Several were displayed within temperature-controlled sections, suggesting great age and fragility.

The pieces now began to fall into place. Marcello tensed. He'd had hazy suspicions. Now they were rapidly solidifying. His radio began to crackle. He ignored it and stepped up to the books for a closer look. The protected titles were Latin. *Malleus Maleficarum*. Where had he heard that before? Then he saw it. *Corpus Hermeticum*. The Hermetic bible the Monsignore had spoken of. His mind was racing now. He studied the unprotected volumes. Taking one down from the shelf he opened it carefully.

On the facing page a small symbol had been stamped in the top right-hand corner. A small black half-sunburst.

Marcello understood. This was a trap. He'd walked straight in. He'd been following a legitimate lead but her scent had disarmed him. He was furious with himself for being so gullible. He closed the book and turned around. De Chesaris was standing next to Alicia. Marcello stared at her. 'Traditio Mystica', he said. De Chesaris applauded quietly, sarcastically, then took a small gun from his left pocket and aimed at this irritant.

Marcello tightened his jaw. Why hadn't he come prepared? He wasn't off duty. He shouldn't have signed in his gun. The radio burst into life. 'Inspector, come in, come in . . .' Brazzi sounded desperate.

De Chesaris nodded. 'Please answer, Inspector, but be careful what you say.'

Marcello picked up the radio and pressed Talk. 'Pronto, Marcello.' The radio crackled again.

'Inspector, can you hear me? The American boy has left the pensione. I am following him. Pronto, Inspector . . .'

De Chesaris smiled and took the radio, turning it off. 'What a pity the storm has rendered your radio useless, Inspector,' he said sneeringly. Pale eyes bored into Marcello's skull. 'It is a pity you will not be able to go to the aid of your colleague, is it not?'

Marcello stared back with nerves of steel. If this snake was going to send him on his way, he was going to make damned sure he learned the truth before departing from this world into the next.

CHAPTER 25

Miles staggered after the fleeting form, oblivious to the stares of passers-by. He looked drunk. In a way he was : punch-drunk. He was soaked to the skin but it didn't seem to matter. On and on he stumbled after the strange inhuman entity he was infatuated with. For a few agonizing moments he lost sight of her. Haunted eyes darted furtively along the dank, dim stone corridors, across the tiny bridges. He gazed longingly into the darkness for a glimpse of accursed midnight blue velvet. He grew panicky, believing she had left him behind. Then, like a mistress whistling to her lost dog, Daniela's high soprano rang out from the echoing gloom of this warren of alleys. Her cloak swished around a decaying corner as Miles ran after her with pitiful steps.

'Daniela, wait for me . . .' His voice was drowned out by the crashing thunder. But she heard him. She waited for a moment then strode cruelly ahead. He would have to walk faster – she couldn't wait forever.

He lumbered around the last corner of his deadly journey, peering after Daniela as she crossed their familiar lichen-covered bridge. Brazzi followed closely and wondered who the boy was calling to. He saw only Miles.

Daniela wheeled around and reached out to Miles, observing his distress with dark staring eyes. He held on to the crumbling wall for support as the rain lashed his face. Daniela leered obscenely. He was once again within her grasp. But no, patience. He reached out to touch her – she was suddenly further away. With a defiant flourish, she turned towards the dark green doors of her destination, leading him on in a mesmerizing dance which he hoped would never end.

Grapper felt in reasonable spirits as he walked towards the pensione. He'd left Bella tucked up in bed, exhausted after their mental and physical tussle. She had at least accepted that he wasn't being unfaithful. Far from it. He was in for a shafting all right but it wasn't the kind she'd been thinking of. He tapped the phial of holy water in his pocket for reassurance. It would prove invaluable if things got out of hand. There were very few things that could contain a malevolent elemental. Holy water was one of them. Of course he'd never come into contact with one, but he'd read up on it. He looked to Mickey Mouse - twenty to twelve. He was late. He hoped Katerina would still be up. It was unlikely she'd be able to sleep until he got there.

He kicked a piece of rubbish with his boot and thought about her tragic life. The poor woman must be beside herself with worry by now. What with this sadistic bastard from her past gnawing away at her like a disease, it was hardly surprising she was afraid. He was glad he knew how to cleanse a house of evil. If anyone needed protection she did. He'd certainly picked an atmospheric night for it. Grapper turned up the collar of his leather jacket to fend off the driving rain which was coursing uncomfortably down his neck.

Turning into the alley he saw a graffiti artist spraying a neo-Nazi message on the wall in dayglow pink. They'd never learn. He muttered a silent prayer for the containment of Fascist evil. Unsure which was worse, the known or the unknown, he walked away.

At the door to the pensione he rang the bell, listening for Katerina's soft shuffling footsteps. He whistled nervously while he waited. Something nagged at him. Alcohol always dulled his gifts, but now they were emerging again he felt uneasy . . . something was wrong. He tried the door. It was open. He could feel pins and needles embracing his lower back. He rushed into the hallway, calling for Katerina. The salon door was closed. He cursed under his breath. He should have known better. He rushed upstairs to Miles's room and threw open the door. The bed was empty. It looked as though there had been some kind of struggle. Physical or metaphysical?

With panic constricting his throat, he checked the bathroom, then bounded down the stairs taking them two at a time, almost tripping on the worn carpet. He wrenched open the door to the salon. Katerina was still slumped in the chair. Her ashen features reflected an ethereal peace which owed nothing to the living. He knew even while he searched for a pulse that she was dead. With tears in his eyes he blessed her, kissing her cold forehead regretfully. This was his fault. If he'd gotten here earlier instead of letting his dick rule his brain. Too late now . . . 'Sleep well, darlin', yer've earned the rest,' he whispered.

The red glow from the fringed lampshade highlighted a serenity that abolished her pained expression forever. For the first time in a decade Katerina looked totally at peace. Her contentment suggested to Grapper that whoever had come for her, it was someone she had known and loved. He gazed down at her wistful smile and asked his mother to keep a watchful eye on her. Respectful to the last, he was about to fetch a blanket to cover her when something distracted him. He glanced at the photograph album. It was back on her table. He took a look, reading the words, 'We were three.' Had Katerina written this? Had she discovered something she wanted him to know before she departed? He doubted it.

'The moving finger writes . . .' the bird in his vision had forewarned him. So that was it. Another kind of message. He didn't have time to find out what it meant. Miles wasn't here. There was only one place he could be.

Grapper ran out of the front door and sprinted towards the little bridge. Then, almost as an afterthought, he turned and ran in the direction from whence he had come.

He pulled a 5000-lire note from his pocket. Waving it under the nose of the startled graffiti artist, he snatched the can of paint from his side, shaking it to make sure it wasn't empty.

'Ta, mate,' he said, pushing the money into the astonished youth's hand. Then he turned and ran back as fast as he could.

De Chesaris smashed the hand radio on the side of the desk with a violence obvious yet contained. Marcello observed, saying nothing.

Alicia admired Marcello's resolve. A pity he could not be initiated. He had an inner strength she found fascinating. As though reading her thoughts De Chesaris turned to her. 'Would you like to amuse yourself with him before he departs, my dear?' He placed a cold skeletal hand on the back of her neck. 'Or perhaps we should show Marcello what you are capable of . . .' De Chesaris's tone was menacing. Marcello felt uneasy. 'Take the knife from our friend, would you?'

She did as instructed.

'Now perhaps you would demonstrate how far you are prepared to go to please me.'

Despite the fact that she had deceived him, Marcello was suddenly afraid for her.

De Chesaris didn't take his eyes from his prey. He merely gave an instruction to Alicia who followed him as though she were taking dictation. 'As your master commands you, cut your left arm. Make the incision six inches. You will feel no pain.' Marcello took a step forward. 'Please, Inspector, do not interfere. I would hate to have to kill you prematurely.'

Alicia held the knife against her skin. Her expression was glazed but her hand was shaking, suggesting repressed fear. With a swift single movement, she slashed her skin. A bright red line appeared. Marcello was certain that if measured it would be exactly six inches long. De Chesaris handed her a handkerchief. 'So you see, Inspector, I can impose my will at random. I trust therefore you will not try anything stupid. Alicia, wake up now. Please go and get the launch and bring it to the front of the building.' His tone suggested this was a request. She knew better. It was another command. In control of her faculties again, she felt disappointed that she would not be party to Marcello's destruction. Winding the handkerchief around the wound, she walked away, high heels clicking on the marble.

'Now, Inspector, I am sure you would like a drink and a cigarette before you die – that is customary, is it not? You do smoke, if I remember rightly.' De Chesaris paused, savouring the moment. Considering himself to be a civilized man, he was graciously granting a last wish. 'Do not make the mistake of reaching into your pocket for your cigarettes, Inspector. One never knows what may be lurking there. As I said, I would hate to kill you prematurely. You will find mine in the ebony box. I hope the brand pleases you.'

Marcello extracted a cigarette and looked around for a lighter.

'There, Marcello,' De Chesaris motioned to a small brass skull. 'A souvenir from Spain. Their festival of the dead is quite an occasion. Press the nose – you'll find it amusing, I'm sure.'

Marcello calmly placed the cigarette in his mouth and picked up the surprisingly heavy skull. He pressed the nose as instructed. A high blue and yellow flame shot out from the central lobe. He lit the cigarette and placed the skull in front of him.

'Perhaps you would do the honours and pour the drinks, Inspector ... as I am otherwise engaged,' De Chesaris said drolly.

Marcello edged towards the cabinet, wisely keeping his distance. With remarkably steady hands he poured two large whiskies. 'Ice?' he asked his captor.

'Dreadful American habit, don't you think? No, not for me.' De Chesaris waved the gun at the desk. 'Put it down there, would you?' He sounded as though he were instructing a slovenly servant.

Marcello went back to his original place behind the desk. The storm over the lagoon raged behind him. 'Perhaps you would indulge me a little as you are being so unusually congenial, De Chesaris.' He could feel death tapping him lightly on the shoulder. 'There are one or two things I'd like to know.'

'Of course.' De Chesaris took a controlled sip. 'I knew your curiosity would eventually get the better of you. In fact, after Alicia failed in her attempt to incapacitate you, I was relying on it. I assumed her charms were entirely secondary.'

Marcello ignored his snide comments. 'I have a theory ...' he said, after taking a long drink.

'And that is?' De Chesaris was in his psychological element – the pedigree cat indulging in a final game of tag with a sewer rat. Rats are highly intelligent.

'After hearing Franco's tape, I thought you might be using hypnosis on some of your patients to test Jung's theory of the alter ego buried deep within the subconscious ...'

'Go on, go on.' De Chesaris waved the gun lazily.

'An alter ego which is capable of certain unnatural acts. Acts which would be abhorrent to the subject's normal behavioural patterns.' Marcello drained the whisky.

'My, my, you have been doing your homework, Inspector. I am quite sure you and I could have enjoyed many a challenging game of chess, were you not about to depart from this world into the next.'

'So, am I right?' Marcello asked, fingering the brass skull.

De Chesaris swilled the whisky in the crystal glass. 'Only partly I'm afraid, Inspector. You see, if you had researched a little deeper, you would have discovered that Jung took his studies much further. He was a great believer in psychic energy – the existence of a parallel psychic energy to our own material state, which could be unlocked through hypnosis. It is that parallel which I am largely interested in bringing to the fore. I have discovered through a great many years of painstaking research that he was right. It does exist.'

'So you used Franco Vercini to kill Belloti. I knew he couldn't possibly have planned the murder alone.'

'Well done, Inspector. In a way you are quite right. However, I must confess it was I who did the actual deed. I merely implanted a memory within Franco. Under interrogation he would have sworn blind that he killed his father. Unfortunately, it was far too important a task to leave to a virtual autistic. He should have been committed years ago.

Marcello breathed a deep sigh. That murder he'd thought he'd solved. One down, three to go.

His captor smiled. 'Now I suppose you are wondering why it was necessary to kill him in the first place. Should I tell you, I wonder? I suppose as you are about to die, it can do no harm.'

Marcello closed his fingers tightly around the brass skull.

'I served with Belloti during the war. We were in the same division in Abyssinia and later in Yugoslavia. He was my superior, of course, but I felt he showed great promise. So I recruited him into a tradition. A tradition he later threatened to expose.

'Traditio Mystica,' Marcello interrupted.

'Good, good. Yes, Traditio Mystica: it means "to keep a great secret". As handed down from the goddess Isis to her son Horus. Our foundations, however, are far from mythological. Mainly, our beliefs stem from a long-standing tradition of witchcraft that has existed in Venice since the fourteenth century. We inherited a network from our ancestors, Inspector. There is a web in the corridors of power. Our methods are somewhat unconventional, but we get results. Belloti achieved a position of great power with the assistance of some of our long-standing members. Of course, as I am sure you have already guessed, that is how he came to be exonerated for his war crimes. However, he was not content with mere freedom. He sought repentance in old age for his so-called sins. He became fearful that he would not be granted a position of power in the afterlife. The stupid fool wanted to avoid damnation at all costs.' De Chesaris smiled. 'Of course, it would have been far too late anyway – he should have had more faith. In my experience the devil looks after his own. It is our belief that the faithful will not only reach Nirvana but will be granted a powerful position in the hierarchy of the after-life. Hell is such an unfortunate word, don't you think? I am sure for mere individuals the prospect of damnation is terrifying. The Catholic Church has held that fear over people for far too long. It is a rather one-dimensional view, in my opinion.'

De Chesaris drew breath. Marcello didn't comment so he continued. 'I apologize, I digressed. We could not take the risk that Belloti might disclose too much about the order. I heard his confession, convincing him under hypnosis that I was a priest, and then the next day eliminated him.'

Now it was clear to Marcello. 'So you are devil-worshippers then – Satanists?'

De Chesaris laughed. 'There I must correct you, Inspector. Nothing so crude. No, we are more concerned with lesser demons who are easier to control and manipulate. I will admit that the odd sacrifice to ensure safe passage of one of our members is necessary. Usually it is woman or a newborn. I am afraid it is a very necessary evil.'

Marcello was horrified. 'And how, may I ask, do you select these victims?'

'Up until now that has been a relatively simple process. Occasionally the mental home, of which I am a director, transfers patients. I make sure they have no living relatives, their treatment is paid for by the state and they come to me for further research instead. The occasional patient has been used to breed from. Mostly they know nothing – they are merely vegetables, Inspector, and would not be suitable for sacrifice themselves. Our demonic masters are discerning. Besides, newborns always produce an immediate result.'

Marcello couldn't believe what he was hearing. He felt sick. 'You said "until recently". What changed?' He tried to sound dispassionate, but his voice trembled a little.

'Investigations into mental care were rumoured to be under way. We simply felt it was not safe to continue. Besides, there is a cache of junkies who would hardly be missed within the city. Where there's a will, Inspector.'

Now Marcello knew. His serial killer was standing right before him. A prime case of 'physician heal thyself'. Why had he killed the others? What possible motive did he have? He took a chance on holding the madman's attention a little longer. 'I accept all this, but why was it necessary to kill Daniela Riaggi? And how did you get in and out of the museum?'

'Daniela was very like her mother, Inspector. Wilful. Antonella was also an initiate into our order, an initiate destined for favours of the highest kind. However, she ran away from the inevitable, depriving us at the last moment. You see, Daniela was to be a sacrificial child but her mother chose to become emotional, denying us the pleasure.'

'Who was Daniela's father . . . I mean, who made Antonella pregnant?'

'That I am afraid I do not know. Antonella was initiated sexually by all members of the order. The multiple conception is necessary in order to avoid any emotional conflict over the infant's fate. When she ran away we used our contacts to try and find her. Given that Daniela was conceived on the 10 August 1971, numerologically her number amounted to three sixes twice over. The number of the beast – doubly powerful. She was destined for us. We could not let her escape her fate. I was delighted when she returned to Venice. She was to be sacrificed on the eve of her eighteenth birthday. To entice her, we told her that after her initiation she would be helped with her audition at the Paris Conservatoire. The Venetian equivalent turned her down. I couldn't understand their decision. I thought she showed great promise.'

The psychiatrist fiddled absently with the gun as he continued with Marcello's sickening enlightenment. 'Anyway, I digress again. As you know Luisa had been sending Daniela to me for treatment for years. She was partially aware of the order but believed it to be a purely Masonic fraternity. Belloti's family, who have been with us since the fifteenth century, naturally did not disclose too many of the facts. Eventually Luisa found out about our origins. She had never questioned her husband's business when he was alive. But after his death her curiosity got the better of her. She had been collecting evidence for years. Daniela took it upon herself to get rid of her. Naturally, as Daniela's mentor and confidant, Daniela felt I would be thrilled to hear of her grandmother's murder – something she had done all on her own, without incentive. She had found a letter from her mother to Luisa begging her to get Daniela away. One night, she listened outside her grandmother's bedroom door and heard her taping a letter to someone. She taped all her correspondence – her arthritis was crippling.'

Marcello felt triumphant; he had been right again. Now he had a true motive for Luisa Riaggi's murder.

De Chesaris droned on. 'It seems she too wanted to draw attention to us. Daniela felt it was quite natural to kill her. She was going to let nothing come between her and a successful audition. I was horrified. This we didn't want. When I read of the English girl's death it confirmed my suspicions that Daniela was psychotic. I knew it was only a matter of time before she was found out. I had given her an initiation task. She was to avenge her grandfather's suicide, thus ridding herself of his visitations, by taking another young life in the place where he died. Franco knew of a hiding place. I didn't doubt for a moment that Daniela would find out about it from him, thus achieving her goal. As I said, she was highly ambitious.'

Marcello felt the need for another drink and looked at the cabinet.

'Please, Inspector, be my guest.' De Chesaris was enjoying the effect these revelations were having on his victim.

Marcello poured another two whiskies and placed the ice in his glass with a delicate chink.

De Chesaris continued. 'The reason for this task was quite simple. Zalchi, who is incidentally one of our members – that is how we knew you would not be at your apartment when Alicia broke in – Zalchi informed me of your diligence. If you had questioned Daniela, I could not be sure that she would not give away far more than we wanted you to know. At least in the museum the young boy could be implicated in her murder, thus tying it up for you and ridding us of her instability.'

'What about the guard and Franco? Who killed them – you?'

'Patience. Franco was never meant to be there, but he had a habit of keeping his cousin company, and despite Daniela's instructions for him to stay away he disobeyed her. Consequently, he saw Daniela slit the guard's throat. The poor fool loved her so much he did not stop her. He was reduced to a gibbering idiot. I was there, I should know. After I broke her neck I left the boy to be implicated. However, after I had seen to it that the boy escaped safely by disarming the security alarm, Franco came at me like a madman. Which I suppose is what he was.' De Chesaris lovingly fingered the gun and smiled with a stomach-churning leer. 'It was not difficult. As a Magus I have certain skills.' He glowered at the chair before his desk. It moved a few inches, demonstrating a telekinetic skill. 'You see, Inspector, there are more things in heaven and earth. I expect my little trick surprised you.'

Marcello looked into the steely eyes and tightened his grip on the skull. 'Not at all, De Chesaris,' he said. 'I am not in the least bit surprised. However, it is a pity we are not living in the Middle Ages – you would have undoubtedly have been burnt at the stake for that little trick. Now, if you are as skilled as you say you are, why don't you simply break my neck just by looking at it?'

De Chesaris yawned pointedly. 'No, no. That wouldn't do at all. After I shoot you, Alicia is going to take your body out into the lagoon and dispose of it. As you have seen, it is extremely easy for me to impose my will on her. She would confess to your murder if pressed on the subject. She could hardly break your neck now, could she?' De Chesaris was growing tired of this mental excursion. Marcello heard the lift juddering. 'Women are so assured these days. I find the feminine need for male domination to be both fulfilling and curious.'

'Yes, I agree, it is very curious,' Marcello said as he aimed the heavy brass skull with precision at the centre of De Chesaris's high forehead.

A look of momentary indignation swept across De Chesaris's stony features, then, as the shadow of defeat clouded his vision, he teetered for a split second that seemed to Marcello like an eternity. Marcello rushed forward and grabbed the gun just as the towering figure crashed to the floor.

CHAPTER 26

The Ca' Rezzonico's dark green doors were open, although not to the general public. Tonight the museum would once again play host to a deadly scenario. No alarm bells rang out to signal intrusion. Only thunder shattered the silence with a series of almost deafening bangs. Torrential rain cascaded on to the slippery cobblestones as Miles ducked under the police tape and moved tentatively through the tiny courtyard.

Beyond the glass doors, Daniela waited patiently. As he approached, she smiled, gliding effortlessly up the grandiose stone staircase as though she were made of air. A will-o'-the-wisp, all light, within and without, not of this earth.

Miles followed her into the ballroom, Brustolon's gigantic painted outrages gazed down at the pair, watching. Somewhere within the vast empty rooms, something stirred. Life returned to a slumbering force, a force that would consume everything in its path.

Outside, in the doorway, Brazzi tried in vain to raise Marcello. He banged the radio in his palm, and spoke into it again. A breeze caressed the back of his neck. Tiny hairs rose on his nape. He spun around. There was no one there. He radioed the station. Mercifully someone answered. Just as Brazzi gave his location, the breeze became a wind which whipped his face and forced the radio from his hands. It fell on the stone. As he cursed and bent down to examine the damage, a hostile shadow hovered behind him.

Daniela laughed, a malevolent laugh, and drifted across the magnificent ballroom as though she were skating on ice. Tendrils of hair wavered like strands of dark seaweed beneath a cruel sea. She led Miles towards the inner staircase that led to the upper floors. He followed, glancing, as he passed the huge mullioned windows, at the fury of the raging storm. The gods were obviously displeased tonight.

Daniela turned, observing his slight hesitation. Was he in control all of a sudden? She spoke for the first time in a distorted voice that sounded like tinkling glass. 'Come along, Miles . . .' Her voice echoed on and on, as though she were calling to him from within a void. She was, a void she desperately wanted him to cross.

The effect on Miles was devastating. He now lost all sense of reason, hauling himself painfully up the staircase after her; not knowing if this was a dream, and not caring.

Daniela sang joyously as she drifted through the Hall of Paintings. The song was an aberration; discordant, without real structure, strangely haunting in its unity with a parallel world which exists in the hearts, but not in the eyes, of men. The ghostly aria filled the marbled chambers with obscene pleasure. Now her confinement would be more bearable – she was going to have company. The exquisite room was periodically illuminated by flashes of bright pink lightning that seemed to accompany her performance, acknowledging her presence.

The dazzling light sent pain searing to the back of Miles's head. He cried out but carried on, shuffling after Daniela, just as a trusting leper follows the healer.

Marcello waited, gun in hand, behind the door. As Alicia entered the office he grabbed her roughly and threw her onto the floor. She cried out, astonished. How had he overpowered her master? She couldn't believe it. Marcello must be strong – mentally and physically.

He relieved her of the keys to the launch. 'Take off your underwear and rip them in half.' Marcello meant business. He knew she was wearing French knickers. They should suffice. For a moment she wasn't sure whether this was a sexual overture or not. She did as he said. He made her tie the unconscious De Chesaris's hands and checked they were tight enough, all the time keeping his eyes on her. She was a clever little bitch. He wasn't going to be taken for a ride again – once was quite enough. He handed her the large linen handkerchief from his breast pocket. 'Now gag him and make sure it's tight. His mouth is the most lethal thing about him.' There was no telling what De Chesaris might be able to do using his hypnotic techniques.

When Alicia had done as he asked, Marcello bound her hands with the remaining strip of silk and pushed her roughly into the chair where he could see her. He opened the window and listened for the sound of the police launch above the storm. They didn't have far to come. He had telephoned for back-up and learned that Miles was heading for the same museum. This confused him. He figured De Chesaris must have something to do with it. Within minutes he heard the distant roar of an engine and felt relieved.

De Chesaris started to come round. Marcello stood close by with the gun. 'It seems the game is not quite over yet, De Chesaris. Now I am going to give you the chance to witness your handiwork first hand.'

Footsteps pounded up the stairs and along the hall. Gianelli rushed in with two other uniformed policemen. All were carrying guns. 'Right, you two, take her back to the station. Gianelli, you come with me.' Marcello handcuffed De Chesaris, leaving the silk that was cutting into his wrists in place. He pulled him to his feet and roughly pushed him towards the lift.

In the launch, Gianelli drove as Marcello observed his captive closely. He couldn't afford to take his eyes off him for a second. Vipers were slippery. They had a habit of escaping.

Gianelli shouted above the roar of the engine. 'We've lost contact with surveillance, sir.'

'Keep trying . . .' Marcello yelled to make himself heard.

Relentless thunder raged above them as they sped across the lagoon to the Grand Canal. He wondered what exactly he would find at their destination. The thought that he might be confronted with a paranormal energy wouldn't have entered his head until yesterday. Before this case he'd been a hardened sceptic. But he had seen something he couldn't explain. He would never take anything for granted again. The core of his conviction was now eroded by the vermin of evil. He mused, with a wry smile, that even his assumed immortality had been threatened.

Grapper sprinted down the deserted alley to the little bridge. Adrenalin pumped through him. He knew he was running headlong into danger, but what possible choice did he have? This was all his fault. He should have known better. He had been defeated and he had to rectify that. He'd been certain Miles would be safe as long as Daniela was unable to enter the house.

He'd felt secure enough to enjoy himself, believing Miles was protected. Of course he hadn't bargained on the stupid bugger going outside. He ran into the museum courtyard and fell over Brazzi's prostrate body, almost knocking himself out. He sat up and banged his chest – he was severely winded. He turned the body. He'd arrived too late for this one. The man was dead.

On the second floor, in a chamber that led to the bedroom where they had hidden, Daniela threw open the picture windows. A stone balustrade overlooked the tiny quadrangle where renovations were taking place. Miles watched her with a naïve longing. 'You see, Miles,' she said, her voice lilting seductively, 'we will be together for all time. We can live here. It is such a beautiful place. You do see, don't you?' This compelling invitation echoed through the vast emptiness. Her cloak billowed in an ethereal wind, once again beneath it she was naked. Translucent skin cried out to be touched. Part of him wanted to run away yet most of him wanted to stay, here with her – forever.

He reached for Necromantic comfort like an unhappy child. Daniela opened her cloak wide and drew him in – a gesture of finality. He wrapped his arms around her, and unnatural warmth flooded his body. She felt so alive. Why wasn't she cold to the touch?

Daniela led him gently on to the tiny stone balcony. 'Look, there below us, Miles . . . it is the pool at home. All you have to do is dive in. You will not be hurt. We will be together again. You can see it, can't you?'

He looked below him, at first seeing only a blur of builder's materials and a tarpaulin which the rain pounded like an army of fingers on a drum. Then, as he focused more acutely, the courtyard became a glittering mirage of the pool he knew so well. Aquamarine water glistened invitingly. For some reason, his dream returned – as though it were still trying to make him aware of something he desperately needed to know. Once again he saw the old woman's wheelchair toppling into the pool. He blinked hard. The glistening water became canvas again.

'Think of it, Miles, we will be together for all time . . .' Outside, a solemn church bell, disturbed by the storm, rang once. A solitary toll.

Miles wanted to believe Daniela with all his heart. He desperately needed release from tortured memories. Death was surely not such a bad option, just like falling asleep – a long peaceful sleep. He closed his eyes and opened them quickly. The pool was there again, looking more inviting than he had ever seen it.

Somewhere, far far away, someone was calling his name. It sounded like Grapper. What did he want? Should he wait for him? Say goodbye? Miles hesitated.

'Almost there now, Miles.' Daniela held out her hands and helped him on to the balustrade. As he prepared to dive in he remembered Grapper's words in the dream. 'Look before you leap . . .' his friend had warned him just as the pool had turned to ice.

Uncertainty washed over Miles. He turned to Daniela for reassurance. She smiled knowingly. For a split second fear returned. He tried to step down but immediately lost his balance, toppling over the edge, screaming as his body flew through the air. He bounced on to canvas and open sacks of cement. A huge dust cloud rose up. Miles heard a ringing in his ears and passed out from the pain.

Like an injured bird that senses its fate, he lay there, motionless, not daring to move. Grey and white clouds of cement dust wafted around him like an impenetrable fog. Dense, surreal. Lukewarm fingers of blood traced the outline of his bruised cheek; broken limbs, now numb, felt as though they no longer belonged to him.

A smothering blanket cloaked his consciousness. He tried to resist the warmth, but the arms of oblivion proved stronger than he, and reached out from a familiar no-man's-land, pulling him ever closer.

Black shapes now whirled in a frenzied mass around the abomination's head as she leaned over the stone balustrade, surveying her conquest. A perverse Juliet calling to her dying Romeo. Dark tendrils of ebony hair framed translucent features with an undulating halo. A creation of the breeze which knew no boundaries. She was transformed – a living Medusa.

With open arms she floated down from her murderous vantage point, moving in for the kill. Her heart-shaped face lingered a breath away from his helplessness. She smiled knowingly. He suddenly understood, opened his mouth to speak, but could utter no sound. Fine white dust covered his face; the silent scream contorted his features into a grimacing mask. He was terrified yet somehow appeared comical – like a redundant circus clown.

Grapper raced down the length of the Hall of Paintings to the bedroom. He saw the open windows immediately and stepped on to the balcony. What he saw made him catch his breath. He felt unprepared, scared shitless. This was for real, 'Don't look at 'er, Miles!' he screamed as he wrenched the top from the phial of holy water. He muttered to himself, praying for strength. Daniela looked up at Grapper shouting incantations for the abolition of evil. He emptied the blessed contents on to the dark quivering shape below him and prayed to God it would work.

Miles kept his eyes tightly shut as Daniela's entity writhed in agony, inches from his face. Quite suddenly her screams stopped. He summoned the courage to look again. Daniela had disappeared.

'Miles, if yer can 'ear me for fuck's sake don't try to move!' Grapper shouted. 'I'm coming down to get yer. Don't open your eyes no matter what 'appens. Just stay there.' Grapper wondered where Daniela had gone. He knew better than to expect total success from one dowsing.

Marcello pushed De Chesaris up the staircase in front of him. He pressed the gun firmly into the small of his back. They could hear Grapper's voice echoing through the museum. Marcello tightened his grip on the gun and wondered if it would be of any real use to him. The mental image of Brazzi's body haunted him. He was a big man, not easy to kill, and he'd been armed.

Gianelli followed close behind. They reached the threshold of the spectacular Salon de Brustolon. The tawdry rococo gods turned above them. Marcello glanced furtively around him, wondering what he was going to find. Why had the boy come back here? His mind was filled with questions.

Suddenly, Daniela's delicate iridescence answered by materializing in the opposite doorway. She floated towards them. De

Chesaris gasped beneath the gag. He had never seen anything like it. Her power was beyond his wildest expectations. He had tried for thirty years to conjure an entity he could actually see. He'd fobbed off his followers with excuses when the great ones chose not to appear. Now he was face to face with pure malevolence. What joy.

Marcello's mouth dropped open. Fear tore into his gut. Daniela shimmered in the centre of the room. She was swaying like a snake, momentarily charmed. She opened her cloak a little, revealing snowy nakedness. Locking Marcello in a gaze that burned like an open furnace, she held out her arms. It was an irrefutable gesture. He was unable to resist, helpless. He moved towards her like an automaton, as though she were a magnet to which he was overwhelmingly drawn. His legs now belonged to someone else. For once he wasn't in control. Gianelli looked on, horrified. He moved quickly behind De Chesaris, taking Marcello's place, and pressed his gun against the doctor's back. For once in Gianelli's long career he'd acted promptly. He couldn't see the creases at the corners of the captive's steely grey eyes.

Daniela stared at Marcello. The room stirred, crackling with electricity. From nowhere, a vibrant polka sprang unnervingly to life, music played by the unseen hands of past musicians.

A spectral host of masked revellers in period costume filed into the room and began to whirl graciously around them, lost in the frenzy of their supernatural dance. Marcello's eyes widened in childlike wonder – the spectacle affirming a power he had so blatantly disbelieved. As ghostly figures cascaded furiously across the elegant ballroom, jagged flashes of nature's anger accentuated their existence – a commanding finger from the nether regions of hell, demanding that the spectators bow to this display from a hitherto unquantifiable power.

Grapper needed to find the inner door to the quadrangle. He ran into the ballroom. The scene was utterly incredible. He caught a glimpse of Marcello and the others through the dance and strode into the midst of the transparent apparitions, ignoring the frenzied spins of these spirit dervishes, passing through them as though they were merely projections on a screen.

Marcello took further steps towards Daniela, to join her in the swirling dance.

'Don't go any closer, Marcello ...' Grapper shouted above the intense musical compression. 'Close your eyes – it's only an illusion!'

Foolishly Gianelli did the same – an act which De Chesaris sensed. He spun around and knocked the gun from Gianelli's hand. Gianelli cried out and opened his eyes wide in surprise. De Chesaris, with his back to the room, locked Gianelli in his gaze. Marcello remained mesmerized by Daniela. In the centre of the ballroom Grapper was hurriedly spraying a dayglow pink pentangle on the floor.

'Don't look at 'er, Marcello. Come over here to me quickly.' Marcello was rooted to the spot – he heard Grapper but couldn't move. The dancers whirled past him as Daniela laughed triumphantly. While Gianelli was being slowly hypnotized into removing De Chesaris's handcuffs and bonds, Marcello stared ahead, unaware.

Abruptly the frenzied dance ceased. The dancers stood rigidly as though they were powered by clockwork and had wound down. With a painstaking slowness they removed their masks and turned to face Marcello, each revealing, hideously, his own face. The phantasmic throng looked to him with black evil eyes that reflected a diabolical force within. They shuffled towards him, their features gradually disintegrating with rapid erosion. Blue-grey flesh crumbled to nothing in the cruel light of the raging storm. Phantom breath blew their ashes into a swirling mass and then inhaled, absorbing their remains.

This demonic spectacle was more than Marcello could bear. A groan of anguish left his lips – he had just witnessed his own decay. Dust to dust. He sank to his knees. Dropping the gun he placed his head in his hands. Daniela mocked his distress, delighted at the effect she was having on her audience.

Gianelli removed De Chesaris's handcuffs, struggling with the key. The gag was still in place. De Chesaris had opted for hands first. If he was going to get out of here alive he would need them.

Marcello rose and, with a supreme mental effort, attempted to regain something of own will. Daniela still held him in her gaze but he looked away quickly. She sent his gun careering down the room merely by glancing at it. Marcello didn't know whether to go after a weapon he knew was useless, or head for the relative safety of the pentangle. Did it work if you didn't believe?

'Gianelli, come on – get inside the circle. Let's go.' Marcello turned and saw what was happening. He leapt at De Chesaris and pulled him away. Gianelli punched his boss full in the face, protecting his new master. De Chesaris's hands were still bound by the silk but his feet were free. He kicked Marcello in the stomach. Marcello fell to his knees with the force of the blow.

Grapper had almost completed the pentangle when the raw wind of Hades tore through the room. Somehow he carried on spraying as he felt himself being lifted with superhuman strength by Daniela's hand.

Marcello sat up, gasping for breath as Daniela lifted Grapper high into the air. De Chesaris, distracted, took his gaze and mind from Gianelli for a split second as Daniela hurled her muscular tormentor against the far wall like a rag doll. It was at least thirty feet away. She smiled as Grapper's head struck the marble corner of a huge period cabinet. Her eyes flickered as a river of blood coursed from his head.

Gianelli blinked hard and looked down at his hands. What was he doing? Marcello shouted to him. 'Don't look at De Chesaris, Gianelli. Do as I do – now!'

Marcello crawled against the wind into the circle. Gianelli followed, leaving De Chesaris at Daniela's mercy. She was ready for him now.

As abruptly as it had arrived, the wind stopped and the museum became still. The deathly hush seemed deafening. Marcello and Gianelli looked on from the safety of the rudimentary pentangle as De Chesaris backed away from the abomination that stalked him with a leer, a deadly inhuman predator. Daniela implored, 'Why did you kill me, father . . . have I not pleased you?'

De Chesaris shook his head. If he had been able to speak he would have said: 'No, it's not possible – you cannot be . . . *my* daughter. We all initiated your mother.'

In fact there was a family resemblance. De Chesaris considered himself all-powerful, but he was no match for her. He looked terrified.

As though reading his thoughts, she said: 'But look into my eyes – don't you see yourself reflected within them?'

Daniela reached out her arms to the Magus who had tricked her. Now he was totally at her command, just as she had once been at his. He glanced at Marcello – knowing instinctively that no one could save him. What did she want from him? He had no way of knowing. But he should, after all she was his creation – a creation of human folly. He backed away, half-glancing behind him as she herded him through the open glass doors to the head of the staircase.

'You always wanted to know the truth about this world, didn't you father. Well, now you will discover it is an eternal nightmare, filled with horrors that even you could not imagine. Fool. Nothing is as you thought it. But why should you believe me? Go, find out for yourself.' With that she blew gently and the wind started again. De Chesaris fell backwards. With his hands tied he could do nothing to save himself. His body rolled over and over until he reached the bottom of the stairs.

Daniela appeared by his crumpled form. His neck was broken yet he was still alive, his agony prolonged by sheer will. He could say nothing, but his eyes reflected deepest regret, a regret that had come too late. As the diabolical stimulus which he had so ignorantly worshipped grasped his life force and pulled him into the depths, a strange transmutation took place. His face, normally so deathly white, turned from grey to black, appearing charred, burnt beyond recognition.

Daniela hovered, satisfied. Now she could return to the place from whence she had come, to rest – for a time.

Without really knowing how, Marcello sensed it was safe to step out of the pentangle. He retrieved his gun and ran to the head of stairs, observing that strange husk which had once housed a monster with a look of extreme relief. He told Gianelli to summon an ambulance and returned to Grapper's crumpled body. As he examined the head wound, Grapper moaned. 'Miles . . . he's out there . . .' He lifted a broken arm and pointed to the quadrangle.

'Don't worry, we'll find him,' Marcello said gently. 'Don't try to move. Someone will come soon. I don't understand what happened – are we safe?' he asked shakily.

Grapper moved his head slightly and groaned. It hurt like hell. 'We're safe for now, yeah. I think Daniela got what she wanted.'

Marcello took off his expensive tie and mopped Grapper's forehead. 'What did she want? Can you tell me?'

Grapper closed his eyes and felt he was in good hands. 'Revenge, mate,' he whispered. 'That's all.'

EPILOGUE

'Do you think about death often, Signore?'

'Yeah, about as often as I think about sex.'

'That does not surprise me. They are much the same in my opinion, mysterious unchartered terrain.'

'The undiscovered country from whose bourn no traveller returns.'

'Shakespeare?'

'I think 'e knew what 'e was talking about. Do you think about death much then?'

'One cannot live in such a place as Venice and not contemplate death, Signore. It is a city of love and of death, of oppressive melancholia and joyous celebration. I myself prefer to think of the romantic but lately – well, let us just say that the afterlife has been prominent in my thoughts.'

'How am I doin', butterfly?' Grapper watched the white three-cornered hat recede. The nurse studied his chart and pronounced that he would live.

Marcello eyed his strange confidant. 'Why did you call her butterfly?' he asked from the leather chair by Grapper's bed.

Grapper grinned, ever the schoolboy. 'Me mother used to make these cakes with wings – butterfly cakes. They 'ad cream on 'em. For some reason the girl's 'ats remind me of 'em.' He winked at a passing nurse. She smiled, flattered by the attentions of the weirdo Inglese in bed nine.

Marcello looked to the plaster-encased limbs of the patient in the next bed. 'To say your friend was very lucky would be an understatement. If it had not been for the builder's tarpaulin . . . Well, perhaps I do not need to elaborate.'

Grapper took a handful of black grapes and tossed them one by one into the air, catching them in his open mouth. He chewed thoughtfully. 'Stupid bugger. I think 'e's learned 'is lesson. Can 'e leave 'ere now?'

Marcello could smell onions wafting from an approaching meal trolley. He felt nauseous. He hated hospitals. 'Of course. His mother arrives tomorrow. I am sure she will want to take him away as soon as he can be moved.'

Grapper scratched at the dressing beneath his spikes. 'That's a bleedin' relief. The sooner 'e gets away from 'ere the better.'

'I cannot help thinking that my investigation would have been made easier if you had disclosed the truth to me in the first instance.'

'What, and let you lock Miles up! Come on, I'm not that much of an idiot.'

This he didn't doubt. Marcello nodded. He felt bonded to this strange individual more by necessity than design. They had shared terrifying experiences which were not of this world. It made them blood brothers – of a kind. 'You may be interested to know that the Riaggis are to be buried in the family vault at Mantua. We are questioning most of the members in the order Traditio Mystica, De Chesaris's vile fraternity. At present we are unable to charge them for murders which happened between two and fifteen years ago, but if I have my way, which is likely, they will be ostracized for some time. Certainly the scandal will do a great deal of harm to their professional reputations.'

Marcello would remember the raid for the rest of his life. The evidence, six exhumed corpses had been discovered so far in the grounds of the Treviso palazzo; also some gruesome tools of their trade and an animalistic junkie in a padded cell who screamed hysterically about demons that were coming for her. She'd reminded him of Sarah at the height of her withdrawal. So frail, hopelessly vulnerable. He stood up to leave.

'You should be quite pleased with yourself then.'

'One is rarely pleased by evidence of human nature at its most debased, Signore. Besides, such images stalk the perimeters of one's consciousness like wolves. I sleep with a light on now, I am ashamed to say.'

'Don't be ashamed, Marcello, that's stupid. What you experienced would have scared the hell out of Hercules. Are you having nightmares?'

'That seems a tame expression for what I am experiencing.'

Marcello picked up his black leather bag.

'There's only two ways to get rid of those, mate.'

'And they are?'

'Say yer prayers and see a psychiatrist.'

'Venice is the city of love and death, of melancholia, and celebration.' Marcello's words rang in Grapper's ears. At Katerina's graveside he felt both emotions. Early morning mist swirled through the plane trees on San Michele, 'Island of the Dead', enveloping the mourners in a premature shroud. Katerina now lay beside her husband, in peace and tranquillity, to be plagued by memories no more.

Miles recited a passage from the Bible. Grapper closed his eyes and watched his mother encircle Katerina's shoulders, a protective gesture. Mario stood to her left. They waved to Grapper and disappeared from his view, off to pastures new, happier times.

Miles struggled to hold back the tears, certain that he was responsible for her death. But death had merely caught up with her at last, relieving her of the burden of life.

Grapper threw his white daisies on to the coffin and added a silent prayer of his own. Miles looked up from the wheelchair and asked his mother to take him away. Grapper squeezed his shoulder and walked silently alongside them. Other mourners turned from the open grave, viewing their departure with mild curiosity. The pair looked like wounded soldiers who had returned from the front line. In a way, they were what they appeared to be.

Celia Hanson spoke first. 'Mr Rice . . . um, Grapper.' She seemed uncomfortable. 'I can't begin to understand what happened to Miles and I am not going to try. However, my husband and I are extremely grateful to you for saving our son's life and I hope you won't be offended, but . . .' she paused. Grapper looked down at Miles and wondered what on earth was coming. 'We would like you to accept this gift as a token of our appreciation.'

Miles held out the envelope he had been nursing and stared thoughtfully out to the edge of the lagoon, to a view he knew he would never see again. Grapper tore open the envelope and couldn't believe what he was holding. This was more money than he had ever seen in his life. 'I can't accept this – it wouldn't be right. I 'elped Miles because I like 'im, I didn't do it for money. I don't need bleedin' charity . . .'

Miles raised a hand in protest. 'Take it, idiot. After all, it's only money.' Mrs Hanson pushed Miles towards the waiting water taxi. 'Not only will you take it, Mr Rice, I hope you will use it wisely,' she said.

The driver helped her with the wheelchair. They edged it, with some difficulty, down a portable wooden ramp.

Grapper bounded after them. 'This is going to come in really 'andy. I forgot to tell yer mate, what with all the excitement and everything, I'm gonna be a dad . . .'

Miles had a sudden mental image of a chubby baby with a green mohican. He threw his head back and laughed. 'You, a dad? This I can't wait to see.'

Grapper extended a grubby hand and helped Mrs Hanson into the launch. 'You will come back and see it after it's born, won't yer?' He instinctively knew that his invitation would never be taken up. Miles wouldn't return.

'Well, let's put it this way. If I don't come back, you and Bella can bring the baby over to stay with us. Are you sure you can't come with us to the station? Why are you going to Mantua now, for God's sake?'

'Family commitments, mate. Of a kind,' he muttered, then he called out, 'Write, you bastard, and 'ave a good trip.'

He waved enthusiastically as the launch sped across the glittering lagoon towards the Grand Canal. He watched until they were safely in the far distance, then returned to Katerina's grave and watched the men piling dirt into the recess.

Miles pushed golden hair from his face as cool winds freshened his skin and his thoughts. This was it, he was finally leaving. He felt as though he had been here forever. Celia Hanson stood behind her son saying nothing, sensing he was surveying the spectacular landscape for the last time.

The launch entered the wide mouth of the glittering Grand Canal and slowly passed the wedding-cake church of Santa Maria della Salute. Miles viewed the buildings with deep regret. Despite everything, he still loved it here.

When they passed the white façade of the Ca' Rezzonico, Miles shaded his eyes and looked up at the second-floor balcony.

Daniela's diaphanous figure watched them pass. Time waited patiently for a moment as the lovers held each other's gaze. She seemed saddened by her solitude, a prisoner of ambition, held within the confines of her beliefs, never to be free. She waved.

Miles, sensing her fate, felt tears welling in his eyes. He lifted an accepting hand in reply, saying goodbye, safely, from a distance.